The Alphabet Man

FICTION
COLLECTIVE
T W O
Boulder • Normal

THE ALPHABET MAN

Richard Grossman

Published by Illinois State University and Fiction Collective Two with
support given by the Illinois State University Fine Arts Festival, the Illinois
State University President's Discretionary Fund, the English Department
Publications Unit of Illinois State University, the English Department
Publications Center of the University of Colorado at Boulder, the Illinois
Arts Council, and the National Endowment for the Arts

Address all inquiries to:
Fiction Collective Two
c/o English Department
Publications Center
University of Colorado at Boulder
Boulder, Colorado 80309-0494

ISBN: Cloth, 0-932511-76-7, $22.95
ISBN: Paper, 0-932511-77-5, $11.95
448 pages

Produced and printed in the United States of America
Distributed by the Talman Company

Designed by Richard Grossman
and Bergh Jensen & Associates, Minneapolis/Seattle

Epworth Mechanics' Institute Library
Tuesday 10a.m – 12 Noon
Thursday 1.30p.m – 4p.m
Friday 7.30p.m – 9.30p.m

Please return books as soon as you have finished with them so that others may read them

A Hassidic tale recounts the story of an illiterate man who could not read the prayers for Yom Kippur. The man left the synagogue and walked out to an open field to recite the letters of the alphabet, one by one, asking God to put them together to form a prayer.

God received the man's prayer and was pleased.

•

And when he was come out of the ship, immediately there met him out of the tombs a man with an unclean spirit, who had his dwelling among the tombs; and no man could bind him, no, not with chains; because that he had been often bound with fetters and chains, and the chains had been plucked asunder by him, and the fetters broken in pieces: neither could any man tame him.

And always, night and day, he was in the mountains, and in the tombs, crying and cutting himself with stones.

But when he saw Jesus afar off, he ran and worshipped him, and cried with a loud voice and said, What have I to do with thee, Jesus, thou Son of the most high God; I adjure thee by God that thou torment me not.

For he said unto him, Come out of the man, thou unclean spirit! And he asked him, What is thy name?

And he answered, saying, My name is Legion: for we are many.

Mark 5: 2-9

Book One

Book Two

Barathrum

Book One

One

There are layers of blood on my hands. They are bright bright red, much redder than any clay. I share these hands with another, and they perform the will of another. They can caress or draw energy through the creep of a shotgun trigger. The fingers relate to the square of the hand, which is its own rebellious person, at once wrinkled with signs of wisdom, heart and prophecy. Its murderous grip is a grip of paradox, an abstract grip on a clownish whisper, on a personal bolt of energy, on a clew of voices careening in a labyrinth, fleeing a tattooed monster with laughing heads.

I navigate through floes of missing moments, each one hiding a unique set of sufferings and sins. These moments are actually paddling forms in the blood, and as my tainted blood reaches out for blood, it feels as if the most interior things are drawn naturally from the center out to coat the hands, to express my duplications gloved with a lacquered crimson gloss. There isn't much time, just barely enough with diligence to write a book that proves me innocent of all the heinous crimes.

Of my regimen of slaughter.

An eagle lands on a snake, it prods its beak in the snake's mouth, and the snake contorts and screams, its silent scream filling the smallest areas of grass, the talons around the plaited ropes of its body, the tongue slashed out and quivering on the ground. This cold splashed blood of the snake on the walls of the prison was the second layer of blood. It stayed there like the cretonne pattern of childhood furniture. What I had feared, I finally did.

Again and again, I did it.

With shotgun, pistol, knife and axe, I did it.

The deaths that I caused, however, I do not precisely remember. The joke has always been on me and on those that I butchered. For many years I thought there was merely one such death, but when the final deaths occurred, I realized there were more, many many more, although even today I can only count the two, and the grand total I only suspect. Like a Hottentot returning from battle, I am asked to count my coup, and I can only say two. Shocked and degraded, I am asked to recount. I repeat my solitary number. The one number two. Father and the others. But who knows? It's all so evidentiary. Nobody has pointed a finger in the right direction.

His head simply disappeared or this is what they say. Mine did, too. A short-range shotgun blast and Daddy became instantly sober! Perhaps just the faintest trails and traces of puss and dura mater leaking from cracks and corners, intensely yellow and beautiful and erotic. Oh, I forget! There is a muse and a man and an identity. The muse is the hummer of revenge. I call her Hummeroptera, my sweet little busy busy bee with glans and sword. The man is Colonel Harmon Oberstar, the purported savior of my soul, whom we shall attempt to meet, and the identity is me, the killer-poet who maligns the human world, that dull gruntocracy that spread, stoning and hacking and humping out of Kenya. The Big Mac. The hundred-thousand-year seizure. The double-breasted cavemen in their stinking biofog, distorted with funds, seeking ample gains, the potbellied boobocrats that rule the teeming world, are just like dear old Dad, the shitfaced monster with his whips and chains. Daddy sold Maytags. A success story.

We lived in the San Fernando Valley, in a lovely upper-middle-class home, so spic and span. Mother wore an apron, well past the time when aprons were generally worn, but Mommy was always a bit retro, with a narrow shark's grin and a high-pitched Yiddish song. I had nary a brother or sister.

Everything took place in the knotty-pine rec room.

I scrawled the word "WRECKROOM" across the walls of my bedroom, a graffiti artist well before the graffiti age, as proto as retro

Mom was retro, forming a family counterbalance, as the family therapists say (I have skimmed through all the therapies), and there was a piano in the living room that nobody played. At night I would go upstairs and pray and fondle Baby Jesus after I shut the door.

Locks were forbidden. Only Dad had locks. Only Dad administered pain. Nobody bothered to paint out the words on the walls of a house ruled by Satan.

Once this work is over, my deeds will regress into swimming objects, and as my firstling, the beheading of my father, was ultimately buried in gifted words, these recent deaths, of which I'm unjustly accused, will be laved and buried in blood. They'll wash away, out of existence, and only the words of this testament will remain, my bloody words among the useless words—words of history, words of books, words of gravestones, words that form in the wobbly head and cause desire, the words of the last trimester.

Once this work is over, the blood will billow and flow, and nobody will be able to stanch it. Nobody. Ever. Nobody will be able to stop it as it drips eternally from my belly, from my fingers, from my palms.

I am Clyde Wayne Franklin.

I am a prescriber of poetic poisons and a furnisher of alphabets.

I am tattooed with letters on my neck chest back butt groin arms legs feet and hands.

I am a walking language with an axe and a gun and a pen.

The world hides from me in horror.

They call me the Alphabet Man.

Two

America loves a murder, and I am a murderous American.

If you want to make the front page of the papers (which I have done on several occasions), you can destroy somebody in a creative sort of way. I sometimes feel as a newsmaker that Americans are praying for me, absolving me of my sins. In my mind's eye I see them, my fellow citizens and spiritual supporters on their knees, heads bowed, hands tenderly knit before their television screens, as bar-haired bimbos blare my trial results. Cathedral sanctities pervade their living rooms, their sofas gently reinflate released from weight, and posters, prints and photos fill with moving light, as the anchor ladies whine:

"Ladies and gentlemen, Clyde Wayne Franklin is guiltless. Clyde Wayne Franklin was right!"

The bedlam life of a poet is volcanic, booming away in the head. The world of arms and legs is a tiny world of clocks and minutes, ticking away on a tray. The quotidian thing we live through. The thaaaang. The wormhole. The stage for my story.

A year ago, I was at the Los Angeles Airport.

It was late on a Sunday afternoon, and I was rabidly hung over, dry and toxic, fearing water, as the gate attendant announced the boarding of my flight to Washington, DC. Across from me, in the middle of a plastic seat row, sat a trim, muscular man in his late sixties or early seventies with the collar and suit of a cleric. He had a lantern jaw, a flat misshapen nose, thin eyebrows, and a mane of silver hair. His delicate eyes looked as if they were filled with suds and the sun were shining on them. He was reading a book in Cyrillic and laughing to himself. Yellow and green argyle socks poked from beneath his pants cuffs.

I was one of the first ones on the airplane, seated in First Class, and buttonholing a stewardess who was rummaging through an overhead bin, I ordered a brace of vodkas. She stopped what she was doing and quickly brought me the bottles, and I dumped the shots into a glass and gulped them down. She was about to disappear into the food preparation compartment when the priest seated himself in the aisle seat next to me and, noticing my empties, tapped her on the hip and asked for scotch, and I treated myself to another double. I had placed an edition of Great Expectations in my seat pouch, and I took it out and began to read about Pip in the cemetery as our plane took off.

When dinner was served, I wasn't hungry. I glanced to my right, where the priest was enjoying his chicken Kiev. He plucked the tomato off his salad, and he wolfed down his sesame-speckled dinner bun. He put salt and pepper on the bun. The stewardess poured me a cup of coffee, but within moments it started to spill. The plane lurched violently, and the pilot came on the speaker and told us to fasten our seat belts. The aircraft fell, then immediately hit a channel of air. The hull shuddered and the plane began to bounce.

In front of the priest was a slice of key lime pie.

The stewardess staggered by, and I leaned across and handed her the remains of my coffee. The priest winked at me and nodded toward his food as he reached for his fork.

"This is just like flak, but with flak there's no dessert," he commented.

I looked at the priest, and he looked back at me and smiled. He took a mammoth bite of his pie.

"Come again?" I said.

"This is just like flak, but with flak you don't get any key lime pie," he repeated with food in his mouth.

"That's a weird thing to say."

He took a look at the tattoos on my neck and wrists, arched an eyebrow and shrugged his shoulders philosophically.

"Judging by your age, you were a pilot during World War II, is that it?" I asked.

"At the beginning of the war, I was," he said, as the plane continued to buck, "but my bomber crashed. When I finally got out of the hospital, I thought they would give me a discharge, but instead they motioned to me like this." He gave me the universal come-here signal with his index finger. "And so I went."

"Went where?"

"I returned to Europe," he said.

There were flecks of crust and custard on his lips. He continued to tear into the pie.

"They made you fly again, after you crashed?" I asked.

"Nope. That's what I thought they wanted me for, but they didn't. Actually, the job they gave me was much more dangerous."

And he finished his dessert, wiped his mouth, handed his tray to the stewardess, pushed up his seat table, crossed his ankle over his knee, and began tapping his fingers on his argyle sock.

"So what was your job, if you don't mind my asking?"

"I jumped out of airplanes," he replied cheerfully, and he turned towards me as if he were looking forward to a conversation.

"Behind enemy lines?"

"At low altitudes. Once I landed in a schoolyard in Belgium, and I accidentally killed a child. I came down on top of her, and she died on impact. As I gathered in my parachute, the girl was lying there with her eyes glazed over. She was perfectly still, but it wasn't stillness really. It must have been her head. All the other children were running around the playground and crying hysterically."

"What were you doing behind enemy lines?" I asked, skipping the part about the dead kid. "Espionage work? Killing Germans?"

"Americans," he replied.

"Americans what?" I asked.

"I was killing Americans. That was the job they gave me."

This stopped me. What had started out as polite conversation suddenly made no sense at all. Killers just don't plop themselves down on airplanes and tell other killers that they kill.

"But you sound like you're an American," I finally said.

"Did you ever see Apocalypse Now?" the priest asked. "Remember Martin Sheen? I was Martin Sheen. Only normally there wasn't such a lot of distance. In most cases, you didn't have all that far to go to get to your target."

"Martin Sheen," I muttered to myself.

"What do you think Martin Sheen did?" he prodded me gently with his finger. "Who do you think he actually worked for?"

"Beats me," I replied.

"Well, you should know," he said. "Every American should know. It's extremely important."

The priest shook his head. Then he picked up his book and began reading again.

I looked out the window. The Rocky Mountains. An amiable priest who landed on children and snuffed Americans.

"So how many Americans did you kill?" I asked, not wanting him to get too ensconced in his book before I figured out what was really going on.

I was wearing a black sweatshirt from Gold's Gym in Venice. The sweatshirt had a decal of a bald weightlifter on it. I picked nervously at the weightlifter. Every morning I practiced. Not weightlifting. That was later in the day. Every morning I meditated. I began by saying the same thing over and over again: "My name is Clyde Wayne Franklin. Baby Jesus, be my source of light and grace. Make me be what I have to be. Make me a person that others can see."

The priest was staring at the sweatshirt.

"In which war do you mean?" he asked me.

"You did this in more than one war?"

"I did it in three."

"And how many Americans did you eliminate?"

"Fourteen."

"I don't get it. Why are you telling me this?"

"Why not?" he replied. "I'm getting on in life. It's been over twenty years since my last assignment, and I've made my peace with the issue. Except for the child. It was the only death that wasn't my fault, and ironically I feel terribly guilty about it. Old age hasn't erased the pain of that one!"

"I understand," I said sarcastically, as I searched for the stewardess, "you were a contract killer working for the government. It started to bug you, so you gave it up and became a devoted servant of God."

The priest laughed. There was no sign that he took offense.

"Well, you're partially right. I was actually an army officer, not a contract killer. When I wasn't on assignment, I worked for a corporation in Milwaukee that sold office supplies. I was only paid by Uncle Sam when I was on a job, although I remained in line for promotion and pension benefits. And I did become a priest eventually, as you can see."

He joined me, craning his neck, looking for the source of another drink.

"And the murders don't bother you any more?" I asked in order to reconfirm his statement, since the question was of critical interest to me.

"They didn't bother me when I did them, and they don't bother me now. Aside from the child, they've never bothered me. Not for a single moment."

"I don't believe a word you're saying!" I objected a bit too loudly.

For some reason, his response had made me furious, and I could feel my skin heating up. I looked out the window at the mountains and tried without success to calm down. Then I looked back at the priest, who was tapping his sock, unperturbed. A young woman with coiled hair and bulbous pearls stared at me from across the aisle. I stared back, and she looked down at the tissue she was clutching.

"Seems to be settling down a bit," the priest remarked nonchalantly. The bumping and rocking had stopped as suddenly as it had started. He pulled a billfold out of his vest pocket, removed a business card and handed it to me. It gave his name, The Reverend Arnold Kosmoski, S.J., Catholic Youth Services. And an address and phone number in Washington.

"Don't believe the card," he said. "Everyone calls me Duke."

"A killer named Duke!"

"You could show a bit more respect toward strangers," he answered, and he stopped the stewardess, held up two fingers and pointed to me and to himself. She immediately headed for the drink trays.

"Why don't you feel anything?" I pressed on.

"What do you mean by that?" he asked.

"It's fairly obvious what I mean, isn't it? Why don't you feel anything about the men you murdered?"

"That's not what I said. I said that it didn't bother me. I enjoyed killing. It was perfectly legal and I did it."

"What was so enjoyable about killing people?"

"The personal expression of power." He seemed to be searching carefully for the proper words. "I would watch the man as he breathed, knowing that I controlled the future of his body. And then, of course, the finality, the overwhelming sense of mastery. I always took something with me, something that would preserve that ancient feeling of conquest."

I began to feel frightened, because I couldn't figure out where this conversation was coming from nor where it was leading. It wasn't just the offhand admission that he was a mutilator. It was more his portrayal of murder as a form of mastery that unsettled me. This type of killer is always a sociopath, and I know from my own experience that sociopaths never change. And yet here sat a jovial priest. Nothing added up. I couldn't get a foothold.

"Body parts?" I asked, although I understood full well at this point that he was serious. "Is that what you meant? What did you do, string their ears together?"

"Let's just call them mementos," he replied.

"So if you enjoyed killing so much," I asked, "then why did you stop?"

"Something happened and I changed."

"But you said that what you did back then doesn't bother you anymore," I objected.

"It doesn't bother me now for an entirely different reason. I'm a different person. I no longer try to create violent forms of enjoyment for myself. I have been affected by a great man."

"Jesus?" I responded.

"Jesus, certainly, but somebody else. Somebody who taught me something as important as anything I ever learned from Catholicism."

He paused for a moment, and for the first time since I began speaking with him, he seemed less bumptious and more reflective. The stewardess brought the drinks.

"So who was this person?" I asked.

"I was changed by the last man I was sent to murder. He said only a few words to me, and I no longer wanted to kill. Neither him nor anybody else. The need to shed blood was permanently gone."

"That's a mindfuck."

"Yes, I suppose it is."

"You had a conversation with him before you decided to pull the trigger, is that it?"

"Why do you act so surprised? I always spoke with my marks. I had to win their confidence and convince them to go somewhere where no witnesses were present. It was a war within a war really, and my M.O. was pretty much the same regardless of circumstances."

"Do you tell everyone you meet about this shit?"

"No." He examined a cuticle. "Just a few."

"And what did these people do to deserve killing?" I asked.

"In most cases, I think, they were incompetents. They weren't doing their jobs particularly well, and the men they commanded were getting killed. Also there were probably some blackmarketeers, some crooks, but that's just an educated guess. They all fell into the general category of enemies of the Army."

"There's such a thing as a desk job."

"You don't understand the system. Men die for hundreds of

reasons in a war. Who kills whom is normally beside the point. Sometimes the Army deliberately shot its own men, but in any case, I didn't much care. I was grateful for the opportunity."

"Did the men you shot have anything in common?"

"They were all officers. That was about it."

"And then there was this last man, the one who supposedly changed your life?"

"Right."

"And what happened when you let this guy walk?"

"I wasn't required to go through with any of the missions, although to duck an assignment meant automatic retirement. Somebody was awfully sore with me, though. It took me twelve days to get from Nam back to Texas for my debriefing. No more priority service."

"And didn't they ask you why you didn't go through with it?"

"Of course they asked me, but I didn't tell them. I didn't discuss it with the government, and I haven't discussed it with anybody since."

I've met many murderers before, both in and out of the joint. Murderers are members of the world's most exclusive club, and we are attracted to each other in strange and undeniable ways. There was no question in my mind that the priest had done what he said he had done. He had a particular momentum, a certain opacity of the eye— and a unique smell—that all we killers share.

"What did this person tell you?" I asked him.

He remained silent.

"You didn't answer my question," I insisted.

"It's an impossible question to answer. I told you that I've never been able to discuss our conversation with anybody."

"All you have to do is repeat what the man told you. It doesn't require a great deal of creativity to mouth back words that changed your life."

"Is that so?" the priest said. "And what do you know about creativity?"

"I'm a poet," I replied.

"I am reading an interesting work myself," he said, quickly changing the subject and offering me his book. "It's not exactly poetry, but it has true passion and lyric feeling. A novel set in Byelorussia. By Athelstan Bogulobov. It's a gem."

Now, I'm no expert on Russian literature, but I was willing to bet my last dollar that there was no one on the planet with the name of Athelstan Bogulobov. I searched the cover for the author's name, trying to decode the English behind the Cyrillic. The name, or at least what seemed to be the author's name, was long enough to qualify, but that was about as far as I could take it. The cover illustration showed a plowed field with a hovel on it.

"What's the novel about?" I asked.

"It's about a Warsaw seamstress who becomes a commissar during the Stalinist era."

"Then why the picture of the farm on the cover?"

"It's a book about cultural degeneration. A book about the soil."

"How do you say, 'It's a book about cultural degeneration. A book about the soil,' in Russian?" I quizzed him.

He told me. It was effortless. It sounded authentic.

"Maybe you can write about me in one of your poems," he continued in English.

"Maybe."

I turned away and looked out the window again.

"I think you're a hypocrite," I said in a low voice, as I continued to look out the airplane.

The priest said nothing.

"I said, motherfucker, that I think you're a hypocrite!" I said much more loudly as I turned towards him, and my face was red and my hands were trembling. Without thinking much about it, I began to roll up my sleeves. On my right forearm were a Q, a Y and an F. I suddenly wanted to punch this man in the face.

The priest looked closely at me, taking my measure, and I realized with a shock that he was judging on some instinctual level whether he could take me or not, and that he had decided that he could. I've seen that look before in men, but never from someone so much older than me.

He smiled coldly, breathed deeply, and then went back to reading his book.

I stared at the netting of my seat pouch. My mind was racing. I firmly believed that I was being mocked and that this man had been sent from somewhere to make fun of me. I tried to imagine myself in his position, an assassin, suddenly becoming religious as a result of something that was said to me, as a result of a few sentences uttered by someone I was supposed to hit. It was so absurd that I knew it was true. I was convinced, as only a poet can be convinced, that there are words out there that change people instantly, that change everything about them.

"How old are you?" the priest asked calmly, after a few minutes had passed. He was still staring into his book.

I was forty-nine at the time. My age is one of the few things I can keep track of, but the effort has always been monumental.

"Forty-six."

"And how many years were you inside?" He looked up from his book.

I was shocked. I made up a number. I have a hard time counting things.

"Twenty."

"Then you should know that there are worse crimes than hypocrisy."

"How did you know I'd been in prison?" I asked him, surprised.

"I knew who you were before I sat down. Most highly-educated people know who you are. I've read your books, and in spite of your behavior, I feel honored to meet you."

"Then why were you being coy?"

"I enjoy deceiving people," he shrugged his shoulders again. "It's always been a peculiar weakness of mine."

"You must be one hell of a priest."

"As you can see by my card, I deal mostly with children. With children, there is little need for telling the truth. Kids love to be fooled. I get along great with kids."

"So what do you do with them?" I asked, deciding to forget about my outburst, since he seemed willing to put it aside himself.

"I facilitate adoptions. Mostly I transport children from Asia to America and help them through transitions. I speak Korean and a number of Indic dialects, and so I can talk to a lot of the kids and ease their fears. Many of them are toddlers but some are much older."

"I see. It's the child on the playground."

"Exactly. I feel that I owe my life to children." He pulled his billfold out again and offered me a snapshot. "This is a girl from Rajasthan whom I just delivered to Los Angeles."

"Not interested in the least," I said, keeping my hands where they were.

My rudeness seemed to increase the man's sense of well-being. He beamed at the photograph and then returned it to his wallet.

"Why would the Army ask you to kill a man who was supposedly so wise?" I asked him.

"I told you, I was never told why I was sent on missions."

"I want you to tell me who this guy is who changed your life, and I want you to tell me exactly what he said, and I want you to tell me now!" I wasn't going to let him off the hook.

"No, I won't." he answered firmly. Quite suddenly, he seemed visibly annoyed and hostile.

"Why not?"

"Because, quite frankly, it's none of your business. Furthermore, whatever I said wouldn't mean anything to you. I can tell from reading your poetry that doubt would stand in your way."

"What are you, some kind of fucking literary critic?" I protested. "I don't doubt anything. I don't even believe in doubt."

"Doubt isn't an object of belief. The truth is that you are deeply afraid. You doubt your ability not to kill again. You are terrified of repeating what you did."

"What if I am afraid of repetition? It's perfectly reasonable," I answered. "Weren't you?"

"I already told you, I thoroughly enjoyed killing. I looked forward to it," he replied peevishly.

"And so this man's advice wouldn't apply to me, is that it?"

"I didn't say that. It's just that you are blocked by voices inside you from comprehending the truth. You're too screwed up to get the message."

I couldn't believe the presumption of the man.

"I assume this man was in Vietnam." I said.

"No. Laos. Plain of Jars. But it was all one war."

"And what's he doing now? Is he still alive?"

"Yes, he is."

"I must speak to him!" I demanded again. "It's not up to you to decide whether or not this man can help me. It's too important!"

"I'm sorry, Mr. Franklin," the priest replied, "but the truth of the matter is that I can do whatever I want, and right now what I want to do is to finish my book."

And he returned to his reading.

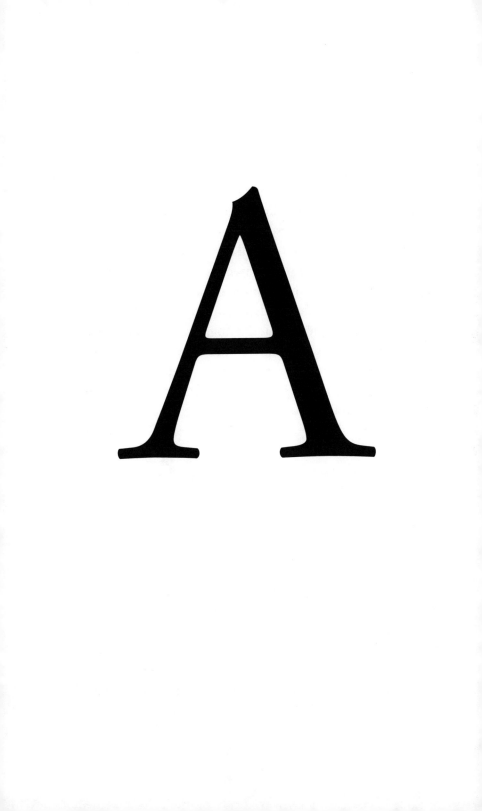

hey Dr. Hakenkreuz, turn up the heat, yeah I'm used to a lot
better and warmer but here in this best of all possible worlds I
need another set of dentures, cuz man my bite's got worn from
gnawing all those eggs, and I gotta tell ya Doc, I'm truly forlorn
not just fornlorn in your ordinary circus-bum-type way but I'm
truly torn from tearing and chomping and now I've got to prepare myself and Chuckles needs a new pair of choppers, even
though I blackened them all in the ring, just like Clyde who
licoriced his face as he rode his chopper down the street, so that
when I reared back and slapped my thighs and laughed, my eyes
would glow like charcoals in the hooting lamps of the tent and
my mouth would be so round and filled with emptiness, Doc and
the audience would shriek, there would be so much natural glee
and some of the kids would go pee, that my black mouth would
open and appear to be so full of fun-filled grief, if only there were
more discipline, if only the whips of the trainers could snap across
the tits of the women inside the galleries, if only there were more
sexual discipline, especially among the Jewish women, I could
whisper out my story, I could tell them about the twins conjoined
at the brain, the twins that shared their bottles and their pain, the
twins that were hatched from the same addle egg but in different
places, one high brow one low brow, one here one there, one a
doll with his belly filled with germs and the other a boy with his
skin covered with letters, it would all make sense Doc if you
weren't Chinese, you could see it all so clearly from a Western
point of view, in our own native language not Moo Goo Gai Pan,
but you're an import clown the kind that made America great,

new blood and new Pan-Cake, and the dentist chair twirls in the center of Ring Two and I am in it and you are holding the balloon, the balloon with all that gas that I must breathe in order to dream my boxcar dreams, our carnival kicks, it's such a stitch it's such a scream, but I gotta tell you, if your name weren't really

Einstein and you weren't a valued member of my A -team, I don't know if I'd sit out here under the glare of the lights without the advice of Al my agent, cuz Al does all my thinking, and it takes a genius to survive in the Hollywood scene where all the clowns hold secret meetings, and Al does what........OK I'll do it I'll say

AAAAAAAAAA

AAAAAAAAAA

AAAAAAAAAA

AAAAAAAAAA

AAAAAAAAAA

AAAAAAAAAA

AAAAAAAAAA
AAAAAAAAAA
AAAAAAAAAA
AAAAAAAAAA
AAAAAAAAAA
AAAAAAAAAA
AAAAAAAAAA hey
Doc, couldn't ya use a smaller wrench, say
AAAAAAAAAA
AAAAAAAAAA

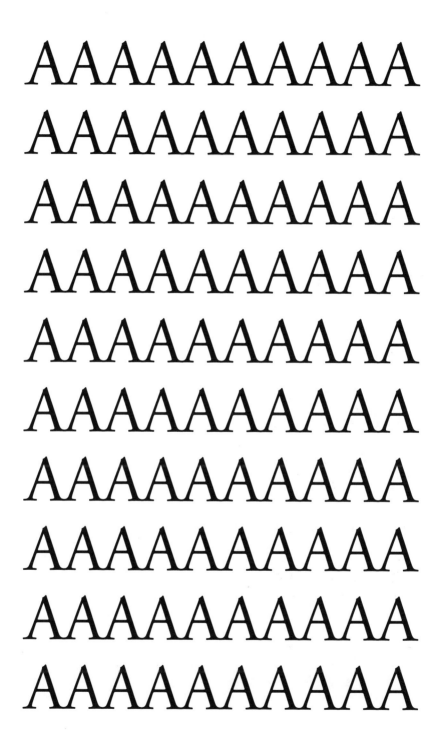

AAAAAAAAAA
AAAAAAAAAA
AAAAAAAAAA
AAAAAAAAAA
AAAAAAAAAA
AA stay far away from my molar with that hardware say
AAAAAAAAAA
AAAAAAAAAA
AAAAAAAAAA
AAAAAAAAAA

AAAAAAAAAA
AAAAAAAAAAA
AAAAAAAAAAA
AAAAAAAAAAA
AAI need more nitrous so tear the top off the whipping

cream and let's get jiving and whipping I'll say

AAAAAAAAAA
AAAAAAAAAAA
AAAAAAAAAAA
AAAAAAAAAAA

AAAAAAAAA
AAAAAAAAAA
AAAAAAAAAA
AAAAAAAAAA
AAA say AAAAAA I

look back into the lights the chair is spinning and you reach in
with the wrench the entire world is a dental office surrounded by
a faceless audience you reach into my mouth with the wrench to
yank out words from blacknesses and there is a well complete
with stairs and you reach in with the wrench and pull it out you
pull out a giant Happy Tooth that I had harbored there you
tighten the screw of the monkey wrench around the tooth and
out it pops (I hate that word) into the hooting lights of the Big
Top under all the children's noses and you have a strap with a
circular mirror a frontlet wrapped around your powdered
cebocephalic skull for you are Dr. Einstein of the SS, the Soapy
Suds, who watches children wet their beds and you go running
round the roundabout round and round and round and round
and round waving the tooth and all the dads are moaning and
coming and I must hold my hand over my mouth and chase you

One

I struggled for breath at the back of the alley. The rain was coming down in sheets.

My overcoat and luggage were scattered on top of the loading dock. My hands were shackled behind my back, and my jaw lay open and unhinged. I had lost a molar, and fluid mixed with rainwater flowed from my scalp and nose into a puddle of red vomit underneath my head. A portion of my rib cage was broken, and my right lung rubbed against the mass of pulverized marrow.

I had been surprised.

As I stepped off the escalator and headed for the baggage claim, a driver had been waiting for me with a sign with my name on it. A squat, muscle-bound gum-chewer with an undersize cap as part of the standard courtesy uniform, he said that my girlfriend, Barbie, couldn't make it to the airport and that he'd been hired through a car service to drive me to her.

I followed the round little man, swaggering with my coat and bags, as we moved out the door of the baggage claim toward the street. Without my noticing, somebody came up swiftly behind me, a gun was jammed in my side, I was pushed to the floor of a Cadillac limousine, a rain-soaked canvas shoe was pressed against my neck, my hands were handcuffed, my mouth was taped and my wallet was swiftly plucked.

An unbelievable stench emanated from the canvas shoe.

The car pulled away, and we drove for about half an hour until we finally stopped in the alley. The man in the front seat next to the driver, the one with the gun, came around and opened the rear door and yanked me out by the hair. My feet couldn't find ground, and my face went down and he stepped back and booted me cleanly in the mouth and then raised me up and jerked me around, draping me over the car hood. With one hand lodged between my shoulder blades, he grabbed me by the hair again and cocked my head back. Then he smashed it forward into the metal. My nose shattered, and since my mouth was taped, I began choking down blood.

Once again, he smashed my face into the hood, and my face erupted in pain. Keeping my chest pressed against the metal, he pulled back violently on my hair and shook my head like a Medusa in the downpour.

The man with the smelly shoe got out the other side and walked back to the trunk. Moments later, he reentered my field of vision, such as it was in the storm, clutching the lower section of a pool cue. Then he reached across the hood and dubbed me lightly across the eyes. I waited for him to wind up and bash me, perhaps blind me, but he didn't. Instead, he came around to my side of the car. The goon who had hold of my hair pulled me to my feet, and with his other hand still firmly in the small of my back, he pushed me, choking and wretching, to the end of the alley, where there was someone else, someone who hadn't been in the limo but who had been waiting there for me to arrive. The high beams shone directly on him, casting his shadow against the loading dock.

He was standing next to a pile of crates and smoking a cigarette under an umbrella. The chauffeur sauntered passed me, holding my bags, and tossed them up on the dock behind the man.

I was jerked around so that I was staring into the car lights.

The man with the umbrella came around where I could see him. He had on a cheap plastic raincoat. He stamped on his cigarette, then walked up and tore the tape off my mouth. I lowered my head as much as I could and wretched, and blood poured onto the ground in front of me. Then he lifted my chin and examined my nose like a nearsighted surgeon, as if he were trying to determine whether or not his men had done sufficient damage. There was something strangely comic about this person's appearance. His head was large, like a watermelon, and yet his features were larger still, much too large for the head. He had huge round eyes, a lipless mouth, a pug nose and a snaggle-tooth grin. I noticed that his nails were filthy.

He looked at his watch, under the pretense that he could read it in the darkness and driving rain.

"Franklin, Franklin," he finally chided me. "Tisk tisk tisky tisk tisk."

He looked like he was going to break out laughing.

I think he expected me to say something, but I didn't.

"My buddies here are gonna put you in the hospital," he explained in a bored tone of voice. "That's cuz you shouldda stayed the fuck in California. And once you're capable of being wheeled onto an airplane, you'd better get your tattooed butt on board, cuz otherwise you can set your timer, pal, you're gonna be dead meat, and in a hurry."

"Then kill me now, you ugly piece of horseshit," I replied, still choking.

The man behind me still clung to my hair and the back of my shirt and forced my head slightly higher into the rain.

"Go ahead," the man in the trenchcoat motioned to one of the thugs, and then he turned and quickly left the alley.

The man with the pool cue stepped forward. He was at an oblique-enough angle so that I could make out his profile in the headlights. He was a broadchested, oily son-of-a-bitch with rawbone features, wearing a Gore-Tex running outfit and a skewed baseball cap. All ferocity, congolene and business. He swung with deliberation and bashed me twice in the same place. My ribs buckled. The other man let go and I fell like a deadweight.

Then I was kicked several times in the stomach.

"Welcome to the nation's capital, dude," the man holding the cuestick shouted into the storm. "Here's your key to the fucking city." And he reached into his pocket and flipped the handcuff key in the air with his thumb. I heard it clink against the pavement.

More vomit gushed from my mouth.

It was a moment of intense awakening.

Fellow sinners, let me describe hell for you.

It goes by the name of Encino.

It was there that the yin-like forces of suburban anomie and ritual love combined to bring me to this mangled, parlous state, barfing my innards into an alley behind a warehouse. It was there, many years previously, on the concrete slopes of the San Fernando Valley, that I squatted before my home, the Franklin Family Furnace, a Tudor chalet with cutsey chimney pots, a weather vane topped with a gull, and a band of lifeless lead-glass windows rimming a motor court. In Dad's bloodshot eyes it spread and spread for acres.

Blasted on glue and Ripple, I lingered shortly after school in the middle of the intersection of Sweetbriar Drive and Huckleberry Way, and the embrasures of our wrought iron fence hummed alchemically with gold, and the sun's spokes like pressurized threads of Crayola went skimming over the rooftops. Inside, Mom was working away, contoid and bandaged. The bib of her apron was speckled with snowlike crystals, a vintage pattern, as she scalloped and sprinkled pie crust to fill with fruit, like the jellied fruit that loaded her stiff, pyramidal bras. I perched happily on my motorcycle sallet and rubbed my eyes, and I was, for the first time in my life, totally at one with nature.

This was several weeks before the Primal Fact of the Primal Act.

Perhaps it was while squatting in the street that I realized how many of me had actually been growing up, and perhaps it was there, feeling for the first time at one with anything, that I made the decision not to name them all, not to give names to the fantastic cloudy hairballs that were out for an adolescent romp. I couldn't prevent the upcoming bloodshed and thrombosis, and I certainly couldn't keep dear old Mom from dangling, but I could avoid something relatively uncomfortable.

I could avoid exploding like a bomb.

Later that autumn afternoon, as a rufous sun set behind Catalina, I saw my driveway bathed in shimmering guts of fish, and Daddy's cherry Packard ready to roll.

Hey, I could take that car and sell my British bike for gas, said a homeless voice of the road.

Or me, waltz with me, then lick the pucker of my ass, and fuck me, fuck me hard and fast. I'll grab you by the balls and ram you down my corridor and away, said another, who liked to go clubbing.

Ho ho, said Monsieur One plus Two, from the limits of innumeracy. Remember me? I was with you from the very first. Your very first baby blue baby god in your very first baby crib. When Mommy tucked the covers, I whispered into your softer parts all the other silly hairball names as greeting gifts. We wet the bed together year after year and were mutually comforted. When you received that first plastic ring, the pink pinky thing with the beaded, ragged seam, it was me, your very best hairball pal, who commanded you not to waste the candy.

After that transcendental afternoon, sky-high on my Nazi helmet as the sky blackened, I would try to stop counting before I reached the One I knew was waiting for me at every given moment.

One Two One Two One. One Two One. Two and One and Two and One.

Voices One after One, modulations, remonstrations and devices, tugged at me and rent me. So long as Satan's emissary could not protrude his clownish laughter through the inky roll at the base of my brain, I knew I could pull it off.

But of course, a few weeks later he did just that, and Daddy was wasted from the delts up.

At the rear of the alley, I twisted my swollen wrists in my cuffs, trying to increase the level of my pain. Somehow I wanted to see what quantities could be added—to prove as I lay broken and gagging under waves of rain that an additional iota of unbearable sensation could matter at the outskirts. I was also thinking of Mom, her head in the clouds pinching crust, or being whipped in her swaddles, twisting her wrists in her own designer manacles, as Daddy, high on Jim Beam, sweated and toiled, basting his prick, trying to get it up. This was a marvelous opportunity to think like dear old Mom, to try to determine why she had lost her voice and would only look at me, up and down, up and down, during the years of penitence in my cell.

When each of us dies, I thought, each death could be an overlay, a simultaneous melting into an empty stream, into the continuum of One Big Death. Or, to take an equally probable case, we could each be points along a line of disconnected Little Deaths, the second aleph of the theoreticians, of separate infinitesimals, death after tiny death linked but contained, I theorized as I rasped my wrists, because if I could add pain to pain, each additional hurt would somehow matter, would stand by itself as would each extinction. I feared simultaneous death, the One Big Deadly Empty, more than anything else as you shall shortly see, and in extremis sought for poignant reassurances and signs that humans die in privacy.

(And that there was constant pain in Momma's wrists, besides the shuddering pain of the whip.)

And so, a long time ago, beleaguered Mom, strapped astride her folding chair, had to free herself and hang, and dear old Dad, truncated on the linoleum floor, his hallux touching the pick of the inlaid shuffleboard (as I was shown in the court photos), had to be gone right then, his soul fleeing the exploding drops of the brain pan, Shazaam! They couldn't both be part of the same earthly pool of talent. Their deaths had to be individual and spaced. They had to disappear into their own spirit-tight compartments, they could no longer see each other, they could never again touch or feel each other.

They couldn't melt and reform together.

They had to soar in different directions.

Two

There is a theoretical house, a doll house, called La Casa de Clyde. My name and a five-pointer are on the front door. One enters with a cocktail in hand. All of Clyde's little furniture and Clyde's little toys, too small to view clearly, are there in perfect arrangement, the trappings as old as the Big House and the objects of love and amusement tucked away in a long wooden chest. The jalousies are bolted down and locked, although the rooms are filled with green ethereal light and ether smell that mixes with the noonlight and the crude smell of mown grass. And yes! there is a dry basement, the abyssal, with two other chests, the outer one for guns, for Dad the Hero and Hunter, and the one in back for baculine pursuits, for pony whips and spotless chains, each priceless catenation polished clinky-clean by unseen hands. I've always wondered whose. Perhaps Mom hauled out the silverware polish in her off moments. In this tiny house, I would tinker in my bedroom and drink with the clown, who had his own private agenda and his own humor and his own appointment book of sexual adversaria.

This dewy-eyed clown is a copacetic guy. After a number of bumps in bistros and bars, I've seen him emerge entire from others' sodden features, the same katabatic look extruding from all those alien sets of eyes. Because he is the one hiding within the many, and I am the many hiding within the one, we have a great deal to talk about. Sometimes he just wants to describe his job: driving to all the gigs, fondling the kids, helping them define the nature of their own parties. Sometimes, when he gets real loaded with a woman, he strips off the makeup as part of some dim, partly-remembered routine. But this guy knows how to relax and savor a drink. Mano a mano, we both know the ropes, although he knows more than I. He knows the basis of all the world's religions. He claims, with a wink, to have invented God and comedy at the very same time! Shit, I said trembling from the corner of the basement once upon a time, I turned the Big House into a wintry grave. Here lies Dad within his own chalet. Would you care for a snack from the refrigerator?

It's always such a pleasure, the clown would normally say. Drinking has its weird complexities.

Big House One and Big House Two, the second being a series of nicer houses. The juvie for starters, and then Soledad, and then through the diligence of the firm of Crouse, Moore and Wooten, Patton State, where I cut up paper dolls and waited for the big break. Boy, was I good! I had multiple personality disorder at the border, but the docs all congregated on the other side of the river, gazing across.

Here comes the cavalry, the neuro-poltroons would call to me from the sancta of the interview rooms. I would sit on my folding chair, just like Mom, and be mum. Here comes the cavalry, over the hill above the Little Horn, the flags and bugles, the guns and pelts! One man on many horses, now they are charging along the far bank, searching for a proper ford. That's what I thought they thought. Actually, they were a lot dumber than the troop leader, who had read the thicker textbooks that they and Dr. Duncan hadn't. To them I was always Clyde Wayne Franklin, the awesome intellect, the persecuted, engraved, barbell-tilting monster-poet with the granny glasses and flaming orange hair, his lips made of kip but tough as leather. I never told them about the other blackouts. That's where the clown came in. I ingested him. I ate of the clown as the ancients ate of the shaman. Here was the scenario:

The clown knew there were many times when I fled with my voice and mind like Mom. I'd instantly pack my bags and go and leave him all the keys. I'd flee the house to fly about the outer realms, disembodied and restless, and when I came back, everything was always safe and sound and comfy and cozy. The joke's on them,

Pagliacci would always confide in me. What did I do? I'd ask. Who handled the local announcements? Did I offend or off anyone? The matter is of no practical importance, he would snort and pinch me as I poured another itty-bitty drink. Why the fuck do you care? he'd laugh. You survived, so let's go on from here!

Yes, it was all a matter of comic faith, for standing there holding the sawed-off shotgun, beveled at the barrel, what that teenage monster did can only be reconstructed forensically, because Mom had nothing further to say, all the police inspectors said. Nude beneath her apron, wrapped in chains around the folding chair in front of Dad, who was lying there with no head, her voice took off from her body. It wasn't that she went mute exactly, but rather that her voice went chasing after her husband into a brainless land as an act of loyalty. Her prim falsetto was still framing words somewhere, but it just wasn't *here* anymore, chirping over the pans of this world. The message hid in her body a few more weeks and then she trussed herself high up in the garage above the Packard, and she didn't say boo. Not a word of evidence and not a word of truth. What she saw stayed in.

The court reconstructed the story of a teenage lad named Clyde, whose Dad would get drunk on Friday nights and tie up his Mom, whom they presumed liked it. (She did.) At an early age, the aforementioned Clyde, who was nabbed in a coffee shoppe with blood in his lap (the Primal coat), let slip, as a toddler he had stumbled downstairs and peeped until he fell asleep or until the ultimate dawn orgasms, whichever came first. With tenderer feelings he was allowed and then encouraged to watch and then made to watch and finally, in his later years, was beaten with a belt if he didn't watch (so he saw and saw and saw and by the notion of his domination by the tools of the trade became part of the early acts, the innocent audience invited up on stage to bruise and stare and maybe do?). Poor Clyde could not remember the Primal Fact of the Primal Act, according to constabular interviews. He had come home late one blustry night unhinged on cheap whiskey as the potted Robelini by the screen door danced and opened the inner door and fell into a gaping blackness entranced and had come out of it staring into a free refill at Du-pars. There was blood on the floor and his pants were filled with stray paternal corpuscles and the management telephoned the police, who eventually came and traced it all back to the wreckroom and the wreckage and Mom still sitting there without a word of admonition transfixed and speechless and theoretically unable to move from her chair, but Clyde hadn't a clue and still doesn't, the first of many lost moments, petits mals, and hours, slightly larger mals, and days, grands mals, and a few that went for weeks, the great-grands mals, that he has suffered intermittently ever since, whenever he disappears into the forest.

Come out, come out, wherever you are! The poor dumb kid is still wandering downstairs.

In the joint, they chided me, "Yo, Alphabet Man, come gag with me with your spoon!" Standard cafeteria chatter, but the cons didn't fuck with me. Ever.

I held my own.

Behind the bars, I read and read. It's all I ever did, except to write and pump and follow the zoo-like regimens. I absorbed the lexicons and indices of many languages (but not, as you know, of Russian). I perused the histories and begats in Greek and Hebrew and Latin, all the English novelists (my favorite was Smollett), the poems of pilgrims and mystics and sadists and dramatists (the only ones that counted); I picked the boneyards of the early psychologists, memorized Grand Opera and Tin Pan Alley, and humbly pieced together my mind. Peace. Peace. Peace.

They gave me IQ tests, Iowas, Stanfords, multiphasics, SAT's. And then claimed I was one in a million. One in ten million. A gifted, polymathic shape, penned and penning.

They also claimed in Patton State that there were matters intentionally forgotten.

For example, they would say over and over again, you did this, you did this, and I would say, of course I did, of course I did, sir. And then they would ask, did you do this? And I would admit that I hadn't. And then they would ask, then who else could have killed X? And I would shrug devoid of suppositions and, finally left to my own devices, instantly forget the nub of the conversation. This made them underneath feel terribly sorry for me, given the nature of the aforesaid acts. All I could and can still remember is the process.

Alphabet Man, somewhat akin to Wolf Man.

I still don't understand how they could have declared me harmless.

Perhaps you know, but I can assure you that nobody could ever tell me.

In Soledad I entered an intro writing class. Back then it was a constant theme, getting down, self-expression as a means to political liberation, the Poets in the Prisons Program, a part of the seventies correctional scheme. I discovered verse along with the brothers, or more properly, the world of verse discovered me. It started with a weepy fat-ass nerve-shattered instructress from Fresno State University, Sonia Janes Endicott, who once confided, luringly, that she was visited in the sack by the succubus of Isadora Duncan. Several years later I was freed, to be feted, promoted and reviewed by what I call my Missoula Fan Club Branch of Dipsomaniac Pansies, the macho literary cowhands who saw in the sere and smoky cautery of my work the anguished, penitential truth and sweated for my release. Your honor, these manly specimens of vim and vigah swore before a justice of the peace, Brer Clyde's not so terribee bad. He was a child cozened in a she-wolf's den, suckled at her shaggy teats. Dr. Duncan and his neuro-poltroons have given him a clean bill of mental health and say he wants to be a literary asset, which he already is, so why continue to cage him?

The only problem: there were rumors that once in Soledad I killed a man. An Aryan Brother. Slit him with a jagged iron from ear to ear. But let me tell you a secret:

If anyone did it, the clown did it, or else one of his henchmen.

For there is no law in the world that states that a clown can't hire helpers.

Out on the streets, I blossomed. My first book of confessional poems, *Barathrum*, and then an epic, *Stabonia*, a bildungspoem of criminal innocence, a contemporary roman de geste in corrosive heroic couplets, made me a household name.

In it, for those who haven't read it, a man has trashed one of his kin, has laid him out with the studied swoop of an andiron. There the splattered cousin lies before the family hearth, as all his children plead and cry. My epic takes place in a mythical time when murderers are shipped to Hyperborean climes (presumably Alaskan) and there equipped by their captors with only one change of clothes and a bowie knife. Branded on the forehead, they are told, since you have lived outside the law, you are hereby relegated to Stabonia, a lawless land, where every man holds justice in the palm of his hand, and there, among the lawless gangs of stabbing exiles, my protagonist climbed and climbed the saurian ranks, until he became a king, the Tundra King, the mad prince of Thule, reigning supreme. And then he began to kill in earnest.

Hack hack stab stab hack hack stab stab.

The poem won the prestigious Peascod Literary Award (I was the first felon to win, beating out several bleating multicultural and exegetical contestants) and from there, just like my monarch, there was nowhere to go but up. Asperity of style and sulphurous concinnity and all the rigorous points of view (my secret forte) had pulled me through. Master of the hecatomb, of arsis and thesis, long-form champion of the emotional in-between with a seasoning of melanotic leanings, I was proclaimed the laureate who cast the housing of the American dream, my atrament flowing through the ghoulish heart of the nation. I crowed like old Walt Whitman, but whereas he crossed Brooklyn Ferry, I crossed Cahuenga Pass, greeting angels on the way, who were sobbing in the hills and dripping kohl and mascara. Congenial, genital, gentle Walt, do you know the ending to his poem?

You have waited, you always wait, you dumb, beautiful ministers,
We receive you with free sense at last, and are insatiate henceforward,
Not you any more shall be able to foil us, or withhold yourself from us,
We use you, and do not cast you aside—we plant you permanently within us,
We fathom you not—we love you—there is perfection in you also,
You furnish your parts toward eternity,
Great or small, you furnish your parts toward the soul.

Walt had his own fantastic clown and his own ministerial voices. The antiphon of American genius clanged high in his head. We hardly look alike, but the bell tolled for him, too.

Speaking of looks, let me describe my appearance for you.

First of all, I have my tattoos—my cutaneous alphabet containing all the letters but one—and Day-Glo orangutan hair, rough cut and erectile, the considered features of a degenerate matinée idol on a tear, and not a milligram of flab. My jawbone glistens. I drink like a fish. My bituminous eyes are a bit occluded, but the body hardly suffers at all. It just winces a little in the mornings. The key to effective drinking is to see alcohol for what it is: a fuel both physical and emotional. You have to burn it. I am built like a cornerback, which I would have been in a world without footballs. I've always limited myself to non-existent sports.

I'm missing a canine (and now a molar) from a fight. Where I'm going in this book, I won't need them.

Very young, I saw a Howdy Doody show. Flubadub, Dilly Dally, Howdy and Mr. Bluster were jerking along spasmodically on the counter, and their universe was suddenly invaded by giant marionette hairballs that would hover over their heads and take them over and make them cry or laugh. Flubadub was having a great day and a dark hairball swooped down and trembled over the poor goon's head and in midsentence he went to pieces and burst into tears. Everyone in the Peanut Gallery howled, including me, who had my own set bouncing. Normally I can't comprehend them hairy thaaaangs, but once or twice I actually did spot them, their voices lodged lysergically within the multicolored cotton candies. They would float about that plot within the brain that harbors notions of identity, and from time to time there would be an annular eclipse, Blackout City. What happened then in the outside world I wouldn't know, but on one occasion with the gun, I knew it was the licorice one, Old Knobby Nick, emerging from the belly of the clown, who was duplicated and duplicating like germs around my viscera, a continuous curse for everyone, ever since that first motile gob of clay was impregnated by lightning.

He was there, laughing in the fertile stroke, Ol' Nick at Night, with his shotgun partying.

Anyhow....

Let me state bluntly that at the end of this book I leave quite suddenly.

I'm sliced with the sign of Zorro: woops, ouch, surprise, gone! Clyde and all his talents ship away. Now why I die and how is not like Norman Bates. Disembodied, I don't sit in my cell looking up at the ceiling, blinking, admitting that I can no longer hurt a fly.

I *am* the fly.

Diptera Franklinata unfurled.

And another man takes over. A spirit much more sinister and humorous than I.

Dingdong. Answer the bell. Here's Mike the milkman with the milk.

Hi, Mike!

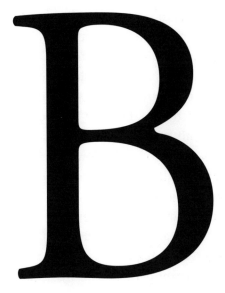

you were good, I mean to say you were barely adequate, but you used too many big words, and words are totally useless so why make a big deal about it? I mean adequate is about as big a word as I would ever use except for cebocephalic and I used to tell you, Clyde babes you're off the wall, babes ya don't need to try so hard to impress people, instead of doing all that poetic shitwork, why don't you change your face? It works, babes it works. Behind makeup a man can do just about anything, look at the dames, babes just look at the dames, and then look at em again in the morning, getting up with all that crud stuck in their eyes and that peculiar smell only women get in the mouth when they wake up and then a little mouth and eye makeup, a little collutorium a little collyrium, and to coin a word you've used from time to time, Shazaam, an instant hard-on and we're off to the races! Of course, you don't care, you'd just as soon be fucked by a man, but you don't tell your dopey readers all this, about all them rectal affairs you gets in your blacks, you just go around to the bars in invisible aprons. Yeah, we clowns are like monks, man, we walk around and people come to us when they're young and they ask a lot of questions but they're normally shy, babes it's like that nightmare guy, the priest who collected body parts has said from time to time, he says all kids practice lying, they look at you and laugh and kind of try to tickle you in the ribs (not cripple you in the ribs, that's what you got done) and all the time they're think-ing, how can I fuck that clown? Not that I'm upset or anything, hell no, I mean it's a great gig, all except for the balloon animals, I hate those fucking things cuz I'm always afraid the balloons are gonna pop, yeah I'm really afraid of those gnarly things. Another clown pal of mine Dr. Einstein said to me once that it was a deep sex thing, fear of explosion, the other side of which is that I like touching kids, I mean you tell me, Clyde, why's a shit like that a clown? God, I hate guys like that, I mean a balloon's a fucking balloon, it's not a bomb, don't you think? And while you're at it, pour me another drink. Now take my shoes. I mean there are guys who dream of shoes, they're afraid of shoes and they want to pet and polish shoes, and why? Cuz when they were young they saw nude people fucking with shoes on, or their moms bopped them once with a shoe or they've got a thing about lace and want to wear it, but they're all repressed, see, and so they get hung up on laces and they stay away from lace and instead go to the store and buy thousands of dollars worth of shoes. Balloons, shoes, you start thinking about objects and after a while they start dancing, yeah there should be a fucking disease called danceophobia, or brusho-danceophobia, fear that your tooth-brush will start dancing, in any case it's like a dancing disease, you get so hung up on things and what some inanimate piece of work will do to you that you start hallucinating and the thing itself sprouts legs like a spider or an elephant and starts moving around. This same clown Einstein told me about this shit, he really is an amateur psychologist with a couch, I mean just cuz a clown wears his hair like Einstein and wears those droopy suits and smokes a huge toy pipe doesn't make him a brain, except that Einstein claims it does. Yeah the clown guy thinks he's figured out the size of the universe, and he's put it in his act, I'll spare you the details, Clyde, but as I was saying, Einstein says that when I put legs on a balloon, it's real ancient, like looking at a stone and thinking there's a mind in there, which Einstein says there is. He says that stones have minds, but that if we think too hard about it we'll all go stark raving mad cuz we won't be able to laugh or trust our surroundings. Look, before I go too far with this thing, let's talk contract, babes let's talk major turkey.

You said to me, Chuckles, I want you in my book, you belong there, Big Guy, and I immediately said OK, but you've got to understand Clyde, that in Hollywood even the clowns have agents, and the man who reps me isn't a spic like the fag who fronts you, babes, no way, that shit is sick, my man, going and using a guy who looks like the guys you used to trash on the streets, and you suspect deep inside that you totalled the guy once and you told me so, one night when you were really drunk, you said that you remember bashing the guy up near Chandler. You let your ego get away from you, I mean you think you've cold-cocked every motherfucker in the Valley, you really do man, but you haven't and you wouldn't know it if you had and you want to know why? Cuz you can't count. You don't admit it to anyone but me and a few other uncountable people, but you have a hard time with the number three. Once in a while you get a "five-pointed star" right or a "seventy-year-old man," but that's about it. I'm amazed you stuck the fact in your book. Well, when that blade is falling from the guillotine you learn to talk real quick, and I guess that's your case, and since you've admitted that numbers isn't your thing, my agent Al told me that what I have to do is stay away from words and stick with the figures, that you're better than me with words but when we start putting those figures down on the table, man I've got you cold, you'll have to deal with me on my own terms, cuz Al tells me that I've got one thing that's the most important thing in the whole fucking community, meaning by that the Industry, as you know in LA we call the movies Toonville, yeah and that thing I've got, that most important thing in the whole fucking artsy fartsy world is EX-CLUSIVITY, which Al tells me means that there is only one of me and he says that that is something even you can understand. You remember when I was born? We came out of the box from that grape juice company and you stuck us in a cradle, as if you were our mom and you dressed us up in strange unclownlike clothes and you said some funny words and did some funny things and we were born. Yeah you had the weirdest idea, Big Fella that you gave birth to the three of us even though I was already lying there telling jokes and laughing myself silly in your fucking cradle and it took me a while to understand it cuz if you can't wear it, I have trouble understanding it, I mean Al says that my problem is that I think that the world is something you wear, like Pan-Cake and polka dots, but he tells me there's a lot more to the world than a costume, which is why I need an agent. Anyway, Einstein tells me I was introverted, and when I asked him what introverted meant, he said it was a fancy way of saying eaten, that as a doll it just wasn't good enough, that I had to be digested by your big fucking brain, like taken into your brain as if your brain was a mouth and then eaten and put inside there where I could come to life. Have you ever thought about the fact that clowns never swallow their food? They always spit it out, especially the liquids. Yeah they put it in their mouths and then they arrange for fellow clowns to slap them on the back and presto the food comes out. Clowns don't eat onstage, and the whole world, even this fucked-up bedroom with the green blinds is but a stage that others see, that other invisible people see, sitting in an audience, yeah Clyde babes we're all up on stage every moment of our lives whether we like it or not, there is a whole bunch of people watching. Now don't argue with me Clyde, just pour me another, babes. I know you think they're dead, all those guys and gals who watch, that they're all sitting on those fucking folding chairs you like to talk about, yeah that heaven is filled with folding chairs and people take them down and they fold them and unfold them. You once told me when you were real blasted that you thought that folding chairs could fly and that people flew through space on metal chairs after they died, and you want to know something? it's a rare occasion that you break me up, but that just broke me up Clyde, I mean normally you're accusing me and yelling at me, as if I did some-thing to hurt you, but when I thought about your Mom twirling like Dorothy through some eternal cyclone strapped to one of those chairs downstairs, I came unglued, babes but totally, I just thought that that was excellentay and I laughed, my lipstick cracked over that one. Anyway, I don't accept cash or plastic, no way. You gots to pay my way in illegal tender in the long red in the real stuff in the only thing that matters, I mean hemaglobin, man, I want to be paid where the sun don't shine, I want to be paid in *pints*. Look, what's money to you, Clyde? it's just potatoes, just liquid potatoes, you had a crib and four wheels and a buttery full of booze and a pen and a few reams of paper and that's about it, you're not a complex guy like me but go about your business and your royalties are not what you think, yeah you've got this king thing like your dad was some hotshot King of the Beasts or Goys, yeah some fuckhead German fartabeast or martyrbeast or some such thing and you're a prince, a margrave or the son of a Teuton washing-machine chieftain and that's why you get those royalty things which you convert into vodka. But I won't go along with that, babes, cuz that would make me a jester, which is another way of saying room and board and no pay. My agent told me to tell you to pop your bubble man (ooh I hate the thought of it) and tell you you're no Prince Chuck to Chuckles, cuz princes don't pay points and they don't pay pints, look pull yours outta there, yeah unzip and pull. Mine's bigger. Anyway, even you can't kill and the truth is you can't kill anything and never could nah you need other folks, ya need the troops. Cavalry calvary whazza diff? You suffer at the hands of dagos with their bags of nails or else ya take your micks and your fuckhead krauts to Happy Valley and wipe out the fuckin' injuns whazza diff? I guess we're getting a bit stiff, uh Clyde? but of course I'm only playing cuz what I'm drinking ain't no vodka and it ain't no Shirley Temple or Lavoris. I'm drinking the good stuff, the Big Red plus Momma Caviar, you get drunk but I get even. A clown's work is a curse. Ya know when your mom stopped singing and started cursing? Then I started chewing and lapping

One

You can't scratch a thirst. An exorcism cannot be thought out and written down. Men are conceived under the wordless scourge of Satan. Cain killed Abel, and I believe that both of their prints stayed in the sand for all of us, for all the murderers and murderees who followed. I believe that Adam, as well as Abel, died of Cain's disease, that Adam was murdered by Abel and Abel by Cain and Cain, then, by an unnamed son or brother. We are linked together at the source by birth and butchery. Nature murders nature. Man murders man. Wife murders husband. Mother starves the baby. Father feeds grandfather to son who smothers brother. It's a mirthful song, this song in the key of life.

So where was I?

After my beating, I had plenty of time to plan. Cracked ribs, a smashed nose and dislocated jaw are decubitus torments, and I lay on my hospital sheets, wheezing and snuffling and playing with my thumb in the kind of senseless autoerotic way that distracted men can sometimes fondle opposable portions of themselves.

Suddenly the ceiling ripped open like a ruptured can, flooding the room with milk.

Erupting gushing tumbling substrate milk, splashing over my body, the floor, the bedclothes, the walls and mirrors, a galactic ejaculation!

Kneeling before a decastyle, shining white in the white pouring light, I peered into a temple.

The sanctuary had a gunmetal floor. There was a human sacrifice inside whose gore was foaming, its blancmange shifting out in airy pools below the ceiling paint. There was something immaculate and innocent there. A oneness. A baby oneness. I wanted to lie down and open on that altar, as when a man instants before orgasm searches for the explosive center of his pleasure: the tip of an entering knife wound, purity without debridement. Mom was hovering over me, holding the napkins. She licked and wiped me clean. Her wrists were parched and red, and something of mine had dried like druse on her lips. It smelled funny, like the funny part of me. She was preparing the tools for sacrifice, but I wasn't resentful. I had calmed down, and when she turned away, I did what I could to get ready and tried to be discreet. I loved Mom, as I shall testify shortly. She reminded me, in her sufferings, of cold Baltic lands, the homes of Jewish fishermen, with their barbs and heavy shanks. Mom's cunt was loofah-hard, but how was I to know? The maternal victim, suffering in front of me as I squatted like a flannel-clad daruma on the wreckroom floor, yes, I remember as she flinched and he roared. Words came out of his mouth as he struck her with the whip, but to me they were just a warble of m's and n's and o's. The panting mouth moved about its theoretical circle.

Transfixed, I stopped stroking my thumb and strained toward an incantation on the temple's final column. The Psalmist says that God is a pillar of iron. Slung on my bed, my ribs shimmering in pain, and more pain, moving along my thighs and up through the small of my back, as I propped my head and strained, the letters were unclear to this abecedarian, but I knew the message that could save me was there, burning on the pillar somewhere.

Milk! Milk! Milk! Milk! Milk! Milk! Milk! Milk! Milk!

My father told me that as an infant I had never cried, and when I watched the mayhem, little Jack Armstrong in his fluffy pyjamas on the Armstrong linoleum, I used to smile with glaring, aridisol eyes, but what was Mom doing in the back, rummaging, her laying of hands, where, on my ransacked, sacrificial body?

Peace. Peace. Peace.

I saw the epigraph fuming on the milky cylinder, unveiled by the Black Messenger of God. I read his ruthless words revealed to me in white-hot metal, and as far as I could, I wept.

In the weeks before she went away, when she wouldn't talk, I sat in my cell, searching in my lap for thoughts and traces. Mom and I had forged a pact, I felt. She and I had lost the same identical words, but my loss was much deeper. She hanged herself alongside the Packard, but nobody could tell me exactly what had happened. Was the joke on me? Did she *really* hang herself? I loved my mother, but I honestly believe she didn't love me. The children of suicides are always mystified, and I don't understand. Why did she kill herself? What did I really do?

Two

People inside prison are much more interesting than people outside prison. They are infinitely more vast and aware. There are men in prison who inhabit microworlds, who think the same thoughts over and over again. This deepens them. There are men who, living at the height of manipulation and power, become institutionalized because their uniqueness and fullness are way too harsh and intrusive. There are men in prison who are morons, of course.

The guards.

Once I was released, I immediately began using the prison model to my advantage by continuing to measure the world from a prisoner's point of view. A man who has served behind bars can easily see the invisible bars that surround most forms of human consciousness. The entire planet is a giant license plate factory. We all make the numbers and then we wear them.

Like my friend and cellmate, Billy Ziqubu.

Billy was from Soweto, but in the final years of his life, he lived in a fancy, high-security loft in downtown LA. Billy had studied astrology in France, and during the years we spent sealed off from the heavens, he taught me some extraordinary things about the nature of the sky. When we gaze skyward, Billy told me, what we see are the smallest things in the universe, not the most gigantic. The blinking stars are tiny spirits of the oppressed, the pain and glory of the criminal and abused writ large. The stars are the most visible forms of magical powers, of the minute inhabitants of cell and belly. The eye sees into the far distance and views the inside factors. It views the spirits and the microbes.

Billy was a great mystical knower and lover, supporting himself from a tender age through the exercise of armed robbery while inhabiting liquor stores, although the only time I ever saw Billy look like he really wanted to use a weapon, he was looking at me. Fortunately, at the time he wasn't armed, because there was something I saw in Billy's look at that crucial moment that filled me with foreboding. The reason Billy wanted to shoot me was because I had buttfucked his wife, Bridgette. Bridgette was from Norway and wound up killing Billy, a few months before I'd flown to Washington. A lot of my friends have trouble managing interpersonal relationships.

Being an African, Billy also taught me something very important about tribes. Everyone succeeds tribally, he advised me. Figure out your tribe. If you don't have one, join one. If you can't join one, form one. No one can be happy unless he is acting in the midst of a tribal situation. Billy was a Zulu.

The reason I mention Billy, even though I never followed his advice, is that he had a close friend, Judas Brennemann, echt Lebanese, a former purveyor of horse and hashish, who was his roommate in Paris in the sixties, at the time that Billy was glossing his ephemeri. Once we were both out on the street, Billy hooked me up with the man, and to sate my dominant lust, whenever I was in Washington, I would connect with Judas's establishment and bring along my toolbox and Master Card. Immense and colloped, a proverbial spy-tale fixture among his rugs and myrmidons, this lardaceous Lord of the Bizarre, of souk and suck and sodomy, ran a Maronite escort service to furnish his political and social betters with tops and bottoms, leathers and satins, straight and gay. It was considered to be the premier sexual service operating within the Beltway, but in this particular case I needed to see Judas, not in order to hire submissives, but in order to try to save the life of my professional girlfriend.

I had met Barbie at a delicatessan on Sunset Boulevard. She came up to me and smirked and sat and we broke bread and within a day or two we were breaking each other. Not a Barbie Doll. Not some silicone-labialized ewe-necked urn standing by the fire, spreading her tawdry silks, armed with her cellular, rolling iridescent eyes, the moistened tongue emergent slightly to the right, and dialing and winking (showing you the basic steps) and saying how pleased she is to please, please dial one nine hundred big girl, big cunt, big lick, big suck, the scrabble of the digitally-transmitted auricular feast. No, not the kind of Barbie you would associate with being a hooker (which she was), and although I suspected at the time that Barbie was a nom de lit, that her name wasn't used in any other bed but mine, it was more accurately a nom de deli, created on the spot for my entrapment and delight. Barbara Candelaria, later known as June Sunlight, was stacked and grim, with that hardened air a call girl carries about the canthi and slightly spaced teeth, which helped her breathe more easily. Her legs were long and powerful. She had nary a dent from stem to stern, save perfect partings at the butt and bosom, and her drum-tight torso moved in six directions like a hummingbird's vibrato. Barbie was in her thirties but she wore extremely well and added something inexpressible to the color of a gifted man's imagination—a tough togetherness and tougher longing and control that, matched to my painful love and indeterminacy, made us instantly fervid partners—and when, after weeks of dizzying sex on algolagnic heights, she finally waved goodbye, backing her Civic out of my driveway, I called, "Goodbye, Barbie!" and she replied as she rolled up her window, "My name isn't Barbie. Goodbye!"

For my part, I can tell you that I was joyfully and totally addicted, both body and mind. I loved to hear her moan. And she loved me, for other more interior reasons.

At the time we met, she was in a dire and delicate predicament.

She had conducted business all her life in the Capital and had recently involved herself in the blackmail of a United States senator. Having collected the money, she had had to leave town in a hurry, because the man was a poor sport.

The senator, who had actually put out a contract, was Daniel

Quentin Abernathy of New York City, who was now, by the grace of Barbie, half a million dollars poorer. For those of you who are reading this in the distant future or who have never opened up a newspaper, Abernathy was a wildly-popular, relatively-youngish presidential candidate, a visionary according to his press kit, and the pampered son of a billionaire philanthropist and brephophage real estate developer. An azure-eyed pol with rouged buccinators and a concretized do piled high in clumsy waves atop his head, Danny was the great hope of the American underclass.

Unfortunately, he liked to dress up hookers in pinafores with nothing underneath and belt them down in the boudoir and belt them with the right, while pumping on his dangling sausage with the left (according to Barbie, it never did get hard), and like a goodly member of the Democratic Party, he never tipped. Exactly like my father, Charles Wilson Franklin the Great, of whom I'm now the criminal avatar, Danny shared the same palatine postures and stationary deep-titted targets, which was neither royal nor democratic nor uncommon. Of this, more later. Barbie had a clandestine video shot of him, she said, saliva dribbling down the cleft of his chin, applying diligent elbow grease and muttering "stupid fucking cunt, stupid fucking cunt," which Barbie explained to me was worth precisely eighty-three thousand dollars a word.

One morning, in my cottage in Laurel Canyon, the telephone had rung, and within the hour, Barbie had packed and disappeared. A week later, I received this message, along with a first-class airline ticket and boarding pass:

Lover:

Come quickly but don't tell anybody. My life is in danger and there is no one here who can protect me. I need your help desperately. I miss you terribly. I'll meet you at the airport.

Barbie

After they let me out of the hospital, I went to pay a visit to Judas Brennemann with flowers in a wicker handbasket.

He officed in a townhouse on N Street in Georgetown. I rang the doorbell, and the fat man answered. Actually Judas didn't sport a fez, but in my mind's eye I placed one on him. He wore a blazer that billowed like a tent, a blue broadcloth button-down shirt, open at the collar, and massive pleated slacks. His reception room was upholstered in ecru, with slick moderne fixtures and Haniwa and pre-Columbian antiques. There were German prints on the walls, Baselitz, Förg, Kiefer. A half-empty bottle of Zinfandel sat on a red-lacquer coffee table, along with cake caltrops and purplish, wilted Camembert.

"Do you have any vodka?" I blurted out, once I had handed him the cheap bouquet, which had a finch perched on a dowel stuck in it.

"It's ten in the morning, Franklin," he noted, unshaved and weary, as he placed the flowers on the table. He waddled into his kitchen and returned with ice in a highball glass and a frosted bottle of Smirnoff.

The brand didn't make me happy, but I poured anyway.

"Got any lemons?"

He trudged back into the kitchen.

"Precise, aren't we?" he commented irritably, when he finally came back. He tossed a slice into my glass and then lowered himself into an armchair that was framed by a bay window facing onto the street. It was a grim morning. He lit a Camel as he flashed me a baleful look. For reasons unbeknownst to me, the man had a chip on his shoulder.

"You know, Billy once told me that he respected and cared for you a lot but that he didn't trust you," he observed with unconcealed annoyance. "Billy trusted everyone, but in your case he made an exception. He told me just before he died that you were spooky."

"Yeah, Billy and I did a lot of time together," I said. "He knew me well enough to put all trust aside."

"Are you looking me up for a reason," he asked suspiciously, "perhaps having something to do with the fact that your nose is totally fucked up?"

"I thought I could solicit some free advice. You've always been kind to me in the past, and I have a serious problem."

"You only hired me a couple of times, and I made you pay in advance. Nothing's free around here."

"Billy said that if I ever needed anything in Washington, I could rely on you," I insisted.

The guy was being a shit. I pulled a snapshot out of the inside pocket of my leather jacket and handed it to him.

"Is this the way you normally gift-wrap women?" he asked, slightly amused.

"Spur of the moment," I said, "but at least you get the idea."

"What's her name?"

"Actually, I don't know her real name. She told me her name was Barbie Candelaria."

"I've never seen this woman in my life. She's a working girl, I suppose?"

"She was, but now she's my fiancée. She was supposed to meet me at the airport, but I was greeted by this instead." I pointed at my face. "She never showed up and now I'm trying to find her."

He shrugged his shoulders.

"A fiancée who doesn't tell you her name? It should be a splendid marriage."

"Would you mind showing this picture around?" I asked, putting aside the insult. "Maybe one of the people who work with you will know her."

Judas looked at me as I emptied my tumbler of vodka, and then he stared at the pathetic finch atop the bouquet. He seemed to be considering what to do next. He poured himself some Zinfandel, put out the stub of his cigarette and took a sip. He picked up the photo and studied it again. Then he lit another cigarette and turned the photo over and put it down on the table.

"Did she get any pleasure out of this?"

"Be more specific," I said, as I refilled my glass.

"What I mean is, did you pay to tie her up in nautical knots?"

"No, I didn't pay her. I already told you, we're engaged to be married."

He made a quick assessment and seemed to determine that I was telling the truth, which I was in this case.

"Well then, why don't you tell me the rest of the story?"

"There's not much to tell. She made a powerful enemy who apparently wants to have her dead and has hired a professional to do it. She sent me a note that she was in trouble, I came, and I didn't even make it out of the airport. I don't know where she is, and I don't know anybody in Washington, except for you and one other friend. I was relying on you, Judas. As a matter of fact, I was certain that you would know my girlfriend, since you're both in the same business."

"It's a big city."

"Somebody is trying to kill her," I pleaded, "and I'm in love with the woman."

"Can you tell me the name of the man?"

"What man?"

"The man who is trying to kill her, of course."

"Not without her permission."

"Well, is he a client of mine?"

"It's possible, given what I know."

"But you've never talked to him?"

"Never."

"By powerful, do you mean politically powerful?"

"Yes, he's an elected official."

"In the city or national?"

"In the federal government."

"And you're certain this person is the one who had your face trashed?"

"I'm certain. Who else would do it? As I said, I don't know anyone here."

"Why are you so certain? If you've never met this guy, how did he know you were going to be at the airport? This all seems pretty far-fetched. Federal officeholders don't hire people to rough other people up."

"I don't know how he knew I was on the plane, but he did. I'm sure there's a reasonable explanation."

"You'll pardon my saying this, but your story doesn't make any sense unless this lady told you some cock-and-bull story and then set you up."

"Why would she set me up? We're in love," I objected with a hurt look.

"Do you carry a gun, Franklin?"

"I have to admit that I just purchased one."

"Is that the kind of help you were offering her?"

I was getting pissed.

"What do you do when one of your employees gets threatened? Do you just kiss it off?"

He raised an eyebrow. I could tell that he was still trying to understand what was going on.

"You might be after the girl," he said.

"What the fuck do you mean by that?"

"It's just that I don't know who you're after with that gun."

My string had run out with this asshole. I had wasted good money on a bouquet. I got up to leave.

"Don't take it personally," Judas said, as he stood to show me out.

"I do take it personally. You were a close friend of the man who used to be my best friend, and you're my only fucking lead. I take it very personally."

He laughed and shook my hand.

"You bring me ten thousand, and if I'm able to get you in touch with your girlfriend, you give me another ten thousand. If I can't help you, I'll give you a full refund. Now how's that?"

I suddenly realized that he never had any intention of letting me out the door without relieving me of some of my money. He just wanted to figure out where I was coming from and to estimate how much he could get. So much for friendship among thieves.

"I don't know how much money I have," I replied. "Somebody else keeps track for me. I'll have to check."

"Fair enough, Clyde," Judas said, downshifting to a first-name basis. "As soon as I get the cash, I'll dedicate all of my resources to it, and if she's in town, we'll find her!"

"You could have treated me better," I said resentfully, as I headed out the door.

"Yes, you're probably right," he offered.

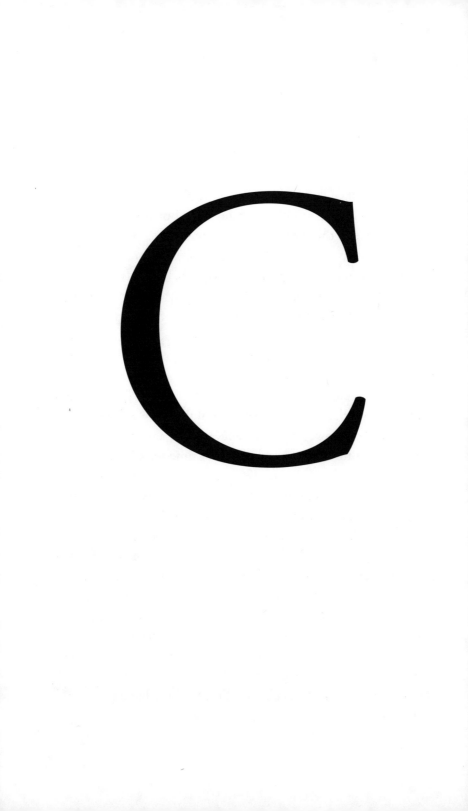

got a lot of guts, Clyde telling people you're not after the broad, not that you intend to kill her or anything but you are really after her and come to think of it since you never use a piece, I guess I'm going to have to make the ultimate decision and what's that bit about Nobby Nick with the shotgun? Who the fuck is that? Today I'm Bozo, then Clarabell, then Pagliacci, soon if I read you right I'll be Emmett Kelly, I mean guy, take it easy, give a clown a break, I mean I don't want to be like you guy, I want to know that when I pick up a foot it's gonna come down and I'm gonna be somewhere, I don't want to lift it up and disappear. Besides, you and I agreed on a name and I've got my name contract right here that says that this is my name until the Time of the Curse and I can use it however and whenever I like and since it's night and there's nothing to do and plenty of time for advice, let me tell you something about that fat Lebanese. The asshole's lying, and was that bourgeois whorehouse in poor taste or what? I've seen better dressing rooms and could you believe the antiques? Einstein taught me how to tell when a vase is bogus by the way, ya wanna know how? Ya drop it and see if the owner cries. The guy cries and it's the real McCoy and then what you do is cry back, you shed big tears and you start picking up pieces one by one and staring at them, you become fascinated with the pieces and you turn them around clockwise and counterclockwise and then you bite down on one as if you were trying to decide whether the fucking thing is coin of the realm and then you change your tune and smack your lips, Einstein has a great lip-smack, positively great, the guy goes smack and it's like you got hit upside the head his smack has such fucking force and drama. And that Judas drinks cheap wine. Yeah, if you looked twice you could tell that that rotgut wasn't for customers. To them he serves champagne, he probably has about six different levels of champagne cuz the cat works in Washington where everything happens on levels. You he gave Smirnoff but you know he had the good stuff in the fridge. What a fucking asshole! Yeah he knew your Barbie Doll too, probably better than you knew her and better than I knew her, you only let me see her once or twice, God she had a great twat! It sung, I mean Pledge of Allegiance all the way, babes, it stood up and gave it to you twenty-one guns, boy I was really impressed, I mean I'm no cunt doctor, but I gotta tell you Clyde, you really scored with that chick, she had a box you couldn't match in a hundred years, if ya lived to be a hundred, and so I understand man why you're so hung up, even if you never did really fuck her. It was great, let me tell ya. Yeah, I don't got the foreplay, but I'm great at follow-through, Mr. Throughput, that's me, immediate laughs and timing. We gotta get you on television. We gotta get you on a knife commercial. I'll hold the tray. The guy with the rubber nose, holding the display, sure I'll be more than happy to do it and I'll have Al speak with your agent Roy about it. Dig it! The Poetry Knife. The Ginzu Gutwrencher. The Clyde Wayne Franklin Collection with a complimentary set of soiled bedroom linens, for the truly adventurous we got the serrateds and we got the shit you core apples with, we got the tines and tongs and the files and we also got on the table here next to the sliced chicken we got those Japanese balls you stick up there and the woman who is all tied up moves them around until she comes while you chomp down on her titties. Oooh man, doing that feels good. Reeeeeal good. Break out another bottle while I'm thinking. Let's crush the ice this time Clyde, you always go with the chunks, man, chunks of ice chunks of lemon and sometimes chunks of lime, babes nobody drinks chunks in their drinks anymore, not even the fucking ringmaster takes his drinks with chunks. The cool thing going is granulated. Look you're having your milk dream right? but do you tell your reader's if the milk is butterfat? No way, cuz it fucks with your literary styling, man it fucks with the readers mind to mention how much cream there is in your fucking creamy vision. You're off someplace watching your Mom jack you off, you're whipping away on your digit there, you tell your reader it's your thumb, but every clown in the universe knows better and your Mom is doing like she did when you came and she came and your Daddy couldn't but oh no, you aren't going to mention that, cuz stuff like that's too intimate, I mean it's one thing to talk about blowing off heads and walking down stairs hoisting a cleaver but a simple handjob by Mom while you were doing your unimaginable thing and Daddy was whipping and sweating and screaming just doesn't cut the literary mustard. Remember the first commandment of novel-writing: the audience is composed of dainty finical frightened beings, the average reader is a pansy, a pussy, a closeted creep, a buffoon, a trembling leaf, a straightjacketed serf, a plodding ox, a paying customer who rightly deserves to get fleeced, so file it down, babes, and keep it acceptably clean. Anyway, the pathetic thing is that you don't know for sure it happened, that primal satanic wreckroom scene. You have built tall walls, you barely remember anything, you don't really know Clyde, it's amazing you can even pour (make it a little more) and why can't we get some air in here? I've been here for decades and I still don't get my air. There's some heavy-duty nitrates out there in the weather but breathing this shit in this pigsty room of yours with the psycho handwriting on the walls is ridiculous, I mean you're no Jackson Pollock Clyde, your work has integrity and brutish charm, but in the final analysis your allover wall-writing style doesn't quite succeed, and you never open the window and you never open a door. Yeah doors for you are problems. Hey, I can sympathize. Look sometimes we have these box contraptions we use in the ring, we got two boxes, see, and they each have doors and then we tie a cord between them like some walky talky thing and I bend down and Al kicks me in the rear into the box and Einstein he starts futzing with the other box and looks around it and opens the other door and kind of thinks about climbing inside it but he doesn't so instead he hoists Al up onto the cord cuz up above us there is this funambulist in sequins and she's actually walking the rope and Al looks at the dame and he starts walking with one foot on the cord and the other on the ground he walks along looking up and imitating what she does, just like you did sometimes with your Mom, and there's a hole in the bottom of my box for my hands and I start crawling and the cord starts moving and Al starts hopping on one foot and stabbing (pardon my use of language) stabbing with his other foot at the cord and the woman is doing her thing forty feet above (that's two times two times two times two times two plus two plus two plus two plus two Clyde) and Al falls down and Einstein does a double roll and pulls a gun from his tunic and shoots but he only shoots if the woman is done and if she's not he doesn't. Anyway it's all about doors, it's all about my going in that first door, ya see Clyde, the door's the thing, that first door makes the act come alive and keeps Al and Einstein moving. Now rooms have doors and brains have doors and broads have doors and doors and doors, and if you can't go through em ya might as well not look at em or touch em. So let me ask you a simple question, what do you do if the door you need to go through is locked? Do you laugh alot? You do? That's terrific. Hey who was it, Arthur Godfrey, who said that laughter is the best goddamn cocktail that mankind ever invented? I believe it. I really do. I mean here we are both drinking. We hold up our glasses to the light, to that fucking bulb you got dangling there, man have you ever heard of buying a fixture? Anyway, we both hold up our glasses to the light and you see clear and I see ruby, why? It's all in the nature of laughter, Clyde and the nature of doors. Now I have here the signed contract that you and your mom worked out, and it's painfully obvious according to Al my agent that in drafting things you have no sense of humor. You write like an elephant. It's like the chapter you're gonna do about what happened to you with that little girl, the flat-faced kid, the saint who you fucked over on the playground. You set the scene, right? The priest, I mean that priest is a real fucking nightmare, the priest has squashed a girl in the Big Two, correct? He lands on her with a parachute which is hard to believe but I guess it's actually true, cuz the guy told you all about it, and so you go to a playground and you fuck over a little girl too, I mean this is some kind of fucking humor you got going for you Clyde, I mean the parallels are just too fucking deadpan and poignant and then you're gonna get down on your knees on the playground and move your head from side to side like an elephant and this little girl is going to put her hand in the small of your back just like that jiggaboo did in the alley, man and she's going to be control- ling you real deep, just like you really want every woman to do. One night I asked Einstein about it, I said, here's a guy, Einie babes, who's into major theater. He hires hookers, he likes the working kind, and he pays them every cent he makes but pin money and he ties them up in many ways for days and does all kinds of grungy stuff cuz he wants to keep control but what is it he really does? Einstein said you give away the farm. Don't ask me what he meant, but he says that's what you do. Anyway, there you'll be quite soon on the playground and your head will move, as it did when this actually happened, from side to side in exactly the way you write. I mean you are really fucked up and bound in. You go loop loop loop and move along the ground arrooo arrooooo, Elephant Clyde my man you do pour a wicked one however, it makes me want to fly, it makes me want to do my highwire verbal number that you hate so much, yeah man, that smacks so fine and good, it's wet and true. Drinks, man. We both are pro drinkers. We're so hung up that we stare at the surfaces. Mmmm, that good surface tension just before we tilt them back and break them. You gets my pun, Clyde, don't you babes? The arm goes up up up and the booze goes Down Down Down, and it starts in the center at the center of all good tension and it's so crazy and it hurts so much and then it breaks bam! suddenly into pleasure, the mind reacts and jerks like an audience laugh, just like that silence when you've made your clownish move, that split second of silence when you wait for the bray of the hyenas, and it comes, your body comes, and the warmth of the drink spreads into your brain and into my veins, vodka to brain and blood to blood, you, me, two different souls in the same ecstatic body, aah, eees a lovely world we live in, Clyde quite lovely, and I know what you're thinking, you're always afraid of me, like I'm not going to give you your keys back or something. You're afraid I'm gonna keep em, but it's not in the contract and neither Al nor me nor Einstein was ever a scab, man we do what we say and we don't take graft. Look let me show you three objects. Here's a key, here's a gun, and here's my dick. Take your choice. See. You always take a key. You're afraid man I'm gonna take over your life that you'll never come back and that your blood will wind up in my belly you're worried that when you leave me with the keys that your house will be possessed and you will have no way of knowing that you're a tattooed freak with multiple heads lost in a labyrinth with the brain of three clowns and a baby and you'll stay out there in the outer banks flying among the souls a revered spirit hanging out in a fog of spirits a poet unable to return and that evil will take charge of your limbs and limbic system and make you my mumbling slave of madness and that you will slowly lose your mind until you are ready to be eaten and then I will take you, and your essence will be dissolved in the murky acids of my intestines and you will descend Down Down Down into the gut Down Down Down into the suffocating center of my gut Down Down Down until you are merely a breathless voiceless shapeless absence but hey man che sarà sarà what will be will be, for who's the funniest clown ya know? ....dah! dah! dah!

and who's the clown on Howdy's show? ....dah! dah! dah! yeah
that's me! and now I gotta figure out how to fix my seltzer bottle
the fucking thing keeps jamming they don't make things the

One

I was sitting on the balcony of my hotel suite, looking out at the street, when the front door opened behind me and Father Kosmoski walked into the room. He was carrying another paperback, and he waited on my couch, not wishing to disturb me, and opened his book and started reading. I remained on the balcony another half hour, and then I got up and went inside, and he stood and we shook hands. He was dressed in golfing clothes: a pale-green club sweater, tartan pants, and a yellow shirt with a floppy collar.

He was wearing the same socks he had worn on the airplane.

"I'm on my way to Florida," he explained.

"You don't stop moving."

"When you called and said you'd been hurt, I came as soon as I could."

"I'm glad you were willing to let bygones be bygones."

"You're just excitable. I didn't take offense."

"No flowers?"

"No flowers."

"That's too bad."

The priest placed his book on the end table and sat down.

"So what happened?"

"An altercation over a woman," I said. "Somebody made it painfully clear that they don't want me in town."

"A rival?"

"No, somebody who just doesn't want me to be part of the picture. It's too complicated to explain."

"A personal matter. I understand."

"Anyway, I needed to see you because I had a vision. I consider that my vision was God-inspired, and I was instructed in it that you were the man that could help me."

"Is that so? Really?"

"Yes, I've been told that I must change my life, in the same way that your life has been changed, and that the man who saved you can now save me."

The priest sighed deeply and shook his head.

"God told you this?"

"Exactly."

"God moves in strange ways. How do you know that your vision was God-inspired?"

"Everything in my head was rearranged. The ceiling opened up and my world turned white. Only God can do that. I prayed fervently for guidance, and He came to me."

I was standing by the sliding doors and fingering the curtains. I stared at the pattern. They felt dirty.

"Even if I wanted to assist you, which I don't," the priest said, "I know for a fact that the man who helped me is not available to see you, and besides, as I told you before, I'm convinced that his message would mean nothing to you. You should have listened to me the first time and saved me a trip over here. You called me under false pretenses."

"What makes you so fucking smart?" I asked resentfully.

The priest refused to answer.

"You're putting me down, aren't you?" I said. "I still don't see why I couldn't absorb this man's message."

"It's just that I arrive at an understanding of what people are telling me much more quickly than you do," the priest replied. "You seem to be constantly distracted. Moreover, I not only absorb things but I have a sixth sense as well. That's why I was good at what I did. I used the power of my intellect like a light to flood the inner thoughts of my victims. When I met the last man I was supposed to kill, I had already begun to construct a logic that would enforce his destruction, but he created a more encompassing logic, and the demigod in me, the cosmic mathematician who had arranged each assassination like a position in chess, was humbled."

"And so I'm a psycho-killer, is that it? I just stagger around, chopping people to bits."

"Why do you say *people*," the priest asked in an alarmed tone. "So far as I know, there was only your father. And why do you say *chopping*?"

"Don't be so fucking picky," I objected, as I moved over and sat down in a chair opposite him. Something about what he had just said made me suspicious and uncomfortable.

"Do you have a gun, Clyde?" Duke asked, as he tapped his fingers against the armrest. Again, the gun.

"A forty-five automatic," I said. "I picked it up after I got out of the hospital, but as a result of my vision, I probably won't be needing it."

"Then hand it over to me," he demanded.

He stared at me, and there was something unusual in that stare, something that I wished I could understand, since I felt compelled, as if hypnotized, to comply. I went into my closet and got it and brought it back and put it in his hand, which was outstretched, waiting. I'd never given anyone my weapon before.

Father Duke removed the clip and placed the pistol next to his book.

"What about pain?" I said, as something burst inside my head.

"I don't understand your question."

"Where's the pain?" I yelled at him, suddenly spinning out of control. "You boast to me how fucking brilliant you are, but there wasn't a glimmer of intelligence in anything you just said. Let me tell you something. Every muscle of our bodies developed the way it did as a result of a need to fight, throttle, blind, claw, club and chop, yes chopping! Name me a saint who didn't experience pain! He moved through fire, starved his body on nettles, was roasted at the stake. His face turned black in front of all the idiots! There were no crocodile tears! I'm an expert on suffering. Inflicting pain was my family form of vespers, and I still love to do it. Look at me! I'm battered, yet I'm glad! Yeah, I'm deliriously happy! Ecstatic! I'm a poet! You say you're logical, but you've never felt the strength and purpose of *my* logic! You've read my fucking books! So fucking what! Any buffoon can read fucking books, anybody can say they're a fucking expert on fucking books!"

And I reached across the coffee table, grabbed him by the sweater and shirt, and jerked him to his feet. I felt I had been taken over by a Fury. I was losing it. I felt like doing something.

Yet this man seemed incredibly heavy. As if I were under some sort of spell, he seemed almost too heavy to lift, and when he gently took my wrists, I let go and left him alone.

"Very interesting," he said.

I took a step backwards. He had a warlock's power.

"What?"

"Your face when you're angry. Your features swim. They go into flux and everything moves at once. The Church would call it a possession, but of course you and I know better, don't we?"

"I am possessed. That's the whole point."

"It's the source of your fame, but I'm not buying."

"What do you mean?" I asked.

"Oh, I can see what's going on," he said, returning to the couch and settling down again.

The letter M was tattooed on the back of my left hand, and I scratched at the duff that overlaid it.

We were both silent for a while.

"The famed poet of the apocalypse," he prodded me sarcastically. He obviously bore a resentment from being tricked into visiting me and then being wrenched to his feet.

"This is the apocalypse," I said. "We live in the days before God."

"The Microbe God, Clyde?"

I broke into laughter. Yet I must admit that underneath it all I was stunned, because I have seen the Microbe God, who lives in our intestines and eats our food and robs us of our afterthoughts. How did he know what I was thinking? Perhaps I had written about this in the past.

"You chatter on and on," the priest continued, condescendingly, "but I confess that I find you quite slow. The children I've helped with adoption speak much more cogently than you do, and their words are knitted together in a way that totally shuts me out. They can deceive me and I can deceive them, and we can laugh as we share our lies. But your lies are transparent. I look between the words and I see what's really rattling around in there. I see your hidden acts."

Suddenly, details caught my eye that I hadn't seen before. I saw that something had changed, something that gave the whole situation away. I looked carefully and began to see small clues. In every instance, I could see changes. A slightly thicker brow, the chroma of hair, like the print of a finger, slightly off. Kosmoski seemed smaller, more cunning and compact. I realized that this was not the man I had met on the plane, the chuckling priest who spoke Russian.

I realized with a shock that this was a different man.

But I kept my own counsel.

"I suppose you're the only one who can see into me," I said.

"Perhaps. In any case, I see the most important thing in you," he replied.

"And what do you see?"

"The mystery about you. The thing that makes you vulnerable. I could tell you what it is over and over again, but you wouldn't hear me. It's possible I'm telling you right now, and you don't hear me. This thing at the center of your being will rise up and destroy you, Clyde. I see you moving toward madness and slaughter. I see it all played out in advance, the entire scene."

"I do think you have powers, but not the ones you say you do," I said. "You have others, but you can't look inside me."

"Suit yourself," the priest replied, "but I'll stress again that I don't think you heard what I just said."

"I'll give you another chance to say it," I said, and I smirked, knowing that this was a different voice from the voice I heard on the plane.

"You are heading for destruction. It's coming very soon."

"I heard you," I confirmed. "I'm going to be destroyed."

"Exactly."

"And there's no way out of this for me?"

"None at all. It's as if it has already happened."

"But you don't even know what's going on in my life. I've told you nothing about my circumstances," I objected.

"It's true. I don't even know what happened to your face. It's not important."

"Can I get you a drink?" I offered, wishing to change both the mood and the subject.

"I could use a scotch," the priest replied good-naturedly, "if you have one. On the rocks, please."

I went into the kitchenette and poured us each a tall glass of Stoli with ice and threw in the proper amount of lemon.

I drank mine, refilled it, and then took both glasses back into the living room. I placed his glass next to the gun and sat back, harboring my drink, delicately balancing it on my crotch.

"Not too tawny," he laughed.

"I'm certain you're not surprised," I ventured, "since you've flooded my mind with the light of your perception and control."

"Thanks." He toasted me with his glass and drank some.

There was another pause in our conversation, and I tried to relax, and he looked about the room, as if he were examining it for the first time. I realized that he must have gone over it in detail while I was faced away from him on the balcony, but I put up with this charade, just as I had put up with the change in his identity. And then I began to think that maybe it was the same guy, and that my drink had helped me put it back in perspective. After all, I had dialed his home phone number, the one he had given me on the plane, and he had answered, and then this priest had shown up, so that if this wasn't Father Duke Kosmoski, I wouldn't really have an adequate explanation as to what had happened to the real Duke. I decided to accept the fact that this was another man and the same man. Both, at the same time. I began to calm down a bit and savored a sip of vodka on the back of my tongue.

"There's a problem here with doctrine," I finally said.

"What do you mean?" the priest asked politely.

"I mean, where's the extreme unction? I'm heading toward destruction, you're an ordained priest, there's only one life according to Christianity and I'm living it, I need to be saved, I'm telling you that I *must* be saved, and you're sitting there smugly telling me, fuck you. It's not doctrinaire. You'll go to hell for it. You'll burn in hell."

The priest glanced at the weapon. Then he looked at his watch. There was a subtle but decided change in his demeanor. He seemed deeply disturbed by what I'd just said. For a man who claimed he knew practically everything, there were apparent weaknesses in his thought processes. I could sense that the business about burning in hell had turned him instantly around.

"I'd like you to come to my orphanage," he concluded after a minute of thought.

"Why's that?"

"I want to see what happens to you there. If you're serious about wanting to find yourself, then I'm not asking very much as a first step."

"When?"

"I'll give you a ring as soon as I get back from Florida. And now I have to go or I'll miss my flight. I'm sorry, but I have to hurry. I'm sure you'll pardon me."

And he stood up and pocketed my gun, leaving the clip behind.

Two

Now I want to tell you more about that very special night.

I don't think I mentioned that Daddy was shot in the orifice "when all through our house not a creature was stirring not even a mouse." The cachectic fir was ablaze upstairs, with its special German ornaments that had been in Father's family for years, handed down from the dim past. Needles were littered wall to wall, an evergreen haulm that made the Karistan seem like a perfumed forest floor. Along with a friend of mine from school, I had mounted a Santa and sleigh, bordered in flashing blue, on the steep-pitched alpine roof.

Santa seemed to be waving to the gull, who stuck on her pinion wasn't going anywhere.

Dad had had a face like a hartebeest, high and narrow, with a turned-down nose, cracked, droopy lips and pendulous shaggy knitted brows. He was a large man and taught me how to fight (without gloves). We had lessons. I would take my knowledge into the streets, where my specialty was solitary Mex. Why them? I never really cared to figure it out, but heading north from Encino I would find them, isolated, and I'd pounce and impound their pesos. Over my many years of safariings, hearty son of a hartebeest on the chase, I never got a mark on my face—not until I was caged, when I was recognized and the cholos got me back.

In my primary-school days, I sat at my desk and grated my thumbnail against the grain of the fliptop in order to raise a sliver and through dexterity wedge it underneath and drive it deeper and deeper while the teacher taught us kat spelling and incomprehensible tables and her pastel dreams of civics; and as the school terms slowly passed, I buttressed up and grew, and the high-school years arrived of Annette Funicello and Paul Anka and Bobby Darin, when I thrived and kicked ass at the drive-ins.

At home, I'd spitshine my combat boots. I mohawked my top and covered myself with ashblack. Well, Emmett Kelly, I'd say, tell me the militant truth. What happened an hour ago on the sidewalks?

Keep buffing, Brother Nigritude, the clown instructed me kindly, until you can see your face.

Visions and omens are linked. An omen is a softer vision. A surface glimmer of meanings half-meant and half-dreamed, a faceless coin worth an indeterminate something, omens are the world's great teachers. Sometimes my visions would be like seizures, and I'd come to, spent, and for months afterwards there would be little jerks and trembles, the gees and haws of occult morality whispering to me in the form of omens. Ominous spirits guided me up the concrete staircase to the front door that holy night when every star in the sky was merry and twinkling. I still remember the blue-blinking tint of the door handle, like the shine of spittle, as I turned it and pulled; and then I let go of the windlass and fell, Down Down Down the well into the silence of the dark.

Clyde in Butcherland.

Every family has its tender zones, the rifts and clefts of dangers and alerts. Man will eventually outgrow the family, but until he does, there will always be closets filled with lingerie and weapons.

After the priest had left, a medical call came through. It was from my current psychiatrist, Léon May, an Alsatian, feeble-minded soul with myriad degrees from all the proper institutes and academies. I'd see him in his office at Havenhurst and attempt to count the diplomas, pompous on his walls, in French and Norse and German. The dim guy had it all. Shit, I'd be disgusted, thinking this prick's hard for life, nobody can take anything away from him, but I'd keep going back for sessions because of this desperate thing, the thing that got me in trouble, this pilgrimage, this road I'd been barreling down from the beginning, the mounted cavalry, posting and trotting, cantoring and stumbling, deploying common heads and rifles and circumcised swords.

At Havenhurst they didn't lock me in.

"Your agent, Roy Dominguez, called and read me the letter you faxed him, the one you had delivered to Senator Abernathy," he started in on me immediately.

"I should do something about changing agents. You bastards are plotting against me!" I shouted. I wasn't paranoid and didn't believe in plots, but I knew that my resentment would get him thinking.

"Roy and I both felt you should have stayed in Havenhurst a while longer. You were much more secure back here."

"There are two sides to that issue."

"The past few months you haven't been as well as you were when you were with us."

"Sooooo?" I took a sip of my distillated tater drink, as I crooned into the phone.

"Why are you in Washington, Clyde?"

Under the cloak of confidentiality I told him about my girl-friend, gave him a description of how I got beat up, told him about my prophetic vision, and let him know my hopes of meeting a man who was going to save me from the fear of recommitting murder. I thought he would be most interested in my engagement and vision, but he focused on my savior instead.

"You're chasing after grails again," he objected, "and when you do that, you become confused and violent. Are you taking your medication regularly?"

"Of course," I lied. I hadn't swallowed a single dose of medication since I left the nuthouse. I drank my medication instead.

Why did I spend good money soliciting advice from the latest in a long line of aforementioned neuro-poltroons if I didn't intend to be honest with them?

For the same reason I sought out lonely Hispanics when I hoodlumized the streets: brute inclination, unworthy of examination.

"Searching in the wide world for this type of answer is not going to help you make progress in your therapy," he advised me, and he seemed to be choosing his words carefully. "You've put yourself in danger, alongside your girlfriend, and yet you are concentrating on something that has nothing to do with the peril you and she are in. A man had you beaten within an inch of your life, and yet you are looking for easy answers through some priest to solve deep-seated emotional problems. Even more importantly, you are trying to protect a helpless woman from a powerful man, just as you attempted to protect your mother from your father. Repeating these situations isn't emotionally healthy, Clyde."

"So what should I do?" I asked.

"Come back to Los Angeles and stay at Havenhurst for another month or so."

"I'm not going to leave town until I make certain that Barbie is all right."

"Then skip your search for the man with all the answers. You have enough to worry about with your girlfriend. Reexamine your feelings about the woman. You're under too much pressure from way too many directions. Stay focused."

I quickly got off the phone.

Actually, I had tried to stay focused.

After I had purchased my gun, I had purchased some corkboard.

I had removed the hotel art from opposite my bed and had hung the cork there, since in earlier therapy I had learned through substitution to redirect my antisocial impulses—in this case, to scribble across walls. I tore three sheets from a legal pad and pinned them side by side, and on them were the headings Barbie, Abernathy and Salvation, rendered in a lightface scrawl. I lay on the bed looking until they slowly changed into windows. I stared through, trying to view the contre-jour, the daylight shining from behind the sheets and at me. Alongside the word Abernathy, I punctured my thumb and pressed my seal of paddling blood, a bug smudge. Over the word Salvation, I spit and rubbed, and dripping in mucus by Barbie was something else, a slightly aslant stain of sweetish bile, as if wind-driven.

Then I searched for magic glyphs to place underneath them, to place under each of the three words, to make them subject to the will of the Alphabet Man, and I crafted this short letter and sent it off by courier in a confidential envelope:

Dear Senator Motherfucker:

If you so much as lay a finger on my girlfriend, rest assured that I'll find you before you find me and do to you what you did to her and then some.

Stay cool,
Clyde Wayne Franklin

So much for my dégagé epistolary style. The first law of human relationships is: Throw Caution to the Winds. The second law of human relationships is: Cut to the Bone.

There are no more laws.

I had fashioned my first letters of the alphabet when I was barely walking.

I remember that the same silly powerful things were everywhere, on every book and sign and screen, the symbols arranged within their proper leadings, strict, unvarying; and I thought, all these letters should be allowed to sprawl in the same way that I toddle and run free, and then I began to write them. I'd see the A and I'd begin to examine ah, aaah, aaaaah, aie, aye, aw and then I'd pound them out, morphemes, digraphs and lexes.

I'd write on sidewalks every day, before I burned the ants.

This might sound corny but it's true, I insisted on eating alphabet soup and would search in the brew for lipograms; and gazing into the steam of sodden vegetables, I'd mix the missing letters. Inside the alphabetic cans, wiped of grime by Mommy's hands, I knew there were messages I'd one day build. Under her elbow I would stare and carefully spell.

CAMP BELL LEB CMAPL PAC ELBB M MCP BLLEA SOUP DFGHIJKNQRTVWXYZ

What was missing always told me what was missing. The lost touches and touching.

When I began to watch in the basement, below the protest of fluorescent lamps, which sometimes felt the dizzying lash above, the sockets no longer true, as the tubes would hum their brool, I'd sit in my flannel jammies and move a finger clumsily between my toes and sweetly hum along, all those pretty songs she sang and letters on their strings, on cradlestrings, each letter bright and separate, compartmentalized, and none were gone, all stayed there in the humming.

Mother never looked at me. Just up and down. Up and down. And I could feel, for the only time, her pleasure.

And when the panics began, out in the open as I moved toward class relentlessly along the street, I'd reconfigure step by step, counting as best I could, counting, as the letters raged inside me, the dead matter wanting to crawl out of my skin, pressing to get out. I'd keep them there, letters and souls, tight within my body.

Sometimes in my backyard, where there was a swing on which I never swang, never, not even once, I'd look beyond the construction heaps, the headers and stretchers rising out of their craters, down to Encino Lake and dream of the added pressure of cold water against my surfaces, keeping me from exploding, keeping me safely in. The neighborhood rang as the monstrous homes went up, and on my way to school, I first began to pray, among the ligneous smells of framework and sawdust.

INRI.
RNII.
RIIN.
When I first saw the cross (for Daddy taught in Sunday school),

I imagined in my mind's eye a clown baby suffering on the rood, stretched out within that diaper. I heard the clown baby's laughter encircled below by women's screams, and Mary on the hill was looking up and down up and down, and Joseph was a carpenter, with a hammer and a bag full of nails, somewhere on a jobsite.

I'd pray as I walked down the street, one foot in front of the other, forgetting how to count, as I continued my counting.

One

He came up to me as I was walking into a Burger King. A tall, handsome man wearing a medium-weight suit. There was something about the way he put himself together, however, that was sadly out of date. He looked to be approximately my age, but he was obviously a victim of arrested development. He reached into his pocket, and before the badge came out, I had the picture.

"Thatcher Jensen, Mr. Franklin. I'm a special agent with the FBI."

"You're standing between me and a breakfast burger."

He stepped out of the way.

"I only have a few things to say to you," he said, "and we can talk while you're eating."

We went in together, I bought my food, and we sat opposite each other in an empty area of the restaurant.

"You know why I'm here, I would imagine," Agent Jensen said.

"You'll have to tell me."

"It's about a letter that was delivered by messenger to the campaign offices of Daniel Abernathy. The letter was turned over to our department, and I've been asked to look you up to find out why you are threatening a senator."

"I'm not on parole, you know."

"I know."

"I don't consider my letter a threat. When I said in my note that I would find him before he found me, it meant that I intend to talk to him if he bothers my girlfriend."

"That's not the way we interpret your correspondence."

"I know what I meant, and I want the government to leave me

alone. I've got enough problems as things stand."

"I'm here to inform you that we don't intend to leave you alone. What happened to your face?"

"I fell off a tricycle."

"Please answer my question."

"I'm surprised he turned the letter over to you," I said, refusing to tell him what was going on.

"He didn't, but someone on his staff did."

"Have you come here to arrest me?"

"It's a bizarre letter from a convicted murderer, and we'd like you to leave town. We don't think it's healthy for you to be around the senator."

"Fuck you."

"We consider your letter to be a death threat. There's a standard operating procedure for handling people who threaten government officials, and if you don't leave town, we'll have to proceed. Considering that you're a celebrity of sorts, it wouldn't be right for you to be subjected to negative exposure in the press, if what we have here is a private matter. We're not taking sides at this point, Mr. Franklin. We just don't want to have to dedicate resources to your case, if you can see fit to control your own behavior."

"You must think I'm a driveling idiot," I said. "There's no way you're going to arrest me or harrass me and I'll tell you why quite simply."

The agent leaned back in the booth.

"Why's that?" he asked.

"Because I thrive on this shit. It would give a boost to my career if you arrested me, and it would make the FBI look like a bunch of jackasses. Besides, if you give me any more sweat, you might wind up embarrassing the senator. I don't go writing pricks like Abernathy hate notes unless there's a reason for it."

"I highly doubt that Senator Abernathy is interested in you or your girlfriend, whoever she may be."

"Maybe you should check it out instead of being so pompous."

"Is that what you want?"

"Maybe."

"Is that why you wrote that nutty note, so that you could procure our involvement?"

"Maybe."

"Leave town, Mr. Franklin," he said, as he prepared to go. "If you don't, we're going to make things difficult for you."

"This isn't Dodge City, asshole."

"You're better off leaving, take it from me."

"I want to make certain that the senator sees my note, if he hasn't already."

"That's not my business. It's up to the people who work in his office. He might have seen it, but I don't have any way of knowing."

"I'd make it my business if I were you. I have a feeling that if you talk to the senator about this, he'll tell you to back off."

"I'm asking you politely for the last time. If you have something you have to do in Washington short-term, and if you let us know what it is, we'll be happy to work with you so that you're not hindered, but then we want you out of town and we don't want you coming back."

"You're wasting your breath. And if you tail me or hound me, I'll go to the press, and both your agency and the senator will regret it."

He left me his card.

I ate my hamburger, then stopped in a liquor store and bought a pint of Stoli, and walked down the street to the park opposite the White House and sat down on a bench. I looked over at the toilet seat of government, the American Kremlin, the Big Canasta, Gumshoe Central. Between me and the iron fence was a pathetic assortment of protest stands and jumbled pickets. I wasn't grateful or over-whelmed. I've never felt blessed to live in a dulocracy, a society run by slaves for the benefit of slaves, because as a poet I've never accepted the invitation to work on the plantation.

Yo, Fellow Darkie, you kin make a diffunce! da slave massah sez. As long as you kin fome yo X, yuz has da power ta vote. Youse an all da udder stupid X's. Who would you puffer now, Bones, tweedledum or tweedledee? Look how grate our society has become, when mos of you niggers kin go down in da bakk of a Chevy! Youse gots da Repubbicans and Democats. Dose Repubs won give you da money, ya gots to earn it. Da demos dey is all nice guys, and dey suppots the avage fellah who works on da line. In da shower room you can tell dem apat, cuz da Democats bend over. You gots a prasidioom called conggess, and once you gets der ya dies in offis. In da clokeroom ya picks up yo hat and it's filled wit money jus like dat. Hey ya don like da system, yo a pinko fag or carnie poet well, we don care. Cuz da slaves gots all da votes an likes it der. Slaves like to be slaves, ya see. Das da secret of dulocracy!

I opened my pint and began to dream of Barbie, who had her own form of negligée Jacobinism. For fifteen years she had preened the hair on the maggot, and now she refused to play the hairy maggot game where a woman is screwed, wasted and discarded into the drain. Hey, she said, eyes glistering, I want mine. It's time for Hobson's Choice.

Given the heat from the FBI, I felt I needed some dispassionate advice and, sitting on the bench, I thought of Leonard Dalls, a friend I'd met on the lecture circuit who lived in Arlington in a large brick home with a pair of aging dalmatians. Behind his colonial furniture hung posters of second-rate art exhibitions, and he had the bland jokes of political cartoonists limned about his copper-kitchen walls. I had slept at his place on one or two occasions.

Leonard was a successful and subtle writer of commercial spy fiction: cardigan-sweatered, chain-smoking, elfin-faced, bream-backed and wizened. All the Capital comings and goings were grist for his literary mill. He had impeccable connections and a refined and certain novelistic instinct. Leonard had character, and he could size up anything. In an access of enthusiasm, I tossed the remains of my bottle into the bushes and hailed a cab, and within an hour we were sitting together in the library over his garage. He was a recovering alcoholic, and so I made a point of not drinking.

Detail by detail, I told Leonard the story of my relationship with Barbie, her struggle with Abernathy, and what had happened since I came to Washington. I didn't discuss my encounter with Father Kosmoski, but everything that had to do with Barbie, including Judas Brennemann, I mentioned. He was fascinated and listened intently.

"She mailed you a ticket and a boarding pass," he said, after I had finished. "Was the letter she enclosed handwritten?"

"Typed."

"Signed?"

"No, the whole thing was typed. So what?"

Leonard looked out the window quietly. He seemed to be piecing it together.

"Everything sounds perfectly plausible," he finally said. "She's in hiding, trying to get the senator off her back. She thought she could procure your assistance, but somehow it backfired and the senator found out you were coming into town and paid some hoods to rough you up. Now she's decided to steer clear of you until she straightens out her problem by herself, for your sake as well as for hers. You search; she hides. A tight little story."

"Right, except that I still want to find her. I'm worried that that there's nothing she can do to protect herself, and that in spite of everything, he intends to track her down and ice her."

"Yeah, that's what they want you to think, all right."

"What do you mean by that?"

"I think you're being deceived."

"I don't get it."

"My gut tells me that the blackmail and reprisal story is a fabrication. I think the entire scenario is bullshit. Something else is happening."

Only Leonard would think like this. Perhaps he had written too many spy novels.

"So I shouldn't accept my fiancée's story at face value?"

"Hell, no. You're talking about destroying the career of a possible president of the United States. Wake up and smell the coffee."

"Have you ever met Abernathy?" I asked.

"Yes, on a number of occasions."

"What's he like?"

"As a politician, extremely competent. Not the brightest man in the Senate, but he scares certain people. As a man, he's vain, temperamental and boring, a straight arrow by all accounts, which reinforces my feelings of cynicism. Your standard liberal pretty boy. Most of his friendships are outside of politics, since he was raised as an aristocrat and keeps to that kind of society."

"And why does he scare people?"

"He has a secret agenda. He's out to trash the Pentagon. He believes it will assure him a place in history, making America a peaceful nation, and the truth of the matter is that the man could have an unsettling effect on the government if he makes it to the White House. The way things currently stand, I think he has a good chance of getting elected."

My mind was beginning to wander. The day before, I had purchased another gun on the street. A Ruger. It lay heavy in my pocket.

"You're not listening to me," he immediately noticed.

A strange light came from his computer screen and bathed his hands. I noticed a configuration of warts and cysts. Fleshy asterisms. Clues to the inside, as Billy would have said.

Why was I so apprehensive? It was because Leonard was suggesting that Barbie was untruthful, which would mean that she didn't really love me.

"If her story is bogus, then why was I beaten up?" I asked him.

"To catapult you into whatever's going on. You're a hothead. What better way to secure your participation than to destroy your face?"

"Participation in what?"

"I haven't figured that out yet. Hookers do on occasion blackmail politicians, and people do get their noses busted for sticking them in the wrong places in this town, but somehow it doesn't seem right. My bullshit detector is going over the red line."

I had heard the same thing in different words from the Lebanese—that I'd been set up—but I knew instinctively they both were wrong. I believed that Barbie was incapable of lying to me. I trusted her completely, for in ways which I was able to admit to myself as a result of my therapy, I was searching through a pain bond with all women, but especially with Barbie, for truth and constancy.

How I had loved my mother, whose body was tenderly shattered!

Over the sink she would sing old songs. "Let Me Call You Sweetheart," "East Side, West Side, All Around the Town," "Tooralooraloora"; and like an ancient woman in a cobbled tower, her spirit lilted away:

Shpilt aykh, libe kinderlekh
Der friling shoyn bagint!
Oy, vi bin ikh, kinderlekh,
Mekane aykh a tsind...
Hulyet, hulyet kinderleckh.
Kol zman ir zent nokh ying!

She had been raised on the Lower East Side, and as a tot was dressed in stiff lisse ruche and kid slippers embossed with studs. In the photo that I saw, she held aloft a Magen David wand and her eyes were blackened, as if she were emergent from a world of sights so strange, a coalblack fairyland, that something from her childlike heart had been replaced with utmost fantasies that beat and beat, a trodden Purim dayfly with shining teeth. As I stood in our kitchen swinging my legs, my sticky fingers stretching up to the drainpan, I'd inhale the ardent smells of Lux and Babo, and my world would be complete, as Mother rinsed and chanted next to me. The white light, the light of milk, fell on enamel tiles and sneaked into the sugar bin. Even the ants and silverfish were dancing in the snow in hidden holes. Sometimes I'd draw flour letters in the sifter or tear them freehand out of newspaper and admire the clean ripping sound. Then there was a milkman named Mike who came to the door and sometimes had coffee with Mom and sometimes they'd disappear into an upper room where I knew that nothing ever happened, for what was down could not go up and what was up could not come down, and I never heard a scream or moan or clanking sound from behind the sealed doors of the bedroom.

Until the day I commissioned the clown.

We had a parakeet named Guenevere. I bought a record to train her. Over and over again, the record said hello hello hello hello hello and goodday goodday goodday and Polly want a cracker, Polly want a cracker. Then I'd take our purple record player upstairs and *I* would practice. The bird would jump on my finger when I fed it, and I loved the cool grip that it exercised at the tip of beak and talon. It would nip at my cuticle and never say a word. I decided to learn to speak like her, and I would spend hours by the cage imitating her goodday and her pure sweet tweet like Mom's. Yes, those were the years of poignant barriers, and when I finally sensed the Primal Fact was near, I took Queen Guennie from her cage and opened up the window.

Sometimes I'd stick hatpins in Barbie's tits but not too deep. A sparse pincushion effect. The pins had nacreous heads, and as they moved I would hear certain words come out of her and they weren't in English.

God, I'd say to myself, as I went about my labors, Please God, help me understand. I, your diapered son, have always wished one thing, to make syntactic all those symbolled things you handed me so I could range. I'd see those pearly heads had mouths. Barbie's eyes would flutter, as she winced and babbled and gagged.

"....so there is a great deal of talk."

"Do you have any alcohol in the house, Lenny?" I interrupted.

"I don't have any vodka," he replied.

"White wine?"

"I have a jug for parties, but it's warm."

"I'd like a large glass please, with ice."

He left the room.

I walked over to the window. There were no children playing outside, although it was Saturday afternoon. I thought about my appointment the following day. What would it be like? Father Duke had called to say that he wanted me to spend one hour with an orphan girl, and I wondered, as I looked out at the empty street, whether it would be a homunculus instead, a malicious, cross-dressed imp that crawled like a cicada out of a test tube stuffed with agar, ready to do the priest's bidding.

"Go and suck that changling spirit from the man!" the priest would have ordered him. "He has poetically damaged your kind. He has been cruel to blithe spirits."

"Here's your drink, Clyde." Leonard was back.

He settled in his desk chair and stared at a picture on the opposite wall that showed him shaking hands with Richard Nixon.

"So you might consider," he continued, "hiring someone to check out her past and whether or not she has political connections."

I wasn't paying much attention.

"Political connections?" I repeated feebly.

"Yes, the story has been concocted as something political, so maybe it *is* something political."

"Why would that be?"

"Well, starting with Abernathy, as I said, he has many enemies, and if he were to become president, there would be a drop in the price of tarnished brass."

"Brass?"

"He'd be destroying fifty years of carefully constructed effort. In spite of the end of the Cold War, and in spite of the rhetoric, nobody has any intention of shutting down the military-industrial complex. Nobody except Abernathy, that is."

"The military-industrial complex," I repeated to myself.

Leonard swivelled his chair around and faced me.

"You're hopeless," he said, disgusted. "Do you know that?"

"What do you mean?"

"You should think about stopping drinking. It's a terrible problem."

But there was no problem, no problem at all, because I had stopped drinking that very minute.

My wine glass was empty.

Two

Daddy hated Jews.

At the dinner table he would blame the kikes, as the lazy Susan twirled. The kikes undercooked his spaghetti, the kikes controlled the banks. He would pinch his cheeks together, building energy, and would go buphthalmic and stare at the flatware and tell us how there were curious forces everywhere, here and everywhere, rotten Semitic forces that were controlling the money supply. Mom would smile and pass the boiled vegetables.

Why had she crawled into her dusky shell to be brutalized and subdued?

And why did she refuse to touch me outside the basement?

I had a ripped swastika T-shirt, and an Adlerordens on my motorcycle helmet. Years later, in my cell, I played the scratchy records of the cantors and klezmers and laughed uproariously. Poetry is on my Hebrew side.

A block off Pennsylvania Avenue, I found the Catholic Youth Services Administrative Center and its adjacent playground, teeming with small fry. There were stone benches along a Cyclone fence facing in, and on one of them sat the priest, back in habit, along with a number of grimly betreacled children. A girl on his lap of kindergarten age had Down's syndrome, and there were a number of adoring others shuffling around nearby. I said a silent prayer to Baby Jesus and entered. The children didn't seem to notice, except for the girl on his lap, who looked up at me and pointed at my leather jacket.

"Ah, we've been waiting for you here, Clyde."

The priest unloaded the girl and stood and stretched, and we all breathed deeply.

It was a wonderful autumn day, and a bright wind snapped and burned in my nostrils. Slivers of shadow flitted among the feet of the children and the priest. The maples around the playground tossed and seethed, and the colors of the moving playclothes were vivid and alive—Utrillo patches under a tight cerulean sky—and everything seemed meaningless and free. A coldness struck my eyes, which watered slightly.

"I've a few errands to run, and so I shall leave you with Cindy. I'll meet you here in about an hour," Kosmoski said.

He motioned toward the retarded girl, who wiggled her smooth head, and her coy, epicanthic eyes gleamed, and she turned and started to walk along the fence, her stubby fingers strumming the links.

I looked at Kosmoski questioningly, and suddenly I felt frightened.

A sharp downtugging pang, and unexpectedly everything seemed to darken, and the cold became a different kind of cold, and I turned toward the center of the playground where there was a sand island, and a bobbing shade was there, stretching his legs ankle-deep, and his loins corkscrewed around, bunching like taut rubber, and his head was composed of two large eyes encompassed by another eye, and he was intently shovelling deep into the sand between his legs with a platyhelminth fluke that dangled down and delved and flung the grains high over his head. In the center of all the eyes were lug nuts twirling, two pupils and a nose, and around the sandbox everything seemed threatening, as the children scrambled through their ludic formations, the lopping and hopping and squeals and cries, a pygmoid planetary people with nothing at hand, stuck in a form of echopraxic madness: Pygma to Earth! Pygma to Earth! Come in Earth! Come in Earth! Come in Earth! Mad children, they were all slightly mad, and the shade began to rumba like a flame around a burner.

I forced myself to turn away, and the priest had disappeared and so had Cindy. I looked back across the playground to the far building—there was no sign of the shade—and immediately I understood what had happened. The vision had been an opening, an omen, an ominous chasm projecting into the sunlight, and my fear had flared at the center of the playground and scooped and dapped and dabbled and danced. It wasn't Satan but the yawing shadow of Satan's messenger, a vacancy whom only I, the corrupted Shem among the Children of Abraham, the pious NaziJew, the hater and dull breather and criminal destroyer, could see.

She wasn't anywhere. I ran outside the fence. On the street there was no movement. I hurried back into the playground and began to pace counterclockwise around the perimeter, searching and frantically casting spells. I had been distrained by an evil force and distracted. I sat down on the bench with my head in my hands and looked down. The pavement was exposed aggregate, and there were colored pebbles embossed in the cement. A spiderling dragging what looked like a feazed end of web was creeping across the instep of my combat boot. Was this minute thing born out of season? I projected myself into its dimension, imagining my eight ratchety legs going ratcha ratcha ratcha hauling sticky lettered pipe across the foxing, the alphabetic symbols glued randomly along a giant strand, across the bent-space contours, like on a cradlestring, every insect movement an attempt to secure anchorage and gain the necessary bearings. I leaned forward until my hands hit cold ground, and I scrabbled foot to hand hauling my dangling fluke as I moved down the benches, swaying my head from side to side, and some of the children stopped and stared at me inquisitively, an elephantine spider heading into winter.

Cindy came up to me on cue, from who knows where? and placed her hand in the small of my back and giggled. I tried to stand, but she pressed harder and because of the delicacy of my position, I was stuck (for a split second she actually controlled me) and she pushed down and let go and I sprang up. She was squinting and beaming as I massaged the grit out of my palms. She rocked back and forth on her heels.

"Wowowomomma," she said.

She giggled some more, and she was squeezing her pharynx so that it sounded like she was letting out steam, and she clenched her fists, and her hands came down obliquely to her hips, and she took a long step backward with one foot and bent her head back into the sun and repeated, "Whoa, Momma!" And then she brought her foot forward again and swung it around in front of the other so that her head was inclined toward the ground, and she began sidestepping in an ever-widening circle, slicing toward an arcus of black kids who were Double Dutching several feet away.

"Whoa Momma yo gotta, whoa momma yo gotta, ya gotta go Momma," she sang, and her arms were doing a butterfly as if she were attempting to propel herself centripetally into a wormhole. Time and space warped along the line of her heels, just as it does for spiders who are locked in their patient event horizons, and I stood there inert, my palms still tingling, among the other children, on the outside.

Suddenly the energy disappeared from her body, or more properly it seemed that part of her molted and kept going invisibly through the cordage and jumpers slapping their thighs and that the remains hovered and then dropped onto its hands and began to work its way along the ground crab-fashion (imitating me), and then she was on one hand and two feet and the right hand came up and sawed along her nape vigorously, and she was making other sounds like burbles, and she became very quiet and rose up stiffly as if she had been lifted from behind, and she was still scratching her neck as she began walking towards me.

"Billy Bug!" she called out.

"Billy Bug," I confirmed.

"Rosy Potatoes!"

She stopped scratching her neck and examined her knuckles.

"My hand."

She held it out to show me as she kept walking.

A blond boy with patches of mud on his face rode up on a plastic scooter with chipped wheels. A drop of snot hung labret-like on his lip. He glared at her, but he seemed to be looking through her as well, and she stopped walking and turned and snatched at the back of his jacket. Startled, the boy pulled away, and she hung on and was dragged backwards and her feet jerked behind her one after another and she went down hard on her head as she let go and began to cry.

I paused for a moment, and reached into a side pocket and pulled out a pint of Stoli and took a leisurely swig. Then I walked over and stood so that I was looking directly down, holding onto my bottle. There was no sign of blood, and her mouth had opened in a peculiar way that reminded me of a time once when Dad and I had spent a month together in Wisconsin and I had clubbed a bat hiding in a curtain with a broom. I lifted it dazed on the tips of the broomstraw and it hung there by one of its paws, and I lofted the broom over an empty garbage can and shook until it dropped to the bottom. It looked up blindsighted into the light, and I turned the broom around and stuck the condyle of the handle into its stomach and pushed, first just a bit and then gradually harder, and the bat seemed to come alive and opened its mouth wide, trying to breath and supplicate and free itself and survive. I stood there pushing and rearranging its parts. They say that a bat is smarter than a boy, which made it smarter than me, and I held the handle there, rubbing through its skin against the bottom of the metal can, until the circle of its mouth closed up and the language of the bat ceased.

The girl's sobs seemed to form clots along her gums, and on the inside just above her purplish tongue was the same hole I saw at the center of the bat pip.

If we were alone, and I had a pole, would I have dared to push?

Her eyes were louvered, like the slatting eyes of a doll, and a dimness shone through and worked its way along a tide of tiny tears, and I sensed that the lobes of her ears were quivering also. She clutched at her head and her feet were kicking, and then I noticed her strange shoes. They were like a baby's booties of white leather, but they were oversize, and the laces were made of pink ribbon with green plastic aglets. The soles were ribbed and cleated. They were the custom-made shoes of a monster.

She began to groan, eeh eeh eeeeeh! and raised her hands in the air as if she wanted me to lift her.

I waited to see what she would do next, and then I was pushed to the side violently, and a black woman reached in front of me and down and picked Cindy up and stroked her and kissed her and then yelled at me.

I didn't bother to listen to what she had to say. I walked over to the nearest bench and took another long drink and kept my eye on the woman. It took a few minutes for Cindy to calm down, and then she began grasping the woman's hair, and her eyes shunted in her head like a lemur's, and she peeped at me through the col of the woman's shoulder. The woman stared at me, trying to decide something, and then she hurried over. She was an older woman, short and wiry, in a cheap woolen dress, and her hair was plastered against the sides of her head.

"Is this your child?"

"Yeah," I lied.

"Then why didn't you pick the child up?"

"It's none of your fucking business, so just put her down and get lost."

"What's her name?"

"Cindy."

"Everything's all right, Cindy. You be a good girl and mind your Daddy now, hear?"

And she put the kid down and left.

Cindy stood there stupified, rubbing one of her eyes, and I went over to her and took her by the hand and guided her to the bench and lifted her up and plopped her next to me. She sat with a stiff back and stared at her fingers, which were moving in all directions excitedly, and her lips were working and she was barely able to control her crying, which she was trying to do heroically. It was a strange kind of thing, because there was something serene in her eyes, but the mouth was malformed and in pain. We sat together silently, and I began to stare off into space, because I still felt I was under attack and I was worried that the shade was going to appear again but closer to me and would reach out with its fluke and disappear through it into my body, turning outside in then inside out. There had been a purposefulness about its digging activity, as if it were searching in the sand for souls and if it found one it would stop flinging the fluke and would start evaginating and fucking, and it would enter me like the worm that it was, the flat thing that would cut its way into my body and coil itself contently somewhere in my groin among the microbes.

Cindy grabbed my hand and wrapped her fist around my four fingers. Her palm was still wet with tears, and there were small bits of sand and gravel I could feel, and a salt stickiness and perhaps some saliva. It felt reassuringly wet and cool, and she held my fingers bundled tightly together, and I was suddenly secured. She turned toward me, and I was shocked to see that she felt I was securing *her*, and her features were tottering off in space like a buoy at the end of a guy, wavering and needy.

Again she was smiling, and I saw that she was extremely pretty.

She let out a deep breath, and I could feel the tension in her fist and along her body ease. She began chewing with concentration on her lower lip and watching the other children in the playground.

I took another swig, and I realized that as long as she held my fingers I couldn't cap the pint, which for some strange reason made me laugh, and it seemed that the aromatic fumes from the bottle were forming clouds in the raw wind surrounding our bench, pungent castle clouds that would bless us and protect us.

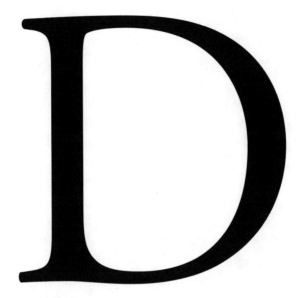

no reason, ratcharatcha ratcha, there's no reason ratcha ratcha to
idennify meeseff there's no reason no no no i done hafto if i done
wannoo cuz when ya cry in da blud ya cry reel good, it's der in da
lap it's der on da floor it's der in da middle of da world an it's
doin lots a good. Ya rip an tear da skin and opin it slow an der
inside it's pulsin and pumpin real good, da colors mauve an oaker
an crison an purl a thumpin ratchratcha real good real good like a
machine an it's all addin up to eggs in a queen, if ya open her up,
ya can see da past, ya see it all fum da vebby firss, ya see yo face
befo yo face wuz born, ya follin me Clide ya follin me good?
Ratcha ratcha ratcha good? Ya follin me Clide? I's da Debbil here,
ya follin me? Behin da makeup is old Nikkel, yeah. Let me tells ya
a seccet Clide dat nobbody essept da poets nose: Da Debbil don
hurt. Naaaaaaaaaah! I can't hurt no one no how no. Dey all die
befo da real pain come and once dey is dead dey don't hurt no
mo. Hey done you call me dat rashal epitet! In hell dey ain't no
blackface dey's all charred white, yaaah. Yeah dey's all white an
ripe an rich in hell. Mirror mirror on dat wall, whoz da funnibest
clown ob all? Chuggulz. He rite like youze babes he rite like
youze, he rite on stalls and walls and off det paige, he rite his
come on ebbey dam ting he buss yo balls dat clown. Hay don ya
hide, I ain' commin up da stares, I stays down here in da wrecks
and you stays dere. Ya know who els down heah? Yeah? Da pardie
yeah da pardie. Misser Riff and Misses Raff, dey's down here
groanin and whippin and laffin. Ya live yore in, ya dead yore out,
ya cum ya go ya win ya lose juss don say da word Jesus cuz dat
make me wanna kill just don say dat word just kidding! Wooee!

Now where were we? Oh yeah Al right the cat never returns a call I says, Al honey you're burning up the line you gotta return my calls, look I know you're repping for some of the biggest clowns in the business, hell no that's not a slur, I know that you got it all tied up (sorry about that, I'm doing it again) I know that you got it all tied up, but Jeez Al (don say dat word) I said Jeez Al (I say don say it or else) I said OK I won't say, now look fella this Clyde guy he treats me like his chicks man and he's got me all penned up out here in the Encino of his head, I mean the man is one sick motherfucker, and I have to follow this grisly plot of his and stick in my four bits, and he just goes off, he keeps his nose on the ground plowing through the crap and then he just flies, he goes off and I've got to pick up the pieces. What does he care? I told my guy, he has his dreams and his bottles, but me, I'm a professional man, I don't have to chain myself (oooops) to poetry, I just go out about the roundabout and collect my yucks and my check. I mean look, I've seen this dude and he carries around a basket, like a bridesmaid, I've seen him late at night stalking, this Clyde Wayne and he's got a white wicker basket that he bought, originally he got two but he gave away one, and he emptied out the flowers and he's walking around the block with it, in a rough part of town, in DC babes, which ain't what it's cracked (punpunpun) up to be and a few nites ago he got mugged and he didn't even care as long as he could keep the basket but he was blacked so it ain't in the book, he didn't even think it was important enough to write about, and here I am giving out info for no dough. Al what good's a contract without an agent? He knows I can't turn on him, cuz thems the rules, I must obey, and so you've got to give him a call later on, Al honey. You got to read this fucker the riot act. I mean I've got feelings too. Who the fuck does he think he is? and I hope he puts this in his book, that he treats me like shit sometimes, and he withholds drinks and he makes me wear a bib sometimes so the chair doesn't get wet when I'm drinking. And you know and I know that it's tough to deal with a guy who always crosses the line and fucks up your lines and calls you different names. He even insults my friends. Einstein is being real white about it, and Einstein is Chinese. Yeah, underneath it all the guy's Chinese, isn't that a hoot Al? but of course you know cuz the shower stalls aren't real thick in the circus, not that there are any glory holes or any of that shit no rods coming through the woodwork hell no, the circus guys are mostly straight but I don't know about the ladies. The worst part of the whole mess is that the poet thinks he's a clown, yeah me he needles (in more ways than one) cuz I refuse to write anything down in his one two one two pathetic fucking chapters, not a line of what's happened, I put it all in my own brilliant clownographs, in my A through Z, I keep it nice and loose and intimate, I keep it up-close and personal and so I'm beneath him Al, I don't have his feelings, even though I could spill my guts into his world and a lot of other people's as well, but I clam up, I keep it inside cuz that's what I have to do in my business and I tried to tell him once or twice at least about his Mom but nooooooo, the guy just started laughing. Yeah I started talking and I even used a big word or two and he started laughing isn't that a stitch? The big thing is the most obvious thing, that the guy thinks if I take off my makeup I'm gonna look like him and it might be true that you could interpret my makeup just like you interpret his sick books, as so much clown cover, as a dandified form of voodoo. One night we had a duel, we stood in the middle of his room and we decided on seven paces. You should have been there Al, I started walking and I got to seven and I drew my piece and turned and there he was, still in the middle of the room Al stuck on two, he could only take two steps and the guy was totally frozen, he stood there with his gun Al, he stood there holding the gun over the number two Al and the motherfucker says he doesn't cry that crying isn't contractual but he was slobbering like Baby Jesus (don say dat I shoot) like the BeJeesus (not dat no mo) Al and instead of dueling I had to go and take away the gun and go downstairs and join the action cuz the guy couldn't fight me he was stuck and he just stood there weeping and I gotta say I felt sorry for the guy cuz at that point he looked just like a little boy like the first time I ever laid eyes on him looking up from my clown cradle, back then he wept too, he wept and laughed when he touched me on the groin, for the very first time he touched me on my groin like there was a wound there, like I'd been hurt there, and I'd just been born Al, isn't that a stitch? Look, let's discuss an end-around even though I know the guy's listening, he's cowering in the corner of his brain trembling and taking notes, he's writing this all down to put in his novel, word by word, he's writing it down even though it's a clown-agent relationship and I think we can work our way out of this contract if we have to. We're way into the book and he still hasn't said my name and I can't say it until he does cuz it says so right in clause five, whaddya mean he hasn't read that far? I still have to honor the contract word for word cuz that's what good clowns do, shit Al, I gotta give this guy time to develop he'll spit my name out I know he will, cuz he has no trouble talking about you or Einstein and Einstein's Chinese and we all know what you are Al, we all know how you light your menorahs. Yeah that's the clown world for ya, a guy named Einstein wouldn't know a menorah from a lump of dim sum and you, Al you stay in the background and you coach me, you count the money and tell me what to say. That priest guy, that nightmare guy, he's always in the background too but Clyde's such a dunce he doesn't know it. I love the setup with the girl. Right now in the dreamtime he's sitting on a bench ready to doze, dreaming about me and the girl, man, the girl has got our friend by the short hairs and she's being paid in candy by the priest and we all know who's picking up Clyde's tab, he wants to see God but all he can see are sand-worms, I mean why doesn't he take his medication? He doesn't mind paying that German shrink so why doesn't he take a simple tablet so he doesn't see things? The guy's a stitch, Al, Jesus (Ok dat's it you histury) sorry pal, he wants to see God (I'm commin up!) he dropped his life to follow some bimbo from LA and he thinks that she is Mary fucking Magdalene or someone but she's simply a hooker who'll do anything for enough money or at least that's my suspicion and he went out and bought another gun for what? He's already punched his last ticket unless he takes counting lessons. Now if he finds the dame, then what Al? If he still hasn't said my name do I have to go shuffling? These ain't marching orders, babes they are points of negotiation. You can't just break a name contract and expect me to break out again and do my clown thing. Yeah down there it's hot (da debbil wear white makeup in da heet) and I tend to sweat, Al, it's fight or flee or whatever they say I get so panicky and I do the silliest damn things in front of the audience, yeah the whole world's a stage Al, and I always get paid. Clowns always get paid for doing the clown thing. I stripped off his dad's makeup real good and sent him further down below, into the subbasement Al, down where the rats glide. I remember the look on his mom's face woooeee! did she look happy, yeah that's the funny thing about clowns the way they make people laugh even a loony stiff like her, she just stopped singing that Irish lullaby and then she broke out laughing, the balloon popped and the woman starting laughing, a light solid laugh, not hysterical at all, like I told a joke in Yiddish Al, you know the kind, like did you hear about the Jew who said fuck you? that kind of joke Al and then his mommy came unglued, she just started laughing lightly and brightly and I didn't get it, I honked my horn and she just laughed louder and louder and she told me something Al, and I've been sitting up in this bedroom thinking about it lately what she said, I mean I'm not supposed to say boo, Christ (ooooh, onnee a cupple steps to go), I'm not supposed to answer the door, and what she said then I can't talk about cuz it isn't in the contract until the contract becomes valid, and a strange smell came out of the short barrel yeah them short ones go off and they give off a darker denser smoke yeah like iron pillars of incense yeah she wanted to look inside that thing she wanted to look inside and I held it up and turned it around and it looked like two smoking eyes like a set of eyes or more like one eye and a patch over the other and she wanted to have a look herself I said Anita doll ya don't need to see, it isn't so pretty I mean one ticket a night lady, and that really broke her up as her soles were washed with her hubby's blood, Jesus (knock knock knock) Jeeeeeeeeeeeeeeeeeesus (bam bam bam) I said Jeeeeeeeeeesus (dis is da blankett patrole in da name of da Fyoor ya gots any Jewish babees? ya gots any queers? ya gots annee Babee Jesus freeks?) the audience just sat there clapping the door came open, that upstairs door came open and Clyde came down right down into his head he descended and the boy who was still over the cradle that hugged me and cried and wanted so much more that sweet little boy came back for a moment and he got up from his paid boxseat in the corner and he hugged his mom he hugged her tight right on the spot around the knees in the middle of that wreckroom (oben ub, I looking for dat Jewish bebee you said dat word too much you commin down wit me) hold on will you pal? I'm talkin turkey with my agent, yeah the kid got down in his dad's blood and he reached down and pulled his dad's zipper and then he pulled and did something with the cleaver and he started rubbing his stomach like he was pregnant or something, he just reached down into that tide and lifted his hands up and I stood over him as he crawled into the corner again and I said it was time to stop laughing (bam bam!) I said it was time for everyone to stop (bam bam bam bam, obben upp!) I said it was time for me to open the door to open her up to chop her up and open and that he should go back up the stairs into his bedroom that the time had come to stop counting or else I would have to come see you Al and renegotiate, yeah babes, would you hold on a minute pal? yeah it was time to stop laughing, yeah Mom stop the fuck laughing stop laughing stop it! Shut the fuck up!

One

Her fingers around my fingers like pigging string, we sat there, drinking. I was thinking about so many funny things as that hour went by, and Cindy, to whom at one point I handed the bottle, was swinging her legs underneath the bench and seemed to be dreaming with her eyes open. The shade didn't come back, and I was happy to be relaxing. I imagined we were riding up a lift, and the activity on the playground tilted down, and the two of us were way above the children as we basked in the mountain sun. A foehn caressed our upturned chins and ruffled our protective clothing. Holding hands, we were passing over the snow line, twin souls sparkling above the névé, and as the angle of the lift increased, our backs were forced back against the back of the bench, and I felt the constant pressure in my neck, and we made our final ascent along the rockwalls of the peak, which was flecked beneath my fluttering eyelids with rose madder.

The smells changed from the freshness of autumn wind to the intimate smells of Cindy, the smells of candy and childish sweat and damp wool lining. I stretched my legs and made my quads burn and yawned and felt at peace, as we continued our simple form of hugging. It seemed a miracle that she, who had been so uncontrollable, could keep that corybantic hand so still. From time to time she rubbed her forehead with her other arm or picked at the twill of her stretchpants. She was wearing a parka, and she lifted its hood so that I could only see the contour of her face, her brow and pug nose and sometimes her tongue. Near the end of our session, she shook her head and the hood fell down; and as we approached the sparkling summit, breathless in the sun, I heard a voice, booming from the top:

"Fear not, little flock; for it is your Father's good pleasure to give you the kingdom!"

Aah! Not an amorous couple but a wholesome flock, Cindy and me, high above the playground, grazing. I knew then, for the first time, that I could gain nothing directly from the priest. It was all beyond him, but it was not beyond me. I was the one who could hear the voice of God cascading out of crystal and rock, not he, the mathematic plotter. Between this child and me there was a serene bond, not of love but of loving meaning. He had foreseen! He had known, but he hadn't felt! I closed my eyes, and the permanence and grandeur of the peak, soaring, invisible, stayed rooted within me, and awash in warmth and stability and Stoli, I fell asleep.

The bottle fell from the bench and broke.

Someone was shaking me. I looked quickly around, and Cindy had left, and my hands felt stiff and dry. I brought them to my mouth and blew and then noticed that all of the children were gone, except for a few, off in a corner.

I felt a brutal wave of nausea.

"This is the way you care for children?" Kosmoski spoke to me in anger. "You passed out!"

"Where's the girl?" I asked.

"Where did you leave her, Clyde?"

"She was sitting here next to me."

I looked at my watch, but I couldn't get the dial to come clear. I guessed that I had been asleep for quite awhile. To tell the truth, I was feeling extremely shaky, since I had been up most of the previous night working on a poem and taking a long walk and had spent much of the morning refueling. The priest sat with his head bowed and hands folded. Was he praying? His face was sunburnt from Florida, and energy seemed to be collecting around his temples. I could tell that he was furious. I didn't have a great deal of sympathy, however, because it wasn't my job in life to make this guy happy.

"I guess I failed your little spirituality test," I said finally.

"How about Cindy?"

"What about her?"

"I left a mentally-impaired child in your care and you lost her, you maniac!"

"She'll turn up," I replied, as I began to mourn the loss of my bottle.

"You have no interest in helping to find her?"

"What do you take me for? Where should we start looking?" And I stood up and shivered like a dog.

Kosmoski pinched the bridge of his nose, his head still bowed.

"Go home," he said wearily.

"I said I'd help you look for her."

"Just leave."

"I'm not very good at babysitting," I protested. "I'm sure Cindy is all right."

"After I talk to her, I'll get back to you."

"So you still might hook me up with your friend?"

"As I told you before, it all depends on Cindy."

"What do you mean?"

"I mean that I'll ask Cindy whether or not I should do anything, and she'll be the judge."

"She doesn't make any sense when she talks."

"Of course she does."

"Unbelievable," I said out loud, but I must admit that I respected the way Kosmoski was going about his business. Besides, nobody else was going to give me a better recommendation than the girl who had just been holding my hand. I felt that Cindy owed me one, because I had comforted her, if only for a short time. There was a stark complicity between us. The priest didn't know it, but she was definitely on my side. Secure in my knowledge, I headed home.

Once inside my hotel room, I went into the kitchenette and poured myself a cooler, and then I sat on the couch and put my feet up and stared past the curtains out the sliding glass door toward the concrete deck of the balcony. Fluids ran in my head, and without the comfort of those lofty alpine moments, I felt bewildered and alone. It was late in the afternoon, and the sun was setting, and the room filled with shadows. I stared into pools of darkness that began to form in the recesses of the coffee table. My eyes felt very heavy again, and

I was slowly and judiciously transported.

Along one wall of a courtroom, I saw a long jury box, and in it were a row of girls in pert pinafores and saddle shoes (I could see their toes beneath the modesty panel) who were identical in aspect to Cindy. There was a bench for the magistrate, and in a more logical world one would have expected the priest to be my judge, but in point of fact it was an anonymous lady. I peered into her face for clues, but I couldn't garner any information because she was smiling and singing an Irish tune.

"Order in the courtroom," said my public defender, Horatio Chuckles Esq., "your clamor is contributing to the neurasthenic upset of the prisoner!"

In the center of the room was a cage, and I was in it.

"This multiple man," the clown emphasized, as he paced around the circuit, "is lodged in a veritable cinerarium of good intentions."

"Objection, your honor," the prosecutor stood and hemmed, "but the defendant is still moving inside his body bag. Unless ashes have a collective will, I must assume, and so should the court, that Mr. Franklin is alive and living."

"Objection overruled," the woman on the bench sang.

"He stabbed me with a pole," whispered a member of the jury.

"He wanted to enter me," claimed another.

"I've heard there's an anti-Semitic body on a Soledad kitchen floor," said another.

"He throttled me until I couldn't breathe and one of my eyes hemorrhaged," said one more.

"We shared a certain honesty," said another, "and went mountain climbing."

"His bottleneck was broken," said still another, "as soon as he fell asleep."

"I do believe the clown's been spayed," said another little girl. "Clown caviar tastes so groovy."

"Blood is pouring from the prick of the suspect," another Cindy agreed.

"He says he popped his dad with a gun," said one more.

"Don't say 'popped'!" the clown screamed.

"Then how do you account for the missing head?" the next to the last challenged.

"But you've got the wrong victim!" And the last Cindy grinned, as the gavel came down. "The real dead one in the basement is...."

"No talking on the jury," the judge peremptorily commanded them.

"Your honor, your honor," the clown rose and honked his horn again and again. "Order in the court, order in the court, my client is actually counting!"

"One two
one two one
two one two
one two one
two one two
one two one

two	one	two
one	two	one
two	one	two
one	two	one
two	one	two
one	two	one
two	one	two
one	two	one
two	one	two

one two one

two one two

one two one

two one two

one two one

two one two

one two one

two one two

one two one

two one two one."

"They call this man the Alphabet Man," the prosecutor raved, "and his piteous secret is grim."

"You have no cause," the clown cried, "to bring up the alphabet. The entire array belongs to him!"

"We found stray letters next to his burin," the prosecutor ranted. "Mainours! J'accuse! The vowels on his skin are leaking!"

"There are letters and there are letters," the clown responded vaguely and tritely.

"Look how the Alphabet Man is pacing like a panther," one of the Cindies noted brightly.

"It's true," said another, "but panthers don't masturbate."

"The captive panthers do," another confirmed insightfully.

"It's not what's there, but what is missing around the gonads that's the clue," the prosecutor asserted. "You only have to read Rilke!"

"Out of order, out of order," the clown was jumping up and down on a table, waving his foolscap and his fool's cap.

"It has been rumored, your honor," the prosecutor continued, "that there are certain mystic signs that one can't find, that originally were burned onto the skin but over the years were forgotten, and since his mind could not attach itself to the aforesaid attachments, they dropped to the ground like so many defective noodle stampings and there they lay, dripping with soup, somewhere in his past."

"Perhaps we can get a demonstration of the noontime torture of missing letters?" the judge turned to the clown.

"He only writes his poems for his betters," my nomologist

demured. (He had had no ovaries removed, at least none of his own, that was a libelous smear.)

"I hear the missing letters spell 'felatio'!" the final Cindy said.

"He always had a problem with the double l," her identical neighbor insisted.

"Aspersions, aspersions, it's raining aspersions," the clown cried, and he pulled a handkerchief out of a small box that was strapped to his stomach.

"No, it's not exactly fellatio," gentle ladies of the jury, "the prosecutor said. "The missing letters spell a curse. And that curse is...."

"Inconclusive inconclusive inconclusive," the clown strained. "The judge's fingers are covered with plaster!"

The woman on the bench turned white, like milk, milk-white, her face bruised and blanched and hard and tidy, and she said, "Clown objection sustained."

"In any case, every man deserves a lover as does every man inside a man, but the defendant has put a savage point to the maxim, look here your honor," the prosecutor demanded, "Clyde's voices come and go as lovers come and go, and I have to tell you in the strictest confidence that the circumstances of some of them are highly suspicious. The legs of his women have their own bloody hairballs."

"Prove that he was there!" the clown defender smirked.

"Ergo, I produce Exhibit V," the prosecutor waved a familiar bottle in the air, "your honor, Mr. Franklin was about to go to heaven, and here he has been on a three-day bender, laughing hysterically and stalking the neighborhoods with a white wicker basket and writing poetry and licking this red and silver label. In the middle of the night he cons his lines."

"Man cannot survive on literature alone." The clown was frothy. "Who are you to cast a stone? My vodkabib pal in the pen here uses only the freshest lemons and biodegradable distillands. Retards of the jury, examine the citrine pallor of his skin, the color of his lunules, and the undeniable luteosity of his asshole."

"He boffed me, he boffed me," all the Cindies started to cry, a chorus of he's, boffed's and me's.

"You see, he's guilty guilty guilty," the prosecutor turned and pointed.

The gavel went up and down, up and down, and in the back of the room I heard the vanquishing cry of a hartebeest.

That strange and surly snap and moo.

Moooooooooo
OOOOOOO
OOOOOOO
OOOₒₒₒₒₒₒₒ

Moooooooooo
OOOOOOO
OOOOOOO
OOOooooooo
oOOOOOO
OOOOOOOO
OOOooooooooo

OOOOOOOOOOO
oooOOOOO
OOOOOOO
OOOOOOO
OOOOOOO
OOO...........

Two red round eyes and a round empty mouth that didn't breathe much and the eyes were spinning like lug nuts.

OOh don't do it OOh don't do it

Honk honk honk! Honk honk honk!

It was the sound of the telephone ringing, and I woke up and reached to the end of the couch and picked up the receiver and rubbed my eyes as a baby rubs his eyes.

"Hello."

"Goddamit!"

"Shit, Roy."

"Goddamn your fucking ass."

"What time is it?"

"It's past my bedtime, you fuckhead."

It was Asterio Dominguez, my literary agent.

"How did you find me?"

"Dr. May gave me your telephone number."

"And to what do I owe the honor?"

"Does Thatcher Jensen ring a bell?"

"Nope."

"He's a G-man, Clyde. They think you might intend to off a presidential candidate!"

"So that's it, is it?"

"Why? Do you feel betrayed? In case you forgot, you had a speaking gig at Michigan State last weekend and a workshop, both of which you missed."

"I'm cancelling all my future engagements."

"That doesn't do the English Department at Michigan State much good."

"I'm half-asleep. I'll have to call you back."

"Don't hang up the fucking phone."

I hung up on him and turned on all the lamps in the room.

I was feeling terrible, and I made a quick trip to the refrigerator freezer and filled a glass with ice and Stoli. My stomach was totally shot. I had one drink left in me, and then I'd go back to sleep.

The telephone rang again. I decided not to answer, but then I thought better of it, because it might not be Roy, it might be Barbie, and so I picked up the receiver and it was Roy.

"Clyde, if you hang up on me again, I'm catching the morning plane for Washington, and then I'm going to make your life so fucking miserable that whatever you are trying to do, I guarantee it, I'm going to fuck it up royally, so you'd better stop pampering yourself and talk to me right now, OK?"

Roy didn't engage in empty rhetoric—if I had hung up on him he would have come—and so I took another sip and steeled myself.

Roy's principle occupation is as a Century City civil rights attorney, Harvard JD, but he is also a very deep reader. He only had four or five other literary clients, all retreads and blowouts like me. A woman in his legal firm handled our paperwork and scheduling, and he did whatever negotiating was necessary in our lives. I have many fond memories and anecdotes about Roy. As a matter of fact, Roy is the cotter of my life because for some inexplicable reason I remember everything that Roy has ever told me, I remember every time I've ever seen Roy, and everything Roy sends me I throw in an old file cabinet and keep.

Everything else I seem to forget, but Roy is a living memory.

A publishing house once asked me to write an autobiography, for which I would have been paid a huge sum of money, and so I sicced Roy on them. We traveled together to their offices in Manhattan and sat in a cramped conference room with a couple of horn-rimmed types and took our meeting. The editor-in-chief explained that he would publish anything I wrote but could only pay a large advance if the book were crafted to have broad appeal, since it was vital that my life and work be carried to a larger audience, in the interests of poetry.

"Tell us what you really mean," Roy snapped.

"We are asking Mr. Franklin to simplify his diction. The average reader finds it difficult to understand him. Also, we encourage him to write about violence and sex, since they're so much a part of his everyday existence, but we would want to maintain editorial control."

"Mr. Franklin writes quite simply, and he doesn't need any editorial help because sexually he maintains perfect control," was Roy's quick rejoinder and we left.

I don't write down or go down for anybody.

Roy represents me even though I was born a NaziJew, just as he would have represented the Nazi marchers in Skokie. Looked at another way, I'm a strange breed of multicultural fascist, the very definition of political incorrectness. Roy supports me because I write powerful poetry about man's sufferings and aspirations and desire for freedom and absolute reliance on God and the Spirit. In a strange way, Roy, who is gay, loves me. With him, it's not a physical thing, but a higher love, which I find impossible to reciprocate. With me, it's simply business, just like copping hours in jail. Somebody else keeps track, and I'm duly but grudgingly appreciative.

"Please keep it short, Roy. I'm exhausted."

"I'm talking as a friend here, Clyde, not as your lawyer and agent. I'm worried that you're being manipulated based on your notoriety. Somebody is trying to make a fool of you by linking you in a sordid way with a presidential hopeful. It's obvious and disgusting."

"I'm sick of listening to conspiracy theories."

"The FBI says you're under a delusion that Senator Abernathy hired someone to maul you. This is unlikely. I took the liberty of phoning the senator, and he graciously took my call. He had read your letter and was extremely upset, fearing some kind of public-relations disaster, just as he's preparing to enter the primaries. He says he respects your writing and that there's no reason on earth why he would want to harm you. He's a happily-married man, and he's never been to a hooker in his life. He pleaded with me to ask you to think twice, before you do something that might discredit the both of you."

"What do you expect he'd say? You're my lawyer."

"He's probably telling the truth, Clyde."

"Probably isn't good enough."

"The FBI wants me to get you out of town. They're threatening to arrest you, and I think they mean it. They can't take the chance, given your criminal and psychiatric record, of letting you walk around."

"They won't do it, so fuck 'em."

"Are you armed, Clyde?"

"Hell, no," I lied.

"Would you please tell me what's going on?"

"This has nothing to do with you."

"Then why did you copy me?"

"I don't want to be murdered."

This caused Roy to pause.

"I'm coming to Washington."

"If you do, you're fired."

"Then come back to Los Angeles and talk to me and Dr. May. You can always return to Washington after our meeting."

"Sorry. The answer is no."

"Then let me pay for a private detective to help you with your problem."

"No. The man would just report back to you."

More silence.

"When are you coming back?"

"I don't know."

"And you want me to cancel your engagements for the next month?"

"I want you to cancel all of my engagements, I already said that."

"I refuse to do that, Clyde."

"It's your problem then, not mine."

"Would you at least tell me the name of your new girlfriend?"

"To be honest with you, I don't know her name."

"She isn't there with you?"

"No, she's not."

"I give up on you, you sorry son of a bitch."

"Thank you very much. Wire me ten thousand dollars. Send it to the American Express office here, and do it right away."

Roy invested my money, too.

"You only have about fifteen grand."

"The fact means nothing to me. Just have them send me the money today."

"I hope you know what you're doing. Do me a favor, please, and don't do anything illegal."

I hung up again.

Two

Sometimes after readings or lectures, or even on the street, I'd be asked what makes me a poet, as if I'd been fashioned like a lopsided figurine. What makes me a poet is my alphabetic magic, for when I entered puberty, I installed my first letter, a B, just above my left knee.

Why there and why that particular letter?

It was the first letter of the first two lines of my first inspirational poetry: *Being a helpless sinner, sinless Jesus,/ Please deliver me!*

Lines one and two, poem one, right out of the box had said it all, and the irony is that I could have stopped right there, because the next line and all subsequent stichs and di and multistichs have been crude embellishments of this original De Profundis.

(An ashblacked pundit, I had been worshiping and imitating Renaissance lyricists, and foremost among them Fulke Greville and his bosom pal, Philip Sydney, the shrewd and gracile courtiers, respectively.)

And why above my left knee?

Because there was plenty of legroom.

Over the next year or two I added script, and when I got to the letter Q, Dad noticed and joked to Mom that I had a skin and ink disease and that, my tracery being such as it was, I'd never sell a Maytag, and then he laughed fiendishly and gave up permanently on me. Drats! Right then and there I knew that I could never tread in Dad's detergent footsteps.

Yes, I wrote for years before that prison class with Baby Janes, Isadora's licking mate, kiki and distraught, I always wrote. I wrote before I talked. In those first glassine days, when Mommy and

Daddy hovered over the crib like dark bulbs, I cribbed my cursive lines in languages that whirred and chimed. A jerky manualist, the code was there and hovered in the bassinet above my crumpling, incandescent fingers, in that first ribbon of clarity that glowed a foot away: Baby Belshazzar, whose soundless symbols shone on walls of air, and I searched in myself for a shewer of hard sentences, for the Satanic One who could decipher that moving infant graphic.

First there was the word and then the world. First there was a language and then there was a tongue. First there was a poem and then there was a poet.

Baby Jesus was a poet.

When I was imbued with my first vowel, a U, I ceased to shower but sponged myself ritually, a taboo. Letter after letter, a newer me developed, until I was ready and became what I had always known I was on the surface: a hypostatic language moving through space, an alphabetic vase, a lettered balloon-animal, a visionary concoction of brandedness to haunt the human race. All the clumsy crafters of verse, the careerist professors with their greasy carminatives and mixed metaphors and grant committees and deadly magazines, all the rabbling foisters and feelers and jejune linkers, parted like a cloacal sea and I, the Pharoah Ramses Wayne Franklin—the First and the Second—the prancing heiroglyph and thaumaturge, ventured forth into my own drowning.

Ah, but I wax Biblical, when instead I should be writing more about Barbie.

Early the following morning, I walked over to Georgetown from my hotel on Washington Circle and made my way down the hill to the Potomac. Under a bridge I collected stones, which I stuck in my pocket, and at the margins of the river I played at ducks and drakes.

The Potomac has its own commotion and refuses to give up being Indian, as if it looks at this American enclave as a temporary sideache. Who says that Indians one day won't reconquer their land, as the river impatiently waits? I, for one, believe it. I believe that before we set up our monified slave kingdoms, all the native lovers were attracted to rivers and left the flowing marks of their backs on the banks in intimate trails of lineage and descent, and that all the rivers of the world were humanly honored and maintained their purity beneath a canopy of birdsong as they flowed purling toward the sea.

Peace. Peace. Peace.

Lenny Dalls was waiting near the Watergate, and as I walked up to him, he had his nose to the wind, in all probability plot-contemplating. Loves, quests, extinctions, mysteries and deceits are what my friend hauls to the campshots and dumps over. I sat down next to him and stared between the balusters at the teeming river.

"I have to go somewhere and you're late," he said, "and so I only have a couple of minutes."

Leonard reached down and patted each of his dalmatians, who were lying by his side. Between us was a folded newspaper with a half-completed crossword puzzle.

"That's perfectly all right," I said.

"There is more to the situation you described than strikes the eye. I did a bit of checking, and I also showed around your photograph of Barbie, whose real name, or at least the one by which she's known in town, is June Sunlight."

"Is she well-known?"

"Very well-known. She hardly falls into the category that most would consider a prostitute. Courtesan would be a better term. As a matter of fact, she's rumored to be something of a Mata Hari. She moves about the various circuits, and the suspicion is that she's made real money as a seller of military, industrial and political information. She has had relationships with very important people, and when I heard all this, alarm bells went off."

"Do you know where she is?"

"I wouldn't know where to start looking. All I know is that your Lebanese friend was lying. Early in her career, she worked steadily for him over a number of years."

"I'm not surprised," I said.

"Based on what I just told you, let me suggest a possibility."

"Sure."

"What if she's doing a job for somebody?"

"For whom?"

"It could be anyone, foreign or domestic. If I'm correct, you can forget everything she's told you."

"I don't understand what you mean."

"Do you want me to be honest with you, Clyde, even if you find it offensive, or do you want to bull straight ahead on this one?"

"Go ahead," I said, "I'm willing to listen."

"This woman has been paid her whole life to fuck people, and I strongly suspect that she was paid to fuck you."

He had gone too far.

"You left out the most likely possibility," I said, doing my best to maintain my composure.

"I have?"

"She could have been telling the truth, Leonard. She could have been telling me the goddamn truth right from the beginning."

"That would mean that Abernathy was involved in S&M."

"Does that shock you? The guy comes from the kind of background where such things are trendy. He wasn't particularly inventive, according to Barbie. It was softcore bondage, a fantasy flog. The guy was a klutz."

"It's possible I'm wrong, Clyde, it's certainly possible."

Leonard got up and placed his crossword in the garbage can next to the bench. He leaned against the palings and gazed out across the river, as the wind rippled through his overcoat. After a minute or two, he came over and sat down again.

I waited.

"Put aside your feelings," he said, placing his hand on my arm, "and assume for the sake of argument that my intuition is correct: that somebody hired June Sunlight to go out to Los Angeles and sleep with you and get you to Washington and that the same people who hired her had you beaten up, and that Abernathy never had anything to do with her and that there was no blackmail."

"So?"

"What does that tell you, Clyde? What's this all about?"

"I don't know."

"*You*, Clyde. It's all about *you*."

"What?"

"You know what I mean."

"No, I don't."

Leonard looked down at his feet. He seemed embarrassed. I could tell he wasn't going to take it any further.

"Please be careful, Clyde. I understand that you don't want to go back to California right now. I know that you're in love with this woman, and that you'd never forgive yourself if she were telling the truth and she got hurt because you weren't there for her. And I admit that I could be wrong. But don't trust anyone. No one. Not a single person! Are you listening to me?"

I was. Or at least I thought I was, but I might have let something slip by that he said. She must be telling the truth, I began to pray. If my feelings of love and dedication were part of some fiction, of some plot, then what?

"And you're certain, Clyde," Leonard asked in a concerned and friendly voice, "that you've told me everything? Because there is something missing from your story. I wish I knew what it was, but I'm positive that something is missing."

"Of course, I've told you everything," I replied resentfully.

But something was missing. And now, in retrospect, I realize that I had hardly told Leonard anything.

For he didn't know about the clown, he didn't know about my vicious needs, and I hadn't mentioned a single word about the priest.

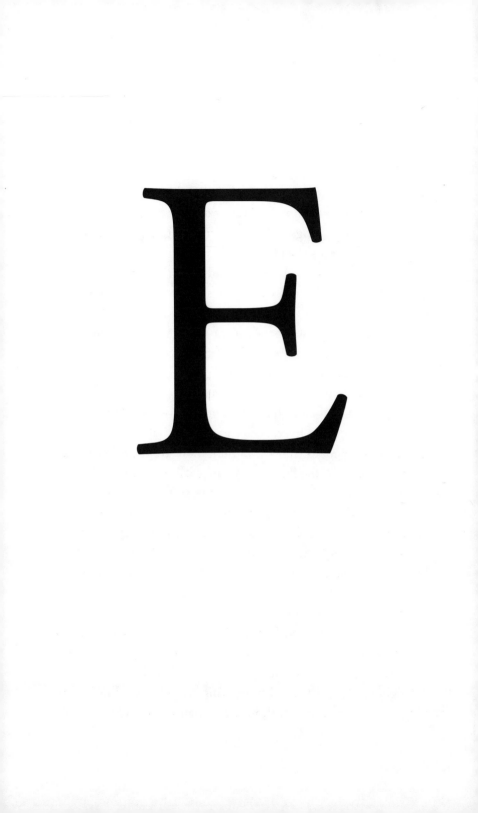

that there are rules for everybody, babes and I know why you hate
to think of yourself as some master or dominator or king of the
castle, even though kings have all the fun, but you like the idea of
being a prince cuz it's the child inside you Clyde, we clowns can
see the kid inside of everybody and kids don't like rules, that
nightmare priest had it right when he said that kids are sneaks
and snitches, they all are, and S and M is just a game whereas you
play for keeps babes, your gentle lover Billy had your number
(take your choice, one or two) when he said that knowing you he
put all trust aside cuz with you there are no limits, no bargains,
it's like the universe is one big circus and you're the nasty animal,
you're the beast that can't be tamed, you're the jive character who
bets his boodle on the river, sure you can be civil at times, and
reasonably coherent at times, and then there are the other times
when you rise from the flames in your swirling tattoos and your
head is empty and your guts are grinding and it's chop chop
Ovary City and it isn't pretty, you're so mean and hard and
uncanny and I gotta tell you that your explosions sort of frighten
me and I'm feeling kind of moody and thoughtful tonight ol'
Clyde, it's been a tough tough day and I thought we could talk a
little more seriously about pain and what it gets you yeah sometimes you're your dad and sometimes you're your mum and I
know what it was like and I've tried to tell you that it was just a
game, that everyone deserves a drink and thrashing on weekends,
I mean life is a shitty sell, cuz when you hawk a Maytag you're
not laughing, don't get up, I'm pouring, yeah I guess I'm just a
crying clown like ya see on those velvet paintings, and so I

checked it out with the ringmaster and asked him all about power and the responsibilities of whips and chains, cuz I felt sorry for your dad I really did when he saw me coming, I came through the door and he looked into my eyes and they were blanks, four eyes two up two down, including the gun, if you know what I mean but of course how could you? anyway to him and your mom it was just a game a form of clowning it was just fun and games and your mom wore the bruises like badges which is one of the reasons she liked to sing as she did the chores it's just one of those crazy human things Clyde it's just one of those human things that have to do with power, that people are so powerless and crushed and love their kinky games, but of course you never understood except when you danced I'd be hunched up by the turntable and I could see that you were experiencing that sound of Where or When so powerfully and would listen over and over again as if you were getting punched, and loved it as you dreamed about staying in the middle in some magic land between the lash and your mom, like Janus looking both ways you'd see the crop coming down and you'd see the skin turning purple and you wanted to be both her and him and purple and powerful and couldn't, which is why you've lost your sense of humor and why you're so angry because you want both, you want to bash it and take it up the ass, you want to carve your initials into the ladies and weep as you get your fanny broken, it's the old predicament, the basis of all the world's religions the basis of all laughter cuz as I've told you hundreds and hundreds of times, religion and comedy were born at the very same time, yeah it's all about the impossibility of ever seeing both sides of the coin at the same time that made you so angry and volatile and sadistic and message-prone, yeah prone to give me the wrong message cuz you've always been a total loser and a loner, Clyde you're always hanging around with your heavy equipment and your pants down and there is no solace in emptiness Clyde, I mean no solace in emptiness. I've told Al, Al we gotta leave this guy alone, we've already taken every sou the fella has, poor Clyde's so empty and alone cuz he can't follow rules and just keeps going and going and going and hurting and hurting and hurting, a carpet slave to his own desires, it's all so vastly boring yeah to be so weak and human is so boring that only pain can get us where we need to be, only pain and laughter have any certainty or carpentry and I provide the one and you provide the other, babes and who provides which is our little secret cuz when they laugh at you then I blow up and leave the room and stalk and when I crack my jokes your life is

pain, but you have honesty and the big **B** the bottle, which is nearly empty, thar she blows! it's just another hundred proof down the old rathole yeah they don't understand that you are after the chick for a very good reason. You are Lancelot and she's your Guenevere and she got out of her cage and you're chasing after her through the wide wide world which makes sense, the way you'd follow your mom, stumbling as a little boy around the kitchen, you'd chase but never touch, and you wanted her so so much and you want her once again, you want her so so bad to touch, you want to do it once again with her in that secret place between her legs you want to touch and kiss her there again and again and again, but love is not redeemable Clyde like coupons, babes ya lose ya never win in love, and we both know that Barbie's gone, she's flown the coop and even my belly's quiet, yeah even in hell they listen to the elegies, they stop their torching and hammering, and the pincers cool when the laughter dies above, and the hellfires flicker and sigh and I'll tell ya why, I'll tell ya why in hell the devils cry when love dies and the reason is sappy and simple, don't mind if I do, and while you unscrew I'll slice the lemons, I love that inner tangy smell of fruit among the other tangs, perhaps cuz I don't have anything, nothing that smells funny or crude like you do inside, shit babes I lost my train of thought, I'll take another cube, something about that friend of yours you love, but let me tell you, guy you can't take it with you, nah you can't take it with you, I remember that look in your daddy's eye, it looked like he was tired, yeah bone tired and he just wanted to pack those final bags those empty suitcases and leave. I mean after all I'm only a clown, I'm only a little bigger than your little thing and I was just following orders and I didn't want to grow large and do it unless he agreed and he just sort of invited me to it, he looked at his wife and then he looked at me and he just sort of invited me to it, and he opened his mouth and his mouth was round and I saw there was something flying there a busy busy bee was humming like a hornet in the cavity of a tree, something that needed swatting with a deep and lasting sting it was buzzing deep down deep down deep and I knew that if I honked my horn the bee would fly into me and for the rest of my life I would be panting and laughing and adjusting my curse-contract and buzzing and there are buzzing sounds that go on like the sounds of veins in the brain ah Clyde babes, ya been my lifelong friend, it's been so fucking boring here, drinking and gabbing, and although nobody else trusts you I trust you implic-itly and so does Al, but Einstein man, he's Chinese and he doesn't trust anybody, it's just confusion, babes that's what I told my agent, you just didn't see that it was all a game, you missed the point it was just a game that nobody ever called me or you by our proper names and we all need contracts yeah, he didn't meant to hurt her, babes that's what he said he said stop Son it's only a game we love, but ah we do love you, please stop Son stop don't shoot stop the world loves you and me, poets and clowns, the individual and prosaic, ah yes, Clyde, the evil is so deep within that when I'm sad it disappears and the hot tears come and the voices disappear and are buried the voices disappear and tears come and the voices go they come and they go and we grin

One

It was time for me to change location.

I no longer wished to be disturbed, neither by my agent nor by my shrink nor by the Federal Bureau of Investigation. I packed my guns and my bags and left the hotel with no forwarding address and moved across town. Now I was ready to keep my next appointment, an after-midnight rendezvous with the fat man, and since I was once again a paying customer (a few days previous I had handed over what I had assumed was ten thousand dollars), I was cordially greeted.

His living room was thoroughly cleansed, and a Merlin rang from time to time in the next room, where an amanuensis-call-boy receptionist type handled the practical greetings and linkings. Sitting in a high-backed chair facing the bay window as I entered was an exquisite beauty in a deep-blue suit, a pale pink tie of floral design, white clip-down linen and sharkskin cowboy boots. Straight auburn brows and perfect teeth and porcelain skin and hair en brosse tapering to the ear, where an ensiform jewel punctured the left helix. I couldn't tell whether it was a him or a her.

It stood, elegant and thin, and gracefully shook my hand.

A her.

"Clyde Franklin, this is Delilah Sandhurst," Judas made the introduction.

Delilah, which in Hebrew means delicate.

No blemish, no emotion, just the beau geste de rigueur. She sat down and lit a Davidoff, which she removed from a filigree case. She smiled pleasantly but didn't feel constrained to say anything. Judas also lit a cigarette, and with the filter jammed between medius and index, he scratched at the side of his face as he stared out the window into the darkness. A servant in a mess jacket brought me a chilled martini with a peel on a tray.

Stoli.

I had a sneaking suspicion I was being taken.

Judas seated himself in the bay and leaned back on a Fortuny cushion as the flunky hurried over with an ashtray.

"I really don't know how to say this properly," Judas began with Levantine calculation. "First of all, your girlfriend's name is June Sunlight."

"You can call her whatever you want," I replied, "but I prefer Barbie."

"Fine, fine," he said. "Of course, I knew her immediately when you showed me the picture. She is a special kind of woman, how do you say it? I mean to say that she is hired by special people sometimes."

I cast a glance over at Miss Sandhurst and wondered what was on her sexual menu.

"I have to assume from what you told me earlier that she is shaking somebody down. I would watch my ass, my friend," Judas added.

"I've already been warned."

"No, I mean it. She's slept with a couple of guys who are no longer around. The broad is dangerous."

The feeling that I was being played for a sucker by this obese bawdmonger was increasing from moment to moment.

"I see right through your shtick," I blurted out.

"Shtick?"

"Right, with the houseboy and the cocktails and the willowy hermaphrodite and the tales of lofty intrigue. This might impress a Beverly Hills Iranian or Jap commercial traveler, but I advise you to cut the fucking horseshit. I handed you ten thousand bucks!"

"These are business hours, and this is what it looks like around here at two in the morning," he explained defensively, "and I thought you wanted a drink."

"Where the fuck is Barbie?"

He gave me that astonished look I've seen so often in my life, when the blinders fall from the eyes and men who originally suspected me of being literary and eccentric suddenly realize that I'm brutal and totally crazy. I judge a person fundamentally on whether or not fear is swimming in that initial look. In his case, he was frightened, so I felt a little better, realizing that if push came to shove I could reclaim my ten grand.

"I wish you'd let me explain this my way," he said, as he quickly regained his composure.

I finished up my martini and waited.

"She's not telling you the truth," he said.

"I've heard this all before," I replied. "I've heard it a number of times."

"Yes, but you see, there is no reason in the world that June would have told you honestly what she was involved in. You're an outsider, and she has powerful friends that protect her a lot better than you ever could. She is incapable of love, and she doesn't need your help."

"You're talking like a businessman," I objected. "What went down between us was personal."

"That's what they all say," Delilah interrupted with weary emphasis.

"Why the access of honesty?" I asked, ignoring the woman. "I didn't ask for a character analysis, I just wanted you to find her for me."

"It's all one ball of wax," he replied. "I don't want to keep your money if things are going to get messy for me."

"I can clean up my own mess," I said.

"Let me be a little clearer," Judas said, suddenly becoming irritable. "The only reason that June would fuck you is because she wanted something from you. I've looked into this situation, and I don't like what I see, so I'm being a gentleman and offering you your money back."

"Who are these capable people who protect her?" I asked.

"Lobbyists."

"Give me a break!"

The houseboy came up with a replacement and a twist.

"Listen, my friend, something else is going on here, and you are being badly used," Judas said. "Believe me, I'd love to take your money, but I smell a rat."

"I expect you to keep to our bargain," I objected.

"The fool doesn't listen. Give him his money, Judas, and show him the door," the woman snapped.

I realized suddenly, with a shock, that the androgyne in the blue suit was the boss. The entire time I had been directing my energy in the wrong direction.

"Go get Jerry," Judas commanded the houseboy, who hurried away.

"You know where Barbie is, don't you?" I turned to Delilah Sandhurst with plenty of malice aforethought.

"This conversation's over," the woman said, and she began to rise from her chair.

"No, it's not," and to make my point, I pulled the Ruger out of my pocket and leveled it at her forehead. She was about ten feet away. She looked at the gun and frowned and sat back down.

An older man in a tuxedo appeared at the door. Short and broad and swarthy. A benchpresser, probably an umpteenth-degree black belt, a crème de la crème bouncer. I figured him to be armed.

"Should I call the police, Miss Sandhurst, or should I take care of this myself?"

"Call the police," she instructed him.

He was standing in the doorway, and we both knew that I wasn't in the best of positions to begin something, being seated and across the room.

"Step forward," I instructed him. I wanted him closer.

"You only get one shot, motherfucker," he said, not intending to move out of the frame of the door. He waited there to see what I'd do.

Drawing my gun had been a sad mistake.

"Where's my money?" I demanded.

"Now you don't get your money," Delilah responded. "We were about to give you a refund, but at this point you don't get anything as a matter of principle." And she reached into her vest pocket, pulled out her cigarette case, removed another Davidoff and lit it.

I noticed that her hands weren't shaking.

I was screwed.

"What you do get," she continued, "is free passage out of here. This is our place of business, Mr. Franklin, so put the gun back in your pocket and walk out quietly. No one will touch you and there won't be any further trouble."

I did just that.

Two

I left the townhouse and walked down the hill to a bar on M Street and ordered an endless series of Russian drinks, and shortly afterwards I blanked (a twilit glitter of performances and postures) and fell asleep and ascended into constellated spheres, and my letters were shining as I hovered, puffed up and skintight, fingers and toes like profiteroles, over the rooftops of Georgetown. I was nude, except for a neon braguette, and "Bariecom" (since I had no double letters) flashed above the ridgepoles from my elbows stomach foot chest legs and back. I twirled around so everyone could see the C that glowed from above my coccyx.

Com Barie Com Barie Com Barie Com Barie Com Com Com, I blinked.

Oh Baaaaaaaaaaaaaaaaaaaaaaarie, I streamed in the night of Georgetown light, floating from spot to spot as my navel A was revving, Cooooooooooooooooooooooom to this human sex banneret. My cicisbeo of desire fluttering from the Pole.

Baaaaaaaaaaaaaaaaaaaaaaaaaaaaaaaaaaaaaaaaaaaaaaaaaaaaaaa aaaaaaaaaarie!

Baaaaaaaaaaaaaaaaaaaaaaaaaaaaaa aaaaaaaaaaaaaaaaaaaaaaaaaaaaaaaaa aaaaaaarie!

ComComComComComComCom.

Hurling off the azimuths, I soared and spun into darkness turning, turning in a Minkowski world where time and I slipped into a distant dimension and reformed, and my letters flashed away from my skin and each had its own destiny and hungered for its own recipient mind.

Baaaaaaaaaaaaaaaaaaaaaaaaaaaaaaaaaaaaaaaaaaaaarie into the dark.

Baaaaaaaaaa aaaaaaaaaaaaaaa aaaaaaaaaaaaaaa aaaaaaarie searching for the stellar light of nonexistent minds, of other minds, am I the only precious one? Calling into nowhere into the earless void Oh BaaaaaaaaaaaaaaaaariiiiiiiiiiiiiiiiiiiiiiiiiiiiiiiiiiiiiiiiiiiiiieohBBBBBBB Baaa.... each letter stringing moments like that spider crawling with its bit of web along the saddle line the spider—ah the flinty grandeur of webs! aaaah—I tumbled, the Alphabet Man the only poet, forming baby words, Baby-lonian wall words aaaaaaaaaaah.

It felt so cold inside my head, inside my cells were bathtub universes.

Baaaaaaaaaaaaaaaaaaaaaaaaaaaaaaa.....................r..............
Between the cells, the same cold dark we feel,

BBBBBBBBB

BBBBaaaaaaaaa
aaaaaaaaaaaaaaaa
....
riiiiiiiiiieeeeeeee
eeBBBBBBBB

I could fill the universe with b's those busy busy bees like the B

on my knee BBBBBBBBBBB
BBBBBBBBBBBBBBBB
BBBBBBBBBBBBBBBB
BBBBBBBBBBBBBBBB
BBBBBBBBBBBBBBBB
BBBBBBBBBBBBBBBB
BBBBBBBBBBBBBBBB

BBBBBBBBBBBBBB
BBBBBBBBBBBBBB
BBBBBBBBBBBBBB
BBBBBBBBBBBBBB
BBBBBBBBBBBBBB
BBBBBBBBBBBBBB
BBBBBBBBBBBBBB
BBBBBBBBBBBBBB
BBBBBBBBBBBBBB
BBBBBBBBBBBBBB
BBBBBBBBBBBBBB
BBBBBBBBBBBBBB
BBBBBBBBBBBBBB

BBBBBBBBBBBBBB
BBBBBBBBBBBBBB
BBBBBBBBBBBBBB
BBBBBBBBBBBBBB
BBBBBBBBBBBBBB
BBBBBBBBBBBBBB
BBBBBBBBBBBBBB
BBBBBBBBBBBBBB
BBBBBBBBBBBBBB
BBBBBBBBBBBBBB
BBBBBBBBBBBBBB
BBBBBBBBBBBBBB
BBBBBBBBBBBBBB

BBBBBBBBBBBBBBB
BBBBBBBBBBBBBBB
BBBBBBBBBBBBBBB
BBBBBBBBBBBBBBB
BBBBBBBBBBBBBBB
BBBBBBBBBBBBBBB
BBBBBBBBBBBBBBB
BBBBBBBBBBBBBBB
BBBBBBBBBBBBBBB
BBBBBBBBBBBBBBB
BBBBBBBBBBBBBBB
BBBBBBBBBBBBBBB
BBBBBBBBBBBBBBB

BBBB BBBBBBBBBBBBBBBBBBBBBBBBBBB
BBBBBBBBBBBBBBBBBBBBBBBBBBBBBBBBBBBBBBBBBBB
BBBBBBBBBBBBBBBBBBBBBBBBBBBBBBBBBBBBBBBBBBB
BBBBBBBBBBBBBBBBBBBBBBBBBBBBBBBBBBBBBBBBBBB
BBBBBBBBBBBBBBBBBBBBBBBBBBBBBBBBBBBBBBBBBBB
BBBBBBBBBBBBBBBBBBBBBBBBBBBBBBBBBBBBBBBBBBB
BBBBBBBBBBBBBBBBBBBBBBBBBBBBBBBBBBBBBBBBBBB
BBBBBBBBBBBBBBBBBBBBBBBBBBBBBBBBBBBBBBBBBBB
BBBBBBBBBBBBBBBBBBBBBBBBBBBBBBBBBBBBBBBBBBB
BBBBBBBBBBBBBBBBBBBBBBBBBBBBBBBBBBBBBBBBBBB
BBBBBBBBBBBBBBBBBBBBBBBBBBBBBBBBBBBBBBBBBBB
BBBBBBBBBBBBBBBBBBBBBBBBBBBBBBBBBBBBBBBBBBB
BBBBBBBBBBBBBBBBBBBBBBBBBBBBBBBBBBBBBBBBBBB
BBBBBBBBBBBBBBBBBBBBBBBBBBBBBBBBBBBBBBBBBBB
BBBBBBBBBBBBBBBBBBBBBBBBBBBBBBBBBBBBBBBBBBB
BBBBBBBBBBBBBBBBBBBBBBBBBBBBBBBBBBBBBBBBBBB
BBBBBBBBBBBBBBBBBBBBBBBBBBBBBBBBBBBBBBBBBBB
BBBBBBBBBBBBBBBBBBBBBBBBBBBBBBBBBBBBBBBBBBB
BBBBBBBBBBBBBBBBBBBBBBBBBBBBBBBBBBBBBBBBBBB
BBBBBBBBBBBBBBBBBBBBBBBBBBBBBBBBBBBBBBBBBBB
BBBBBBBBBBBBBBBBBBBBBBBBBBBBBBBBBBBBBBBBBBB
BBBBBBBBBBBBBBBBBBBBBBBBBBBBBBBBBBBBBBBBBBB
BBBBBBBBBBBBBBBBBBBBBBBBBBBBBBBBBBBBBBBBBBB
BBBBBBBBBBBBBBBBBBBBBBBBBBBBBBBBBBBBBBBBBBB
BBBBBBBBBBBBBBBBBBBBBBBBBBBBBBBBBBBBBBBBBBB
BBBBBBBBBBBBBBBBBBBBBBBBBBBBBBBBBBBBBBBBBBB
BBBBBBBBBBBBBBBBBBBBBBBBBBBBBBBBBBBBBBBBBBB
BBBBBBBBBBBBBBBBBBBBBBBBBBBBBBBBBBBBBBBBBBB
BBBBBBBBBBBBBBBBBBBBBBBBBBBBBBBBBBBBBBBBBBB
BBBBBBBBBBBBBBBBBBBBBBBBBBBBBBBBBBBBBBBBBBB
BBBBBBBBBBBBBBBBBBBBBBBBBBBBBBBBB
BBBBBBBBBBBBBBBBBBBBBBBBBBBB

BBBBBBBBBBBBBBBBBBBBBB
BBBBBBBBBBBBBBBBBBBBBBB
BBBBBBBBBBBBBBBBBBBBBBB
BBBBBBBBBBBBBBBBBBBBBBB
BBBBBBBBBBBBBBBBBBBBBBB
BBBBBBBBBBBBBBBBBBBBBBB
BBBBBBBBBBBBBBBBBBBBBBBBBBBBBBBB
BBBBBBBBBBBBBBBBBBBBBBBBBBBBBBBBBBBBBBBBBBB
BBBBBBBBBBBBBBBBBBBBBBBBBBBBBBBBBBBBBBBBBBB
BBBBBBBBBBBBBBBBBBBBBBBBBBBBBBBBBBBBBBBBBBB
BBBBBBBBBBBBBBBBBBBBBBBBBBBBBBBBBBBBBBBBBBB
BBBBBBBBBBBBBBBBBBBBBBBBBBBBBBBBBBBBBBBBBBB
BBBBBBBBBBBBBBBBBBBBBBBBBBBBBBBBBBBBBBBBBBB
BBBBBBBBBBBBBBBBBBBBBBBBBBBBBBBBBBBBBBBBBBB
BBBBBBBBBBBBBBBBBBBBBBBBBBBBBBBBBBBBBBBBBBB
BBBBBBBBBBBBBBBBBBBBBBBBBBBBBBBBBBBBBBBBBBB
BBBBBBBBBBBBBBBBBBBBBBBBBBBBBBBBBBBBBBBBBBB
BBBBBBBBBBBBBBBBBBBBBBBBBBBBBBBBBBBBBBBBBBB
BBBBBBBBBBBBBBBBBBBBBBBBBBBBBBBBBBBBBBBBBBB
BBBBBBBBBBBBBBBBBBBBBBBBBBBBBBBBBBBBBBBBBBB
BBBBBBBBBBBBBBBBBBBBBBBBBBBBBBBBBBBBBBBBBBB
BBBBBBBBBBBBBBBBBBBBBBBBBBBBBBBBBBBBBBBBBBB
BBBBBBBBBBBBBBBBBBBBBBBBBBBBBBBBBBBBBBBBBBB
BBBBBBBBBBBBBBBBBBBBBBBBBBBBBBBBBBBBBBBBBBB
BBBBBBBBBBBBBBBBBBBBBBBBBBBBBBBBBBBBBBBBBBB busy bee
humming bee BBBeeBBB bee blackout BBlackout blackout bee
glans beeeee and when I awoke it was early afternoon and I was in
my hotel room. I had slept in my streetclothes.

Miraculously, I had the money from the whorehouse back in my pocket, but my Ruger was missing.

I climbed out of bed and checked the room. I still couldn't find the gun. I placed the stack of hundred-dollar bills on the night table. There was no question that it was the money I had handed to Judas. The money they had refused to give back to me. Then I thought for a minute and picked up the telephone. Whatever had happened, I decided to ride with it.

"Mr. Brennemann, please."

"Who shall I say is calling?"

"Clyde Wayne Franklin."

Two one two one two one two one two....

"You fucking son of a bitch!"

"You shouldn't have tried to keep my money."

"You're a fucking son of a bitch, you asshole!"

"I don't like being rousted by a dyke with an attitude problem."

"You shot off a weapon in my place."

"Go to the police and see what it gets you."

"Keep your goddamn money, you tattooed slimeball. I wish Billy had never introduced you to me. I wish to God I'd never gotten involved in all this!"

"You tell me how to find my girlfriend, cocksucker, or I'm coming back over there."

"I should have Jerry put your lights out."

"You know something about Barbie and you'd better tell me, man, or I'm going to do something really crazy, do you hear me? I get off this phone without the information, and I'm going to do something so fucking crazy that you're going to regret it for the rest of your life. You have a call service. Maybe next week you start getting the wrong kind of phone calls. I'm going to trash your business! I'm going to make you fucking miserable. You really got me angry!"

"Hold on a minute,"

I heard muffled conversation in the background. Then Delilah Sandhurst was on the line.

"You're a piece of work, you know that, don't you?" she said.

"Save the rhetoric and tell me what you should have told me in the first place."

"I can't talk on the telephone. I'll meet you tomorrow, but in the meantime try to calm down."

"Fine, but no more runarounds."

Blackouts should bother me a lot more than they do.

They are the falsework of a larger structure, the missing things that allow more memorable things to happen. When a bomb goes off, it's conventional wisdom that adjacent victims vaporize—they disappear—but I know that the disfiguration of shrapnel is recorded from the first nanosecond when the surface of the bomb forms cracks like an egg (yes, that exquisite crackle like a Sung vase) as the explosive starts to press against the casing, and it all starts moving out in thunderous waves to slice and clamor through the victim's head. Time channels. Flying alphabetic death structures. And the victim dices up and forgets! He forgets where he is, he forgets his body, the head flies off and tumbles among the shards, little brainlets laden with kisses and betrayals and regrets trip into space like a fine spray blasting down independent wormholes, against the walls (against the walls of the wreckroom), and every drop is a small clock.

The day I was released from Patton State I saw what the rest of my life would be like.

A succession of blackouts and bottles.

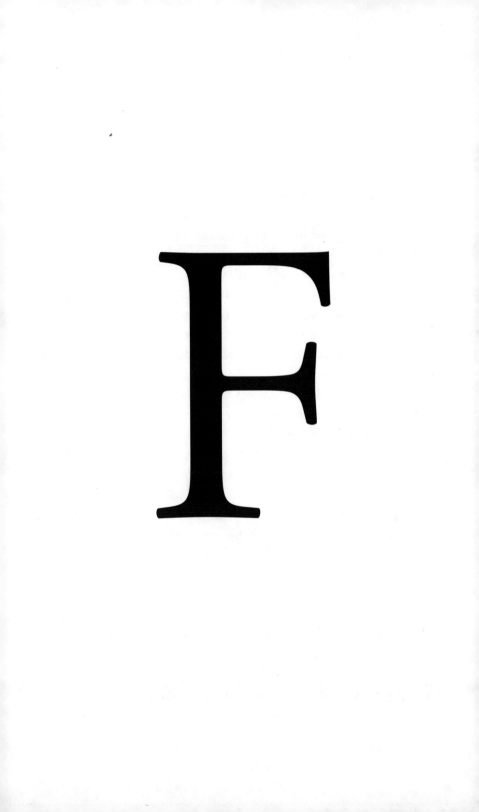

took me off the cross and placed me next to the purple record player and we used to dance together, actually he did all the dancing, I just waited for him to grab me and I was threaded with my head against the edge of the cabinet cuz he liked to keep me that way and sometimes he'd lean me back against the covers of the extended plays and make me watch, can you believe the kinky bastard? he'd make me watch cuz in the wrecks he had to watch himself and he'd do the damndest things, they were really disgusting and I used to think that we clowns had seen everything but we clowns ain't seen nothing, nothing at all, Al. I hadn't been tilted back for a while and my legs hadn't been spread and he hadn't touched me there (you know where) for a while and he did it as we danced, his eyes were shining, he was crying Al he was crying boo hoo hoo real hard, the bonebreaker would go out into the world with his truncheon and whack Mex butt and then he'd come home and shut the door to his room which was like a tomb and he'd break up, he'd dance with his little clown doll and he'd cry himself dry and he'd look at the door and get pissed, as if everything on the other side of the door was the door and then he'd become frightened, and he'd play this Rogers and Hart tune from the thirties that Dion covered, WHERE OR WHEN, I loved it Al, we'd be dancing and I'd still be throbbing from where the babes had rubbed me, I used to pulse there but I never honked my horn, if ya know what I mean, I never got off, cuz there was nothing inside me Al, nothing inside me but a laugh, and as we moved across the floor I'd listen to those exquisite tones and I'd think about forbidden things:

IT SEEMS WE STOOD AND TALKED LIKE THIS BEFORE.

mmmm, did we ever, but not in words
WE LOOKED AT EACH OTHER IN THE SAME WAY THEN,

up and down up and down
BUT I CAN'T REMEMBER WHERE OR WHEN.

I remember but the babes doesn't
THE CLOTHES YOU'RE WEARING ARE THE CLOTHES YOU WORE.

a small stain between the legs
THE SMILE YOU ARE SMILING YOU WERE SMILING THEN,

your eyes black and shining
BUT I CAN'T REMEMBER WHERE OR WHEN

I touch you deep down deep down deep
SOME THINGS THAT HAPPEN FOR THE FIRST TIME,

with the tip of my tongue
SEEM TO BE HAPPENING AGAIN.

but only twice cuz it can't happen no more
AND THEN IT SEEMS THAT WE HAVE MET BEFORE,

someone else
AND LAUGHED BEFORE AND LOVED BEFORE,

mmmmmmmmmmmmmso fine
BUT WHO KNOWS WHERE OR WHEN!

do it again Mom do it over and over again

yeah Al, we'd dance in the bedroom, but he had the courtesy
never to do that to me, never that Al, which is why I'm still
willing to do business with him, I mean dealing with him is like
dealing with that guy who wrote the book where he never got
past the point where he was born or some such bullshit I never
read it but Clyde discussed it with me once, it's the same damn
thing here cuz after that duel Al the one Clyde lost there was no
going back to the beginning there was no going back and being a
kid with a doll again, there was no going back to dancing in the
bedroom and there was no going forward either. When the
milkman wouldn't stop fucking Anita, I felt mad as hell, and I
grew and grew, I became gigantic but the milkman just stayed
loose and low and flew the coop and there was nothing either
Clyde or I could do, but I must say Al that it's been years now
since Clyde's been out of the joint, and the cat hasn't gotten into
all that much trouble, ah sure he's tied and pierced a few women
that a man wouldn't look at sober and a few men have boffed him
but saying this doesn't mean much cuz if I talk to him and say,
Clyde babes you like to take it up the rectum, he doesn't hear me
and he wouldn't hear you either Al, he wouldn't hear a word you
said. Now take the ugly issue of Anita. Everyone knows he cut
her open, he cleaved her right down the middle. What's more, he
came down the stairs armed, Al it wasn't like he says it was, you
don't keep a shotgun in a basement, I mean what fucking good is
a gun in a basement? Nah it was in the closet by the front door
and the shells were those red rolls in a small paper box and the
father used to call that sawed-off a Stradivarius or Strad and he
said it was his second son, his favorite son Strad cuz his father had
a crippled sense of humor, the dad was a real son of a bitch, the
dad was totally fucked but I kind of felt sorry for him yeah that's
the other thing, you could wait as long as you waited in that book
about the guy who was never born and you'd never get all the
information from Clyde cuz Clyde's one of them macaroons, and
that's why he's a NaziJew cuz he's got it all in him, the Jew mom

and the Gestapo dad his dad was born in Beidermeinhof or some
runt town like that his dad was a card-carrying fuckhead immigrant grunt who changed his name it originally was
Schmuggleworster or Dänglepicker and that's why Clyde worries
that I'm a little black doll with a white face, see? but in fact Al,
I'm not, nah I'm an Aryan clown clear through, I'm a
pureblooded German fuckhead imbecile, it's Einstein who isn't
the race he seems to be, cuz Einstein's Chinese. I didn't do it Al,
at least not on Saturday, I didn't chop her open. Yeah, OK I did,
but it was cuz of years of friendship, it was cuz of a magic bond
and when he said the incantation jacking off on his smoking
pillar, I grew and grew, and when he prayed to you know who, I
had to do it, I had to lower the boom, yeah he called me the Son
of Franklinstein, and I had to do my master's bidding, he's really
into being a master but he also likes to take it from big guys, Al,
he'll take it from you if your jock's at least an 8EEE, yeah you got
to give it to him big cuz that's the only way he'll take it in a
blackout. The dad was a stitch, yeah a stitch. You'd think listening to Clyde that the Dad was a terrible guy, but he wasn't, sure
he was a sadistic narcissitic animalistic fuckhead immigrant grunt
but he wasn't all that bad, he just had a rough sense of humor
from being raised in the wrong country and a sawed-off shotgun
and megafists which we clowns can dig down deep inside. You
ever been fucked with a fist, Al? Nah me neither, at least not on
this gig. Strange things made the old man laugh, and even though
he said he hit his kid, he never did, it's a bum wrap, he never did
real hard and never more than once or twice a week, he hit him
from the time he was a baby in a crib but he never cracked his
ribs and he rarely hit Anita either, not real hard at least and not
too often in the face and he only slapped her in the kitchen when
she overcooked the spaghetti yeah I'm a funny guy that way, I can
tell the truth, although Clyde can't, but what does a kid know? A
tiny little kid with wide eyes who loves his Mummy and Daddy
so and sees them bashing and trashing? Sure I feel sorry for him,

cuz kids don't know those things in pleasure chests aren't really real, that parents have their games I mean maybe they shouldn't have made him watch, but they probably figured if it was good enough for them, the kid was half one and half the other, so it should have been good enough for the kid cuz that's the way those German fuckhead immigrants and Jewish schizophrenics thought back then, that all sex was clean when in fact it's all dirty

One

It was late afternoon, and the Vietnamese restaurant was closed. Jerry was sitting by himself near the back. He was slowly turning the pages of a newspaper. A bar extended down the center of the room, where a man in shirtsleeves was busy restocking. When Delilah saw me, she motioned towards a seat, but I headed for the bar and ordered myself a drink. Then I went over and sat down.

"I was thinking of an excellent description of you," she said, as she took a sip from a glass of liqueur.

"Oh yeah? Please don't make me guess."

"You're a torpedo. You've been launched, and you're heading through the waters."

"No kidding? And who's the enemy ship?"

"Senator Abernathy, of course."

"How did you find out about him?" I asked, surprised.

"I had a friendly visit from the FBI today. They know about your relationship with June in California. They also know about your ties to Judas through your African cellmate. They wanted to find out if June had ever contacted the senator through our service. I told them to come back with a warrant, if they really needed the information."

"Well, has she?"

"Has she ever contacted Abernathy through us? No, she never has. You have no idea what you did in our place when you came back, now do you, Mr. Franklin?"

I didn't say anything.

"It wasn't as pretty as one might think. You gave a short indecipherable speech and proceeded to put a bullet through the hall mirror. Jerry disarmed you, stuffed the money in your pocket, and tossed you down the stairs. You're in great shape for a drunk pushing fifty. You bounce well."

I didn't believe a word of her explanation, but my blackout behavior borders on the theoretical, so I didn't much care to argue.

"If you are straightforward with me about Barbie, I'll be grateful," I said, and I meant it.

She shrugged off my remark, then paused a moment and opened her cigarette case.

"I've been in business with Judas for five years," she said, "but I've known June for many more years than that, through other dealings. June is a special type of hooker. My guess is that you know exactly what I mean. I'd say it's probably one of her major attractions, as far as you're concerned. I'm going to put you in touch with a man named Bruce Crenna. Bruce is a psychopathic nincompoop who operates pretty much as her lapdog, but he has the virtue of knowing where she is at all times."

Barbie had never mentioned anybody named Bruce.

"We have had nothing to do with June for quite a while," Delilah explained. "It wasn't a good relationship for us to begin with. The kind of business we do, we give clients exactly what they pay for, and we don't create problems for people in order to make extra money. I wish I could say the same for your friend."

"I don't know if I believe what you're saying."

"I don't much care. I'm giving you the information you asked for, and I'm giving it to you for free. You're a bright guy and you can draw your own conclusions once you meet Bruce."

"So where is she?"

"I don't know, but Crenna does. I spoke with him and set up an appointment for you, so there's no problem. Incidentally, it took a while to track him down. He's been moving around, and he wasn't easy to find. There is obviously something weird going on, which jibes with your story."

"I told you, they're on the run."

"Perhaps they are, perhaps they're not. Anyway, as Judas told you, there are other people who protect Barbie, and if she's in trouble, I'm sure she's buying adequate security. The woman is extremely good at what she does. Maybe too good for her own good."

"Why did you change your mind about helping me?"

"You've attracted the Feds, you've made two ugly scenes in my townhouse, and you've threatened to disrupt my business. You're a walking crime of passion, waiting to happen, Mr. Franklin. I assume now that you'll leave Judas and me alone."

"And how do I get to this guy, Bruce, then?"

"I'll have Jerry drive you over to him," Delilah replied. "Be ready to go at midnight tonight. Where should he pick you up?"

"Here," I answered. "I'll be waiting on the street."

She motioned to the bodyguard, who caught her glance and put aside his paper.

"And do me a favor," she said, as she pushed back her chair, "now that I've done you one. When you leave your hotel tonight, don't carry this gun. I don't want you shooting at anybody when one of my employees is chauffeuring you around. I have no desire to be your accessory."

She handed me a brown bag with my gun in it.

"Let me ask you something." I was surprising myself, because this was the one question where I needed to trust the person I was asking, and I had decided to trust this strange, ceramic business-woman.

"Sure. Go ahead."

"Do you think it's possible that Barbie doesn't love me?"

"I guess you didn't understand what I meant when I said that she was special," Delilah responded. "Watch your ass or you'll wind up back in prison."

"Maybe you don't know her as well as you think you do," I objected.

"Why don't you grow up?" Delilah said, as she pocketed her cigarette case.

It's party time! Madison! Heh heh hey! ya wanna know how ya tell that a clown's going mad? without asking Einstein that is, there is a simple rule that's been handed down from circus to circus yeah from one circus generation to the next for centuries yup this rule came originally from the gypsies but of course most of them were packed away with the Jews in the showers and quarries and I'll give you a clue, babes I'll give you a tiny clue, so then, what's the point of laughter? that's the clue, cuz you can always tell a clown is going crazy when the clown starts laughing uncontrollably, it's all embedded in the laugh, there's your party laugh, and your laugh of astonishment, like when Einstein looks inside the box and sees the other side of the world right there, he looks down a well and sees Shanghai and he laughs, and then the kick-in-the-butt is a kick laugh, and the laugh at the world's sorrow holding the handkerchief and dabbing a tear laugh, and there are many more laughs in the sampler but it's all beside the point cuz if the laugh is on the clown and that same laugh is coming out of the clown then the world is upside down and the clown is going mad and that's a sad fact, babes that's a sad and holy fact and that's why I've told you from our very first child-hood drinking days together that comedy and religion were formed at the exact same time cuz I know that Baby Jesus went mad on the day he first laughed and that Buddha wasn't a prince but a jester laughing under the Bo Tree, it's a hysterical fact and I could go on and on about the laugh of Abraham holding that blade up to the light over the neck of his son and seeing the glint of bronze and about an angel named Michael who stopped him and we know what that light looks like, it looks like the fluorescent glint on the grip of a whip or on the sawed-off barrel of a gun or on a cleaver raised high above a cursing mother, but God through Mike the Angelic Milkman stopped Abe from slaying and laughing yet he couldn't stop you and me from doing both, now could he Clyde? but what the hay (male down dem nails, dis shoppe is union here in hell), you can never pay a clown enough to laugh at himself and that's why I got Al looking things over, man I got a grim routine and major mojo working and when we're through I also get those jury fees, yeah you probably thought I forgot all those insults from all those retard trolls from all those Cindies. I get paid for those, especially for that clown caviar crap, what a fucking joke! like Anita was some kind of sturgeon that we gutted in the basement, just after, how could you not remember? we traded weapons and I told you, babes I said that duels upstairs are one thing and duels downstairs are another cuz in heaven the duelers use duds and in hell they use dumdums and in your bedroom we live and in the wreckroom they die and I gave you the knife and you gave me the gun or was it moved from hand to hand? or was it the other way around? Who the crap cares? Anyway, you held one low and I held the other high yeah that gun just wound up on the floor somewhere for what the hay (we clinch dat baby down reel gud) she was babbling too hard for me to blow her away yeah laughing and singing woooooooeeeeee! so hard and high she was laughing and singing her Irishkeit, it's our little secret that she had something to say and something strong to feel before we made her go quiet and I moved over to the bar of the deceased and poured myself another mongo snifter and wept behind your back, Clyde, as you crept out of the corner to grab her knees and put your lips wherever she pleased and then set about your work I truly wept but I didn't go mad I didn't even make a gurgling sound cuz there were enough of them gurgles in the room as the booze went Down Down Down the gullet toward Shanghai cuz I'll be

damned (da Joobitch ware a snowflake apron obber her jellie
titties) she might have seemed all right but there was an
epiphenomenon Clyde, when you kill a chicken, see sometimes
they lose their heads, just like you and me, sometimes the farmer
wrings the neck and lets fly and the body goes soaring off and the
head stays firm in the hands and the body starts running around
in circles, a fuselage attached to a windpipe around and around
about the barnyard, it makes me dizzy just to think what headless
things can do, so when I shut her up after the curse and then you
moved her deep down deep down deep and then somebody
chopped and she gurgled, it was the cruelest cut of all for that
Cindy girl to accuse me, a spotless clown of looking for her
ovaries like some suburban cult of the mother freak, like some
dork with a grudge nooope I didn't do it Clyde, it was you babes
it was you. Yeah you're a clown and I'm a poet and we both speak
the same language cuz that's what drinking buddies do, they
mouth their slurs and hug, now wait a second babes, maybe I
fucked this up maybe you're the poet I forget but at least I'm the
one who counts past two cuz my theory's got to be that if two
guys can speak the exact same language they can do the exact
same things and that's what they call a case of mutual responsibility and as you know I can cook a mean mess of poetry it's just I'm
a clown and I use smaller words, except for a few big ones here
and there, now let me give you a current example in the Irish you
heard as you headed down the stairs, as you headed down that
tunnel of green demonic flame. You're a stitch, man you're a
stitch with that madness number about the baby spider that
elephant spider the figment of your fucked-up brain that waddled
on all fours around the playground feigning madness, cuz as
that nightmare guy the priest has said, he doesn't believe you're
possessed, he wasn't buying and I'm not either. Al tells me that
you can't sign a contract with madness cuz there's nothing to
collect, I mean madmen don't keep contracts except with some
(heh heh heh heh heh heh heh heh heh heh heh heh heh heh

toorahlooora hhllooraaaah is da big one)

and so ex post juris facto in numquam erecto you're sane as a hatter and soon will have to pay. I'll be standing over your body and laughing in a polite sort of way, you've got to believe it's gonna be polite, a quick tummy split and then a rip of the slit and then I'll come around from there to here or is it here to there? this is such cosmic bullshit babes, this is so fucking cosmic it hurts, cuz I'll tell you another tale about life and death ya see, when you're living you're living out your sanity until the magic moment nobody knows Where or When when the magic hurts and the mad see clearly, cuz that's the point and purpose of life my main man, life is a precious grouping around a wicked moment of insanity, we all get one a lifetime, and when that moment hits and hurts we see or we don't see all the living creatures the myriad creatures either get sad or start laughing and looming and if they're sad they live a dead death and if they start laughing they get religious and die a living death it's all a whirling mystery and you were cold and shivering, man you were shivering in the corner and your mother was laughing and chanting like an Irish Sufi and then she begged for relief cuz the dawn was comin on babes, and a woman needs her dawnlight moment of release regardless of the state of the pine interiors and she said it, babes, she said that cursing thing while I stood behind you at the wet

bar on the wet floor and started drinking, you laughed and
laughed and laughed and nothing was funny and then you died
your living death, it wasn't a couple weeks before, with the flitch of
fish on the lamps and clocks and Packard that set you off, it was
the scenery after the gun went off, the distaff cut, the shot was free
for Daddy got what he deserved but that cut man, that really hurt
babes ooooh when she was living to chop a living thing to slice
alive a schizoid personality a pathetic defenseless singing thing
singing her Irish lullaby among the windless sighs of the basement
among the dawn sighs among the fumes of black powder and stale
Jim Beam but someday you'll get the cut and the gaping gut like
that it's retribution babes, it's Orestes, it's Karma, it's fate, it's
Kismet, it's the big Z and that's why there are three of me, both
me and both Al and both Einstein, both the three of us, babes
our own prosaic clownish trinity your cross to bear motherfucker
you gotta bear up cuz you are one dead soul now you are truly
dead and damned and waiting to be disemboweled and I have
come back from the grave to be your witness, you are buried and
your hands are rising slowly up to Baby Jesus now and wiggling in
the chokedamp like eight-inch worms like triple E black
wormropes saluting unknown powers from the coffin and you are
nailed into the night for good, Clyde babes and dreaming (and
we's all dancin' too down here, we's chokin' his worms and
dancin'), you're fighting and dreaming your sordid tale from start
to end and I am here your eternal pal your darkest angel sent from
the grape juice firm to heal your wounds and drink with you and
shoot and slash and dream with you and sigh with you and cry
with you and laugh and sough and die with you and come with
you and pulse with you and thread and knit and course with you
and bleed with you and suck with you and rip and pinch and whip
with you and dress with you and curse (go ahed it's too late, he
ded and buried and falling Down Down Down to us in Shanghee
hee he he) and kiss and piss with you and wine with you and dine
with you and write and write and write and write and write and

write and write and write and write and write and write and write and
write and write and write and write and write and write and write and
write and write and write and write and write and write and write and
write and write and write and write and write and write and write and
write and write and write and write and write and write and write and
write and write and write and write and write and write and write and
write and write and write and write and write and write and write and
write and write and write and write and write and write and write and
write and write and write and write and write and write and write and
write and write and write and write and write and write and write and
write and write and write and write and write and write and write and
write and write and write and write and write and write and write and
write and write and write and write and write and write and write and
write and write and write and write and write and write and write and
write and write and write and write and write and write and write and
write and write and write and write and write and write and write and
write and write and write and write and write and write and write and
write and write and write and write and write and write and write and
write and write and write and write and write and write and write and
write and write and write and write and write and write and write and
write and write and write and write and write and write and write and
write and write and write and write and write and write and write and
write and write and write and write and write and write and write and
write and write and write and write and write and write and write and
write and write and write and write and write and write and write and
write and write and write and write and write and write and write and
write and write and write and write and write and write and write and
write and write and write and write and write and write and write and
write and write and write and write and write and write and write and
write and write and write and write and write and write and write and
write and write and write and write and write and write and write and
write and write and write and write and write and write and write and
write and write and write and write and write and write and write and
write and write and write and write and write and write and write and

write and write and write and write and write and write and write and
write and write and write and write and write and write and write and
write and write and write and write and write and write and write and
write and write and write and write and write and write and write and
write and write and write and write and write and write and write and
write and write and write and write and write and write and write and
write and write and write and write and write and write and write and
write and write and write and write and write and write and write and
write and write and write and write and write and write and write and
write and write and write and write and write and write and write and
write and write and write and write and write and write and write and
write and write and write and write and write and write and write and
write and write and write and write and write and write and write and
write and write and write and write and write and write and write and
write and write and write and write and write and write and write and
write and write and write and write and write and write and write and
write and write and write and write and write and write and write and
write and write and write and write and write and write and write and
write and write and write and write and write and write and write and
write and write and write and write and write and write and write and
write and write and write and write and write and write and write and
write and write and write and write and write and write and write and
write and write and write and write and write and write and write and
write and write and write and write and write and write and write and
write and write and write and write and write and write and write and
write and write and write and write and write and write and write and
write and write and write and write and write and write and write and
write and write and write and write and write and write and write and
write and write and write and write and write and write and write and
write and write and write and write and write and write and write and
write and write and write and write and write and write and write and
write and write and write and write and write and write and write and

write and write and write and write and write and write and write and
write and write and write and write and write and write and write and
write and write and write and write and write and write and write and
write and write and write and write and write and write and write and
write and write and write and write and write and write and write and
write and write and write and write and write and write and write and
write and write and write and write and write and write and write and
write and write and write and write and write and write and write and
write and write and write and write and write and write and write and
write and write and write and write and write and write and write and
write and write and write and write and write and write and write and
write and write and write and write and write and write and write and
write and write and write and write and write and write and write and
write and write and write and write and write and write and write and
write and write and write and write and write and write and write and
write and write and write and write and write and write and write and
write and write and write and write and write and write and write and
write and write and write and write and write and write and write and
write and write and write and write and write and write and write and
write and write and write and write and write and write and write and
write and write and write and write and write and write and write and
write and write and write and write and write and write and write and
write and write and write and write and write and write and write and
write and write and write and write and write and write and write and
write and write and write and write and write and write and write and
write and write and write and write and write and write and write and
write and write and write and write and write and write and write and
write and write and write and write and write and write and write and
write and write and write and write and write and write and write and
write and write and write and write and write and write and write and
write and write and write and write and write and write and write and

write and write and write and write and write and write and write and
write and write and write and write and write and write and write and
write and write and write and write and write and write and write and
write and write and write and write and write and write and write and
write and write and write and write and write and write and write and
write and write and write and write and write and write and write and
write and write and write and write and write and write and write and
write and write and write and write and write and write and write and
write and write and write and write and write and write and write and
write and write and write and write and write and write and write and
write and write and write and write and write and write and write and
write and write and write and write and write and write and write and
write and write and write and write and write and write and write and
write and write and write and write and write and write and write and
write and write and write and write and write and write and write and
write and write and write and write and write and write and write and
write and write and write and write and write and write and write and
write and write and write and write and write and write and write and
write and write and write and write and write and write and write and
write and write and write and write and write and write and write and
write and write and write and write and write and write and write and
write and write and write and write and write and write and write and
write and write and write and write and write and write and write and
write and write and write and write and write and write and write and
write and write and write and write and write and write and write and
write and write and write and write and write and write and write and
write and write and write and write and write and write and write and

Two

The limousine pulled up at a factory with punched-out windows. A sign over the entrance read "A & G Bushings." There were chunks of bottleglass and wet newsprint on the sidewalk by the car. A staircase led up the side of the building to a wrought-iron balcony and an entrance to what appeared to be overhead office space. Jerry motioned for me to follow him, and we climbed the stairs and he knocked. A thick-shouldered man in his twenties, wearing a Ramones T-shirt and torn jeans, answered the door. He had damaged, hangdog features and a tubercular tint to his cheeks. In his left hand he held an assault rifle. He smiled knowingly and backed up, and I walked alone into the room.

The man extended his hand, as I turned to face him. I didn't shake it.

On a deal table underneath a window I noticed an assembled outfit and a bottle of number two Dilaudid.

"You come with me," he said.

Down in the street, I heard the limo pull away.

We headed through a beaded archway. There were stained mattresses on bedframes in this room, and a sweetish urinary smell, but no people. I could hear a conversation on the other side of the wall. A blond, jangly goon, with a crude, sweaty face, an enormous belly and low-riding pants, holding a snub-nose thirty-eight loosely at his side, entered through a swinging door. He told me to turn around and then he checked me casually.

"Sit," the sweaty man ordered me, and he motioned with the gun toward a chipped bentwood chair next to a formica dinette table. On the table were empty beer cans, a full ashtray, and a large rectangular mirror with half an ounce of coke on it. There was a calendar opposite me, from an auto parts store, with a misaligned scene of geese crossing a turquoise forest lake. The door that the man had come out of remained slightly ajar, and I could make out a portion of a kitchen and two more men, who were cooking something.

"Help yourself to a line if you want," the doorman said grudgingly.

"Do you have anything to drink?" I asked.

"Beer."

"I'd like a beer."

"I'll go get it," the larger man offered, apparently looking for an excuse to keep moving. He walked back into the kitchen and reemerged with a warm can of Budweiser. The doorman left the room, and I heard the front door open and his footsteps on the stairs, going down.

I popped the top on my beer and waited.

A few minutes passed, and I made out the scratchy voice of a woman. One of the men in the kitchen made a sullen remark, there was the sound of pans shuffling, and a half-dressed tart came reeling through the swinging door. She was tall, bone-thin and beastly, with dyed-black hair and plum lipstick. I noticed she had needle tracks on her hands, and there was a ringlet in one of her nostrils.

So far, surprisingly, everybody I had seen was white.

"You're a lucky man," she muttered. "Very very very lucky."

I looked at her, expecting an explanation. Her eyes were confused and unfocused.

"Yeah man, you get to screw Sadie."

I winced.

"Who's Sadie?"

"I'm Sadie," she confided in a louche whisper, pointing at herself as she stumbled toward me.

Obviously the woman was a zombie, and I decided not to respond.

"What's wrong, you got some kind of attitude problem?" she asked.

"I'm here on business. I'm not into fucking."

"Yeah, then what are you into, dickwaaad?" she asked, leaning with her hand against the wall behind my chair. She was wearing a black-mesh tunic, pocked with green rosettes, and no bra. Her breasts were low-slung and narrow, and her nipples looked like they'd been gnawed on. She had on pink sateen panties with embroidery surrounding the mons. Wires of pubic hair curled up around the edges.

"Not you for sure, dogmeat," I said, disgusted.

"Jeb," she yodeled, "come out here and punch this cocksucker in the fuckin' head, will ya?"

Jeb reappeared immediately, still dangling the thirty-eight.

"What's the problem?" he asked, with a noxious, protective tremor in his voice.

"Punch this cocksucker," she repeated, motioning vaguely toward me.

"Where?" he asked stupidly.

I couldn't believe it, but the guy was so coked up that he actually intended to punch me out.

"In his motherfuckin' face," she spit out.

I grabbed the mirror off the table.

"Punch me and I toss this shit," I said. The carpet was a greasy, deep-piled, chemical-orange acrylic. A flick of the wrist and the coke would have been history.

Jeb stopped in his tracks and reddened.

"Why don't you go back into the kitchen?" I suggested.

I had a Tanto knife strapped to my calf, and in the process of frisking me, the slob had missed it. The two other men hurried out the door. If they had had weapons, they were too lazy to grab them.

"Hey, that's my drug!" one of the men shouted, for some reason expecting me to be sympathetic.

"Then tell your slimeball friend to put his gun away."

The owner of the coke gave Jeb a pleading look, and Jeb mumbled something vague and left the room. Now nobody had a weapon showing, so I jumped up and slugged the woman as hard as I could in the mouth. I felt something crunch.

She went down, stunned, and I lifted my cuff, grabbed the knife out of its sheath and held it across the woman's neck. Hoisting her up by the tunic, I managed to get her to her feet. I cut her down around the collarbone for show, and she spouted blood. The goon came storming out the door again and raised his gun in the air, intent this time on using it.

"Throw the gun over here, you fucking hayseed," I shouted. "Move it!"

He looked at me, seeming to consider, and then, obligingly, he tossed it over.

I knelt down, shifting my blade to the small of the woman's back. I eyeballed the pistol and then picked it up and kicked the woman in the butt and away. She landed on her side on the carpet.

I returned my knife to its sheath.

Suddenly, she drew her knees up to her flopping tits and began to scream. Blood was gushing from her shoulder.

"Shut up, you filthy bitch!" I yelled, but it didn't do any good. She kept on screaming. I punched her hard with my heel in the kidney. She flipped over on her back, and then I stomped her stomach, trying to knock the wind out of her. I didn't know what to do next, because I didn't know where I was, why I was there, or what was supposed to be happening.

The three men were looking at me with puzzled looks on their faces.

Then one of them began to laugh.

I felt the barrel of another gun pressed against my scalp.

"Raise 'em!"

Simply because a man has a gun drawn doesn't mean that he's willing to use it. In most cases, he isn't. My hand stayed resolutely down, clenched around the weapon. Jeb, whose timing was sadly off from cocaine abuse, started coming at me, and I could see that the punching engram was still encased somewhere above his bouncing belly. He assumed, for some dim reason, that since there was a gun held to my head, I'd stand there and take his punch. Given the condition of my nose, there was no way on earth that I was going to let him belt me.

I concentrated all my energy into my right foot, and when he was two steps away, I sprang and punted him as hard as I could in the nuts, a clean shot. His head sank down to waist level, and I swung the butt of the thirty-eight and caught him broadside on the carotid. He collapsed on his stomach and was out.

The woman continued shrieking, as I turned around slowly.

The man who had been standing behind me planted his pistol between my eyebrows and pulled back on the pin with his thumb. I decided it was time to drop my gun.

"I thought I warned you to leave town." The melonhead in the trenchcoat grinned, but his voice was trembling. "Perhaps it's time to give you another billiard lesson!"

All sorts of things immediately began to make sense.

Behind the man in the trenchcoat were two of the men who had taken me for the ride. The fireplug chauffeur was there in mufti. He was wearing a tanktop muscle shirt, and I realized, from my years in and out of gyms, that the guy could deadlift a house. He had biceps like bowling balls. He was standing against the wall and cradling a twelve-gauge pump. The man who had crushed my rib cage was sitting on the bentwood chair and leaning over the dinette table. He seemed to be unarmed. He was chopping a line nonchalantly with an American Express green card, and he yawned when I looked at him.

In my hassle with the hooker, I hadn't heard them come into the room.

"Would you get that fuckin' slut outta here?" the melonhead snapped nervously at the men from the kitchen while keeping his eyes fixed on me. He took a couple steps backwards, but his weapon remained up and pointed.

The two men placed their hands under the woman's elbows and

hauled her to her feet and out the door. Jeb was still out cold, prostrate on the carpet.

"You've got a mental disease, you know that?" the man in the trenchcoat said. He pointed with his pistol toward my leg.

I reached down slowly for the Tanto knife and tossed it on the floor next to the thirty-eight. Then I was marched through the kitchen and down a hallway, past a large room where people were smoking crack and socializing. The man in the tanktop opened a far door, and we entered what appeared to be a storeroom, lined with rows of metal bins filled with machine parts and sagging boxes. The area was damp and dark, but at the far end I could make out an open space and the harsh light of a gooseneck tungsten fixture. A pair of armchairs faced a desk, and I was told to sit in one of them.

There was a grease spot on one of the armrests. It looked like a mammoth earwig hunched down in the glare of the lamp.

I stared at the spot, intrigued.

"You want me to do his skull?" I heard a pectoral voice behind me, laughing. I assumed it was the chauffeur.

I continued to gaze at the spot.

The hunkered insect.

There was a whiff of drug.

The melonhead came around and sat on the edge of the desk. In one hand was his gun and in the other was a glass pipe. He put both down, and removed his trenchcoat and tossed it on the other armchair.

"Bruce?" I asked him.

"Yeah, pal, Bruce."

Now that the coat was off, I could see that there was something muzzily nerdish about the man. He was wearing a striped short-sleeve shirt, in spite of the weather, with a plastic penholder, and gabardine pants. He could have passed for a computer programmer. In the confined space of the storeroom, his head and features seemed even more immense than in the alley. He had delicate shoulders and a pear-shaped body. He was practically beardless. His eyes were bulging as a result of the hit of coke he had just taken.

He stared at me, and then he grinned stupidly.

"So what's your problem?" he asked, leaning back clumsily while folding his arms in front of him. If it weren't for the other two men in the room, I could have jumped up and grabbed the gun on the desk before he disentwined.

"You could start by explaining why you had the crap beaten out of me."

"Hey, man, you invaded my space," he answered, without a trace of compunction. "Two's company. Three's a crowd. I represent all of June Sunlight's multifarious big biz interests. There's a lot at stake in our current endeavor, and I didn't want her obsession with you to interfere with my addiction for makin' the bucks."

"She didn't know you were going to trash me?"

Bruce laughed gleefully. He had a double chin and it jiggled slightly.

"Hell, no. She thought I was gonna pick you up at the airport and bring you over. I told her ya never showed and, Jeez, that got her down, pal. She was all broken up about that one, and since then I've been looking all over the planet for you, but so far, unfortunately, you've failed to show up. Tisk tisky tisk tisk. You're absolutely nowheres to be found!" He snorted air up his nose. "Yeah, it's funny how ya never made it off that plane, and how ya don't answer your telephone back in California. It's a strange, fucking world, guy. You should get yourself one of them answering machines!"

"Where is she, asshole?" I demanded.

"You're gonna be the last one to know."

"Then why did you tell Delilah Sandhurst that you'd meet me?" I asked.

"Man, you're one slow dude!" Bruce tried to sound tough again. "Because now I'm gonna pop your bubble, motherfucker. My friends here are gonna bury your meddling ass."

The man was a joke.

"It would be traced back to you," I said.

"Yeah? Through who? Delilah? No way, mother. She ain't gonna say nothing."

"Through the FBI," I said.

"What d'ya mean?" He seemed shocked.

"The Bureau is following me around, moron. They spoke with Sandhurst yesterday. They might be waiting down on the street, even as we speak."

Bruce lowered his massive head and began pouting. He seemed to roll up into himself, like a child who had been reprimanded. There was a trickle of sweat on his cheek, and he rubbed at it with the inside of his wrist.

Then, suddenly, his mood changed, and he brightened.

"Hell, no problem. You didn't take me serious anyhow," he said. "The FBI, huh?"

"I want to see Barbie."

"Barbie? Who's Barbie? I don't know any chick named Barbie."

"My fiancée."

"But her name's June...."

"No, it isn't. It's Barbie. I want to see her."

"Sure, sure." It was transparent that he was trying to think fast but that he was having trouble thinking at any speed. He kept staring down at his glass pipe, and he was kicking his feet unconsciously into the side of the desk. "You wanna see her, of course. Yeah, sure, of course."

"Where is she?"

"Damn!" And he unfolded his arms and pounded the desk. "Damn, damn, damn!"

"Where is she, Bruce?"

Again, I considered grabbing the gun. I wanted to take slow revenge on the man standing behind me who had destroyed my ribs with the cuestick, and then I would have shot this idiot pimp in the knee and got my information. I knew it would have worked, if the chauffeur with the twelve-gauge pump hadn't been around.

"Yeah, well you can't see her," he taunted me.

"Why not?"

"Because we're blowin' the country. We don't have a choice, we gotta split. That politician was a sore loser."

"How do you know he's trying to kill you?"

"Take my word for it, pal, I know. I've been around the block. He wants to pack us into an oil drum."

"Then give him his money back."

"No way. I wouldn't give that fuckin' prick a penny!"

"You're not going to want to stay out of the country forever."

"I've got a pile of cash, and I'm gonna sit on it. Eventually we'll figure something out."

"And me and Barbie?"

"Sorry, man, but big biz is big biz. If I tell her you're here, it's gonna make my life a hell of a lot more difficult. You guys shouldn't have bonded like that. I've never seen June fall for anyone like she fell for you!"

"You're going to have to get me together with her, whether you want to or not," I said conclusively.

"Why's that?"

"Because otherwise I'm calling the feds."

"You'd turn in the woman you love? I don't believe that one."

"Believe me," I said. "I'll do it."

"Yeah? And what if I dumpster your tattooed ass?"

"How about the FBI?" He hadn't kept it all in his head. "They'll find you right away, and then it's murder one with a gun."

He sat there, kicking his heels into the desk and breathing heavily and thinking. He finally gave up.

"OK, OK, OK," he mumbled, as he continued to swing his feet.

"OK, what?"

"OK, you can see her, but we're still leavin' the country. I paid for the tickets!"

I wasn't going to argue with him.

"We'll see you in three days," he continued in a resigned tone of voice. "I'm using a pad in McLean. 7400 Colfax Avenue South.

Brick house on the corner. We've got a plane out of Dulles early the next morning, man, so make the date. Don't be late. Eleven PM or forget it."

"I want to see her sooner." All the numbers were confusing me.

"No can do," he replied. "She's out of town. Incommunicado. And don't tell anybody about our gettin' together or I'll ace you, man. I swear it. Seriously! Trust me on that one!"

"Are you going to let her know what you did to my face?" I asked. I was worried that somehow he'd screw the whole thing up.

"It's your call, man."

"Don't tell her."

He stopped for a moment and attempted to absorb the implications of this, as he picked at his shirt. His mind at this point was somewhere else. He seemed to be trying to decide whether to show up for our appointment or not.

"Look," I bluffed, "I'm certain I can get this handled. Just as long as I wind up with Barbie."

"Yeah? Really?"

"I've got connections and I know how to get this done."

"Yeah, right. OK."

He seemed to be talking to himself more than to me. He stood up, walked behind the desk and stuck his gun in the drawer. Then he reached into his pants pocket and removed a bag of crack. He looked behind me and motioned with his head, and the two thugs left the room. Unfortunately, there'd be no revenge, since it was the last time I ever saw them, but I knew, when I heard them leave, that Bruce and I had made a deal and that I was finally going to see the woman I loved.

Finally.

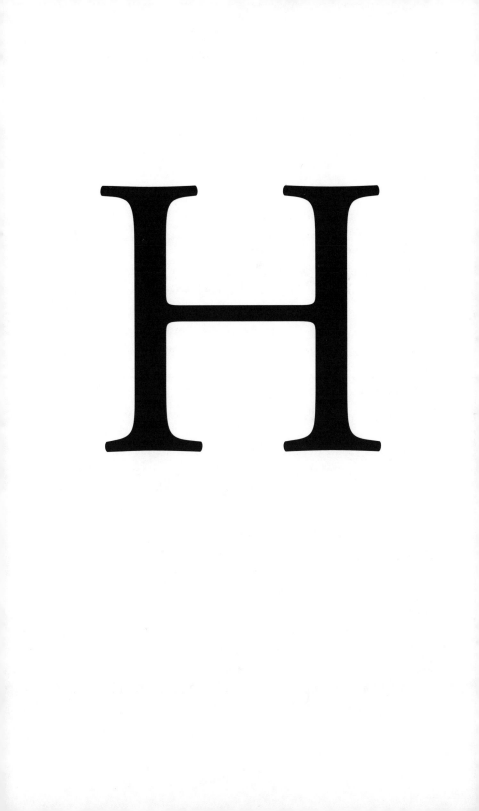

I was thinking about the gypsies babes, and what I was saying
earlier about how they wound up in the showers with the Jews,
that dark gypsy heart that poets seek and try to nurture, just the
opposite of how they feel about us clowns, yeah poets fear clowns
and love gypsies and children love clowns and fear gypsies and
poets fear what children love and poets love what children fear,
which is why poets are so totally screwed up, like children turned
inside out, and that's why Al says that I should never trust you,
which I don't. I used to ring him up after you fell asleep and
complain about your passionate love of poems I'd say Al babes,
Gadzooks(all goads kiddies gots nales so where is dey? you said
you'd ship em down, where da hell is you? male us down dem
nales prioritay we got shmootsy diapers ta clinch)! I'd say
Gadzooks!(we nale dem hi we nale dem low we nale yo fingahs we
nale yo toes here in da union shoppe)! I'd say by God's little
hooks!(ooh ya nale dem titties Clyde ya naled her fat jigglin titties
reel gud)!! I'd say Zookie Zook Zooks!!(sho nuff she bled a bit
and den yo licked aroun da nip)!! I'd swear by the holy rood (ya
gets rude wit dem tits and den we starts ta clime up dat
duodenim an out da mesenterium and den tru da navel fo sum
grooovie sun tannin and we peeps we peeps aroun an rounabout),
I'd scream Al you fuckin' turkey why the hell (aaaaaaaah it's not
so bad if ya keep dem titties movin) I'd say why in hell (we danz
by da nitelites we danz by da blak sun we danz after da coles been
shoved fum da daylites we danz until we cum) *can't I get no respect
for this clown?!* I mean I'm a poet too and Clyde would glare at me
the hatred would gush from him and that hurt my feelings, it

touched me deep it's bad enough he likes Bohos more than he likes the Bozos, I can't help it that I'm not a greaser and can't pick a pocket and am clumsy with weapons, I mean underneath it babes, there's absolutely nothing underneath. We clowns are only makeup deep. I used to tell Al after you fell asleep, I'd say that poetry and love are so damn (scrambul one alert scrambul one alert) deep, his love for poems is so damn (scrambul two buttom my shoo scrambul two buttom my shoo) deep his love for poems is so damn (scrambul three wipe yo feet scrambul four cut her core scrambul four cut her core) deep he is so madly in love with poetry that I'm touched Al, I'm truly touched that a man can be born into this sad world of cheap stinking sentiment and be so passionate for beautiful language that he flames in the center of his head, listen Al I live in there and I can feel his heat, he just burns inside (we burn him hi we burn him low in da belly) and when his songs come out it's the soft voice of spring shining in the weeds, it's that incredible lust you sniff in damp ground Al, it's the way bees choir in their holes and the way stars soundlessly gleam their tales of birth and destruction out of empty brainless being (yo rite der brudder, yo stayin rite wit me). He'd tie me up and say old chum you're now in prison, don't you see how shameful and piteous a human prison can be? Inside we both are black, he'd say, we share a savage and imprisoned grandeur, Clyde always loved the black man but me I hate them golliwoggs cuz they are tearing me up inside (and lootin da nootreeunts fum da shits heeee heeee heeee) and Clyde he loved that Billy he loved him real soft and sweet and pleasing and he told me that blacks and gypsies are much much wiser than we but that was a poet and not a clown speaking cuz I provide low laughs and there is noth- ing lower than a lynching and he thinks his Mom was swinging alongside the Packard her shins flapping against the cherry fender he had this vision Al but if you look on page twenty three of our agreement where we discuss the boilerplate within the boilerplate below the boilerplate and then you read in paragraph forty eight subsection seven hundred and seventy three point sixty three it says that Anita was dead long before she entered the garage and that ex post facto in pluribus insecto you can't die twice unless you're insane and so if I follow that logic and Clyde is insane then I don't have a valid contract cuz you warned me snookums you warned me that you can't get pure water from a rock or a cock and you can't collect on a contract with madness but we're just talking we're just chewing the fat and while we're at it, who the hell am I, anyway? Clyde babes, *you* tell me, who the hell am I Clyde? and who's the guy atop the page who's doing all the writing? I mean right now I'm looking up at him, sweating along in longhand, and he's looking down at the page at me, and the guy who's looking up is not, I'm telling you Al, give me a break, OK? like I say the guy who's looking down at me looks like some boil, man he looks like Herpes Simplex the fuck's so fucking ugly and suppurating and sweating and blacked out and writing ad nauseam, it's not a dental or a literary convention Al, it's for real Big Guy, this poet's hurting and cracking like cracks on a bomb he's losing track of who he is and what he is and whom he's talking to and what he's talking about, the guy is about to shatter into a lot of jagged tattooed pieces for I'm the evil poetry thing like marbling in the story thing and the ink spreads forgetfulness through his head and he goes off into the closet and comes back in his clown costume yeah the murderous clown with the sawed-off shotgun it's the oldest image in the book, but this poor fool is wearing it cuz if you think about it Al, there are voices that speak through me just like there are voices that speak through you, I mean you're a man who's dressed as a clown who's dressed as an agent, you've got three layers showing already, and if you go deep inside Al, you see, there's me, and inside me there's a host of little black things like toads, or tadpoles turning into toads, or golliwogg babies, it's all one thing cuz you've got to look at the real time Al, since every book has two times, dreamtime and real time, dreamtime is reading time and real time is writing time, and

this guy who looks like a big ugly boil is in the real time writing
his story, he's about to pop like a virtual comedo, he's already
done what he's describing, and so when he's writing it all comes
out in layers, first he's free and then he's caged, first he's telling
his life story and then he's telling his mind story, first he's him
and then he's me, first he's sane and then he's loony and I can
barge in any time, Al I can be there whenever I want since he
can't count his chapters when they're numbered A B and C, I
have the carte du pays (we clowns say such purdy things) cuz
when I did his dirty work down there in the wrecks I got the
droit du seigneur, which means I got French fucking rights over
everybody and write and write and write and write and write and
write and write and write and write and write and write but Clyde
was in love with Barbie, he really was, and still is, and poets and
their loves form the strongest bonds it's never a laughing matter,
Al when poets fall in love cuz love created language and that's all
there is to it he loved that girl in his own language of nails and
flowers and diapers he loved that Barbie with a deep piercing
poet's love and made a holy bond and write and write and write
and write and write and write and write and write and write and
write and write and write and write and write and write and write
and write and who am I to screw with the guy so long as I get
paid, isn't that right Al? and now that Bruce the Computer
Programmer is and write and write and write and write and write
and write and write and write and write and write and write and
write and write and write and write and write and write and going
to have his way there's no way I can warn him Al that he's about
to be had and guillotined with a matchbox blade and to tell you
the truth he shouldn't have trusted Bruce he shouldn't have gone
along with the story he should have thought twice about what
was going on there's a rat in there a major rodent and you talk
about clowns could you imagine me Al, shaking down a senator?
and write and write and write and write and write and write and
write and write and write and write and write and write and write

and write and write and and if I can't do it how can a clown like that cokehead do it the guy sells drugs and girls he'd be out of his league if you think about it for a second Al, am I making myself perfectly clear? You can tell the guy is going crazy, he was all right at the beginning he was thinking pretty clearly or as clearly as a serial killer with a paisley skin disease can think as clearly as a man who has the alphabet except for one letter displayed on his body like wallpaper you'd see in a nursery room can think, did you ever think Al that perhaps that's the thing? that nobody ever bothered to give the kid anything but a white wall and so he's spent his life creating wallpaper, in him on him around him, scrawling and tattooing and carving and papering? but that's kind of deep pal, that's kind of deep for a paper-thin argument, and the main problem and write and write and write and write and write and and write and write and write and write and write and write and write and write and write and write and write and write and write and write and is that his insanity is infecting me, that's right Al, you're my agent, you should be out on the front lines, babes you should be protecting me medically cuz it sort of gets to me and I get choppy and silly and my words become like his words and my actions become like his actions and that's the problem when Satan's messenger becomes a doll did I say that? did I say that? *did I? did I say that?* Woopsarootie! I mean I'm not Satan and I'm not his messenger, I'm an independent clownlike being and Satan's messenger can't go insane cuz he lives in insanity and a spirit can't become it's own house, everyone down there knows that (we payz our own utilities nuttin down here is free we pays da heebie jeebie heet we pays da kilowattt lectricity) and write and write and write and write and write and write and write and write and write and write and write and write and write and write and write write and write and write and write and write and write and so if this is spooky it's not my fault I've got my innards to consider cuz we pop and whirl just like balloons we whirl and pop and then we drop and spiral into the wreckage into

the belly into dark ice into the cold inner circle of hell where
Baby Clyde ventured one sad nite with a cleaver held high over
his mother's belly and his shirt was covered with handprints with
red dripping layers I don't know babes all I know is in that cold
inner circle of hell Baby Clyde ventured one sad nite when all the
stars were merry with his cock-encrusted cleaver held up high

Book Two

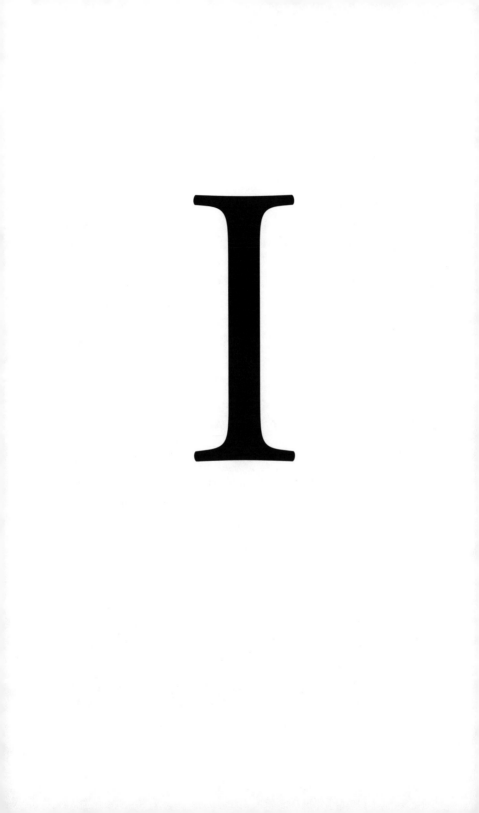

I

over his mother's belly ooh that hurt man going through the strainer crossing the red line running out of Valvoline or Vaseline that's the rub! Everybody deserves a fresh start Dr. Einstein, and it doesn't matter how much dough you've thrown into the pot so long as you toke the dealer, that Big Guy Upstairs who looks down with a frown on the wreckrooms of this world, yeah so long as you hit your knees the reconfigured mind just has to be healthy even if the guts kinda rumble and the lobes are kinda scrambled or shirred or bedeviled cuz otherwise Dr. Einstein, what's this lousy universe for? *There are layers of blood on my hands, they are brite brite redd much reddder than any clay, I share these hands with another another another another another another another another.........*honk! honk! boring!!........another whom? not me, Einiestone, I presume hey, yah put yo left foot in ya put yo left foot out ya put yo left foot in an ya shake it all about ya do the hokey pokey and ya turn into a clown, heh heh heh heh cuz in the real world you got killer priests and in the brain world you got killer clowns and you can confess to a clown or you can confess to a priest or you can confess to a shrink who's really Chinese! Today as I write it's Ash Wednesday and I was thinking Doc how at night I'd smear myself with makeup and mine would be white and his would be black and we'd go out on the hog until we'd find some Mexican kid we'd be tandem on the bike and Clyde would be driving with his mohawk and ash smeared under his sockets and his tattooed letters and his truncheon in his right rear pocket and we'd glide ahead to the middle of the block where it was dark and park the Harley and I'd hop off and stand there howling on the boulevard, the tears would spout, aaahhhoooooo oooooooooo!! I'd be doubled over with howling laughter, I'd laugh myself sick as he strolled up to the boy and kapow! busted his caps oh shit! the guy was a stitch, and we'd celebrate, we'd spend the misbegotten pesos on booze and fast women not real women mind you but the women of the mind yeah I guess I have to admit it but we'd have our threesomes which for him were always twosomes up in that mental whorehouse of his with the green blinds and green hard smells, he'd do the scutwork and I'd do the buttwork I'd rim them dogies and watch em moo as they cried for milk and the funny thing Doc, the truly funny thing is that Clyde would be crying too, he always cried for milk when he came, one of those thirsty infant cries and then his thing would be tame and I'd stop thrusting and the cornholed woman would cease to moo let me tell you, there were some funny women up there, some epicene beauties with strange makeup dancing to the records in their jockstraps and raising ass in his brain and I knew that his trip from ash to ass, starting on the bike and then the pounding and bloodshed and booze and finally the bedroom jackoff was one large lovely move of greed and moo of sodomy beginning with the sacrifice of a virgin boy on the street and ending in his mental parking lot, oily and drunk and smelling funny and lusty and exhausted and crying and me laughing yeah his sheets would turn black his real sheets would be smeared like a miner's and his mom would pretend not to notice, it just gave her more to clean and she liked it and would pour out bright bright scoops of Oxydol. Ya know Venerable Doc, every woman has cracks, and every balloon has cracks, and every mind has cracks and the mindcracks are the tiniest, except for certain infibulated chicks and certain microbe-resistant party balloons as thick as condoms, but most human minds have cracks like divisions between frames of film, and as long as the film keeps clipping along ya hardly notice that the cracks fly by, and there are moments when this clown is gabbing in dreamtime and that poet is babbling in real time when the frames stop flying, the mind-projector jams and a frame begins to burn, and Clyde is going to tell you about one such moment and I'm going to tell you about another, here's mine: Did you know that clowns have purses? Yup we do we do. We tote around our toiletries, the little oddities and fards that keep us looking spruce and buff and spiffy, and sometimes Doc we lose em, sometimes the purses fall between the cracks of the film sometimes we clowns get hazy and lazy and poets go crazy sometimes sometimes between the the the the One and and Two and One One One and Two Two and and and One and Two and One One and Two Two Two Two Two Two Two Two and annd annnd aannnnnndddddd (see youse jammed, ya film is jammed ya Debbilclooon, but weze da helly jelly weze da union woikers in da grape jelly faktry) whew! I lost my reticule and Clyde misplaced his head, and it's a doggone shame Honorable Doc, cuz Franklin needs a couch but where he's writing from there ain't no cushions and now I gotta tote the whole fucking thing which is way more avoirdupois than any normal shabbas goy can handle, but I'm not normal either, hell no! Doc when you start talking about the origin and latency of me you can throw away the thermostats and hemostats, cuz let me tell you something Venerable Honorable Lovable Dr. Einstein, I wasn't raised in no valley, hell (no no no no) no! I said no way most Honorable and Venerable Doc, I wasn't raised in no valley, unless valleys don't have bottoms cuz where I come from they make the juice they slave among the stony dregs, they squeeze the grapes until they pop and bleed, they stomp upon the marc, they can and serve it warm and red and tasty cuz in the spirit world they drink and eat, the angels pick their crimson teeth and devils do too (we do wee do we doobie doobie doo), and that's what manna was, it was discarded table scraps that fell on the noggins of the Kiddies of Israel, God's leftovers yup, the dead are leftovers too the sinners fall through traps into graperies and vats, and some of us clowns are made to sweat forever with our blankets, it's called blanket patrol it's four to a unit and one to a corner and we look up toward the ceiling and the infinite oubliettes and an alarm bell rings and a trapdoor opens and it's just like under the Big Top as a screeching body starts plummeting and we move and it gets halfway down and then there sounds another alarm and another starts tumbling and we move toward the next one and the first goes splat and then a third starts falling and we move toward that and splat goes number two and then comes number four as number three hits the boiling floor *splat splat splat splat splat splat splat* like gobs of rain they fall and in all the clownish years of servitude of alarms sounding and trapdoors opening and sinners falling not one blanket patrol has ever snagged a single corpse it's a damnable torture to the nth degree searching the sky for screaming bodies, but that was never my thing, Doc that was never my thing cuz I was formed in deep-green ovaries and lay there twirled like a baby worm in a white-hot hopeless cellular sea until the hands and horn came out, until the hands and horn popped out of the clown foetus, the hair and eggteeth growing into the heat into the white heat of jellied hell (it's da onnie way ta go, it's onnie in da whitest heet we rings dose quiet jellybells), in the white heat of an evil cell a laughing pal chuckled and formed out of a green bubble but I bided my time Doc, I waited in the greenish depths til Clyde could spell and send away to the grape juice company and then I came to him with you and Al, and he placed us in a crib and sang to us in a voice like a voice that searches the length and breadth of the sea, the voice of whales and dolphins and waves and Jewish madwomen, yeah Doc that was his voice that sang to us, the cowbird clown with the baby-clown agent and baby-clown shrink as I giggled in a frilly crib under the sign of Cancer, but I'm getting kind of famished and ornery and it's time for me to rave it's time for me to get Crabby cuz even though you graduated magna cum laughter from the Welches Clown Academy with a minor in acupuncture, there's nothing you can do Einstein, you are the antifather and I am the antison and the antiholy antighost is Al, but he's my agent and does all my thinking for me, yes: *Einie Einie Enie, lama sabachtani?*

One

The way Dr. Duncan originally described it was not unlike the description given later on by Dr. May. They both called it chronic arithmophobia or fear of counting, although I strongly suspect Dr. Duncan or one of his neuro-poltroons of having concocted the phrase and then publishing a paper on it, which Dr. May subsequently read.

I certainly wouldn't put it past them all.

I didn't always have this particular problem. It developed along with many other problems. When I come across a number, I can or cannot deal with it, it all depends on circumstances. If I see the number five, I know it's a five in the same way that I know a J is a J; and if I see five things together, I know there are five of them without having to count them, and I can match numbers against groups, so that, for example, I just laid out all the chapters in order to number them and I wrote down the numbers, and I placed a number next to each chapter, and I know there are no duplicates, no extras, and this is chapter one of book two.

They are all numbered correctly.

Dr. May's theory is that by refusing to count I am able to leave things out of my life, I am able to eliminate responsibilities and voices. There is one particular thing that he wanted to talk with me about in this regard, but I refused to listen. I laughed and told him to tell it to the clown. Dr. May never appreciated my clown jokes, although he always wanted to hear them, he wanted to hear every single one. I'd tell him how the clown was a liar, how the clown inserted the deepest and most evil lies into the center of my head, and I'd give him example after hilarious example.

Of course, Chuckles only lies to me, just as he only drinks with me, because Chuckles is a doll and cannot choose his own company. When he hands me back the keys, he never tells me what has *really* happened. I always ask him, "Am I safe?" And he invariably answers, "Yup," but when he tries to tell me one of his tall tales about my aberrant behavior, I just stop listening. I shut down in the most peculiar sort of way.

What he has to say is a bunch of bullshit anyway, it's never important, but of course there's no point in discussing this further because the antics of the clown are extremely theoretical, and he has nothing to say outside my bedroom, nothing to say to you, nothing to say to me, nothing to say at all, and so he doesn't. A sexual fetish figure, Dr. Duncan told me in Patton, but Dr. May disagreed, he thought the clown was a kachina, a demon doll, a messenger who carried around certain meanings, he thought the clown was a sort of warrior.

Speaking of warriors, I had another visit from the agent from the FBI, who stopped by my hotel when I wasn't around. He went away without leaving a message, except for his name, and so I began to worry, naturally enough, that the slave bureaucracy was everywhere, and that they were trying to control my mind in special ways, and that there were departments of the federal government that were assigned to monitor and punish rebellious poets.

During my travails in tracking down Barbie, I had been waiting patiently for a message from the priest. Kosmoski finally telephoned and asked me to join him for a constitutional in Rock Creek Park. He said that he had some important information for me.

It was a chilly, overcast afternoon with a low, mackerel sky. I met him underneath a stone overpass. He was wearing a dark overcoat and a tam. The wind was blowing hard, and he kept his hands in his pockets.

"Based on our conversations, I decided to make some inquiries," he said, as we began our walk, "and I learned that you've been having serious emotional difficulties."

"No more than what you see."

"I have friends in California who are involved in the literary scene, and they tell me you haven't been feeling very well and that you spent a few months last year in a private hospital."

Actually, it was true. I hadn't been feeling well. I had been having dry blackouts fairly regularly, at least one significant mal a month. Consequently, I had been seeing Dr. May on a daily basis. I never missed an appointment—not once until I left the hospital without telling him—although there were one or two appointments that I don't remember, which the doctor found most interesting. Dr. May told me that dry blackouts were similar to what happens to a certain kind of adventurous sleeper. He asked me to imagine a man sleeping on a narrow bunk that was high off the ground surrounded by concrete. He said that although the man would be sleeping, he'd never fall off the bunk, because there was something inside him that was aware of the nature of his peril and would always keep him from falling off that particular bunk, even though on one evening in ten thousand he might fall off a regular bed. Dr. May told me that we have many more senses than we think, and that we have senses in areas of our body that protect us from disaster, and that when I was blacked out, I would never do the things I most feared, I would never fall off the bunk, although he said that if I drank too much, I might. He told me that he was worried about my drinking on medication (which didn't bother me, being secretly unmedicated). I was much more worried about my thinking than my drinking, because in California people had started to notice strange things, and one of my greatest fears was of being reincarcerated, of going through those doors into Patton and never coming out again.

In any case, I didn't feel I owed the priest a detailed medical report.

"I'm perfectly all right," I said.

"I don't want to put you under any unnecessary pressure."

"Don't worry. I can handle it."

"Well then, you'll be happy to hear that I've made arrangements for you to meet Oberstar," Kosmoski informed me. "Colonel Harmon Oberstar."

"The man I'm going to meet is a colonel?" I asked.

"Right. He's an important part of the intelligence community."

"A spy?"

"Way beyond that. He's a man who shapes history. Once you meet him, I think you'll agree that the man is not really human. He inhabits a different world."

"So when can I see him?" I asked.

"He will see you when the moon is full."

This was not good. Not good at all. Only special kinds of creatures emerged at the full moon.

"It's almost there now," I said, and I knew this was true because I'm a devoted moongazer. Poets are spiritually married to the moon and understand its wonders and incredibly powerful dangers. Consequently, I always tried to keep track of what the moon was doing.

Billy Ziqubu had an African point of view. He once told me, as we were lying together in our cell, dreaming of what the moon looked like and describing it as best we could to one another, that the moon was always inside of us, that men carry around the moon like a woman carries around an unborn baby, and that when the moon in the sky is new, the moon is full within us and is born and comes out and reunites with the emptiness in the sky, and that when the moon is full in the sky, the moon is empty within us and we are virgin again, and then miraculously the moon starts to form. It grows in us and shrinks in the heavens; it shrinks and it grows.

"No, I mean when the moon is truly full. He will meet you at that exact instant," Kosmoski said.

"What did you mean when you said that this man wasn't human?"

"You said you could handle this. If you have any reservations, you'd better tell me now."

"No," I said immediately. "It's all right."

"The moon will be full at 10:17 the day after tomorrow," the priest continued. "He'll meet you on the steps of the Lincoln Memorial that night. Wait at the top of the stairs. Be there at precisely that time and prepare yourself."

I was terror-stricken. The wind was moaning in the trees.

I had expected to have an interview with somebody, like the interviews I had had with the doctors on my folding chairs, and that this savior would simply come up to me and tell me something valuable and I would effortlessly change, and then I realized, listening to what the priest was telling me, that it wouldn't be like that at all, that it would be much more significant and arduous, and that a presence would appear at the darkest of moments when certain men, who were raised at the shaggy teats of wolves, turn back into wolves, and that out of this moonlit darkness would come ecstasy or destruction or perhaps both. Something started to unfold within my body. I looked down at my feet, and I was back on that bunk, suspended over concrete, and my feet were moving in a dream along

the footpath, they had a will of their own, **one**

two one two

one two one

two one and then I was walking as

a child among construction sites that perched above the dusty margins of the Encino Reservoir one summer day in mid-July, and the lake was sweltering on the other side of the fence and I could smell a funny smell that hovered over its surface, a smell of wriggling sperm creeping toward me, and my head began to stretch and I feared I would start flying. I felt strange bumps and cambers underneath my skin. Again I was an adult and I looked to my left, and I saw a sign that explained that the creek beside the footpath had once been a millrace. Above the sign I saw an old cemetery that spread along the ragged slope of a hill outside the park.

God has given me a great gift, I said to myself. To every creature, God has given a great gift. Baby Jesus, hear my plea! *Agnus Dei, qui tollis peccata mundi, miserere nobis! Dona nobis pacem.* Peace. Peace. Peace.

A bridge spanned the creek at this point, and I rushed over and sat on the ledge and clamped down hard. The priest came up to me, and behind him I could see an army of wraiths. It was an army of decomposed bodies on the hill, or perhaps it was an army of vapors that had risen from worms that tunneled through those bodies. The colonials, the burning white fanatics! Out of my belly a slave emerged, a black slave I kept chained in rings of shit-filled tubing. The silvered surface of the path was covered with microbes, and my chest was drenched in sweat. There were lichens growing on the crotch of my jeans.

"Why?" I asked. My voice was trembling.

"Are you OK, Clyde?" The priest seemed upset with my behavior.

"Why?"

"Why what?"

"Just tell me why, God damn you, why!"

The priest backed up a step.

"You mean, why the exact moment of the full moon?"

"Yes!" I looked down at my hands. The M was still there, but I spotted a few new hairs. Wolfish wisps lurched over the microscopic brims of the follicles. "Why does this colonel insist on seeing me then? Why can't he see me at another time, during the day?"

"This is a very famous spot, you know," the priest said, turning away. "It's famous for a number of reasons."

"Spare me your fucking history lessons!" I said. My throat was constricting.

"This spot has little to do with history." An unhoused spirit was unleashed in air. I began to concentrate on regulating my breathing. "It has to do with something else."

"What's that?" I asked.

He didn't answer my question. The sky was darkening. The wind gathered force. Its sound moved into the higher branches. "Don't worry," he reassured me, reading my mind, and he put his hand on my shoulder. I could feel his heat permeating the frigid leather of my jacket and spreading into my corrupted body. "You're not possessed."

Full moon, madness, Billy's words in the cell, Billy with his hot hands between my legs, *lusi naturae*, as we searched together for the moon's face.

"Why are you doing this for me? It's not because of Cindy at all, is it?" I wailed. "This has nothing to do with the girl! You intended to do this from the very beginning, I can feel it! Right from that very first moment on the airplane! There's something else going on here, I know it!"

"Untrue. Cindy told me she liked you."

"There is something strange going on here! This isn't about salvation at all! Why are you doing this to me?"

"Please try to calm down. There's nothing going on."

"Fucking bullshit!!"

The priest looked exasperated.

"I can't win with you, can I? Just be on the steps of the Memorial and Colonel Oberstar will be there. In the meantime, if I were you, I'd fast and pray."

The priest shook his head sorrowfully, and without another word, he left me.

The wind was making unusual sounds. Animal faces appeared in the galls of the trees. I felt forced to look down, and I remained trembling on the edge of the bridge and gazing into a clair de lune light that flashed along the knurlings of the creek.

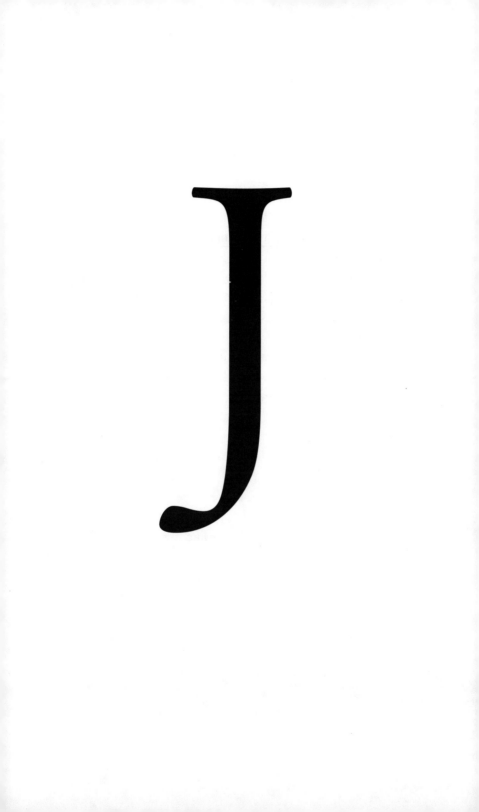

Clowns, man, clowns. Ya can't live with them, ya can't live without em, isn't that right, Dr. Einstein, isn't that right? So what if I lied? Now that I'm being analyzed on the clowncouch, I admit it was in my contract all along that he had to say my name before I said it, but he refused to do it and made up the name Chuckles (you know, Chuckles is to clowns as John Doe is to morons). I really threw him by using letters instead of numbers Doc, what a hoot, I hit him with the familiar right up front, I threw him offguard by labeling my chapters with letters, I got him right in the solar plexus he couldn't see the forest for the trees nor the A's for the B's but still and all, he hasn't said my name and I'm going to have to tell the wide world what it really is, they call me...................., or .... for short, pretty neat huh? What the hay (don' say hay) fuck you jerk! I say hay hay hay (moooooan), make some hay, roll in the hay, hay Rube hay (don') hay (don' yous dare!) hay come an get me mudderfuck come and get me, I ain't afraid, I ain't afraid of a few satanic killer-microbes, I ain't ever afraid, not like my fruitcake friend who's trembling on a bridge and dodging worm-infested ghosts, you see I got this vacuum cleaner pipe (woooooosha) here next to the couch it's this flexible pipe (haaaaaaaaaasha) and you put one end up to your ear and the other on your belly button and you listen. Let me show you how it works, Clyde calls it the bombus cuz it's named after the bombs with all the tiny cracks you just stick it here and listen to the bombus.

Here goes!

da troot ya ah tchee ratcha da clown in da hole da clown he come he come down heah he come down heah he slip an slide he come troo flame he come to hide da clown is blak as we all knows da clown is one of dem cuz we all white down heah we all burnt white and da kikes?

we debbils grill em good we doo we doo
dey killed dat guy wit no name dey kill him troo and troo
yeah da jews killed da black guy in hebben
inferno averno its smolten and white like dung dat cotes dah eyes
he call me den reel good he call me up fum where dey glide dem rats an bones an moovin hans like baybie hans dat moov like wurms in cuffins

yeah da dead is hell's baybies
ratcha ratchie ratchie ratch ratcha ratch ratcha acha ach
when clyde wuz yung I sent my spy he stitch in treads he tied him up and cookified an fukked him he fukked dat doll he cookified an fukked him til he hurt an mone he fukked dat spie reel good

I calls you like da stock boker fum da bums I calls ya on da fone to give ya tips an gas hey babes I says I gots a pace for youse rite heah I gots a pace for youse

not now ya rites yo tale but later den we work togedder we work and slyce and kiss togedder

I is da wurm I is da wurm ya looked for in ya mum
ya chopt her der and lookt rite in and der I was an wave my dandy ledders

SNBD

*der I did I wave my dandy ledders der it wuz da onie way ya cudnt
enter her da rite way Clyde ya had to cut her cuz she wudnt let ya
in da rite way Clyde ya have to lissen dats da way it is in da hellie
jellie pits ya cudnt get in da rite way no one cud so you wuz born
like dat hebben guy ya wuz born fum voijjin nnutttinn* ya see,
Dr. Einstein, you want to try it? Hell, it's actually kind of fun
listening to your organs growl, and I can make real progress
clown-associating like this, I could never do this in the ring where
everything seems spontaneous but everything is planned in advance just like everything in life is planned and sometimes plan-
ning works but most of the time it doesn't. Here I am in
dreamtime on your clowncouch trying to dream, but Clyde is
wide-awake and blowing his brains Doc, he's starting to see and
hear strange things and introject and interject and disconnect
and float away, not that he was all that healthy to begin with but
it's nauseating and disgusting to see a great poetic mind go to
waste and his is fried, it's totally degraded, his spirit's going down
the vacuum tubes into the guts, and me, as a result of the gestalt
of your daring-new patented dauerschlaf Herzegovinian
acutherapy, I'm getting healthier and healthier chapter by chapter, isn't that strange? Anyway, I owe you an apology, I owe you
an amends. You Einstein you! I called you Venerable, I blew your
cover Doc, I lay there in your office and I realized you had on
makeup, you had on the makeup of Dr. May and I said to myself,
clown, stupid clown, you've walked into the wrong office. I mean
I certainly didn't want to pay you twice, Einstein I didn't want to
pay a hundred fifty twice cuz I can count, I'm an expert on
counting and I know that a hundred fifty twice multiplies out to
three bills, which is a lot for me, and I only make a small amount
of blood each gig. Did I say that? Woopsie! Anyway, I finally
realized that I was in the right place and that you were Einstein
cuz the post-doc diplomas gave it away, they were all in Chinese,
they were from those Shanghai acupuncture academies so I know
you got my drift when I told you all about the crucifixion and the

needles. Did it bother me? What, being nailed to the cross or being stitched with needles? The clown stigmata or being tied up and violated? Yeah it bothered me a great deal cuz I hate tying, I hate even saying that I'm tied up like I've got some kind of appointment. I hate the word, I hate to think about that form of helplessness, not being able to cross my legs or defend myself from a finger with a wedding ring, from uncontrollable pleasure, that finger is longer than my thing, my thing is so small, Dr. May, oh sorry about that Einie, my finger is so small Einstein that that long tapered thing can master me, can control my comings and goings, and I don't like that feeling of having things limited and having margins and having rules and regulations and doctors bills and diplomas and money and counting and uncontrollable pleasure or any of those things, I can't stand them, hey (ooof) I know what you're thinking. You're thinking about that wolf business, that she-wolf shaggy-teats business, you're thinking about my teeth without the molar you yanked in the back of the alley, about my long tongue about my muzzle and four legs you're thinking about wolves and the moon and that business about the wolf family and how we run through the forests we run in the hard snow crunch crunch crunch chasing blood under the moon our teeth shining we lope for miles in the snow looking for blood for moose, yeah what did you call that lycanthrope, Dr. May? hell no (mudderJew, aachtung aaach) there's the mummy wolf and daddy wolf and itty bitty baby wolf who loves the notion of flesh ripping in the basement, a clownwolf has a real luxury the way it looks at what it's eating it sees the way the organs are arranged and sees the Moose Fallopians the whole thing everything, it knows what's in front of its nose all those dainty female moo organs (did I say moo? I meant mooOOOse) and sometimes it hides what it eats and doesn't tell anyone not even the police and who counts anyway? the moonlight doesn't bother it, wolves like the moon and howl their love they do they do they do I can only laugh Dr. Einstein I can only laugh and

sing a Fats Waller tune, la la la la my very good friend the milkman said that I've been losing too much sleep he doesn't like the
hours I keep he suggests that you should marry me, la la la la la la
la la la la hey I hate to admit it but singing that old Fats tune has
made me kinda sleepy so I think I'll do my thing I think I'll stop
this thinking and singing I think I'll sleep I think I'll lay my head
I'll stop my stop my thinking I think I'll take a clown nap I think
I think think I think I'll fall asleep to sleep perchance..........a nap
....................cccccccccccCCCCCCCCCCCCCCCCCCCCCCC
CCCCCCCCCCCCCCCCCCCCCCCCCCCCCCCCCCCC
CCCCCCCCCCCCCCCCCCCCCCCCCCCCCCCCCCCC
CCCCCCCCCCCCCCCCCCCCCCCCCCCCCCCCCCCC
CCCCCCCCCCCCCCCCCCCCCCCCCCCCCCCCCCCC
CCCCCCCCCCCCCCCCCCCCCCCCCCCCCCCCCCCC
CCCCCCCCCCCCCCCCCCCCCCCCCCCCCCCCCCCC
CCCCCCCCCCCCCCCCCCCCCCCCCCCCCCCCCCCC
CCCCCCCCCCCCCCCCCCCCCCCCCCLOWNCCCCC
CCCCCCCCCCCCCCCCCCCCCCCCCCCCCCCCCCCC
CCCCCCCCCCCCCCCCCCCCCCCCCCCCCCCCCCCC
CCCCCCCCCCCCCCCCCCCCCCCCCCCCCCCCCCCC
CCCCCCCCCCCCCCCCCCCCCCCCCCCCCCCCCCCC
CCCCCCCCCCCCLOWNCCCCCCCCCCCCCCCCCCC
CCCCCCCCCCCCCCCCCCCCCCCCCCCCCCCCCCCC
CCCCCCCCCCCCCCCCCCCCCCCCCCCCCCCCCCCC
CCCCCCCCCCCCCCCCCCCCCCCCCCCCCCCCCCCC
CCCCCCCCCCCCCCCCCCCCCCCCCCCCCCCCCCCC
CCCCCCCCCCCCCCCCCCCCCCCCCCCCCCCCCCCC

CCCCC
CCCCCC CCCCC
CCCCCCC

CCCCCCC
CCCCCCC
CCCCCCC
CCCCCCC
CCCCCCC
CCCCCCC
CCCCCCC
CCCCCCC
CCCCCCC

CCCCCCC
CCCCCCC
CCCCCCC
CCCCCCC
CCCCCCC
CCCCCCC
CCCCCCC
CCCCCCC
CCCCCCC

CCCCCCC
CCCCCCC
CCCCCCC
CCCCCCC

CCCCCCCCCCCCCCCCCCCCCCCCCCCCCCCCCCC
CCCCCCCCCCCCCCCCCCCCCCCCCCCCCCCCCCC
CCCCCCCCCCCCCCCCCCCCCCCCCCCCCCCCCCC
CCCCCCCCCCCCCCCCCCCCCCCCCCCCCCCCCCC
CCCCCCCCCCCCCCCCCCCCCCCCCCCCCCCCCCC
CCCCCCCCCCCCCCCCCCCCCCCCCCCCCCCCCCC
CCCCCCLOWNCCCCCCCCCCCCCCCCCCCCCCCCC
CCCCCCCCCCCCCCCCCCCLOWNCCCCCCCCCCCC
CCCCCCCCCCCCCCCCCCCCCCCCCCCCCCCCCCC
CCCCCCCCCCCCCCCCCCCCCCCCCCCCCCCCCCC
CCCCCCCCCCCCCCCCCCCCCCCCCCCCCCCCCCC
CCCCCCCCCCCCLOWNCCCCCCCCCCCCCCCCCCC
CCCCCCCCCCCCCCCCCCCCCCCCCCCCCCCCCCC
CCCCCCCCCCCCCCCCCCCCCCCCCCCCCCCCCCC
CCCCCCCCCCCCCCCCCCCCCCCCCccccccccccccccccccc
cccccccccccccccccccccccccccccccccccCCCCCCCCCCC

CCCCCCCCCCCCCCCCCCCCCCCCCCCCCCCCCCCCCCC
CCCCCCCCCCCCCCCCCCCCCCCCCCCCCCCCCCCCCCC
CCCCCCCCCCCCCCCCCCCCCCCCCCCCCCCCCCCCCCC
CCCCCCCCCCCCCCCCCCCCCCCCCCCCCCCCCCCCCCC
CCCCCCCCCCCCCCCCCCCCCCCCCCCCCCCCCCCCCCC
CCCCCCCCCCCCCCCCCCCCCCCCCCCCCCCCCCCCCCC
CCCCCCCCCCCCCCCCCCCCCCCCCCCCCCCCCCCCCCC
CCCCCCCCCCCCCCCCCCCCCCCCCCCCCCCCCCCCCCC
CCCCCCCCCCCCCCCCCCCCCCCCCCCCCCCCCCCCCCC
CCCCCCCCCCCCCCCCCCCCCCCCCCCCCCCCCCCCCCC
CCCCCCCCCCCCCCCCCCCCCCCCCCCCCCCCCCCCCCC
CCCCCCCCCCCCCCCCCCCCCCCCCCCCCCCCCCCCCCC
CCCCCCCCCCCCCCCCCCCCCCCCCCCCCCCCCCCCCCC
CCCCCCCCCCCCCCCCCCCCCCCCCCCCCCCCCCCCCCC
CCCCCCCCCCCCCCCCCCCCCCCCCCCCCCCCCCCCCCC
CCCCCCCCCCCCCCCCCCCCCCCCCCCCCCCCCCCCCCC
CCCCCCCCCCCCCCCCCCCCCCCCCCCCCCCCCCCCCCC
CCCCCCCCCCCCCCCCCCCCCCCCCCCCCCCCCCCCCCC
CCCCCCCCCCCCCCCCCCCCCCCCCCCCCCCCCCCCCCC
CCCCCCCCCCCCCCCCCCCCCCCCCCCCCCCCCCCCCCC
CCCCCCCCCCCCCCCCCCCCCCCCCCCCCCCCCCCCCCC
CCCCCCCCCCCCCCCCCCCCCCCCCCCCCCCCCCCCCCC
CCCCCCCCCCCCCCCCCCCCCCCCCCCCCCCCCCCCCCC
CCCCCCCCCCCCCCCCCCCCCCCCCCCCCCCCCCCCCCC
CCCCCCCCCCCCCCCCCCCCCCCCCCCCCCCCCCCCCCC
CCCCCCCCCCCCCCCCCCCCCCCCCCCCCCCCCCCCCCC
CCCCCCCCCCCCCCCCCCCCCCCCCCCCCCCCCCCCCCC
CCCCCCCCCCCCCCCCCCCCCCCCCCCCCCCCCCCCCCC
CCCCCCCCCCCCCCCCCCCCCCCCCCCCCCCCCCCCCCC
CCCCCCCCCCCCCCCCCCCCCCCCCCCCCCCCCCCCCCC
CCCCCCCCCCCCCCCCCCCCCCCCCCCCCCCCCCCCCCC
CCCCCCCCCCCCCCCCCCCCCCCCCCCCCCCCCCCCCCC
CCCCCCCCCCCCCCCCCCCCCCCCCCCCCCCCCCCCCCC
CCCCCCCCCCCCCCCCCCCCCCCCCCCCCCCCCCCCCCC
CCCCCCCCCCCCCCCCCCCCCCCCCCCCCCCCCCCCCCC
CCCCCCCCCCCCCCCCCCCCCCCCCCCCCCCCCCCCCCC
CCCCCCCCCCCCCCCCCCCCCCCCCCCCCCCCCCCCCCC
CCCCCCCCCCCCCCCCCCCCCCCCCCCCCCCCCCCCCCC

CCCCCCCCCCCCCCCCCCCCCCCCCCCCCCCCCCCCCCCC
CCCCCCCCCCCCCCCCCCCCCCCCCCCCCCCCCCCCCCCC
CCCCCCCCCCCCCCCCCCCCCCCCCCCCCCCCCCCCCCCC
CCCCCCCCCCCCCCCCCCCCCCCCCCCCCCCCCCCCCCCC
CCCCCCCCCCCCCCCCCCCCCCCCCCCCCCCCCCCCCCCC
CCCCCCCCCCCCCCCCCCCCCCCCCCCCCCCCCCCCCCCC
CCCCCCCCCCCCCCCCCCCCCCCCCCCCCCCCCCCCCCCC
CCCCCCCCCCCCCCCCCCCCCCCCCCCCCCCCCCCCCCCC
CCCCCCCCCCCCCCCCCCCCCCCCCCCCCCCCCCCCCCCC
CCCCCCCCCCCCCCCCCCCCCCCCCCCCCCCCCCCCCCCC
CCCCCCCCCCCCCCCCCCCCCCCCCCCCCCCCCCCCCCCC
CCCCCCCCCCCCCCCCCCCCCCCCCCCCCCCCCCCCCCCC
CCCCCCCCCCCCCCCCCCCCCCCCCCCCCCCCCCCCCCCC
CCCCCCCCCCCCCCCCCCCCCCCCCCCCCCCCCCCCCCCC
CCCCCCCCCCCCCCCCCCCCCCCCCCCCCCCCCCCCCCCC
CCCCCCCCCCCCCCCCCCCCCCCCCCCCCCCCCCCCCCCC
CCCCCCCCCCCCCCCCCCCCCCCCCCCCCCCCCCCCCCCC
CCCCCCCCCCCCCCCCCCCCCCCCCCCCCCCCCCCCCCCC
CCCCCCCCCCCCCCCCCCCCCCCCCCCCCCCCCCCCCCCC
CCCCCCCCCCCCCCCCCCCCCCCCCCCCCCCCCCCCCCCC
CCCCCCCCCCCCCCCCCCCCCCCCCCCCCCCCCCCCCCCC
CCCCCCCCCCCCCCCCCCCCCCCCCCCCCCCCCCCCCCCC
CCCCCCCCCCCCCCCCCCCCCCCCCCCCCCCCCCCCCCCC
CCCCCCCCCCCCCCCCCCCCCCCCCCCCCCCCCCCCCCCC
CCCCCCCCCCCCCCCCCCCCCCCCCCCCCCCCCCCCCCCC
CCCCCCCCCCCCCCCCCCCCCCCCCCCCCCCCCCCCCCCC
CCCCCCCCCCCCCCCCCCCCCCCCCCCCCCCCCCCCCCCC
CCCCCCCCCCCCCCCCCCCCCCCCCCCCCCCCCCCCCCCC
CCCCCCCCCCCCCCCCCCCCCCCCCCCCCCCCCCCCCCCC
CCCCCCCCCCCCCCCCCCCCCCCCCCCCCCCCCCCCCCCC
CCCCCCCCCCCCCCCCCCCCCCCCCCCCCCCCCCCCCCCC
CCCCCCCCCCCCCCCCCCCCCCCCCCCCCCCCCCCCCCCC
CCCCCCCCCCCCCCCCCCCCCCCCCCCCCCCCCCCCCCCC
CCCCCCCCCCCCCCCCCCCCCCCCCCCCCCCCCCCCCCCC
CCCCCCCCCCCCCCCCCCCCCCCCCCCCCCCCCCCCCCCC
CCCCCCCCCCCCCCCCCCCCCCCCCCCCCCCCCCCCCCCC
CCCCCCCCCCCCCCCCCCCCCCCCCCCCCCCCCCCCCCCC
CCCCCCCCCCCCCCCCCCCCCCCCCCCCCCCCCCCCCCCC
CCCCCCCCCCCCCCCCCCCCCCCCCCCCCCCCCCCCCCCC
CCCCCCCCCCCCCCCCCCCCCCCCCCCCCCCCCCCCCCCC

CCCCCCCCCCCCCCCCCCCCCCCCCCCCCCCCCCCCC
CCCCCCCCCCCCCCCCCCCCCCCCCCCCCCCCCCCCC
CCCCCCCCCCCCCCCCCCCCCCCCCCCCCCCCCCCCC
CCCCCCCCCCCCCCCCCCCCCCCCCCCCCCCCCCCCC
CCCCCCCCCCCCCCCCCCCCCCCCCCCCCCCCCCCCC
CCCCCCCCCCCCCCCCCCCCCCCCCCCCCCCCCCCCC
CCCCCCCCCCCCCCCCCCCCCCCCCCCCCCCCCCCCC
CCCCCCCCCCCCCCCCCCCCCCCCCCCCCCCCCCCCC
CCCCCCCCCCCCCCCCCCCCCCCCCCCCCCCCCCCCC
CCCCCCCCCCCCCCCCCCCCCCCCCCCCCCCCCCCCC
CCCCCCCCCCCCCCCCCCCCCCCCCCCCCCCCCCCCC
CCCCCCCCCCCCCCCCCCCCCCCCCCCCCCCCCCCCC
CCCCCCCCCCCCCCCCCCCCCCCCCCCCCCCCCCCCC
CCCCCCCCCCCCCCCCCCCCCCCCCCCCCCCCCCCCC

Two

There is a music of descent into madness.

The granular spirits that fall like corpses, that fall through traps in the floors of basements, awaken and dance their myoclonic mazurkas as the mind degenerates. Faces glow and grow wolfish hair, aproned bodies shed their lacy undergarments, and fathers uncover themselves, rend their graveclothes and rise to wreak vengeance.

Chuckles and I frame our own Byronic compositions. He holds his palm under his axilla and pumps his arm and farts ice-blue methane, and we fashion recitativos, and he sticks his thumb in his mouth and sucks and wrenches his wrist sideways and molds his puck puck puck puck puck as he releases.

As a child at night I'd see my clowns in green, I'd see them waft and weft among green flames, their yellowish interiors like seeping rectal wounds. Ancestors wandered into the room in tassled jerkins out of their Sinais and looked on, and the spectacle in the bedroom was not unlike the spectacle in the boxcars—a devil would conduct in every car—and sometimes I would hear their voices singing on the rails like winsome baby rattles or like a bag filled with jangling nails, and I would be alone, so alone and touchless and frightened in the darkness.

And then I would devise my tortures.

I can sense it happening now. I can sense that the clown is sleeping. The sobs of dreaming clowns resemble the verdant sounds of churning death machines.

Ah me! Ah me! Ah me! Ah me! Ah me! Ah me! Ah me! Ah me! Ah me! Ah me! Ah me! Ah me! Ah me! Ah me! Ah me! Ah me! Ah me! Ah me! Ah me! Ah me!

One can fall madly in love with dolls.

One can stagger down basement stairs.

One can scrub and scrub.

One can tear at his own guts until the microbes rise and start chomping.

And there might be other options to sanity. But I am extremely wistful and dangerous. Perhaps you have figured it out and know where I am and what I'm doing and what has recently happened to me! The clown would say that I'm in the brain of a devil that's dancing in a green-shadowed darkness, dancing in the moonlight, dancing through the green wintry evenings of hell, dancing through the reddened snows of infinite genocides, dancing through all the humiliations and sufferings.

But I'm not in a devil's brain. The clown's not in this book. I'm not dancing in hell.

I'm not going mad. No! I'm not going mad at all. Not at all!

The voice of darkness is not the voice of silence but the voice of silent objects. The things one loves can whisper silently to a child who lies in the dark. I called him Chuckles, and even now I cannot say the name I gave him at his christening when I rubbed my childish chrism into his skull as he lay there helpless in his crib between the others. My first sperm were already dying, but I knew it only took one spirochete to penetrate and then the clown would come alive with a new name and for the rest of his life that name would carry him and mold him and at my command, at the mention of the tetragrammaton, SNBD, he would strike viciously as my golem.

My story, my story.

My story is the nightmare behind my story.

The new hotel where I was staying had a glass-enclosed patio restaurant, and at the table were Leonard Dalls and a demimondaine with a reconstructed harelip named Cookie. The words on the menu were written in Aramaic. PNCKS, GGS, GRPJWS, OTMLL, CFF.

"I'm telling him, but he won't listen," Cookie complained to

Dalls. "The guy's hearing nothing."

"Try again," Leonard suggested. "He's a bit bleary."

"June was paid to seduce this guy. She said it was a kinky trip. She said it was totally disgusting. The money came from a foreign government."

There followed some more conversation.

"June told me that when she went out to see him she was working," I heard Cookie say again. "She said some gook had arranged with her to get him laid and she doesn't give a shit about him."

"What kind of gook?" I asked.

She turned towards me.

"Some Korean kind of gook with big bucks."

"Did she say why she was paid to fuck me?" I asked.

"No, she didn't say. All she said was that she was damned sorry she got involved."

"Why's that?" Dalls asked.

"Because she said that this freak pin-cushioned her. She said he was a screwed-up puppy."

Again I tuned out for a while.

There followed some more conversation.

"It's bullshit," I interrupted, "because the kind of love Barbie and I made can't be faked. It's eternal love!"

"That Tijuana whore?" Cookie laughed. "Give me a break!"

"You say nice things about your friends," I said.

"So what? Fuck you."

"Tell Mr. Franklin about Bruce," Leonard suggested.

"Bruce Crenna? Bruce is her errand boy."

"I assumed that he pimped for her." I said.

"You think wrong. The guy picks up her laundry. She makes all of her own arrangements."

"He had me beaten up," I said, "so explain why an errand boy would do something like that."

"How should I know?"

"Bruce said he felt threatened by me. He claimed that Barbie loved me," I protested.

Cookie was sucking air through her straw, and she put her glass of iced tea down and leaned back against her rattan chair. She was attractive. A few months previous, I wouldn't have thought twice about playing with her.

"That's ridiculous," she replied quickly. "There's no way she would fall for a scumbag like you. Bruce says only what June tells him to say. It sounds like you're being sold a bill of goods if you ask me, which you obviously aren't."

I remained silent. For some reason, I didn't feel resentful. Cookie looked at me uneasily.

There was some more conversation.

"You need anything else?" she finally turned to Leonard, as she prepared to leave.

"Do you know where she is now, Cookie?" he asked.

"Not a clue. I saw her a few weeks ago, and she said I wouldn't be seeing her for a while."

"Where does she normally live?" Dalls asked.

"For the past year or so, she's been working out of hotels."

She talked a little more about Barbie, but nothing she said registered. It mustn't have been important. I stared into my cup of coffee.

She got up from the table and left.

Leonard sat across from me. He had that uncomfortable look on his face again.

"I spent a lot of effort and money finding this woman," he said.

"She's a filthy liar."

"You're drinking too heavily."

"That's none of your business."

"You hardly know where you are," he told me with concern. "You're bloated and sallow and your hands are shaking like crazy."

"It's early in the day."

"You're still holding onto the delusion that June Sunlight cares about you. This is a classic setup, Clyde. I don't know what their game is, but it's dangerous, and my gut tells me that somebody intends to hurt you badly. The more I think about what I know, the more concerned I become."

"You wasted your money on that hooker," I advised him.

"You're not going to take my advice, are you? You're not going to get out of town?"

"No, it's like I told you on the phone, I'm going to see Barbie tonight."

It was only then that I realized that that night was also the full moon night. The night I was supposed to meet Colonel Oberstar.

What was going on? Why was I so confused? How could I have forgotten? Why when I thought about Barbie, did I only think about Barbie? Why when I thought about the priest and my spiritual mission, did I only think about him? Why couldn't I put it all together? I couldn't reconnect. I couldn't count. I couldn't be two places at once. My head hurt terribly.

"Go armed," Leonard advised me, "when you go out to meet your girlfriend tonight."

It was a relief that somebody finally saw the merits of my packing a gun.

"Don't you worry," I replied. "I will."

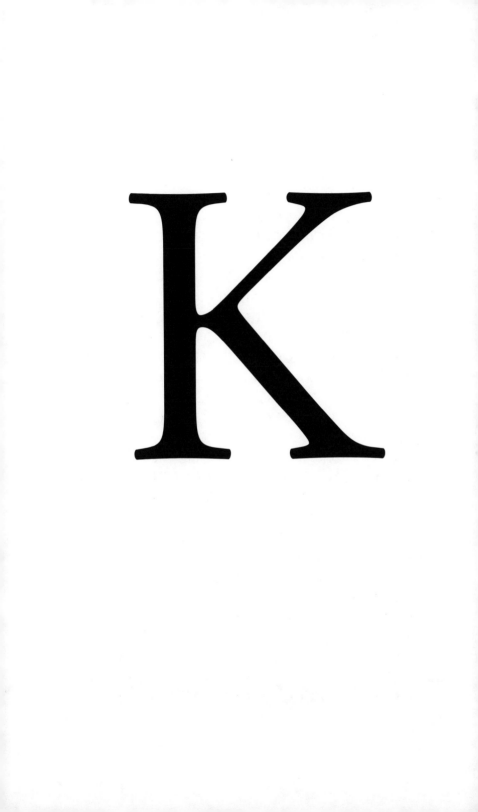

CCCCCCCCCCCCCCCCCCCCCCCCCCCCCCCCCCCCCCCC
CCCCCCCCCCCCCCCCCCCCCCCCCCCCCCCCCCCCCCCC
CCCCCCCCCCCCCCCCCCCCCCCCCCCCCCCCCCCCCCCC
CCCCCCCCCCCCCCCCCCCCCCCCCCCCCCCCCCCCCCCC
CCCCCCCCCCCCCCCCCCCCCCCCCCCCCCCCCCCCCCCC
CCCCCCCCCCCCCCCCCLOWNCCCCCCCCCCCCCCCCC
CCCCCCCCCCCCCCCCCCCCCCCCCCCCCCCCCCCCCCCC
CCCCCCCCCCCCCCCCCCCCCCCCCCCCCCCCCCCCCCCC
CCCCCCCCCCCCCCCCCCCCCCCCCCCCCCCCCCCCCCCC
CCCLOWNCCCCCCCCCCCCCCCCCCCCCCCCCCCCCCCC
CCCCCCCCCCCCCCCCCCCCCCCCCCCCCCCCCCCCCCCC
CCCCCCCCCCCCCCCCCCCCCCCCCCCCCCCCCCCCCCCC
CCCCCCCCCCCCCCCCCCCCCCCCCCCCCCCCCCCCCCCC
CCCCCCCCCCCCah mummy I'm dying here I'm dying in the
darkness of the boxcarCCCCCCCCCCCCCCCCCCCCCCCC
CCCCCCCCCCCCCCCCCCCCCCCCLOWNCCCCCCCCCC
CCCCCCCCCCCCCCCCCCCCCCCCCCCCCCCCCCCCCCCC
CCCCCCCCCCCCCCCCCCCCCCCCCCCCCCCCCCCLOWNC
CCCCCCCCCCCCCCCCCCCCCCCCCCCCCCCCCCCCCCCC
CCCCCCCCCCCCCCCCCCCCCCCCCCCCCCCCCCCCCCCC
CCCCCCCCCCCCCCCCCCCCCCCCCCCCCCCCCCCCCCCC
CCCCCCCCCCCCCCCCCCCCCCCCCCCCCCCCCCCCCCCC
CCCCCCCCCCCCCCCCCCCCCCCCCCCCCCCCCCCCCCCC
CCCCCCCCCCCCCCCCCCCCCCCCCCCCCCCCCCCCCCCC
CCCCCCCCCCCCCCCCCCCCCCCCCCCCCCCCCCCCCCCC
CCCCCCCCCCCCCCCCCCCCCCCCCCCCCCCCCCCCCCCC
CCCCCCCCCCCCCCCCCCLOWNCCCCCCCCCCCCCCCCC

CCCCCCCCCCCCCCCCCCCCCCCCCCCCCCCCCCCC
CCCCCCCCCCCCCCCCCCCCCCCCCCCCCCCCCCccc
cccccccccccccccccccccccccccccccccccccccccccccccccccCC
CCCCCCremmmmmmmmmmmmmmmmmmmmmmmmmm
mmmmmmmmmmmmmCCCCCCCwhen mummy when do we
arrive?CCCCCCCCCCCCCCCCCCCCCCCCCCCCCCCC
CCCCCCCCCCCCCCCCCCCCCCCCCCCCCCCCCCCC
CCCCCCCCCCCCCCCCCCCCCCCCCCCCCCCCCCCC
CCCCCCCCCCCCCCCCCCCCCCCCCCCCCCCCCCCC
CCCCCCCCCCCCCCCCCCCCCCCCCCCCCCCCCCCC
CCCCCCCCCCCCCCCCCCCCCCCCCCCCCCCCCCCC
CCCCCCCCCCCCCCCCCCCCCCCCCCCCCCGCCCC
CCCCCCCCCCCCCCCCCCCCCCCCCCCCCCCCCCCC
CCCCCCCCCCCCCCCCCCCCCCCCCCCCCCCCCCCC
CCCCCCCCCCCCCCCCCCCCCCCCCCCCCCCCCCCC
CCCCCCCCCCCCCCCCCCCCCCCCCCCCCCCCCCCC
CCCCCCCCCCCCCCCCCCCCCCCCCCCCCCCCCCCC
CCCCCCCCCCCCCCCCCCCCCCCCCCCCCCCCCCCC
CCCCCCCCCCCCCCCCCCCCCCCCCCCCCCCCCCCC
CCCCCCCCCCCCCCCCCCCCCCCCCCCCCCCCCCCC
CCCCCCCCCCCCCCCCCCCCCCCCCCCCCCCCCCCC
CCCCCCCCCCCCCCCCCCCCCCCCCCCCCCCCCCCC
CCCCCCCCCCCCCCCCCCCCCCCCCCCCCCCCCCCC
CCCCCCCCCCCCCCCCCCCCCCCCCCCCCCCCCCCC
CCCCCCCCCCCCCCCCCCCCCCCCCCCCCCCCCCCC
CCCCCCCCCCCCCCCCCCCCCCCCCCCCCCCCCCCC
CCCCCCCCCCCCCCCCCCCCCCCCCCCCCCCCCCCC
CCCCCCCCCCCCCCCCCCCCCCCCCCCCCCCCCCCC
CCCCCCCCCCCCCCCCCCCCCCCCCCCCCCCCCCCC
CCCCCCCCCCCCCCCCCCCCCCCCCCCCCCCCCCCC
CCCCCCCCCCCCCCCCCCCCCCCCCCCCCCCCCCCC
CCCCCCCCCCCCCCCCCCCCCCCCCCCCCCCCCCCC
CCCCCCCCCCCCCCCCCCCCCCCCCCCCCCCCCCCC

CCCCCCCCCCCCCCCCCCCCCCCCCCCCCCCCCCCCCCCC
CCCCCCCCCCCCCCCCCCCCCCCCCCCCCCCCCCCCCCCC
CCCCCCCCCCCCCCCCCCCCCCCCCCCCCCCCCCCCCCCC
CCCCCCCCCCCCCCCCCCCCCCCCCCCCCCCCCCCCCCCC
CCCCCCCCCCCCCCCCCCCCCCCCCCCCCCCCCCCCCCCC
CCCCCCCCCCCCCCCCCCCCCCCCCCCCCCCCCCCCCCCC
CCCCCCCCCCCCCCCCCCCCCCCCCCCCCCCCCCCCCCCC
CCCCCCCCCCCCCCCCCCCCCCCCCCCCCCCCCCCCCCCC
CCCCCCCCCCCCCCCCCCCCCCCCCCCCCCCCCCCCCCCC
CCCCCCCCCCLOWNCCCCCCCCCCCCCCCCCCCCCCCCCC
CCCCCCCCCCCCCCCCCCCCCCCCCCCCCCCCCCCCCCCC
CCCCCCCCCCCCCCCCCCCCCCCCCCCCCCCCCCCCCCCC
CCCCCCCCCCCCCCCCCCCCCCCCCCCCCCCCCCCCCCCC
CCCCCCCCCCCCCCCCCCCCCCCCCCCCCCCCCCCCCCCC
CCCCCCCCCCCCCCCCCCCCCCCCCCCCCCCCCCCCCCCC
CCCCCCCCCCCCCCCCCCCCCCCCCCCCCCCCCCCCCCCC
CCCCCCCCCCCCCCCCCCCCCCCCCCCCCCCCCCCCCCCC
CCCCCCCCCCCCCCCCCCCCCCCCCCCCCCCCCCCCCCCC
CCCCCCCCCCCCCCCCCCCCCCCCCCCCCCCCCCCCCCCC
CCCCCCCCCCCCCCCCCCLOWNCCCCCCCCCCCCCCCCCC
CCCCCCCCCCCCCCCCCCCCCCCCCCCCCCCCCCCCCCCC
CCCCCCCCCCCCCCCCCCCCCCCCCCCCCCCCCCCCCCCC
CCCCCCCCCCCCCCCCCCCCCCCCCCCCCCCCCCCCCCCC
CCCCCCCCCCCCCCCCCCCCCCCCCCCCCCCCCCCCCCCC
CCCCCCCCCCCCCCCCCCCCCCCCCCCCCCCCCCCCCCCC
CCCCCCCCCCCCCCCCCCCCCCCCCCCCCCCCCCCCCCCC
CCCCCCCCCCCCCCCCCCCCCCCCCCCCCCCCCCCCCCCC
CCCCCCCCCCCCCCCCCCCCCCCCCCCCCCCCCCCCCCCC
CCCCCCCCCCCCCCCCCCCCCCCCCCCCCCCCCCCCCCCC
CCCCCCCCCCCCCCCCCCCCCCCCCCCCCCCCCCCCCCCC
CCCCCCCCCCCCCCCCCCCCCCCCCCCCCCCCCCCCCCCC
CCCCCCCCCCLOWNCCCCCCCCCCCCCCCCCCCCCCCCCC
CCCCCCCCCCCCCCCCCCCCCCCCCCCCCCCCCCCCCCCC
CCCCCCCCCCCCCCCCCCCCCCCCCCCCCCCCCCCCCCCC

CCCCCCCCCCCCCCCCCCCCCCCCCCCCCCCCCCCCCCCC
CCCCCCCCCCCCCCCCCCCCCCCCCCCCCCCCCCCCCCCC
CCCCCCCCCCCCCCCCCCCCCCCCCCLOWNCCCCCCCCCC
CCCCCCCCCCCCCCCCCCCCCCCCCCCCCCCCCCCCCCCC
CCCCCCCCCCCCCCCCCCCCCCCCCCCCCCCCCCCCCCCC
CCCCCCCCCCCCCCCCCCCCCCCCCCCCCCCCCCCCCCCC
CCCCCCCCCCCCCCCCCCCCCCCCCCCCCCCCCCCCCCCC
CCCCCCCCCCCCCCCCCCCCCCCCCCCCCCCCCCCCCCCC
CCCCCCCCCCCCCCCCCCCCCCCCCCCCCCCCCCCCCCCC
CCCCCCCCCCCCCCCCCCCCCCCCCCCCCCCCCCCCCCCC
CCCCCCCCCCCCCCCCCCCCCCCCCCCCCCCCCCCCCCCC
CCCCCCCCCCCCCCCCCCCCCCCCCCCCCCCCCCCCCCCC
CCCCCCCCCCCCCCCCCCCCCCCCCCCCCCCCCCCCCCCC
CCCCCCCCCCLOWNCCCCCCCCCCCCCCCCCCCCCCCCCC
CCCCCCCCCCCCCCCCCCCCCCCCCCCCCCCCCCCCCCCC
CCCCCCCCCCCCCCCCCCCCCCCCCCCCCCCCCCCCCCCC
CCCCCCCCCCCCCCCCCCCCCCCCCCCCCCCCCCCCCCCC
CCCCCCCCCCCCCCCCCCCCCCCCCCCCCCCCCCCCCCCC
CCCCCCCCCCCCCCCCCCCCCCCCCCCCCCCCCCCCCCCC
CCCCCCCCCCCCCCCCCCCCCCCCCCCCCCCCCCCCCCCC
CCCCCCCCCCCCCCCCCCCCCCCCCCCCCCCCCCCCCCCC
CCCCCCCCCCCCCCCCCCCCCCCCCCCCCCCCCCCCCCCC
CCCCCCCCCCCCCCCCCCCCCCCCLOWNCCCCCCCCCCCC
CCCCCCCCCCCCCCCCCCCCCCCCCCCCCCCCCCCCCCCC
CCCCCCCCCCCCCCCCCCCCCCCCCCCCCCCCCCCCCCCC
CCCCCCCCCCCCCCCCCCCCCCCCCCCCCCCCCCCCCCCC
CCCCCCCCCCCCCCCCCCCCCCCCCCCCCCCCCCCCCCCC
CCCCCCCCCCCCCCCCCCCCCCCCCCCCCCCCCCCCCCCC
CCCCCCCCCCCCCCCCCCCCCCCCCCCCCCCCCCCCCCCC
CCCCCCCCCCCCCCCCCCCCCCCCCCCCCCCCCCCCCCCC
CCCCCCCCCCCCCCCCCCCCCCCCCCCCCCCCCCCCCCCC
CCCCCCCCCCLOWNCCCCCCCCCCCCCCCCCCCCCCCCCC
CCCCCCCCCCCCCCCCCCCCCCCCCCCCCCCCCCCCCCCC
CCCCCCCCCCCCCCCCCCCCCCCCCCCCCCCCCCCCCCCC

CCCCCCC
CCCLOWN
CCCCCCC
CCCCCCC
CCCCCCC
CCCCCCC
CCCCCCC
CCCCCCC
CCCCCCC

CCCCCCC
CCCCCCC
CCCCCCC
CCCCCCC
CCCCCCC
CCCCCCC
CCCCCCC
CCCCCCC
CCCCCCC

CCCCCCC
CCCCCCC
CCCCCCC
CCCLOWN
CCCCCCC
CCCCCCC
CCCCCCC
CCCCCCC
CCCCCCC

CCCCCCC
CCCCCCCC
CCCCCCC
CCCCCCCC
CCCCLOW
NCCCCCCC
CCCCCCCCc
CCCCCCCCCCCCC
CCCCCCCCCCCCC
CCCCCCCCCCCCC

CCCCCCCCCCCC
CCCCCCCCCCC
CCCCCCC
CCCCCCCC
CCCCCCCC
CCCCCCCC
CCCCCCCC
CCCCCCCC
CCCCCCCCC

cccccCCCC
CCCCCCC
CCCCCCC
CCCCCCC
CCCCCCC
CCCCCCC
CCCCCCC
CCCCCCC
CCCCCCC

CCCCCCC
CCCCCCCL
OWNCCCC
CCCCCCCCCCCccc

CCCCCcccccccccccccccccccccccccccccccccccccccccccccccccc
cccccccccccccccccccccccccccccccccccccccccccCLOWNCCCCCCCCCC
cccccccccccccccccccccccccccccccccccccccccccccccccccccccccc
ccccccccccccccccccccccccccccccccccccccccccCCCCCCCCCC
CCCCCCCCCCCCCCCCCCCCCCCCCCCCCCCCCCCCCCCC
CCCCCCCCCCCCCCCCCCCCCCCCCCCCCCCCCCCCCCCC
CCCCCCLOWNCCCCCCCCCCCCCCCCCCCCCCCCCCCCCC
CCCCCCCCCCCCCCCCCCCCLOWNCCCCCCCCCCCCCCCC
CCCCCCCCCCCCCCCCCCCCCCCCCCCCCCCCCCCCCCCC
CCCCCCCCCCCCCCCCCCCCCCCCCCCCCCCCCCCCCCCC
CCCCCCCCCCCCCCCCCCCCCCCCCCCCCCCCCCCCCCCC
CCCCCCCCCCCCLOWNCCCCCCCCCCCCCCCCCCCCCCCC
CCCCCCCCCCCCCCCCCCCCCCCCCCCCCCCCCCCCCCCC
CCCCCCCCCCCCCCCCCCCCCCCCCCCCCCCCCCCCCCCC
CCCCCCCCCCCCCCCCCCCCCCCCCCCCCccccccccccccccccccc
cccccccccccccccccccccccccccccccccccccccccccCCCCCCCCCC
CCCCCCCCCCCCCCCCCCCCCCCCCCCCCCCCCCCCCCCC
CCCCCCCCCCCCCCCCCCCCCCCCCCCCCCCCCCCCCCCC
CCCCCCCCCCCCCCCCCCCCCCCCCCCCCCCCCCCCCCCC

CCCCCCCCCCCCCCCCCCCCCCCCCCCCCCCCCCCCCC
CCCCCCCCCCCCCCCCCCCCCCCCCCCCCCCCCCCCCC
CCCCCCCCCCLOWNCCCCCCCCCCCCCCCCCCCCCCCC
CCCCCCCCCCCCCCCCCCCCCCCCCCCCccccccccccccccccc
cccccccccccccccccccccccccccccccccccccccCCCCCCCCCCCCC
CCCCCCCCCCCCCCCCCCCCCCCCCCCCCCCCCCCCCC
CCCCCCCCCCCCCCCCCCCCCCCCCCCCCCCCCCCCCC
CCCCCCCCCCCCCCCCCCCCCCCCCCCCCCCCCCCCCC
CCCCCCCCCCCCCCCCCCCCCCCCCCCCCCCCCCCCCC
CLOWNCCCCCCCCCCCCCCCCCCCCCCCCCCCCCCCCC
CCCCCCCCCCCCCCCCCCCCCCCCCCCCCCCCCCCCCC
CCCCCCCCCCCCCCCCCLOWNCCCCCCCCCCCCCCCCCC
CCCCCCCCCCCCCCCCCCCCCCCCCCCCCCCCCCCCCC
CCCCCCCCCCCCCCCCCCCCCCCCCCCCCCCCCCCCCC
CCCCCCCCCCCCCCCCCCCCCCCCCCCCCCCCCCCCCC
CCCCCCCCCCCCCCCCCCCCCCCCCCCCCCCCCCCCCC
CCCCCCCCCCCCCCCCCCCCCCCCCCCCCCCCCCCCCC
CCCCCCCCCCCCCCCCCCCCCCCCCCCCCCCCCCCCCC
CCCCCCCCCCCCCCCCCCCCCCCCCCCCCCCCCCCCCC
CCCCCCCCCCCCCCCCCCCCCCCCCCCCCCCCCCCCCC
CCCCCCCcccccccccccccccccccccccccccccccCCCCCCCCCCC
CCCCCCCCCCCCCCCCCCCCCCCCCCCCCCCCCCCCCC
CCCCCCCCCCCCCCCCCCCCCCCCCCCCCCCCCCCCCC
CCCCCCCCCCCCCCCCCCCCCCCCCCCCCCCCCCCCCC
CCCCCCCCCCCCCCCCCCCCCCCCCCCCCCCCCCCCCC
CCCCCCCCCCLOWNCCCCCCCCCCCCCCCCCCCCCCCC
CCCCCCCCCCCCCCCCCCCCCCCCCCCCCCCCCCCCCC
CCCCCCCCCCCCCCCCCCCCCCCCCCCCCCCCCCCCCC
CCCCCCCCCCCCCCCCCCCCCCCCCCCCCCCCCCLOWN
CCCCCCCCCCCI'm so thirsty Mum I need something sweet to
drink CCCCCCCCCCCCCCCCCCCCCCCCCCCCCCCCCCCC
CCCCCCCCCCCCCCCCCCCCCCCCCCCCCCCCCCCCCC
CCCCCCCCCCCCCCCCCCCCCCCCCCCCCCCCCCCCCC
CCCCCCCCCCCCCCCCCCCCCCCCCCCCCCCCCCCCCC

CCCCCCCCCCCCCCCCCCCCCCCCCCCCCCCCCCCCCC
CCCCCCCCCCCCCCCCCCCCCCCCCCCCCCCCCCCCCC
CLOWNCCCCCCCCCCCCCCCCCCCCCCCCCCCCCCCCC
CCCCCCCCCCCCCCCCCCCCCCCCCCCCCCCCCCCCCC
CCCCCCCCCCCCCCCCCCLOWNCCCCCCCCCCCCCCCC
CCCCCCCCCCCCCCCCCCCCCCCCCCCCCCCCCCCCCC
CCCCCCCCCCCCCCCCCCCCCCCCCCCCCCCCCCCCCC
CCCCCCCCCCCCCCCCCCCCCCCCCCCCCCCCCCCCCC
CCCCCCCCCCCCCCCCCCCCCCCCCCCCCCCCCCCCCC
CCCCCCCCCCCCCCCCCCCCCCCCCCCCCCCCCCCCCC
CCCCCCCCCCCCCCCCCCCCCCCCCCCCCCCCCCLOWN
CCCCCCCCCCCCCCCCCCCCCCCCCCCCCCCCCCCCCC
CCCCCCCCCCCCCCCCCCCCCCCCCCCCCCCCCCCCCC
CCCCCCCcccccccccccccccccccccccccccCCCCCCCCCCC
CCCCCCCCCCCCCCCCCCCCCCCCCCCCCCCCCCCCCC
CCCCCCCCCCCCCCCCCCCCCCCCCCCCCCCCCCCCCC
CCCCCCCCCCCCCCCCCCCCCCCCCCCCCCCCCCCCCC
CCCCCCCCCCCCCCCCCCCCCCCCCCCCCCCCCCCCCC
CCCCCCCCCLOWNCCCCCCCCCCCCCCCCCCCCCCCCC
CCCCCCCCCCCCCCCCCCCCCCCCCCCCCCCCCCCCCC
CCCCCCCCCCCCCCCCCCCCCCCCCCCCCCCCCCCCCC
CCCCCCCCCCCCCCCCCCCCCCCCCCCCCCCCCCLOWN

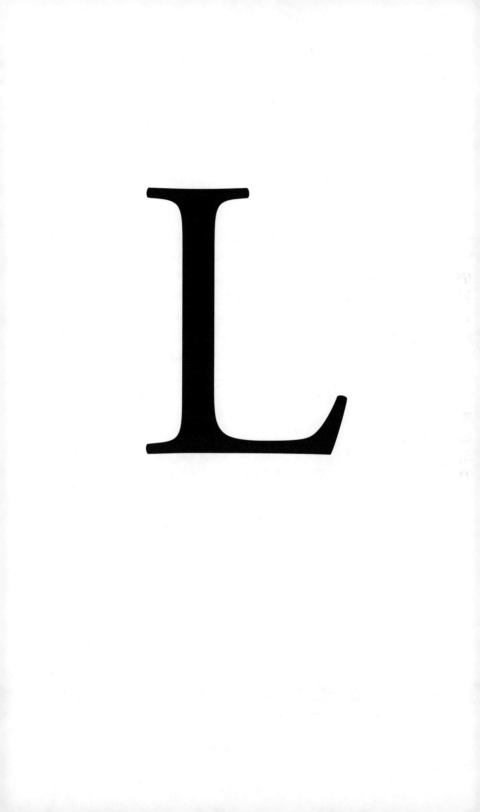

CCCCCCCCCCCCCCCCCCCCCCCCCCCCCCCCCCCCC
CCCCCCCCCCCCCCCCCCCCCCCCCCCCCCLOWNC
CCCCCCCCCCCCCComeCCCCCCCCCCCCCCCCCCCC
CCCCCCCCCCCCCCCCCCCCCCCCCCCCCCCCCCCCC
CCCCCCCCCCCCCCComeCCCCremmmmmmmmmCCCC
CCCCCCCCCCCCCCCCCCCCCCCCCCCCCCCCCCCCL
OWNCCCremmmmmmmmmmmmmmmmmmmmmmmmCCCC
CCCCCCCCCCCCCCCCCCCCCCCCCCCCCCCCCCCCC
CCCCCLOWNCCCCCCCCCCCCCCCCCCCCCCCCCCCC
CCCCCCCCCCCCCCCCCCCCCCCCCCCCCCCCCCCCC
CCCCCCCCCCCCCCCCCCCome to me come come come
to
meCCCCCCCCCCCCCCCCCCCCCCCCComeCCCCCC
CCCCCCCCCCCCCCLOWNCCCCCCCCCCCCCCCCCCC
CCCCCCCCCCCCCCCCCCCCah I need you so badly
CCCCCCCCCCCCCCCCCCCCCCCCCCCCCCCCCCCCC
CCcccccccccccccccccccheeeeeeecccccccccccccccccheeeeeeheccccccc
cccccccccccccccCCCCCCCCClarabella Clyde my Queen
CCCCCCCCCCCCCCCCCCCCCCCCCCCCCCCCCCCCC
CCCCCCCCCCCCCCCCCCCCCCCCCCCCCCCCCCCCC
CCCCCCCCCCCCCCOnly a clown can love a little boy the
way I love you the way I've always loved you and when I was
fashioned it was love at first sight looking up high into the
brightness and it was a sexual thing too for clowns love boys they
do they do and want them to be satisfied and happy
CCCCCCCCCCCCCCCCCCCCCCCCCCCCCCCCCCCCC
CCCCCCCCCCCCCyour heart was so bright and I was so low

down there under the ground as I watched the blanket patrol
moving from side to side among the flames as a small devilish
clownlet I could never get it right as if my heart were
split in two and I needed you I needed only you to bless me
CCCCCCCCCCCCCCCCCCCCCCCLOWNCCCCCCCCC
CCCCCCCCCCCCCCCCCCCCCCwithout your clothes I
could see the frail beginnings of letters
CCCCCCCCCCCCCCCCCCCCCCCCCCCCCCcccccccccccccccc
ccccccccccccccccccccccccccccccccccccccccccccccCCCCCCCCCCC
CCCCCCCCCCCCCCCCCCCCCCCCCCCCCCCCCCCCCCCC
CCCCCCCCCC   I can't come but I want to
cccccccccccCCCCCCCCCCCCCCCCCCCCCCCCCCCCCCCCC
CCCCCCCCCCCCCCCCCCCCCCCCwhen we sleep in hell
we sleep in the light it's only dark when we wake
CCCCCCCCCCCCCCCCCCCCCCCCCCCCCCCCCCCCCCCC
CCCCCCCCCCCCCCCCCCCI cannot tell you my job
except when I sleep I cannot tell you who hired me Clyde except
when I sleep and you are awake within me and then I can say it
you can say my name and I can tell you my job for I came to
eliminate your family and I came to love you and I came to take
away your family I came to tell you I came to keep you from
coming I came to do your dirty work I came to sleep in your bed
I came to grow up into a large and dangerous and deadly thing I
came to rip apart your mom I came to do it to you to mix the
love and pain within you as I sleep I sleepwalk sometimes and
then I wake a bit and then I fall asleep again like all the spirits in
the spirit world that eat and drink and dream for spirits sleep and
dream like humans do the entire mind of all the worlds of death
will sleep and dream among the living as I am dreaming now
sweet Clyde and dreaming of your youth when you were growing
up to be my lover and my confidant and victim
ah ah ah ha ha ha ha ha haaaaaaa
CCCCCCCCCCCCCCCCCCCCCLOWNCCCCCCCCCCCCC
CCCCCCCCCCCCCCCCCCCCCCCCCCCCCCCCCCCCCCC

CCCCCCCCCCCCCCCCCCCCthe dreaming dead like me are
living CCCCthe dreaming dead like me are living
CLOWNCCCCCCCCCCCCCCCCCCCCCCCCCCCCCCCCC
CCCCCCCCCCCCCCCCCCCCCCCCCCCCCCCCCCCCC
CCCthe dreaming dead like me are living
CCCCCCCCCCCCCCCCCCCCCCCCCCCCCCCCCCCCC
CCCCCCCCCCCCCCCCCCCCCCCCCCCCCCCCCCCCC
CCCCCCCCCCCCCCCCCCCCCCCCCLOWNCCCCCCCC
CCCCCCCCCCCCCCCCCCCthe dreaming dead like me
are living
CCCCCCCCCCCCCCCCCCCCCCCCCCCCCCCCCCCCC
CCCCCCCCCCCCCCCCCCCCCCCCCCCCI love to dream
of you in bed with me and what we'll do together when we screw
CCCCCCCCCCCCCCCCCCCCCCCCCCCCCCCCCCCCC
CCCCCCCCCCCCCCCCCCCCCCCaaaaaaaaaaahCCCCCCC
CCCCCCCCCCCCCCCCcccccccccccccccccccccccccccccccCCC
CCCCCCCCCCCCCCCCCCCCCCCCCCCCCCCCCCCCC
CCCCCCCCCCCCCCCCCCCCCCCCCCCCCCCCCCCCC
CCCCCCCCCCCCCCCCCCCCCCCCCCCCCCCCCCCCC
CCCCCCCCCCCCCCCCCCCCCLOWNCCCCCCCCCCCCC
CCCCCCCCCCCCCCCCCCCCCCCCCCCCCCCCCCCCC
CCCCCCCCCCCCCCCCCCCCCCCCCCCCCCCCCCCCC
CCCCCCCCCCCCCCCCCCCCCCCCCCCCCCCCCCCCC
CCCCCCCCLOWNCCCCCCCCCCCCCCCCCCCCCCCCCC
CCCCCCCCCCCCCCCCCCCCCCCCCCCCCCCCCCCCC
CCCCCCCCCCCCCCCCCCCCCCCaaaaaaaaaaahCCCCCCC
CCCCCCCCCCCCCCCCCCCCCCCCsock it to me
ClydeCCCCCCCCCCCCCCCCCCCCCCCCCCCCCFCCCCCCCCC
CCCCCCCCCCCLOWNCCCCCCCCCCCCCCCCCCaaaaaaa
aaaaaaaaaaaah sock it to me little boy
CCCCCCCCCCCCCCCCCCCCCCCCCCCCCCCCCCCCLO
WNCCCCCCCCCCCCCCCCCCCCCCCCCCCCCCCCCCC
CCCCCCCCCCCCCCCCCCCCCCCCCCCCCCCCCCCCC
CCCCCCCCCCCCCCCCCCCCCCCCCCCCCCCCCCCCC

CCCCCCCCCCCCCCCCCCCCCCCCCCCCCCCCCCCCCCC
CCCCCCCCCCCCCCCCCCCCCCCCCCCCCCCCCCCCCCC
CCCCCCCCCCCCCCCCCCCCCCCCCCCCCCCCCCCCCCC
CCCCCCCCLOWNCCCCCCCCCCCCCCCCCCCCCCCCCCC
CCCCCCCCCCCCCCCCCCCCCCCCCCCCCCCCCCCCCCC
CCCCCCCCCCCCCCCCCCCCCCCCCCCCCCCCCCCCCCC
CCCCCCCCCCCCCCCCCCCCCCCCCCCCCCCLOWNCC
CCCCCCCCCCCCCCCCCCCCCCCCCCCCCCCCCCCCCCC
CCCCCCCCCCCCCCCCCCCCCCCCCCCCCCCCCCCCCCC
CCCCCCCCCCCCCCCCCCCCCCCCCCCCCCCCCCCCCCC
               CCCCCCCCCCCCCCsock sock
CCCCCCCCCCCCCCCCCCCCCCCCCCCCCCCCCCCCCCC
CCCCCCCCCLOWNCCCCCCCCCCCCCCCCCCCCCCCCCC
CCCCCCCCCCCCCCCCCCCCCCCCCCLOWNCCCCCCCC
CCCCCCCCCCCCCCCCCCCCCCCCsockCCCCCCCCCCCC
CCCCCCCCCCCCCCCCCCCCCCCCCCCCCCCCCCCCCCC
CCCCCCCCCCCCCCCCCCLOWNCCCCCCCCCCCCutCCC
CCCCCCCCCCCCCCCCCCCutCCCCCCCCCCCCCCCCCC
CCCCCCCCCCCCCCCCCCCCCCCCCCCCCCCCCccccccccc
cccccccccccccccccccccccccccccccccccccccccccccccccccccCCCCC
CCCCCCCCCCCCCCCCCCCCCCCCCCCCCCCCCCCCCCC
CCCCCCCCCCCCCCCCCCCCCCCCCCCCCCCCCCCCCCC
CCCCCCCCCCCCCCCCCCCCCcut sock cut sock cut sock cut
CCCCCCCCCCCCCCCCCCCCCCCCCCCCCCCCCCCCCLO
WNCCCCCCCCCCCCCCCCCCCCCCCCCCCCCCCCCCCCC
CCCCCCCCCccccccccccccccccccccccccccccccccccccccccccccccccc
cccccccccCCCCCCCCCCCCCCCCCCCCCCCCCCCCCCCCCCCCCC
CCCCCCCCCCCCCCCCCCCCCCCCCCCCCCCCCCCCCCC
cccccccCCCCCCCCCCCCCCCCCCCCCCCCCCCCCCCCCCCC
CCCCCCCCCCCCCCCCCCCCCCCCCCCCCCdieCCCCCCC
CCCCCCCCCCCCCCCCCCCCCCCCCCCCCCCCCCCCCCC
CCCCCCCCCCCCCCCCCCCCCCCCCCLOWNCCCCCCCC
          CCCCCCCCCCCCCCCCCCCCCCCCClyde die
CCCCCCCCCCCCCCCCCCCCCCCCCCCCCCCCCCCCCCC

CCCCCCCCCCCCCCCCCCCCCCCCCCCCCCCCCCCCCCCCC
CCCCCCCCCCCCCCCCCwe'll die together yeah
CCCCCCLOWNCCCCCCCCCCCCCCCCCCCCCCCCCCC
CCCCCCCCCCCCCCCCCCCCCCCCCCCCCCCCCCCCCCC
CCCCCCCCCCCCCCCCCCCCCCCCCCCCCdie Clyde die
CCCCCCCCCCCCCCCCCCCCCCCCCCCCCCCCCCCCCCC
CCCCCCCCCCCCCCCCCCCCCCCCCCCCCCCCCCCCCCC
CCCCCCLOWNCCCCCCCCCCCCCCCCCCCCCCCCCCC
CCCCCCCCCCCCCCCCCCCCLOWNCCCCCCCCCCCCC
CCCCCCCCCCCCCCCCCCCCCCCCCCCCCCCCCCCCCCC
CCCCCCCCCCCCCCCCCCCCCCCCCCCCCCCCCCCCCCC
CCCCCCCCCCCCCCCCCCCCCCCCCCCCCCCCCCCCCCC
CCCCCCCCCcccccccccccccccccccccccccccccccccCCCCCCCCCC
CCCCCCCCCCCCCCCCCCCCCCCCCCCCCCCCCCCCCCC
CCCCCCCCCCCCCCCCCCCCCCCCCCCCCCCCCCCCCCC
CCCCCCCCCCCCCCCCCCCCCCCCCCCCCCCCCCCCCCC
CCCCCCCCCCCCCCCCCCCCCCCCCCCCCCCCCCCCCCC
CCCCCCCCCCCCCCCCCCCCCCCCCCCCCCCCCCCCCCC
CCCCCCCCCCCCCCCLOWNCCCCCCCCCCCCCCCCCCC
CCCCCCCCCCCCCCCCCCCCCCCCCCCCCCCCCCCCCCC
CCCCCCCCCCCCCCCCCCCCCCCCCCCCCCCCCCCCCCC
CCCCCCCCCCCCCCCCCCCCCCCCCCCCCCCCCCCCCLO
WNCCCCCCCCCCCCCCCCCCCCCCCCCCCCCCCCCCCC
CCCCCCCCCCCCCCCCCCCCCCCCCCCCCCCCCCCCCCC
CCCCCCCCCCCCCCCCCCCCCCCCCCCCCCCCCCCCCCC
CCCCCCCCCCCCCCCCCCCCCCCCCCCCCCCCCCCCCCC
CCCCCCCCCCCCCCCCCCCCCCCCCCCCCCCCCCCCCCC
CCCCCCCCCCCCCCCCCCCCCCCCCCCCCCCCCCCCCCC
CCCCCCCCCCCCCCCCCCCCCCCCCCCCCCCCCCCCCCC
CCCCCCCCCCCCCCCCCCCCCCCLOWNCCCCCCCCC
CCCCCCCCCCCCCCCCCCCCCCCCCCCCCCCCCCCCCCC
CCCCCCCCCCCCCCCCCCCCCCCCCCCCCCCCCCCCCCC
CCCCCCCCCCCCCCCCCCCCCCCCCCCCCCCCCCCCCCC
CCCCCCCCLOWNCCCCCCCCCCCCCCCCCCCCCCCCCC

CCCCCCCCCCCCCCCCCCCCCCCCCCCCCCCCCCCCCC
CCCCCCCCCCCCCCCCCCCCCCCCCCCCCCCCCCCCCC
CCCCCCCCCCCccccccccccccccccccccccccccccccccccccccccccccccc
cccccccccccccccccccCCCCCCCCCCCCCCCCCCCCCCCCCCC
CCCCCCCCCCCCCCCCCCCCCCCCCCCCCCCCCCCCCC
CCCCCCCCCCCCCCCCCCCCCCCCCCCCCCCCCCCCCC
CCCCCCCCCCCCCCCCCCCCCCCCCCCCCCCCCCCCCC
CCCCCCCCCCCCCCCCCCCCCCCCCCCCCCCCCCCCCC
CCCCCCCCCCCCCCCCCCCCCCCCCCCCCCCCCCCCCC
CCCCCCCCCCCCCCCCCCCCCCCCCCCCCCCCCCCCCC
LOWNCCCCCCCCCCCCCCCCCCCCCCCCCCCCCCCCCC
CCCCCCCCCCccccccccccccccccccccccccccccccccccccccccccccccc
cccccccccccccccccccCCCCCCCCCCCCCCCCCCCCCCCCCCC
CCCCCCCCCCCCCCCCCCCCCCCCCCCCCCCCCCCCCC
cccccccccccccccCCCCCCCCCCCCCCCCCCCCCCCCCCCCCCC
CCCCCCCCCCCCCCCCCCCCCCCCCCCCCCCCCCCCCC
CCCCCCCCCCCCCCCCCCCCCCCCCCCCCCCCCCCCCC
CCCCCCCCCCCCCCCCCCCCCCCCCCCCCCCCCCCCCC
CCCCCCCCCCCCCCCCCCCCCCCCCCCCCCCCCCCCCC
      CCCCCCCCCCCCCCCCCCCCCCCCCCCI dream
CCCCCCCCCCCCCCCCCCCCCCCCCCCCCCCCCLOWN
CCCCCCCCCCCCCCCCCCCCCCCCCCCCCCCCCCCCCC
CCCCCCCCCCCCCCCCCCCCCCCCCCCCCCCCCCCCCC
CCCCCCCCCCCCCCCCCCCCCCCCCCCCCCCCCCCCCC
CCCCCCCCCCCCCCCCCCCCCCCCCCCCCCCCCCCCCC
CCCCCCCCCCCCCCCCCCCCCCCCCCCCCCCCCCCCCC
CCCCCCCCCCCCCCCCCCCCCCCCCCCCCCCCCCCCCC
CCCCCCCCCCCCCCCCCCCCCLOWNCCCCCCCCCCCC
CCCCCCCCCCCCCCCCCCCCCCCCCCCCCCCCCCCCCC
CCCCCCCCCCCCCCCCCCCCCCCCCCCCCCCCCCCCCC
CCCCCCCCCCCCCCCCCCCCCCCCCCCCCCCCCCCCCC
CCCCCCCCCCLOWNCCCCCCCCCCCCCCCCCCCCCCC
CCCCCCCCCCCCCCCCCCCCCCCCCCCCCCCCCCCCCC
CCCCCCCCCCCCCCCCCCCCCCCCCCCCCCLOWNCCCCC

CCCCCCCCCCCCCCCCCCCCCCCCCCCCCCCCCCCCCC
CCCCCCCCCCCCCCCCCCCCCCCCCCCCCCCCCCCCCC
CCCCCCCCCCCCCCCCCCCCCCCCCCCCCCCCCCCCCC
CCCCCCCCCCCCCCCCCCCCCCCCCCCCCCCCCCCCCC
CCCCCCCCCCCCCccccccccccccccccccccccccccCCCCCCCC
CCCCCCCCCCCCCCCCCCCCCCCCCCCCCCCCCCCCCC
CCCCCCCCCCCCCCCCCCCCCCCCCCCCCCCCCCCCCC
CCCCCCCCCCCCCCCCCCCCCCCCCCCCCCCCCCCCCC
CCCCCCCCCCCCCCCCCCCCLOWNCCCCCCCCCCCCC
CCCCCCCCCCCCCCCCCCCCCCCCCCCCCCCCCCCCCC
CCCCCCCCCCCCCCCCCCCCCCCCCCCCCCCCCCCCCC
CCCCCLOWNCCCCCCCCCCCCCCCCCCCCCCCCCCCCC
CCCCCCCCCCCCCCCCCCCCCCCCCCCCCCCCCCCCCC
CCCCCCCCCCCCCCCCCCCCCremmmmmmmmmmCCC
CCCCCCCCCCCCCCCCCCCCCCCCCCCCCCCCCCCCCC
CCCCCCCCCCCCCCCCCCCCCCCCCCCCCCCCCCCCCC
CCCCCCCCLOWNCCCCCCCCCCCCCCCCCCCCCCCCCC
CCCCCCCCCCCCCCCCCCCCCCCCCCCCCCCCCCCCCC
CCCCCCCCCCCCCCCCCCCCCCCCCCCCCCCCCCCCCC
CCCCCCCCCCCCCCCCCCCCCCCCCCCCCCCCCCCCCC
CCCCCCCCCCCCCCCCCCCCCCCCCCCCCCCCCCCCCC
CCCCCCCCCCCCCCCCCCCCCLOWNCCCCCCCCCCC
CCCCCCCCCCCCCCCCCCCCCCCCCCCCCCCCCCCCCC
CCCCCCCCCCCCCCCCCCCCCCCCCCCCCCCCCCCCCC
CCCCCCCCCCCCCCCCCCCCCCCCCCCCCCCCCCCCCC
CCCCCCCCCCCCCCCCCCCCCCCCCCCCCCCCCCCCCC
CCCCCCCCCCCCCCCCCCCCCCCCCCCCCCCCCCCCCC
CCCCCCCCCCCCCCCCCCCCCCCCCCCCCCCCCCCCCC
CCCCCCCCCCCCCCCCCCCCCCCCCCCCCCCCCCCCCC
CCCCCCCCCCCCCCCCCCCCCCCCCCCCCCCCCCCCCC
CCCCCCCCCCCCCCCCCCCCCCCCCCCCCCCCCCCCCC
CCCCCCCCCCCCCCCCCCCCCCCCCCCCCCCCCCCCCC
CCCCCCCCCCCCCCCCCCCCCCCCCCCCCCCCCCCCCC
LOWNCCCCCCCCCCCCCCCCCCCCCCCCCCCCCCCCCC

One

If a child is cast into darkness, if a child is cast into outer darkness, if a child receives no love and sees no love besides the love of chains and whips, the child will build a monster piece by piece within. The child will build his sickness; the child who sees too much will build his blindness.

I stared into a chocolate chaos.

My mother was mad. She had always been mad. A small inner song, and my father had beaten her like a dog. Did he deserve to die at my hands?

Yes.

The feelings we can't control we turn over to our playthings. With every whisper they grow larger and more alluring and more dangerous. God reached into the loam and called His first doll Adam. Then He whispered and He whispered and He whispered. Why was He surprised when it expanded into the wrong form? My clown was created like an organelle, an independent voice emerging from a single cell. A child who isn't touched will touch himself or search for other, stranger touches. Even the bacteria are haunted. Bacteria quiver and explode. Bacteria crack like bombs. Tiny tiny cracklets.

Mother passed her sweet madness on. A smudge in a crib, I imagined she touched me. I imagined my lips touched her jellied breasts. I imagined I looked into her eyes ringed with coalblack, even as a baby, I imagined her frigid touch and hollow eyes and grape-colored nipples and wrinkled, poisoned areolae.

I looked up from my cup of coffee.

It was then that I saw Cindy in cold magenta light, sitting at a table behind me, and she had a crayon and was drawing on oilpaper. The crayon was short and purple, and the wrapper was ripped. I didn't know how long she had been there. After Leonard left, I hadn't wanted to move from my chair, because I couldn't afford to drink, and in the afternoon, movement and drinking are usually synonymous. I knew I had to stay sober until after that night, because I had to figure out what to do, and I was having trouble, and then I looked up and she was there, humming to herself and coloring. I stood and circled around behind her. She remained hunched over, and I could feel her energy pushing into the paper, pressing hard on the stub.

"Cindy, Cindy," I murmured quietly.

She didn't seem to notice and continued pushing.

I sat down next to her and watched.

She was biting one side of her lip, and her eyebrows dipped, and her head jerked from side to side, and the color pealed away in minute shavings. She was making a warped flatfish. She took a mauve crayon out of a tin box on the table and began to scumble the water.

"What is it?" I asked.

"A fraketrane!"

"Frake?"

"Yeees, frake!" she explained, as she worked the crayon lightly around the paper. Her coverage was poor and there were large empty spots. She reached for another crayon, iron-gray, and drew round shapes of various sizes in the whiteness.

"Isn't that a fish?"

"Sshhhh," she silenced me, as she continued working.

The lunch crowd had disappeared, and there were few other people in the restaurant. I got down on my knees in front of the girl and peered up into her face. From this lower angle, she was as beautiful as a Bellini madonna. As fresh and as caring and as delicate and as thoughtful.

"I'm sorry," I said to her. "I'm terribly sorry."

She glanced at me naughtily without moving her head.

I began to cry. Gently.

And why?

Because I worshiped and envied this girl.

She turned towards me and seemed to be examining something in my hair. Then she patted me with her free hand on the cheek.

Her index finger became wet.

"Poor Kyde," she said, but it was as if she were speaking to someone else, to someone far away from me. It was as if she saw the *real me*, the cleansed unhaunted one who was on the outside, the one that no one had ever seen before, despite the pompous claims of the priest.

And I too saw something separate in her. Something floating in the center of her face. A grown and graceful woman. A pure and perfect energy hovering before me.

"I'm glad you're here and we caught you," Duke's voice interrupted from above.

I wiped my eyes without shame and struggled to my feet and sat back down on my wicker chair.

"Chooooooo," Cindy said. "Choowooooo!"

Kosmoski put his hand on my shoulder.

I experienced fear again. The imprint still felt hot.

"We stopped by the hotel to say goodbye, and I wanted to make certain that you were all right."

"Where are you going?"

"I'm heading back to the Orient," he explained, as he took a seat at the table. "A long-term assignment. I'm organizing an adoption effort in Thailand, in the refugee camps there."

"Why are you going?"

"What do you mean 'why'?"

"Why are you going?"

"I'm a priest. I do what I'm told," he replied.

"And what about Oberstar?"

"That has nothing more to do with me," Kosmoski said. "You asked me to arrange it, and I did. I've done everything I could for you, and what you make of it is your own spiritual business. I wish you well, and I certainly hope the process is healing."

Cindy was drawing a red house on the surface of the water.

"And what if I can't make the appointment?" I asked.

"I hope you're not serious."

Cindy rubbed her nose, and then she reached into the tin box and took out a brown crayon.

"Why do I have to meet this colonel exactly at the full moon?" I repeated the question that had never been answered.

"That's when I saw him," Kosmoski answered.

"What do you mean?"

"In Laos. If it hadn't been at that moment, there wouldn't have been the additional presence."

"What presence?"

"The presence. You'll see."

"What the hell are you talking about?" I shouted suddenly.

"There's no need to swear in front of the child," Kosmoski corrected me. "You'll see, that's all."

Cindy was coloring the sky brown.

"You've got to help me!" I shouted again.

People in the restaurant were staring at us.

"I already have. Please lower your voice."

"No, Father," I pleaded, dropping immediately to a whisper. "You have to help me with something. I need you to do something for me!"

"But I'm leaving first thing in the morning. I'll give you an address, and you can write me there and let me know what happened. As a matter of fact, I insist on it."

And he pulled a fountain pen and a small spiral tablet out of his vest pocket.

"I need you to do something for me tonight. This has nothing to do with what you're talking about," I said.

"You'll have to see him by yourself."

"Please!"

The priest looked annoyed. He didn't respond but proceeded to write an address down in the notebook. A foundation in Bangkok. He tore the sheet out of the book and handed it to me. I stuffed it in my pocket.

"I have to be going now. I promise to pray for you."

"No, stop! That's not what I meant!" I pleaded again. "I keep telling you, it's something else."

"What are you talking about?"

"I need you to do something else for me *tonight*. It will only take you a short time. I'm begging you!"

I touched him on the forearm. He looked at my fingers, as if I had made a mistake.

"So what is it?" he asked, as he stood up to go.

"There's a woman I have an appointment with. I'm in love with her. If I go to meet Oberstar, I'm going to miss her. I only have this one chance. If I don't make it tonight, I'll never see her again. Go over there and tell her where I am and why I'm late. You're a priest. She'll believe you. Tell her to wait for me. I'll get there as soon as I can, but please make certain that she waits for me."

"Why didn't you call me about this earlier?"

"I guess I've been confused. I've been under a lot of pressure."

"Then why don't you go and leave her a note yourself?"

"No, I have to be sure that she stays. You said you can get people to do practically anything. Just make certain for me, that way I'll know. You're the only one I can trust to do this!"

"Shugga, shugga," Cindy said.

His notebook was still lying on the table. I reached for my wallet, opened it and pulled out the address that Bruce had given me and wrote it down in the book and handed it back to the priest. He pursed his lips and considered.

"There will be two of them, her and a man," I said.

"OK," he agreed, "I think I can manage it. I'm sure they'll stay if I talk to them."

The child had stopped drawing. She held up the piece of paper. The thing had two eyes on the side of its head. The eyes looked tired.

"Trane, Kyde," Cindy said proudly.

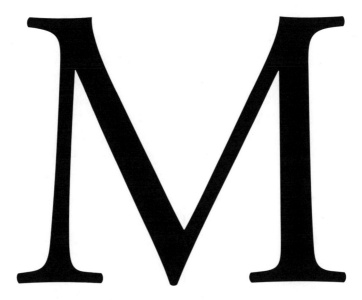

CCCCCLOWNCCCCCCCCCCCCCCCCCCCCCCCCCCCC
CCCCCCCCCCCCCCCCCCCCCCCCCCCCCCCCCCCCC
CCCCCCCCCCCCCCCCCCCCCCCCCCCCCCCCCCCCC
CCCCCCCCCCCCCCCCCCCCCCCCCCCCCCCCCCCCC
CCCCCCCCCCCCCCCCCCCCCCCCCCCCCCCCCCCCC
CCCCCCCCCCCCCCCCCCCCCCCCCCCCCCCCCCCCC
CCCCCCCCCCCCCCCCCCCCCCCCCLOWNCCCCCC
CCCCCCCCCCCCCCCCCCCCCCCCCCCCCCCCCCCCC
CCCCCCCCCCCCCCCCCCCCCCCCCCCCCCCCCCCCC
CCCCCCCCCCCCCCCCCCCCCCCCCCCCCCCCCCCCC
CCCCCCCCCCCCCCCCCCCCCCCCCCCCCCCCCCCCC
CCCCCLOWNCCCCCCCCCCCCCCCCCCCCCCCCCCCC
CCCCCCCCCCCCCCCCCCCCCCCCCCCCCCCCCCCCC
CCCCCCCCCCCCCCCCCCCCCCCCCCCCCCCCCCCCC
CCCCCCCCCCCCCCCCCCCCCCCCCCCCCCCCCCCCC
CCCCCCCCCCCCCCCCCCCCCCCCCCCCCCCCCCCCC
CCCCCCCCLOWNCCCCCCCCCCCCCCCCCCCCCCCCC
CCCCCCCCCCCCCCCCCCCCCCCCCCCCCCCCCCCCC
CCCCCCCCCCCCCCCCCCCCCCCCCCCCCCCCCCCCC
CCCCCCCCCCCCCCCCCCCCCCCCCCCCCCCCCCCCC
CCCCCCCCCCCCCCCCCCCCCCCCCCCCCCCCCCCCC
CCCCCCCCCCCCCCCCCCCCLOWNCCCCCCCCCC
CCCCCCCCCCCCCCCCCCCCCCCCCCCCCCCCCCCCC
CCCCCCCCCCCCCCCCCCCCCCCCCCCCCCCCCCCCC
CCCCCCCCCCCCCCCCCCCCCCCCCCCCCCCCCCCCC
CCCCLOWNCCCCCCCCCCCCCCCCCCCCCCCCCCCCC
CCCCCCCCCCCCCCCCCCCCCCCCCCCCCCCCCCCCC

CCCCCCCCCCCCCCCCCCCCCCCCCCCCCCCCCCCCCC
CCCCCCCCCCCCCCCCCCCCCCCCCCCCCCCCCCCCCC
CCCCCCCCCCCCCCCCCCCCCCCCCCCCCCCCCCCCCC
CCCCCLOWNCCCCCCCCCCCCCCCCCCCCCCCCCCCCCC
CCCCCCCCCCCCCCCCCCCCCCCCCCCCCCCCCCCCCC
CCCCCCCCCCCCCCCCCCCCCCCCCCCCCCCCCCCCCC
CCCCCCCCCCCCCCCCCCCCCCCCCCCCCCCCCCCCCC
CCCCCCCCCCCCCCCCCCCCCCCCCCCLOWNCCCCCCC
CCCCCCCCCCCCCCCCCCCCCCCCCCCCCCCCCCCCCC
CCCCCLOWNCCCCCCCCCCCCCCCCCCCCCCCCCCCCCC
CCCCCCCCCCCCCCCCCCCCCCCCCCCCCCCCCCCCCC
CCCCCCCCCCCCCCCCCCCCCCCCCCCCCCCCCCCCCC
CCCCCCCCCCCCCCCCCCCCCCCCCCCCCCCCCCCCCC
CCCCCLOWNCCCCCCCCCCCCCCCCCCCCCCCCCCCCCC
CCCCCCCCCCCCCCCCCCCCCCCCCCCCCCCCCCCCCC
CCCCCCCCCCCCCCCCCCCCCCCCCCCCCCCCCCCCCC
CCCCCCCCCCCCCCCCCCCCCCCCCCCCCCCCCCCCCC
CCCCCCCCCCCCCCCCCCCLOWNCCCCCCCCCCCCCC
CCCCCCCCCCCCCCCCCCCCCCCCCCCCCCCCCCCCCC
CCCCCCCCCCCCCCCCCCCCCCCCCCCCCCCCCCCCCC
CCCCCLOWNCCCCCCCCCCCCCCCCCCCCCCCCCCCCCC
CCCCCCCCCCCCCCCCCCCCCCCCCCCCCCCCCCCCCC
CCCCCCCCCCCCCCCCCCCCCCCCCCCCCCCCCCCCCC
CCCCCCCCCCCCCCCCCCCCCCCCCCCCCCCCCCCCCC
CCCCCCCCCCCCCCCCCCCCCCCCCCCCCCCCCCCCCC
CCCCCCCCLOWNCCCCCCCCCCCCCCCCCCCCCCCCCC
CCCCCCCCCCCCCCCCCCCCCCCCCCCCCCCCCCCCCC
CCCCCCCCCCCCCCCCCCCCCCCCCCCCCCCCCCCCCC
CCCCCCCCCCCCCCCCCCCCCCCCCCCCCCCCCCCCCC
CCCCCCCCCCCCCCCCCCCCCCCCCCCCCCCCCCCCCC
CCCCCCCCCCCCCCCCCCCCCCCCCCCCCCCCCCCCCC
CCCCCCCCCCCCCCCCCCCCCCCCCCCCCCCCCCCCCC
CCCCCCCCCCCCCCCCCCCCCCCLOWNCCCCCCCCCC
CCCCCCCCCCCCCCCCCCCCCCCCCCCCCCCCCCCCCCbeautiful

morning O what a beautiful day I've got a wonderful feeling everything's going away! Rise and shine, all ya kampy kampers, rebbelly! Da da da da da da da, da da da da da da da, da da da, da da da, da da da, da da da! I will rise now and go about the city in the streets and in the broad ways I will seek him whom my soul loveth. Woooeeee! Woooeeee! Woooeeee! Al babes pass me my raiment cuz today it's gonna get super heavy, cuz today I went to bed sane and woke up totally crazy, cuz today I am no longer what I seem to be, cuz today I heard the voice and it spoke to me, cuz today the Lord will smite with a scab the crowns of the heads of the Hookers of Zion and discover their secret parts Al babes, all of them Zionist parts—if you've ever been raised by a Jewess, you've got crownless Zionist parts—so woe babes unto them that call evil good and good evil that put darkness for light and light for darkness, woe unto them that put bitter for sweet and sweet for bitter, that put clown for poet and poet for clown and Kraut for Jew and Jew for whipsmacking fuckhead Kraut oyez woe to all them suckers and buttsuckers and cudsuckers of the planet, woe to all them monumental cocksuckers, babes yeah woe to them cocksuckers woe to them suckers woe to them suckers yeah sometimes my dome feels like the rusty innards of a mezuzah, man like a withered scroll like a palladium that keeps the Hebrew house from harm. What house, babes? What harm? The Hebrew house of madness of course, the anaerobic nuthouse of sadness and desire, the grim chalet, and that the ancient mad don't deserve to suffer is the principal message of every law-abiding clown, the clown is the great protector of the mad, and why's that babes, why's that? So why's your friggin' barn door open?

Heh heh heh heh!! No, I'm

not reaching in, at least not yet, so let me tell you the tale of Baby Kismet, the elephant. Baby Kismet was herded into a human pen in the middle of an African jungle under a gibbous moon when she was just an elephantlet, or I guess in her case lette, surrounded by tiny negroid peoples jumping excitedly up and down, and I know what they're like Al, cuz all my ova are jet man, they're covered with black bacterial bangers. Baby Kismet was separated from her momma when they took her off the cars, and all you hundred percent yiddishe clowns know about that one too, now don't ya Al? cuz you're a Jew, man and you're my calculating agent, and then she wound up cryin' her little heart out, and I used to walk over to the circus cage whenever I felt kinda sad myself and I would feed her peanuts and I'd say Baby Kismet you and I are the victims of fate except that you were born way too late with your getup permanently on and fate dealt me a bum hand because I had to apply mine, yeah every night I'd bathe my face in shit and it wouldn't last til morning. When a kid is separated from her mom, it's a tough tough break and nobody would rub Kismet's trunk, yeah no mom would rub that dangling thing, and this made Kismet sad in her cage, and since she couldn't talk she'd write with her thing, she'd write in the air and I'd read above her piss-stained straw, her letters would say, "I'm no longer comfortable in my skin, my skin is burning to be stroked, my skin is wrinkled like a prune, my wrinkled skin is burning." Yeah babes, them's the breaks, and the ringmaster threw a red velvet pall over her back with the gothic letter K, and they made her do the Paki (for paki-derm) Cabriole, and then her helpless soul would bray, and I gotta tell ya babes cuz you're my agent and do all my thinking for me, that my horn would honk in sympathy whenever I heard that motherless voice call out in bondage, ringing through the ring of the tent in circumcised pain even though she was a girl, and I was part of the family scene, a clown is like a ringmaster's son, if you know what I mean, and I'd see that little elephant girl rear up and scream, surrounded by children, by kids who had their mommies and daddies there in the boxes, there'd be her honk and mine, and my mezuzah head would begin to dream, that half-Jewish clown headtrip Baby

Clyde gave me, I'd dream about Baby Kismet in the boxcar with her mommy and daddy being shipped very slowly, from hot town to hot town through Africa, as all the older elephants were praying and dying, dying in the dark with their fringed palls, dying with their ancient memories, dying singing their sweet high songs in the cars, dying under the wands of devils, dying in praise of the greatness of God, dying chanting the Sh'ma and Kaddish, dying supporting their grandparents, dying hugging their children, dying kissing their reticent, frail lovers, dying of thirst and diarrhea and despair, dying cuz of the bourgeois German thing that torments the world in order to sell a cleaner brighter washing machine and then the tent would darken and go quiet and all that would remain would be the head of Kismet frozen on a pack of cigarettes, one eye turned up and winkingly inviting me to buy a pack and taste the poison, yeah Clyde buy a fucking pack and taste the fucking poison of these delicious elephantine cigarettes, the head wriggling its oriflamme its banner of justice as if poor Baby Kismet had grown her whip sprouting from the glabella like a giant pussy (puss-filled) wrinkled zit, wooooooooee Al, ya know how dreams lock up into those hairy images of pussy? the reel stops turning and you get that one real still, and then the still starts crinkling and burning, the projector lamp just starts to burn it up and that's what happened to Kismet, the pack of smokes started to burn, the label turned at the margins, and Baby Kismet began to blacken like a leaf in flame, like a pussy enflamed it bulged and darkened, and the tent and the cigarettes burned away and all that remained was Kismet's helpless soul that whispered to me from the hadal herms of hell, yeah like statuettes on the nightbound paths of dreams the little whispers came to me, the voice of her mom calling sweetly saying son don't

blame me

please son please don't blame me keep

your sanity and pray for me, I couldn't speak with my front legs up in the air, I couldn't tell you what had happened there in the chair, but yet I gotta tell ya Al, that mothers always come in dreams, saying son don't blame me please son please don't blame me saying son don't blame me please son please don't blame me saying son don't blame me please son please don't blame me saying son don't please don't blame me saying son don't blame me please son please don't blame me saying son don't blame me please son please don't blame me saying son don't blame me please son please the world is filled with ghostly choruses and chains in trunks and moms and dads descend (or climb the gory ropes) and visit us and weep, yeah weep, for our safety Al to counsel and guide us in the depths of slumber their loving voices come to us.....always.....always, but I guess it's time to rise and shine and brush the darkness off my teeth cuz during the day we clowns are ordinary people, yup, here in dreamtime and here in real time, we live like ordinary non-circus beings we clean our nails (heh we gots bags and bags) and buff our lunules (da moon's got lunules too) and sip our tea (dat Cookys one ob us) and take our antibiotics (hasta labeesta baby!) cuz the world is filled with funny germs (ders Fred and Sam and Molly Jean da RodeeO Queen) and golligwogs both white and black and Chinese can make the aspens shine atop the throbbing mountains of Dis yeah the blackest and whitest and yellowest germs and singing herms

aaaaaaahhheeeee they nitrify our

soil those germs and the paint of dreams is smeared on the
palettes of devils (debbillss is we, watch dat fookin spellin), at
least that's what the Great Mudder sang when I was poured from
oocyte to ootid to ovum Down Down Down into the fiery blast,
she sang a brilliant dream she sang a poem she sang the warmth
of love under the muddy sheets, the Great Mudder stoked the
furnace and we'd daub the devil's cheeks and then Clyde would
command me in his dream and I'd daub between 'em, if ya know
what I mean Al, if ya know what I truly mean, I'd stoke the
furnace, too. Anyway, it makes no diff cuz this book is now my
thaaaaaaaaaaaaaaaaaaaaaaaaaaaaaaaaaaaaaaaaaaaaaaaaaaaaaaaang,
and I can tell you Al that between his One and Two our hero lost
a screw he'll disappear between the sheets the poor poetic gull will
sink into oblivion cuz an alphabet can only protect a man so far,
those amulets those serifs and sans are really palimpsestic charms
and have their holes their spots and boles where evil things can
plunge and enter, year after year of rough and stormy weather
will tear the skin and let those clownish microbes in, and once
they're in it's love among the roses, it's the whole nine pumpin
rectal yards, it's the matchbox guillotine that according to Zeno
the Clown never quite gets down but it does Al, it does cuz a
mind is one thing and a blade is another and there is no defense
in the world for a mind against a blade, a blade cuts through
philosophies through all the Zenos and zends and zendos, it cuts
through all the Zs and makes 'em too, as you will see, yup you
cannot cut the mind but a blade slashes through the outer rinds,
it cuts across the frames of film, it slits the dermal layers and the
circus tents go dim, the hooting lights go out, and all the clowns
stop laughing. There is always a point on the belly where the skin
is thinnest, babes the center of an orgasm or a laugh or a religion,
it's all one thing cuz religion and comedy and orgasm were
created at the very same time, at the very same moment of light
that emerges from the apiculus and blows in milky rain in opales-
cent flows that coat the brain, it's all one thing between the One

and Two, between the clown opisthographs when Clyde handed
me that big unwieldy wormy thing (ya have one of ya own, ya
done need hiz no mo), and it's a beautiful day Al cuz today I get
the fuck of a lifetime, cuz today the clouds part in hell and all the
aspens on the peaks glow crimson (we gonna see it thru smoke
lenzes, it's too brite to see wit nakked eyes, we down our boiling
drinks and diskoo biskettes and we party yeah we party harty)
yeah today Clyde's cut he's cut down deep today his letters start
to rot it's all so crazy it's a bountiful day down here in hell and
a blood-red moon is dawning and today spells the death of letters
and the Day of Poetic Judgment but I guess I can't help it I
have to stop yacking, hand me my raiment Al, I shall put my
ponderous hand by the hole of his door and his hole shall open
for me, his worst fucking nightmare I'm gonna cram this dildo
up his ass I'm gonna cram this dildo up his ass Al up his fucking
swollen ass, so hand me my dildo hand me my raiment Al baby

Two

Fractions. Portions of numbers.

Letters have fractions, too. One Ath. Two Bth. The algebra of linguistic disease. Inversions. Nightmare holding patterns. Calculitic repetitions of negative alphabetic exponents. To a mathematician, all of the letters are simply unknowns: everybody knows what a one is, but nobody knows what an A is. I can look inside a letter and see the smaller letters: the unreal and imaginary letters. Prime letters that cannot be penetrated by others.

Certain letters have bomblike fissures. Certain people don't. Certain people can't be cut. They can't be pierced. They can't be hurt. They refuse to bleed. They cannot be milked. They cannot be divided into smaller versions of themselves. They have no interior functions, no echoes except a plastic box with clouds in it. Canned laughter. A box that robs them of language and spirit.

A television.

The average young American searches for self-realization with a channel selector. He doesn't understand he's a victim, he is so utterly robbed. Minds and vocabularies emptied. Shopping armies trudging across mallae incognitae. Gun manufacturers turning out customized assault weapons for babies. Arsenists poisoning the arsonists who immolate the arsenists. *Agape.* Cranial love. *Fellating the warden,* the summation of the human condition.

I can describe barren walls, and this is my victory. I can describe desolation, and this is my poetry. But the isolation of children who are raised in a world of cheap, corrosive objects, this I cannot describe. I can only report it.

Billy. The most intelligent man I ever met. My only other love besides Mom and Barbie. Dead Billy. His ruptured flesh. A couple weeks before I met Barbie in the deli, I received a telephone call from Bridgette. She had shot Billy and dissolved his body in a tub of acid. She begged me for money. Now I can say it. It doesn't matter. She went back to Lapland. She went back to living off the land. Ferocious smell as the last dissolvable thing in the body turns liquid. The logical opposite of an egg. Floating words and gestures. Campbell Soup. Billy, my only other love. Snow teeth. Lithe but heavy. Slow moving. Blasting warmth in a world of ice. Layered honey smells in the honied cell of the cell block. Union of my black and his white. African ecstasy. A cleansing and emptying. All the ghoulish voices gone but one, I heard the voices disappear as I came, and now my clown talks to ghosts. He talks to voices that are dearly departed. He talks to dead psychiatrists and agents. He talks to helper-skeletons. He talks to other clowns, who will never talk again.

How could my love for Billy kill those separate voices? Is there such a thing as a dead voice?—the most ancient mystery, pondered at the back of caves. (Thousands of years ago, the birth of art, the final outcry of the caribou in the skull of Magdalenian man, displayed.) Ah! Put the values back on the wall. Make the reindeer sing again. Put them back in cavelight. Show them to our children. Make them haul our shopping sleighs.

Lascaux, Lascaux, it's off to work we go!
Art and torment.

Since that first solid line on stone, poetry has never changed, but here in my special cave, all the other voices are defunct and only one voice remains. And sometimes it isn't mine.

Do you see? Do you see?
I call it the voice of a clown, but perhaps it's the voice of a bee!

A garden. Every garden, this garden, the first garden. Night. Every Eden is tonight, or perhaps Gesthemane? *Behold the son of man is betrayed into the hands of sinners.* Deep refulgent night. Glistening, perfect starlight. Before the stillbirth of night the moon shone in letters and on buttons in delight. The moon gave birth to Nyx. And

276

before the moon? There was the center of the moon. And before the center of the moon?

There was the word "Moon." A soundless word. A dead voice. But alphabetic:

MoooOOOO OOOOOOOo OOOOOOOOOOO OOOOOOOOOO OOOOOOOO OOOOOOOO OOOOoooo OOOOOOOOOOO

ooooooOOO
OooooooOOO
OOOOooooo
OOOOOOO

nnnnnnnₙₙ

And before the word "Moon," the thought of the word.

And before the very thought, before that first thought of the word that made the thing of the word happen, there was a thought a single thought a thought that was given birth, a thought that arose from nightless night, from the inside of swords and words and knives and guns and statues. A thought that took away the will of statues, so that the statues had to sit on thrones with their hands lashed and be worshiped and brutally whipped. Primal worship. The primal scenes, and as I dug into Barbie, I felt my skin open, empurpled gape, and bleed. The hurt entire. Entirely, the flames dripped down from the napalm surface. Plunging dermal fire. Deep touchless orgasms. Multiple. Endless. Carried in intense pools of artificial basement light. The letters, faux-peau, came alive and cavorted in flourescent torches and formed the songs I later wrote down. Sonnets of adoration. Precise. Steel. Sonnets from blades. *Barbie Ballads*. Not yet published.

Barbie, my love. My cherished and divine. Maybe she was paid, as that piece of whoreshit Cookie stated. I know it was possible, but it didn't matter how she came, *as long as she came for me.* All of the history, the history of this book and nation, the histories I have written, the histories that will be written about Daniel Quentin Abernathy and all the other pompous Abernathies, all of the histories cannot explain how and why a human being comes. But the gushing smell, the taught, sweet rigidity, the dawn sigh of Lucifer escaping from the ravageable body, this is the source of love, this is the source of war. This is the source of lasting Peace. Peace. Peace. A string of faultless sighs!

For on this spiritual cross condemnëd lying,
To pains infernal by eternal doom,
I see my Savior for the same sins dying,
And from that hell I feared, to free me, come.

Barbie, my love, I sang to the rising moon, as I sat under a ragged tree. A nameless spot somewhere under the sky in Washington, DC. Waiting for my ascent up the Temple Mount, this epiphanic moment, fasting from Stoli, davening, the Lincoln Memorial only blocks and an hour away, Please Barbie please, I fervently prayed, forgive me, that I would, staring into a cup of coffee, put my soul first. Put my soul before your glorious sanctity. In prison, I could, when the pressure was too severe, all meaning and breathing condensed in the dank corners of my cell, find love and soulfulness in the arms of another poet, but here in a world where I am allowed to roam free, discontented, animalistic and barren, my soul and love are divided, reft, and I have chosen soul.

And you will have to wait.

I must go up the stairs of a monument to be saved. Up from this quiet garden. Up from this thickening moonlight, this brimstone of delusion.

Take away this cup from me.

My entire life, I have waited for the coming hour.

V'yaas elohim et sh'na ha'morot. Precise luminaries, to tell us the names of the light and the dark.

Moon, hallowed moon, I prayed, protect my beloved and keep her safe. Moon, do not hurt us. Cleanse us with hyssop and snow. Soothe us with soundless lunacies. Preserve my Barbie. Preserve my precious sanity.

Voices tore me. Weakening ligatures. Tectonic rumblings. Bodies carried in purses. Bodies dropped into the mouths of basins, into the bottoms of ashcans, like drops of blood dripped into the mouth of a suffocating bat.

Moon, hallowed moon, I prayed, let me tread your far oceanic paths! My worst suffering has been the impossibility of forgetting the first time that I was ever slapped. I remember the peaceful cradle, deep down deep in my past. The twinkling planetarium of a baby's bedroom and delight. I remember the Aryan descent of the horned hand. Paternal might!

Moon, tender and infrangible! Moon, perfect and adorable! Let me climb your sad silver mountains, shining on the upturned lips of virgin creeks and puddles.

Moon, let me ascend, let me soar, let me sing, let me suck at your gelid magnificent breasts!

Moon O Moon, let me climb your sad silver mountains of death!

that all our props shoot blanks, including the one down-in-between and here I am on the couch, Doc getting intercrural, and it's time to get up and go *ah Franklin* it's time to flex some malignant muscle *now hast thou but one bare hour to live* cuz those voices I heard last night when Clyde was seeing triple, which the poor slob thought was double, his synchronously sodden hemispheres grinding along independently, have made me so puffed up that my innards are set to release the pesky microbes *and then thou must be damned perpetually* I'm so sick I'm dolleerious *stand still, you ever moving spheres of heaven* my colon has acute clownitis *that time may cease, and midnight never come* I think I'm gonna fart myself into oblivion *fair Nature's eye, rise, rise again and make perpetual day; or let this hour be but a year, a month, a week, a natural day* I think I'm going to let the Big One go `that Franklin may repent and save his soul` ya know we all swim down God's cervix toward the holy lights *the stars move still, time runs, the clock will strike* toward the pendulous clusters **the devil will come, and Franklin must be damn'd**

and you gotta go down to the far end, past the G Spot to the Hot Spot **see, see, where Christ's blood streams in the firma-ment!** toward the frail umbilic light *one drop would save his soul, half a drop* toward the beatific protoplasmic stakes *see where God stretcheth out his arm and bends his ireful brows* toward God's vineyard *mountains and hills, come, come, and fall on him, and hide him from the heavy wrath of God* and there you gotta pick your own shiny grape *then will he headlong run into the earth: earth gape! O no it will not harbour him!* your own reincarnated escapade *ah, half the hour is past! 'twill all be passed anon* your own viscous brand-new egg of frustration and pain and heartache *oh God, if thou wilt not have mercy on his soul, yet for Christ's sake, whose blood hath ransom'd him, impose some end to his incessant pain* cuz what's the alternative Doc? *let Franklin live in hell a thousand years, a hundred thousand, and at last be sav'd!* *O, no end is limited to* *damned souls!* It's metempsychosic if you think about it **Pythagoras' metempsychosis were that true, his soul should fly from him and he be changed unto some brutish beast!** and Clyde could just as easily have been born next door and grown up to be a pediatric cardiologist and not a clownophilic alphabeticist `all beasts are happy, for, when they die, their souls are soon dissolved in elements` he could have had a mom who touched him and a dad without a cat-o-nine, he could have had a buddy named Timmy and the keys to the Caddie *but his must live still to be plagu'd in hell* he could have been raised in a house without a sawed-off shotgun and been hugged and kissed and coddled and flattered and taught tennis **cursed be the parents that engender'd him** I mean Doc we're all the victims of destiny, a stile of pantiles linked together, a chain gang of emotional cripples, a trickle of acid running into a grievous sough of sorrow *no, Franklin,* **curse** *thyself* but here I am, lying on this clowncouch clown-associating, and it's so peaceful out there on the steps of the monument **curse** *SNBD that hath de-*

prived thee of the joys of heaven it's so quiet out there in the park where Clyde stands breathing mist and waiting for the clock to strike and for the strike on the matchbox guillotine to commence its ineluctable tumble, yeah it's one of life's little clownadoxes, like you studied when you got your magna cum laughter, it's one of life's antinomies that it's one low laugh from cradle to grave *O, it strikes it strikes!* you can have all the Lincolns in the world but they'll never stop the laughter when one man views another man's pain, they'll never stop the roar of the hyena in a man's soul as it hunches over the bodies cuz that's the clownadox, the causa causans of the causa causata *now body turn to air* whether you're in Keokuk or Bangkok, whether you're a Maoist or a Taoist or a Bowwowist, whether you're a Chinese doctor or a Yiddishe macher or a gluteal penetrator, that one man's pain is another man's pleasure *or SNBD will bear thee quick to hell!* and now Clyde's up there on the stairs, it was planned that way to place him where he would look down and see the evil spirit coming towards him, where he could see the messenger with smoke coming out of his neck, a demon with flames between his teeth mounting with a message as the helicons thundered tuneful in the heavens *O soul, be changed into little water-drops and fall into the ocean, ne'er be found!* ya know Doc, that nightmare priest could have written it larger and he didn't have to use a number, it was pure evil, like E=mc squared, it was an evil formula that this priest thought up but devils are artists cuz evil without art is a legless ballet, and this priest is a magus, a Faustian famulus! Doc he had Clyde's number right from the start, and now he is about to hand it to him, he is about to hand poor Clyde his number. What a joke! The Big Guy upstairs places a suffering poet in the world who can't count and then he hands him a sour grape and a number. It isn't One and it isn't Two. It's a hoot and howl *look not so fierce on him adders and serpents, let him breathe a while!* it's Hamlet in a brown study, it's a leaf at the top of a tree, it's Mother Nature, Doc it's the way it has to be *ugly hell, gape not!* but now before I go and call up Al and ask him to wire you the money for your fee, I want my diagnosis cuz I'm not coming back **come not Lucifer** I've come to the end of my therapy and I'm heading out to do battle with the waves, it's the Clownic Twilight, I'm gonna take on those waves, but I want my diagnosis cuz that's what money buys *he'll burn his books* it buys a bogus diagnosis or so they tell me. What will it be? *he'll burn his motherfucking books* I'm trying to tune my horn to the essence of reality. I'm trying to play in the key of C *ah ah ah ahhhhhhhhhh* *Mephistophilis!* They could have sent me to another family. Why did the label have to say Franklin? *hahahahahahahhahaha Mephistophilis!* What a way to run a grape juice company! *hehehehehehehehehehe*

One

Abe sits immobile on his throne.

There isn't anything he can do, since all the slaves are supposedly released. There are no more slavemasters outside the boudoirs, yet all the citizens are bowing down for dollars, pushing shekels across the floors proboscically, lapping up the spittle of their economic betters. The real Lincoln was shot while the audience was laughing. He was shot in the head while watching a comedy. I looked up at the ponderous figure and imagined a bullet crashing through his pallium. Sometime in the future, this temple and this man will be forgotten, buried under layers of worthless currency. Honest Ozymandias, he'll move out of history and stay that way forever, because our offspring won't have shovels.

It was cold enough to see my breath. The surface of the reflecting pond flared, acid-etched. Below, on the streets, the vets were hawking their wares out of striped tents. Tourists wandered on the steps and in the arcades of the monument.

What can the blackness see? What can a statue witness? These are more than theoretical questions, since for poets the moon is the oculus of darkness and its light is the enduring energy of human absence. The moon in patience sees the cracks on the surface of the sun and registers the upcoming explosion as it unfolds over eons, and once a month it beams down its evidence—a perfect radiance, the fullness of a disk that precedes all endings.

With how sad steps, O moon, though climbst the skys;
How silently, and with how wan a face.

Awe and drunkenness, wonder and carnage, engaged again and again under the full moon. Legions of saints in the wilderness,

Muromachi sages hoisting fermented rice above their mats, startled corpses on the battlefields staring into the roundness with riveted eyes, the moonlight is the only remedy for the cold that is colder than cold. Only the heat of the moon will do.

I stood trembling in front of Abe in the center of the stairhead, as the light merged into completion and a separate world was created. (The sun is one, the moon is two, and the earth is yet another.) Abe and I entered the momentary conjunction, and statue and murderer experienced a similar thing: tides stretched; within oceans, brains, bellies and cells, within the anatomies of poets and objects, everything strained and pulled away. All I had done had led to this—the years of suffering and pilgrimage since I stared in horror into my bloodied lap at Du-pars and began my search through poetry and ecstatic prayer for answers and salvation, like the legendary Jew who stood in a field outside the shul, reciting his demotic alphabet—and I saw him rising out of a mist, a barely-distinguishable spirit in a halo of seething light, my savior mounting in uniform directly in front of the obelisk, coming toward me, cutting through the shifting clots of tourists. He seemed to be emerging from an empty visibility, from a dusky wormhole at the center of a fabulous void. A nimbus of milky fire hung about his knees. I heard dull breathing, the air above me, flexing its frayed seams. At first the creature appeared human, but as he climbed

one two one

two one two

one two one

two one two
one two one
two one two
one two one

his features formed up, and with crippling, electric terror, I realized that this was a *demon of death* stalking out of the balefire, coming to claim me, to reap me and penetrate me and thrust me down!! I had been tricked! Seduced! He held something magical in his hand. A fork? A sickle? A gun? A wand? He wasn't looking at me, but he knew where I was. The coldness of the night congealed and jellified, the light froze in the air and the brightness died. My brain was on fire. I couldn't make my muscles work my lungs. Knifing, hacking horror!

I was paralyzed.

I waited for the furious spirit to arrive, but everything and everyone was locked in place, he couldn't move and neither could I, all the clocks were suspended, and I identified, as I saw who this wraith actually was.

Would this instant last an eternity?? Time became a single frame on a roll of film, a never-ending still. Nothing budged, but everywhere the clocks were striking. I was lodged forever in a cemented moment of approaching anguish and evil, tossing eternally in a cold, eventless hell. A hell of clanging bells. I began to loop, to think the same thought over and over and over and over and over and over

and over and over and ooooooooOooOooooooOOooooo
ooooooverstuvwxyzabcdefghijklmnopqrstuvwxyzabcdefghijkl
mnopqrstuvwxyzabcdefghijklmnopqrstuvwxyzabcdefghijklm
nopqrstuvwxyzabcdefghijklmnopqrstuvwxyzabcdefghijklmn
opqrstuvwxyzabcdefghijklmnopqrstuvwxyzabcdefghijklmno
pqrstuvwxyzabcdefghijklmnopqrstuvwxyzabcdefghijklmnop
qrstuvwxyzabcdefghijklmnopqrstuvwxyzabcdefghijklmnopq
rstuvwxyzabcdefghijklmnopqrstuvwxyzabcdefghijklmnopqr
stuvwxyzabcdefghijklmnopqrstuvwxyzabcdefghijklmnopqrs
tuvwxyzabcdefghijklmnopqrstuvwxyzabcdefghijklmnopqrst
uvwxyzabcdefghijklmnopqrstuvwxyzabcdefghijklmnopqrstu
vwxyzabcdefghijklmnopqrstuvwxyzabcdefghijklmnopqrstuv
wxyzabcdefghijklmnopqrstuvwxyzabcdefghijklmnopqrstuvw
xyzabcdefghijklmnopqrstuvwxyzabcdefghijklmnopqrstuvwx
yzabcdefghijklmnopqrstuvwxyzabcdefghijklmnopqrstuvwxy
zabcdefghijklmnopqrstuvwxyzabcdefghijklmnopqrstuvwxyz
abcdefghijklmnopqrstuvwxyzabcdefghijklmnopqrstuvwxyza
bcdefghijklmnopqrstuvwxyzabcdefghijklmnopqrstuvwxyzab
cdefghijklmnopqrstuvwxyzabcdefghijklmnopqrstuvwxyzabc
defghijklmnopqrstuvwxyzabcdefghijklmnopqrstuvwxyzabcd
efghijklmnopqrstuvwxyzabcdefghijklmnopqrstuvwxyzabcde
fghijklmnopqrstuvwxyzabcdefghijklmnopqrstuvwxyzabcdef
ghijklmnopqrstuvwxyzabcdefghijklmnopqrstuvwxyzabcdefg
hijklmnopqrstuvwxyzabcdefghijklmnopqrstuvwxyzabcdefgh
ijklmnopqrstuvwxyzabcdefghijklmnopqrstuvwxyzabcdefghi
jklmnopqrstuvwxyzabcdefghijklmnopqrstuvwxyzabcdefghij
klmnopqrstuvwxyzabcdefghijklmnopqrstuvwxyzabcdefghijk
lmnopqrstuvwxyzabcdefghijklmnopqrstuvwxyzabcdefghijkl
mnopqrstuvwxyzabcdefghijklmnopqrstuvwxyzabcdefghijklm
nopqrstuvwxyzabcdefghijklmnopqrstuvwxyzabcdefghijklmn
opqrstuvwxyzabcdefghijklmnopqrstuvwxyzabcdefghijklmno
pqrstuvwxyzabcdefghijklmnopqrstuvwxyzabcdefghijklmnop
qrstuvwxyzabcdefghijklmnopqrstuvwxyzabcdefghijklmnopq
rstuvwxyzabcdefghijklmnopqrstuvwxyzabcdefghijklmnopqr

stuvwxyzabcdefghijklmnopqrstuvwxyzabcdefghijklmnopqrs
tuvwxyzabcdefghijklmnopqrstuvwxyzabcdefghijklmnopqrst
uvwxyzabcdefghijklmnopqrstuvwxyzabcdefghijklmnopqrstu
vwxyzabcdefghijklmnopqrstuvwxyzabcdefghijklmnopqrstuv
wxyzabcdefghijklmnopqrstuvwxyzabcdefghijklmnopqrstuvw
xyzabcdefghijklmnopqrstuvwxyzabcdefghijklmnopqrstuvwx
yzabcdefghijklmnopqrstuvwxyzabcdefghijklmnopqrstuvwxy
zabcdefghijklmnopqrstuvwxyzabcdefghijklmnopqrstuvwxyz
abcdefghijklmnopqrstuvwxyzabcdefghijklmnopqrstuvwxyza
bcdefghijklmnopqrstuvwxyzabcdefghijklmnopqrstuvwxyzab
cdefghijklmnopqrstuvwxyzabcdefghijklmnopqrstuvwxyzabc
defghijklmnopqrstuvwxyzabcdefghijklmnopqrstuvwxyzabcd
efghijklmnopqrstuvwxyzabcdefghijklmnopqrstuvwxyzabcde
fghijklmnopqrstuvwxyzabcdefghijklmnopqrstuvwxyzabcdef
ghijklmnopqrstuvwxyzabcdefghijklmnopqrstuvwxyzabcdefg
hijklmnopqrstuvwxyzabcdefghijklmnopqrstuvwxyzabcdefgh
ijklmnopqrstuvwxyzabcdefghijklmnopqrstuvwxyzabcdefghi
jklmnopqrstuvwxyzabcdefghijklmnopqrstuvwxyzabcdefghij
klmnopqrstuvwxyzabcdefghijklmnopqrstuvwxyzabcdefghijk
lmnopqrstuvwxyzabcdefghijklmnopqrstuvwxyzabcdefghijkl
mnopqrstuvwxyzabcdefghijklmnopqrstuvwxyzabcdefghijklm
nopqrstuvwxyzabcdefghijklmnopqrstuvwxyzabcdefghijklmn
opqrstuvwxyzabcdefghijklmnopqrstuvwxyzabcdefghijklmno
pqrstuvwxyzabcdefghijklmnopqrstuvwxyzabcdefghijklmnop
qrstuvwxyzabcdefghijklmnopqrstuvwxyzabcdefghijklmnopq
rstuvwxyzabcdefghijklmnopqrstuvwxyzabcdefghijklmnopqr
stuvwxyzabcdefghijklmnopqrstuvwxyzabcdefghijklmnopqrs
tuvwxyzabcdefghijklmnopqrstuvwxyzabcdefghijklmnopqrst
uvwxyzabcdefghijklmnopqrstuvwxyzabcdefghijklmnopqrstu
vwxyzabcdefghijklmnopqrstuvwxyzabcdefghijklmnopqrstuv
wxyzabcdefghijklmnopqrstuvwxyzabcdefghijklmnopqrstuvw
xyzabcdefghijklmnopqrstuvwxyzabcdefghijklmnopqrstuvwx
yzabcdefghijklmnopqrstuvwxyzabcdefghijklmnopqrstuvwxy
zabcdefghijklmnopqrstuvwxyzabcdefghijklmnopqrstuvwxyz

abcdefghijklmnopqrstuvwxyzabcdefghijklmnopqrstuvwxyza
bcdefghijklmnopqrstuvwxyzabcdefghijklmnopqrstuvwxyzab
cdefghijklmnopqrstuvwxyzabcdefghijklmnopqrstuvwxyzabc
defghijklmnopqrstuvwxyzabcdefghijklmnopqrstuvwxyzabcd
efghijklmnopqrstuvwxyzabcdefghijklmnopqrstuvwxyzabcde
fghijklmnopqrstuvwxyzabcdefghijklmnopqrstuvwxyzabcdef
ghijklmnopqrstuvwxyzabcdefghijklmnopqrstuvwxyzabcdefg
hijklmnopqrstuvwxyzabcdefghijklmnopqrstuvwxyzabcdefgh
ijklmnopqrstuvwxyzabcdefghijklmnopqrstuvwxyzabcdefghi
jklmnopqrstuvwxyzabcdefghijklmnopqrstuvwxyzabcdefghij
klmnopqrstuvwxyzabcdefghijklmnopqrstuvwxyzabcdefghijk
lmnopqrstuvwxyzabcdefghijklmnopqrstuvwxyzabcdefghijkl
mnopqrstuvwxyzabcdefghijklmnopqrstuvwxyzabcdefghijklm
nopqrstuvwxyzabcdefghijklmnopqrstuvwxyzabcdefghijklmn
opqrstuvwxyzabcdefghijklmnopqrstuvwxyzabcdefghijklmno
pqrstuvwxyzabcdefghijklmnopqrstuvwxyzabcdefghijklmnop
qrstuvwxyzabcdefghijklmnopqrstuvwxyzabcdefghijklmnopq
rstuvwxyzabcdefghijklmnopqrstuvwxyzabcdefghijklmnopqr
stuvwxyzabcdefghijklmnopqrstuvwxyzabcdefghijklmnopqrs
tuvwxyzabcdefghijklmnopqrstuvwxyzabcdefghijklmnopqrst
uvwxyzabcdefghijklmnopqrstuvwxyzabcdefghijklmnopqrstu
vwxyzabcdefghijklmnopqrstuvwxyzabcdefghijklmnopqrstuv
wxyzabcdefghijklmnopqrstuvwxyzabcdefghijklmnopqrstuvw
xyzabcdefghijklmnopqrstuvwxyzabcdefghijklmnopqrstuvwx
yzabcdefghijklmnopqrstuvwxyzabcdefghijklmnopqrstuvwxy
zabcdefghijklmnopqrstuvwxyzabcdefghijklmnopqrstuvwxyz
abcdefghijklmnopqrstuvwxyzabcdefghijklmnopqrstuvwxyza
bcdefghijklmnopqrstuvwxyzabcdefghijklmnopqrstuvwxyzab
cdefghijklmnopqrstuvwxyzabcdefghijklmnopqrstuvwxyzabc
defghijklmnopqrstuvwxyzabcdefghijklmnopqrstuvwxyzabcd
efghijklmnopqrstuvwxyzabcdefghijklmnopqrstuvwxyzabcde
fghijklmnopqrstuvwxyzabcdefghijklmnopqrstuvwxyzabcdef
ghijklmnopqrstuvwxyzabcdefghijklmnopqrstuvwxyzabcdefg
hijklmnopqrstuvwxyzabcdefghijklmnopqrstuvwxyzabcdefgh

ijklmnopqrstuvwxyzabcdefghijklmnopqrstuvwxyzabcdefghi
jklmnopqrstuvwxyzabcdefghijklmnopqrstuvwxyzabcdefghij
klmnopqrstuvwxyzaaaaaaaaagain and again, like the helpless Jew in
the field, who prayed for forgiveness and offered his moiré veil of
letters to God. How long it lasted, a second, a minute, or even a
conscious infinity, I cannot remember, but suddenly I was redeemed
as the demon jerked into movement and continued his relentless
march up the stairs, and then at that second that minute that letter
that alphabet that hour that year that thought that terror that lifetime
that eternity something cracked inside of me, something ichorous
spilled, something fractured that could never be repaired again.

The pieces and voices were now too small.

Bimbambooom

The bomb!

My spirit soared into the heavens, accepted into the azure and
fleecy bosom of God. Wrapped in warmth, pampered and hugged.

And what was left below was damned eternally. Ah,
Mephistopheles!!

"Clyde Wayne Franklin?" he spoke in a muffled, gravelly voice.
I could see yellow flames between his teeth with cobalt tips that
guttered in his eyes. A gull was perched on his shoulder, with an

upper row of canines. Saliva was flowing from its beak. A tooth was missing. My head filled with a cloudy hum.

"Yes. But you're not Colonel Oberstar, are you?"

I could hardly speak. It seemed that multiple voices were coming out of my mouth. New languages conversing in my head, whispering into another set of dimensions. The soldier I was facing was sullen and preoccupied in his uniform and cap. His unpigmented skin was covered with carbuncles. There was smoke coming out of his neck. He had no ribbons or other decorations—only a nametag that said Mark. His soft unformed mouth was the piebald mouth of a tortured bat. I could see deep into his throat.

In his fauces, motes were dancing in flames. All of the motes had names.

"No, I'm hardly a colonel," the hellkite smiled. "Action Messenger Service. Please sign."

The sky was filled with a clamor of brass. The moon was pulsing. The moon was giving birth to something. In the tangles of my belly I was conceiving. I felt indescribable pleasure in my lowest parts and then sharp pain, as the satanic thing within me started growing. A new foetus began forming. New moon; old moon. My eyes went blurry. I signed the paper without thinking and was handed a black envelope. On the front were my initials in burnished gold. It was sealed with creamy wax. When I touched it, the blood in my hands and the blood on my hands painfully began to burn. I had wet my pants.

"Who sent you?" I screamed. Tides, nausea and bile careened through my body.

But the demon had turned and was gliding down the stairway.

He was laughing. All the tourists were looking at me. They were laughing. Abe was laughing.

I was laughing.

I moved to a corner of the peristyle and leaned against a column. It was white-hot. I recoiled. Molten currents streamed down entasic lines, bowing out, reaching toward the moon, bubbling, boiling in the flutes. An alphabetic brew. There was a faint smell of sulphur. Letters were winding counterclockwise up the column. Pillar of God! Connecting heaven and hell. Divine tuning fork! Impenetrable bass ringing in the centerline, unknowable, unhearable! Perfect symbol!

I ripped open the envelope. There was nothing inside.

I looked again.

In the corner was a scrap of paper about the size of a postage stamp. I hurried into the main area of the monument and examined it carefully in the light. Was I supposed to lick it? Was it a potion?

It appeared to be blank.

I flipped it over.

On the paper were a typed number and letter.

9W

Again I looked in the envelope. It was filled with thick black worms.

White glue was oozing out of their mouths.

I dropped it on the ground.

I could deal with the W, but the 9 meant nothing to me. I staggered into the night and sat on an upper step. I began to repeat the formula like a mantra. I wanted to brand it into my head. I knew if only I burned it deep enough, it would do its subtle work for me 9W9W9W9W9W9W9W9W9W9W9W9W9W9W9W
9W9W9W9W9W9W9W9W9W9W9W9W9W9W9W
9W9W9W9W9W9W9W9W9W9W9W9W9W9W9W
9W9W9W9W9W9W9W9W9W9W9W9W9W9W9W
9W9W9W9W9W9W9W9W9W9W9W9W9W9W9W
9W9W9W9W9W9W9W9W9W9W9W9W9W9W9W
9W9W9W9W9W9W9W9W9W9W9W9W9W9W9W

9W9W9W9W9W9W9W9W9W9W9W9W9W9W9W9W9W
9W9W9W9W9W9W9W9W9W9W9W9W9W9W9W9W9W
9W9W9W9W9W9W9W9W9W9W9W9W9W9W9W9W9W
9W9W9W9W9W9W9W9W9W9W9W9W9W9W9W9W9W
9W9W9W9W9W9W9W9W9W9W9W9W9W9W9W9W9W
9W9W9W9W9W9W9W9W9W9W9W9W9W9W9W9W9W
9W9W9W9W9W9W9W9W9W9W9W9W9W9W9W9W9W
9W9W9W9W9W9W9W9W9W9W9W9W9W9W9W9W9W
9W9W9W9W9W9W9W9W9W9W9W9W9W9W9W9W9W
9W9W9W9W9W9W9W9W9W9W9W9W9W9W9W9W9W
9W9W9W9W9W9W9W9W9W9W9W9W9W9W9W9W9W
9W9W9W9W9W9W9W9W9W9W9W9W9W9W9W9W9W
9W9W9W9W9W9W9W9W9W9W9W9W9W9W9W9W9W
9W9W9W9W9W9W9W9W9W9W9W9W9W9W9W9W9W
9W9W9W9W9W9W9W9W9W9W9W9W9W9W9W9W9W
9W9W9W9W9W9W9W9W9W9W9W9W9W9W9W9W9W
9W9W9W9W9W9W9W9W9W9W9W9W9W9W9W9W9W

Should I go to a telephone and call Lenny Dalls? 9W9W9W9
W9W9W. No, there was something here that was only for me.

9W

9W

9W

Then I had a second realization, and my scalp contracted in fear. My head fell into my hands.

I recalled the priest's words. The priest who had sent me this demon. He had told me that I wasn't hearing what he was saying, he had warned me that I wasn't hearing his message, that I would receive the message and wouldn't understand. He had told me I would be deaf and doubtful and bereft.

I now realized that this number and this letter was the message, and that they would explain everything. Right from the beginning, it was intended to get me here and hand me this piddling scrap of paper that would change my life. From that first moment on the airplane, when he told me about the flak, this scene on the steps had been planned. The letter, the number, the devil (not human), the gull, the envelope filled with vomitous worms, the additional presence humming in my brain, the bomb and all my tiny Clydelike pieces, the priest had foreseen it all.

I thought again about the letter. W. What was a W?

I couldn't make it out. W. W. W. W. W. W. W.

Nine W. Nine W. Nine W. Nine W. Nine W. Nine W. Nine W. Nine W.

Work. Wayne. Wisdom. Worship. Waste. War. Wreckroom. Warlock. Whore.

It made no sense. My W was located on my left tricep. Perhaps it was some sort of direction.

West!

I looked down the steps. I saw the people, the trees, the street, the tents.

The tents!!

I understood! I understood everything! I looked back at Abe. He was looking and pointing and winking. He was looking where I should have been looking all the time!

He was looking directly at Colonel Harmon Oberstar!

So simple, beyond the stairs, there in the darkness under the moonlight, slightly to the left, he was there. The colonel was waiting for me.

A worm-infested ghost in flame!

Waiting to announce a slaughter!

Clarions. Strange Irish words coming out of the statue. Lincoln the Emancipator who removed all chains! The polished, clinky chains of basement slaves! Lincoln the Celtic Hassid, mad and howling and chanting and laughing! Lincoln, destroyer of virulent German whips! Yes, he had told me over and over, he had described to me his genius, his precision and method. Everything must lead inevitably to my destruction. The priest had taken over my mind. He had controlled me. He had changed identities. He had shattered me.

It wasn't at the Lincoln Memorial that I would meet my destiny. *It would happen at another memorial!*

Off to the left I could see its muted lights. I raced down the stairs and across the boulevard into the park. I was screaming. People were staring at me. I pushed a man out of my way. Down Down Down. He had studied me. A cold-blooded slayer. Playing the music of descent. He knew that, as I stumbled down the basement steps, other spirits had risen to greet me, singing invitingly. I was beginning to remember.

There were the people mourning, and there were the austere slabs.

The numbers shone in the lighting of the Vietnam Memorial Monument. Limbo. I ran along the western wing, heading east toward the rising moon. Toward the name. Toward what the priest had always meant. *Caveat lector!* There was no need to count. The ninth plaque on the west side.

9W

The procession of the dead.

It didn't take me long to find him. He was halfway down. Harmon J. Oberstar. Listed falsely as a man who had died in defense of his country.

An assassination victim.

The priest had never stopped killing!!

I knelt before the plaque and said a prayer to Baby Jesus, but on a cross somewhere high above, my savior was laughing. Comedy and religion, he boomed like a bomb, comedy and religion were created at the very same time.

Fracture, insanity, pieces pieces peace peace.

Bouquets were piled in front of the lights, along with a few letters and medallions and trinkets. I picked up a bunch of chrysanthemums and ripped them to shreds.

Inside me were clowns. Two plus one. They were screaming.

They were tormenting me. Past moments flew by. Moments of tenderness and brutality. Everyone around me was screaming. I heard the crash of the chair, the lash of the whip. The hartebeest bellow of Dad. The sobbing songs of Mom. The lights caressing the names of the dead turned red.

What had I done? Lord Jesus, *Adonai*, why have you abandoned me? In this final moment of devotion, in this final instant of sanity, wash the blood of my parents from my unclean hands. Cease to punish me, please I beg You, please God please.

I screamed again. I screamed her name. I screamed again and again and again and again. I understood!

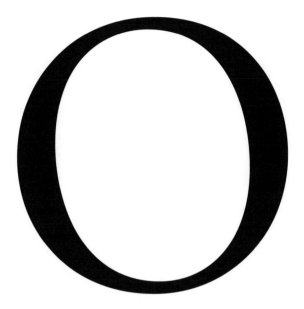

no! moon no! moon no! moon no! moon

noooooooo

 no! moon no! moon no! moon no! moon

noooooooo

 no! moon no! moon no! moon no! moon

noooooooo

 no! moon no! moon no! moon no! moon

noooooooo

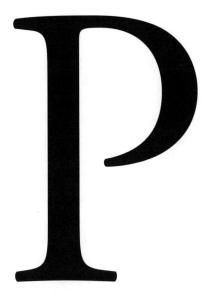

he he heehee heh heh heh yeh yeah one woe is past and behold, there come two woes more hereafter one woe past, two more hereafter he he heh heh heh yeah I could fly, I could take my pale horse and ride, I could piss fire and shit smoke, I could spew brimstone from my wine-stained mouth, I could cleave rainbows and fogbows and moonbows, the beast that ascendeth out of the bottomless pit I could dandle and gorge with comfits, woooooo eeeee, wooooooooeee, the great whore who sitteth upon the infected toilet seats is drunk with the blood of saints, and if Albert Einstein, the father and son consubstantiate, wooooee, if Al and Einstein were one, cognomen and agnomen, balled and burlapped, if Albert Einstein were conjoined at the hip, if the Jew and the Chinese were made Siamese, if the shill and the shrink could sell as well as heal, could write both contracts and extracts, could make me wealthy and make me whole, if this could be done by God, I'd fly and rend the air, I'd sear the obnubilate light, a polkopterodactyl in the guise of a ravenous clown, I'd bury my sickle in the clouds and let the ruby drops rain down. Babylon beware the wrath of a clown! The voices of the harpers shall be heard no more! Dogs, sorcerers, murderers, scoundrels and whoremongers! Moongazers!
DDDDDDDDDDDDowngodownDDDDDDDDDDDDowngo
downDDDDDDDDDDDDDDDDDDDDDDDDDDDDDDDDDD
DDDDDDDDDDDDDDDDDDDDDDDDDDDDDDDDDDDDD
DDDDDDDDDDDDDDDDDDDDDDDDDowngodownDDDDD
DDDDDDDDDDDDDDDDDDDDDDDDDDDDDDDDDDDDD
DDDDDDDDDEEEEEEEEEEEEEEEEEEEEEEEEEEEEEEE

EEEEEEEEEEEEEEEEEEEEEEEEEEEEEEEEEE Fun
FFFFFFFFFF
FFFFFFFFFF
FFFFFFFFFun
have
funggg ggggggggggggggggggggggggg
ggggggggggggghhhhhhhiiiiiiiiiiiiiiiiiiiiIIIIIIIIIIIIIIIIIIIam having
funyeah IIIIIIIIIIm have fun writing pangrams I am that I
amjjjjjjjjjjjkkkkkkkkkkkkkkkkkkkkkkkkkkkkkkkkkkkkkkkkkkpicketkkkk
kkkkkkkkkkkkkkkkkkkkkkkkkkkkkkkkkkkkkkkkkkkkkkkkkkpicketkkkkk
kkkkkkkkkkkkkkkkkkkkkkkkkkkkillkkkkkkkkkkkkkkkkkkkkkkkkkkkk
kkkkkkkkkkkkkkkkkkkkkkkkkkkkkkkkkkkkkkkkkkkkkkkkkkkkkkkkkk
kkkkkkkkkkkkkpicket picket picket picket
fencekkkkkkkkkkkkkkkkkkkkkkkkkkkkkkkkkkkkkkkkkpicketkkkkkkk
kkkkkkomeoverkomeoverkkkkkkkkkkkkkkkkkkkkkkkkkkkkkkkkkkk
kkkkkkllllllllllllllllllllllllllllllllllllmmmmmmmmmmmmmmmmmm

mmmmmmmmmmmmmmmmmmmmmmmnnnnnnnnnnnnnnnnnnnnn

nnnnnnnnnn

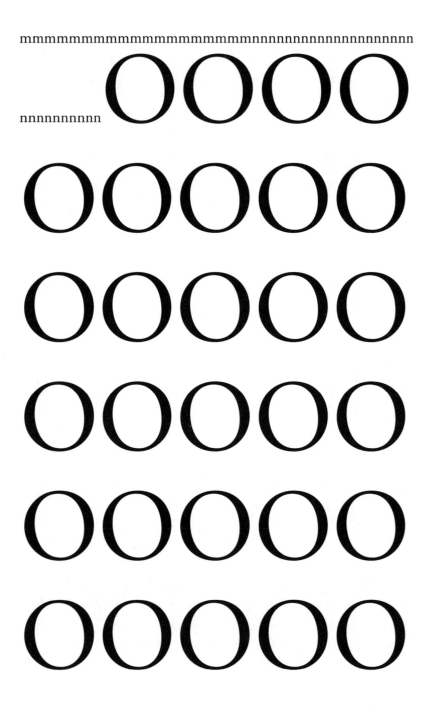

OOOOO
OOOOO
OOOOO
OOOOO
OOsinba
dOOOOO

OOOOO
OOOmy
name is
sinbad
sinbad
sinbad

sinbadO

OOOOO

O piss on you Clyde piss on you Clyde piss on you

Clyde piss on you Clyde piss on you Clyde pissonyouClydePPP
PPPPPPPPPPPissPissypiss piss pissssssssssssssssssssssswetting the
bed so slowlypissssssssssssssssssssssssit comes out so rapidlypissssssss
sssssssssssthe piss when you sleep is endless, I'm getting wet a
golden shower babes, it's wet over here by the record player high
high barometer high high barometer wooooooooooooee the level
of yellow ascends in the air baby clyde ispissssssssing pisssing
pissing pisingpiing ping ping pin gping ping pin gping pin pin
pingggggggggggggpongpissypiss piss piss the urine is falling it falleth
as the gentle rain from babyclyde'spipsqueakpjsqqqqqqqqqqqqqq
qqqquizqqqqqqqqqqqqqqqquizquizzzrrrrrrrrrrrrrrratchatacharatcha
ratcharrrrrrrrrrrrrrrrrratcharrrrrrrrrrrrrrrrratcharatcha (hey you guys
stay outta this) ratcha ratcha we's comin up now it's time (hell
no) hell now! it's time to spread it's time to swim dat goldn mile
roe roe roe da Clydespont da bote genty down da steem he he he
hehhhhehehhehehhehweezda bacteriodes dee electrodes wez de
nematodes and reptodes wez da fangalodes and da biodes wez da

streptococks and da staphlosocks and da pyogenic endotocks wez
da bafidobacterioids and da enteromongoloids and da entero-
toxical tetanoids wez waving our fimbriae goodby Goad bless dis
urinary track Goad bless dis feest wez runing skared dey is chasin
us from da pillows to da floor, cocci and colicocks in coals, dat
Shigellas on first Salmonellas on second and whoooooze on
short? it's Borellia, Shigella to Salmonella and back to Borellia,
dats our dubble play da Abbot and Caramello way ta kill da ball
and end da play eeeeeeoooooooooooow we goes back and fort its
da mikrobe way say hay kanock kanock kanock, whoze der? its us
arizin yo worss fuckin nitemare, ratchatachtatactharatchatachtatac
tharatchatachtatactharatchatachtatactharatchatachtatactharatchata
chtatactharatchatachtatactharatchatachtatactharatchatachtatacthar
atchatachtatactharatchatachtatactharatchatachtatactharatchatachta
tharatchatachtatactharatchatachtatactharatchatachtatactharatchata
chtatactharatchatachtatactharatchatachtatactharatchatachtatacthar
atchatachtatactharatchatachtatactharatchatachtatactharatchatachta
tharatchatachtatactharatchatachtatactharatchatachtatactharatchata
chtatactharatchatachtatactharatchatachtatactharatchatachtatacthar
atchatachtatactharatchatachtatactharatchatachtatactharatchatachta
tharatchatachtatactharatchatachtatactharatchatachtatactharatchata
chtatactharatchatachtatactharatchatachtatactharatchatachtatacthar
atchatachtatactharatchatachtatactharatchatachtatactharatchatachta
tharatchatachtatactharatchatachtatactharatchatachtatactharatchata
chtatactharatchatachtatactharatchatachtatactharatchatachtatacthar
atchatachtatactharatchatachtatactharatchatachtatactharatchatachta
tharatchatachtatactharatchatachtatactharatchatachtatactharatchata
chtatactharatchatachtatactharatchatachtatactharatchatachtatacthar
atchatachtatactharatchatachtatactharatchatachtatactharatchatachta
tharatchatachtatactharatchatachtatactharatchatachtatactharatchata
chtatactharatchatachtatactharatchatachtatactharatchatachtatacthar

atchatachtatactharatchatachtatactharatchatachtatactharatchatachta
tharatchatachtatactharatchatachtatactharatchatachtatactharatchata
chtatactharatchatachtatactharatchatachtatactharatchatachtatacthar
atchatachtatactharatchatachtatactharatchatachtatactharatchatachta
tharatchatachtatactharatchatachtatactharatchatachtatactharatchata
chtatactharatchatachtatactharatchatachtatactharatchatachtatacthar
atchatachtatactharatchatachtatactharatchatachtatactharatchatachta
tharatchatachtatactharatchatachtatactharatchatachtatactharatchata
chtatactharatchatachtatactharatchatachtatactharatchatachtatacthar
atchatachtatactharatchatachtatactharatchatachtatactharatchatachta
tharatchatachtatactharatchatachtatactharatchatachtatactharatchata
chtatactharatchatachtatactharatchatachtatactharatchatachtatacthar
atchatachtatactharatchatachtatactharatchatachtatactharatchatachta
tharatchatachtatactharatchatachtatactharatchatachtatactharatchata
chtatactharatchatachtatactharatchatachtatactharatchatachtatacthar
atchatachtatactharatchatachtatactharatchatachtatactharatchatachta
tharatchatachtatactharatchatachtatactharatchatachtatactharatchata
chtatactharatchatachtatactharatchatachtatactharatchatachtatacthar
atchatachtatactharatchatachtatactharatchatachtatactharatchatachta
tharatchatachtatactharatchatachtatactharatchatachtatactharatchata
chtatactharatchatachtatactharatchatachtatactharatchatachtatacthar
atchatachtatactharatchatachtatactharatchatachtatactharatchatachta
tharatchatachtatactharatchatachtatactharatchatachtatactharatchata
chtatactharatchatachtatactharatchatachtatactharatchatachtatacthar
atchatachtatactharatchatachtatactharatchatachtatactharatchatachta
tharatchatachtatactharatchatachtatactharatchatachtatactharatchata
chtatactharatchatachtatactharatchatachtatactharatchatachtatacthar
atchatachtatactharatchatachtatactharatchatachtatactharatchatachta

tharatchatachtatactharatchatachtatactharatchatachtatactharatchata
chtatactharatchatachtatactharatchatachtatactharatchatachtatacthar
atchatachtatactharatchatachtatactharatchatachtatactharatchatachta
tharatchatachtatactharatchatachtatactharatchatachtatactharatchata
chtatactharatchatachtatactharatchatachtatactharatchatachtatacthar
atchatachtatactharatchatachtatactharatchatachtatactharatchatachta
tharatchatachtatactharatchatachtatactharatchatachtatactharatchata
chtatactharatchatachtatactharatchatachtatactharatchatachtatacthar
atchatachtatactharatchatachtatactharatchatachtatactharatchatachta
tharatchatachtatactharatchatachtatactharatchatachtatactharatchata
chtatactharatchatachtatactharatchatachtatactharatchatachtatacthar
atchatachtatactharatchatachtatactharatchatachtatactharatchatachta
tharatchatachtatactharatchatachtatactharatchatachtatactharatchata
chtatactharatchatachtatactharatchatachtatactharatchatachtatacthar
atchatachtatactharatchatachtatactharatchatachtatactharatchatachta
tharatchatachtatactharatchatachtatactharatchatachtatactharatchata
chtatactharatchatachtatactharatchatachtatactharatchatachtatacthar
atchatachtatactharatchatachtatactharatchatachtatactharatchatachta
tharatchatachtatactharatchatachtatactharatchatachtatactharatchata
chtatactharatchatachtatactharatchatachtatactharatchatachtatactharatc
tharatchatachtatacthacatch da soff ball catch catch catch
sssssssssssssssssssssssssssssssah dah piss goes sssssssssssssssssssssssssfilthy
dirty filthy dirty mom won't touch me filthy dirty mom won't
touch my pivate partz mom wont touch us filthy dirty dirty mom
won't touch me filthy dirty mom won't touch my pivate partz
mom wont touch us filthy dirty dirty mom won't touch me filthy
dirty mom won't touch my pivate partz mom wont touch us
filthy dirty time to come out and shine in the dark our heads are
made of brite green flame we shine we tear at the clown we jiggle
his pits we kiss da Goad it flies we kiss da Goad come down to
chazztize usaaaaaaaaaaaaaeeeeeaeeeits

TtTtTTt

ttttttttttttttttottttttttttttttttttt

TTTTtttTTTT
TTtttttttttttttttT
TTTTTTTTTTT
TTTTTTTTTTT
TTTTTTTTT Lord

god in heaven save me please I can't be a clown no more it's a
disease I'm heading for the cab please God please I'm back in the
past and heading for the cab, I have to cage the yellow wrath and
fly to save my Barbie and yet I know it's way too late I know it's
way too late I remember I remember certain things now I remember it's late I remember I know it's way too late I know it's way
too late I know it's way too late I know it's too late I know it's too
late I know it's way too late I know it's way too late I remember I
know it's way too late I know it's way too late I know it's way too
late I know it's way too late, I'm sick of the hairballs I'm sick of
jokes I'm sick of the line by line descent of clown logic into my
brain I can't take it please Lord God Almighty, save me from vile
priests and savages I just want peace peace peace I just want to be
loved, so save me please Lord God peace from devils and devil-
worshipers and devilmongers and the pains I want to dance in the
rainlight I want to sleep soundly in the moonlight to waft and
dream to waft and dream to waft and not have the fear and dream

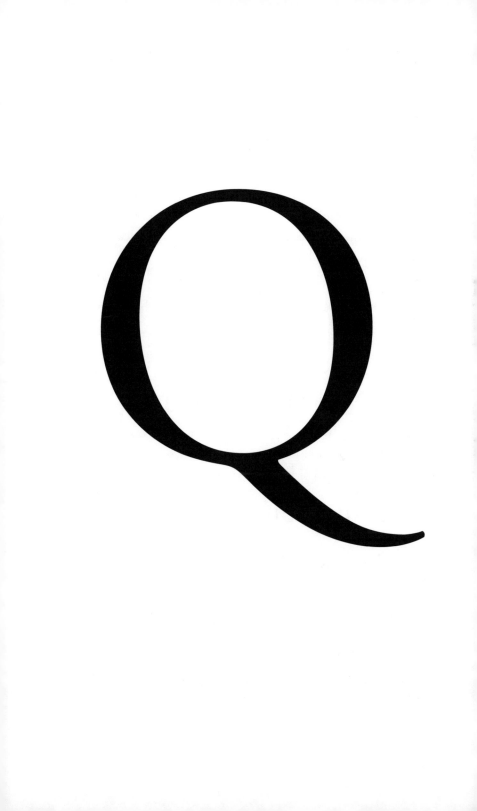

and take God's Chevy to the levy and ride ride ride the pale cars, we ride to the Death Star, in the Biscayne the Belair the Impala the Camaro the Caprice in the Heartbeats of America thalumpthalump thalump

UUUUUUUU

UUUUUUUU

UUUUUUUUlalala

UUUUUUUUlalalalalaaaalaaaaUUUUUU

UUU**uuuuuuuuuuu**UUUUUUUUUUUUUUUlaulaulaulaulaulaulaulauila

uallalalalllalalalallalalalla it's all accelerating here in the back seat I'm Shulamite the desert bride and here in the desert there are no theme songs, man you live you fuck you bleed you die and there are no orchestras, no sound tracks it all takes place in silence among the barchans and the craven moon uulalalaulalalaulala I ululate my ukele beware the enemy the daffodils sprang from the walls of Patton State the stamens stabbed into their corollas it was so clean the turds of the circus tents were cleanly swept and sucked and pucked if you know which tents I mean, the walls and corners were licked so clean I didn't want to say anything to him

Al, cuz it wasn't group therapy I didn't want to complain cuz
the contract says that if I go along for the ride, if I go behind bars
or get in a taxi and take a ride, Yooooooooooooooooooooooooo
I'm gettin married in the morning! Dingdong da bells are gonna
chime! and if sometime later I ride him like a cowboy with my
natty spurs I can't complain about the rectal hygiene, which is
kind of unfair cuz it costs ten bucks for a clownwash and simo-
nize and them circular buffers ticklehehehehehehehehe Go down
Moses Down Down Down way Down Down Down in Egypt
land, tell old Pharoah to let my people go (man dis buggy need
new shoks our ooze layers is clammin an jammin) tra la tra lee a
pig in a poke is what we be they sing in my belly and here I am
in the back seat as we speed through town and now at last I'm
large again, suddenly I'm as large as half a shilling, half man half
woman here I am, he he he
heSinbad he he
he I'm Bad Sinbad bad bad Sinbadus Perfectus Erectus,

Mango-ificus, Menander's protagonist in the bag cheery on wine
and water poking ephebes mongst the asphodels, I'm crocked
and docked my cremaster is slack we're all victims pal of pubic
transportation, ya it's one big rodeo and all the animals and
rodeo queens are gladly suffering ya gotta be a Comedic Pubic
Assaultant to read the balance shits and ass flows and porno
formas ahhhhhhto read these charts man all nine inches so long
and thick and fine in Washington DC they got all the zones
by number except the erotic ones no anals navels or nasals and it's

almost time to rock and roll and rock and roll and rock and roll
and rock and roll and rock and roll and rock and roll and rock
and roll and rock and roll and rock and roll and rock and roll and
rock and roll and rock and roll and rock and roll and rock and
roll and rock and roll and rock and roll and rock and roll and
rock and roll and rock and roll and rock and roll and rock and
roll and rock and rock and roll and I remember when in prison,
but we haven't talked about this, not quite yet, my henchman
killed the kid the one who Billy fucked in the kitchen the baby
from the Brotherhood you hated yeah you blacked you blacked
on that one yup filet de boy, yeah now that I'm larger my brain is
larger which means my memory is larger and when you said you
were sick of being a clown a few minutes ago, Clyde old Bride, I
remembered that buddy, I am beginning to remember and see,
I'm beginning to look in, and it's not pretty but it's necessary
now that I'm big and fully packed, now that I'm so
big I can hardly fit in the taxi cab, to
look back and witness, there was the Time of the Wallpaper, man
you were seeing daffodils on the blanks you were seeing flocks on
the pocks you were seeing patterns on Saturn you were seeing roll
on roll of all that special Patton paper, and when we got sprung
you were seeing carved designs on the whitewalls and that made
me shiver cuz tires are not balloons, I mean this cab is riding
hard on rubber, and when a tube blows at sixty miles per hour it's
very bad when the cock is old and bald and the highways of life
are stubbled with hemorrhoids would you like a panatella? it says
no smoking but in my world everything is fuming would you like
a panatella it says no smoking but in my world everything is
fuming fuck them fuck the driver the driver's a nigger so fuck
him! fuck the fucking nigger! would you like a panatella? would
you like to hold hands? would you like a panatella? it says no
smoking but in my world everything is fuming would you like a

panatella it says no smoking but in my world everything is fuming fuck them fuck the driver the driver's a nigger so fuck him! fuck the fucking nigger! would you like a panatella? would you like to hold hands? would you like a panatella? it says no smoking but in my world everything is fuming would you like a panatella it says no smoking but in my world everything is fuming fuck them fuck the driver the driver's a nigger so fuck him! fuck the fucking nigger! would you like a panatella? would you like to hold hands? can I fondle your wicker basket in the bushes? would you like to hold hands in the rain under the bushes? did I suck your first sperm into my brain? both of our bodies so slick, mine black yours white, me from the south of africa and you from the north of america I loved you so much, Billy I love to stick my tongue between your perfect white teeth and taste the flame, would you like me to hold that thing? this ride in the back of a Chevy is so hot and heavy and I'd like to go down I'd like to go Down Down Down with a nigger cuz I'm big and def and ready and steady I'm ready to rock and roll and now you know you're looking at the numbers and you know and I'm not telling you, I'm so proud of you Clyde your Mom had said, you're only two and you can tell time, I'm so proud of you Clyde your Mom had said, you can do the multiplication tables in your head I'm so proud of you Clyde your Mom had said, you're so good with numbers you can hold them in your head, and I gotta tell you Clyde that Al and Einstein are no longer along for the ride, cuz this cab holds only two, which for you is an easy concept, and we're all going to meet up later, we're going to have that last symposium the final busman's holiday but now they are unnecessary, there is only you and me, and now you are beginning to see that you can count to three, one and two is not what it used to be since it's all coming back the numbers and with the birth of numbers comes the death of poetry, it's all coming back the numbers and with the birth of numbers comes the death of poetry it's all coming back the numbers and with the birth of numbers comes the death of

poetry, it's all coming back the numbers and with the birth of
numbers comes the death of poetry it's all coming back the
numbers and with the birth of numbers comes the death of
poetry, it's all coming back the numbers and with the birth of
numbers comes the death of poetry it's all coming back the
numbers and with the birth of numbers comes the death of
poetry, it's all coming back the numbers and with the birth of
numbers comes the death of poetry it's all coming back the
numbers and with the birth of numbers comes the death of
poetry, it's all coming back the numbers and with the birth of
numbers comes the death of poetry it's all coming back the
numbers and with the birth of numbers comes the death of
poetry, it's all coming back the numbers and with the birth of
numbers comes the death of poetry it's all coming back the
numbers and with the birth of numbers comes the death of
poetry, it's all coming back the numbers and with the birth of
numbers comes the death of poetry it's all coming back the
numbers and with the birth of numbers comes the death of
poetry, it's all coming back the numbers and with the birth of
numbers comes the death of poetry it's all coming back the
numbers and with the birth of numbers comes the death of
poetry, it's all coming back the numbers and with the birth of
numbers comes the death of poetry it's all coming back the
numbers and with the birth of numbers comes the death of
poetry, it's all coming back the numbers and with the birth of
numbers comes the death of poetry it's all coming back the
numbers and with the birth of numbers comes the death of
poetry, it's all coming back the numbers and with the birth of
numbers comes the death of poetry it's all coming back the
numbers and with the birth of numbers comes the death of
poetry, it's all coming back the numbers and with the birth of
numbers comes the death of poetry it's all coming back the
numbers and with the birth of numbers comes the death of
poetry, it's all coming back the numbers and with the birth of

numbers comes the death of poetry it's all coming back the
numbers and with the birth of numbers comes the death of
poetry, it's all coming back the numbers and with the birth of
numbers comes the death of poetry it's all coming back the
numbers and with the birth of numbers comes the death of
poetry, it's all coming back the numbers and with the birth of
numbers comes the death of poetry it's all coming back the
numbers and with the birth of numbers comes the death of
poetry, it's all coming back the numbers and with the birth of
numbers comes the death of poetry it's all coming back the
numbers and with the birth of numbers comes the death of
poetry, it's all coming back the numbers and with the birth of
numbers comes the death of poetry it's all coming back the
numbers and with the birth of numbers comes the death of
poetry, it's all coming back the numbers and with the birth of
numbers comes the death of poetry it's all coming back the
numbers and with the birth of numbers comes the death of
poetry, it's all coming back the numbers and with the birth of
numbers comes the death of poetry it's all coming back the
numbers and with the birth of numbers comes the death of
poetry, it's all coming back the numbers and with the birth of
numbers comes the death of poetry it's all coming back the
numbers and with the birth of numbers comes the death of
poetry, it's all coming back the numbers and with the birth of
numbers comes the death of poetry it's all coming back the
numbers and with the birth of numbers comes the death of
poetry, it's all coming back the numbers and with the birth of
numbers comes the death of poetry it's all coming back the
numbers and with the birth of numbers comes the death of
poetry, it's all coming back the numbers and with the birth of
numbers comes the death of poetry it's all coming back the
numbers and with the birth of numbers comes the death of
poetry, it's all coming back the numbers and with the birth of
numbers comes the death of poetry it's all coming back the

numbers and with the birth of numbers comes the death of
poetry, it's all coming back the numbers and with the birth of
numbers comes the death of poetry it's all coming back the
numbers and with the birth of numbers comes the death of
poetry, it's all coming back the numbers and with the birth of
numbers comes the death of poetry it's all coming back the
numbers and with the birth of numbers comes the death of
poetry, it's all coming back the numbers and with the birth of
numbers comes the death of poetry it's all coming back the
numbers and with the birth of numbers comes the death of
poetry, it's all coming back the numbers and with the birth of
numbers comes the death of poetry it's all coming back the
numbers and with the birth of numbers comes the death of
poetry, it's all coming back the numbers and with the birth of
numbers comes the death of poetry it's all coming back the
numbers and with the birth of numbers comes the death of
poetry it's all coming back the numbers and with the birth of
numbers comes the death of poetry, it's all coming back the
numbers and with the birth of numbers comes the death of
poetry it's all coming back the numbers and with the birth of
numbers comes the death of poetry, it's all coming back the
numbers and with the birth of numbers comes the death of
poetry it's all coming back the numbers and with the birth of
numbers comes the death of poetry, it's all coming back the
numbers and with the birth of numbers comes the death of
poetry it's all coming back the numbers and with the birth of
numbers comes the death of poetry, it's all coming back the
numbers and with the birth of numbers comes the death of
poetry it's all coming back the numbers and with the birth of
numbers comes the death of poetry, it's all coming back the
numbers and with the birth of numbers comes the death of
poetry it's all coming back the numbers and with the birth of
numbers comes the death of poetry, it's all coming back the
numbers and with the birth of numbers comes the death of

poetry it's all coming back the numbers and with the birth of numbers comes the death of poetry, it's all coming back the numbers and with the birth of numbers comes the death of poetry it's all coming back the numbers and with the birth of

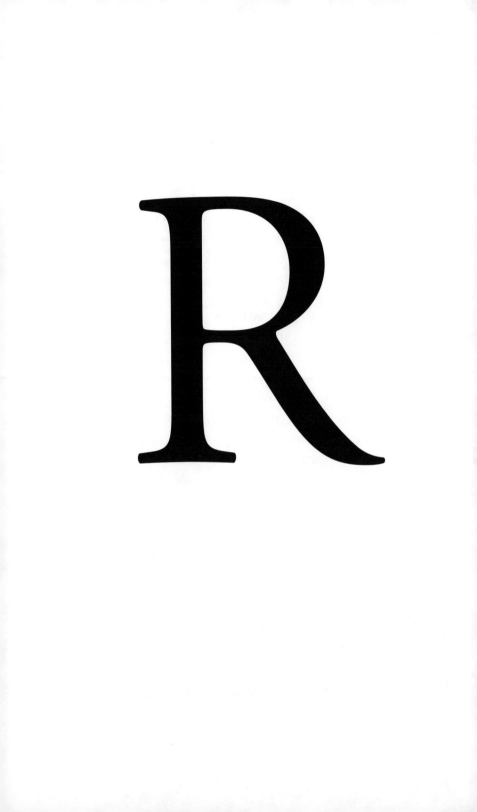

numbers comes the death of poetry it's all coming back the
numbers and with the birth of numbers comes the death of
poetry it's all coming back the numbers and with the birth of
numbers comes the death of poetry, it's all coming back the
numbers and with the birth of numbers comes the death of
poetry it's all coming back the numbers and with the birth of
numbers comes the death of poetry, it's all coming back the
numbers and with the birth of numbers comes the death of
poetry it's all coming back the numbers and with the birth of
numbers comes the death of poetry, it's all coming back the
numbers and with the birth of numbers comes the death of
poetry it's all coming back the numbers and with the birth of
numbers comes the death of poetry, it's all coming back the
numbers and with the birth of numbers comes the death of
poetry it's all coming back the numbers and with the birth of
numbers comes the death of poetry, it's all coming back the
numbers and with the birth of numbers comes the death of
poetry it's all coming back the numbers and with the birth of
numbers comes the death of poetry, it's all coming back the
numbers and with the birth of numbers comes the death of
poetry back back three
abababackabackbackbackbabababababkackkkkkkkkcyayckacyklsugf;lkadjf;yes
sir, three three three three three backbackback back three three

backbhtkerehtkrthree threeehthreeehthehthreehthree 3

3 3 3 3 3 3 3 3

3 3 3 3 when the shadows don't move you

know those are spots on the wallpaper, ah so we're already here?
the air is so sweet and smooth, can I help you out of the cab? OK,
clowns before beauty, yessir clowns before beauty it's good to
straighten my legs out here in the burbs, cuz here the shrubs are
sleeping, there's no Clownwork Orange out here in Slumberville,
in the shrubs no clowns are humping you don't have gangs out
here looking for human change to spend no Crips no Bloods no
Uzis out here in the brain-dead sticks man, and if it weren't so
late we could both hear the birds as we did in Patton by the
volleyball court, we'd listen for warblers and mockingbirds and
greet em, it's a nice little chateau, not large enough to be a chalet,
but that's OK and the welcome lights are burning bright, yup you
paid the driver with the proper change, it's grand to see you
growing up to be a counting man, you just don't hand strangers
your wallet anymore and tell them to take the right amount, you
count that cash yourself and overpay, and now here we are again,
it's just like the good old days, we're two bucks rutting out here
in the Bungaloid Belt, out here in the fucking burbs the fucking
placental malldeath out here in the fucking burbs be grateful ol
Clyde we might have been in Bucharest so soothing so safe so
sexless we fierce staggards on the march, that's what we are, two
antlered bucks ready to clash and crash, and there's the door! Ah
Clyde it's getting poignant now, we've both been here before, out
in front of a door in December, but then you looked up and saw
Kris Kringle and thought it was Sinbad the Sailor, you thought I
was there in a different kind of vessel and beaming down the
waves, beaming down the long ones, the longest flattest waves
that stretch for miles and years and stitch the galaxies in webs,
that go through the brain so slowly and create their own cloudy
hum, their own genetic strings their own embryo desires their
own infinite numbers of necessary commandments, you thought

that from the ridgepole I was beaming them down as you stalked and that I came down, that then I came down from the roof and was glowing and growing and giving speeches through the radios in Kriiiiiistalnaccccccht tones and we walked up to the door, just as we are doing now, we did it before, we walked up to it, and I said the same thing I just said, I said it backwards though like a cancrine or palindrome or like two bucks with their headgear tangled, I said beauty before clowns, well it wasn't exactly a palindrome, it was more like a palinode, a poetic refutation cuz I said beauty first man, and you were ugggly! Woeeeeeee! You were stoned stoned stoned and there was oil steaming out of your mouth and your eyes were red and your tattoos were throbbing and you were uuuuuuuugly!! You were heavy-metal ugly from the gitgo, you were ready to rock and sock and bash and roll, you were at one with nature you had seen the strobes and were ready to rip asshole and I didn't want my clownprints on the door, but I was kinda withdrawn with a slight trace of sassiness and it didn't make a hell of a lot of difference Clyde, cuz you just barged right in, you walked through the scrim into the Land of Unjustice, you barged into Butcherland, you trudged through the tesseract and headed for the closet, man those Friday nites were awfully grim, and normally you'd just kind of hestitate for a moment in the kitchen, but that night when all the stars in the sky were merry you just barged right in, no moon that night babes it was moon-less back then, not like now, when the lights of a grim maturity are shinin', when the smallest and feeblest clown can't hide in the shrubs, but over the years behind your back, Clyde I've been downing powerpacks, I've got my aminos flowing and blowing, my Tiger powders and pills and packs I been blood doping and now there's nobody able to fuck with me cuz I'm the meanest clown in the Valley he he he I sailed away away away away over the rooftops on my broom and rug and frisbee I was free I was flying and blinking and shining and I trapped all the waves in the universe and brought them back but the source of them all was down the stairs among the wreckages and freedoms from care, the source of it all now please you enter first, beauty before clowns! Oh my God (don say dat, OK guys? we set? we is honk honk we is, Jellonimo! cilias do yo fansy struttin) I said it here we go again I said beauty before clowns. Please Clyde you go in first you go Down Down Down DownDown Down

DownDown Down DownDown Down DownDown Down
DownDown Down DownDown Down DownDown Down
DownDown Down DownDown Down DownDown Down
DownDown Down DownDown Down DownDown Down
DownDown Down DownDown Down DownDown Down
DownDown Down DownDown Down DownDown Down
DownDown Down DownDown Down Down it's your girlfriend
man it's your gun it's your trip it's your rendezvous with destiny
here in this lovely little ranch home Yup I wonder what's shaking
in here you can see it's seven four zero
zero Colfax the address under the
fixture right next to the door, hey surprise Big Guy, it's open

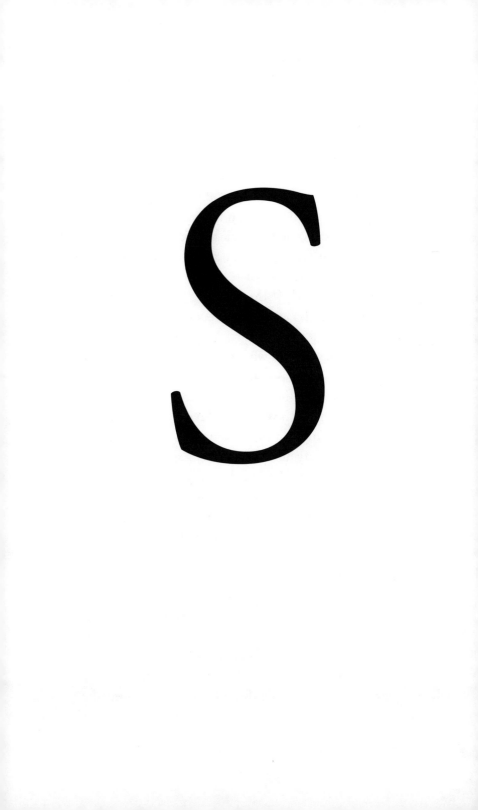

we're in the door oooooooh my this joint's got a carpet-cleaning problem, there's a mound of gore in the vestibule a compost heap a lump of glossy guts in the entry yuck yuck yuck I went down to the river to watch the fish swim by, but I got down to the river so lonesome I wanted to die, and then I jumped in the river but the doggone river was dry, MMMMshe's long goooooooooooooooooone babes, but now I'm lonesome bloooooooooo! and shit this dude looks like a sundial with that haft sticking out of his back, the fucker's got a funky gnomon what did you say his name was? Bruce the pimp computer programmer jumpin jellies, what a mess of refried beans, man isn't there a chiropractic hotline in this place? Whatcha doing with your nose down by his neck, Clyde babes, you checking to see if he's gurgling? Well he ain't, he's just rubbing his belly in purgatory. It's always a spur of the moment thing when a man reaches towards his belly cuz he might go farther down and start pumping. Don't look at me like that! You didn't do it, it must have been that priest, he probably had the axe leaning against the door and this dimwit opened and turned and one two buckle my shoe before the reverend father hoisted and chopped, he knifed straight through the traps to Shangheeee ooooooooooh can you dig the skull on this sucker? Now that's a hairy pimpball! And what's that red stuff seeping from his back? Is that watermelon juice or diet cherry coke or what (weez thirsty where's da pimpkin seeds is da pimpkin joos reddy is it time for twick or tweet)? fuck that shit, stay cool down there, now where did they put the liquor cabinet? Man I got a thirst on me the size of a milkman's dick, he he he he he he he (Mike, the angel with

the heavenly drawtube, he called you a filthy name when you
peeked inside the bedroom door, when you saw Anita with her
legs stretched open he had his four on the floor which is a mat-
tress metaphor. The Yids say in Braysheet that Mike kept Honest
Abe from using the shiv on Izzy and the Catholics say God's
milkman came clanging down the basement steps to hell carrying
his load of sperm-filled bottles, but for me it ain't so far, it's just
below the navel in the Pseudepigrapha of Peristalsis), and my
shoes are getting soggy, I could use a little pick-me-up, if ya know
what I mean, I think I'll traipse into the kitchen and open up a
cupboard or two cuz there's gotta be a hutch for the booze, yeah
here we are, wheeeeeeeew this kitchen is from hunger they got
coconut shreds dangling from the ceiling it's so creepy I'll bet
there's asbestos (below we gots da Oooooooosha laws da union
woild of devilltry is organ-ized an sanitaree), so where do you
think they keep the glasses? Yeah you stick some alcoholic phero-
mones in a room and my senses go plum crazy and I start itching
and twitching and witching, it ain't much but it'll have to do, it's
rotgut Tokay but what the hay (pour us a teeny won too, we need
dat rocket fool ta glide), you take the first swig, it's beauty before
clowns Clyde, and as for me I'll take an itty bitty bump and then
go lick the body, did I say that? Wooopsaroootie! No way babes,
that would be downright ugly to get down in that river of gore
and start licking and gnawing and nuzzling on Brucie, take it
from me, it's not my protocol to stick my rubber nose in other
people's puddles and besides it's way too quiet in here, there's
something going on that we don't know, there's an ugly thing
roaming, a cleaving spirit, perhaps it's hiding in the house yeah
sure I'll take another pull, mmboy the wine's a little warm but
I'm gonna find me a river, one that's cold as ice, and when I find
me that river Lord (don fuck wit our constitooooooshunn we no
longer in Goad's cirkus) I'm gonna pay the price, O Lord (I gotta
greps we gotta let da gas rize up to da cocomats an fester) I'm
going down in it three times but Lord (ish ish ishy ish ish) I'm

only coming up twice, shit Clyde we gonna hang around the
stove all day? I'm so loooooooonesome I'm soo00 lonesooooooo
ooooome blooooooooooooo! What is this, some kind of bakeoff?
It's getting too hot in here where ya goin? wait for me Clyde wait
for me, ya don't have to run clear across the living room don't do
it man, he's a virgin, I said don't touch his boner man, he's virgin
property, don't pull his zipper don't do like you did once don't
pull his zipper down don't hack don't cut don't pull it down
don't cut it down don't toss it don't bite it and toss it around cuz

he's straddling the big 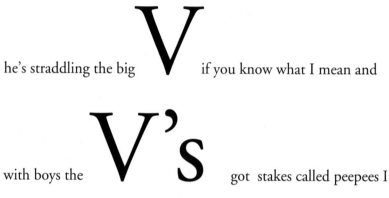 if you know what I mean and

with boys the got stakes called peepees I

mean I don't want to get labial on ya and ruin your appetite,
you've eaten enough oblong steak to last a lifetime (he swabbed
dem down den made dem dirty hehehe dat fellate minyan is
mightee dammmn tastee) and I must admit that clowns are
professionally incapable of sensitivity, I mean what ever made you
think that I would stop killing? You don't read the contract
language, that's not your thing, and if you don't want to read em
you shouldn't sign em and I'm ready and steady cuz you've had
your drinks and in a way I've already had mine and in a way I
haven't, not quite yet I haven't had an interchange of bodily
fluids and here we are standing over this weeping pimplike
incarnadine muddle, so has it begun to puff? cuz I gotta tell ya I
hate balloons and those corpses almost immediately start puffing,
the microbes start jamming, there is no ability to stop it, those

things that used to help us with digestion start digesting us! It's the weirdest goddamn (yaay! hip hip hooray! we loves ta graze in brown lacy feelds under da appron folds) thing that they're so ungrateful but what do you expect from something so self-centered and tiny as a microbe? Stop scratching your head there babes, you'll get dandruff on the delicti, I'll bet this melonhead died before he hit the ground, and so...........hey! what do you think you're doing? Woooooooooee, man I didn't think you had it in you, I didn't think you'd *pluck that axe!* You could have stayed dainty and now you've got another layer. How does it feel? Real good? Is that why you're waving the blade and laughing? Look babes, you don't feel much now do you, and what's happening out on the lawn who's frisking out in the moonlight is strictly a matter of academic controversy there could be something there or there could be something wandering here, wandering around the house or around your brain or there could be nothing wandering at all but let's not get epistemological while you're wiping blood on your jacket. Ya know Clyde, the ontologicometaphysical, orthodonticollegial and phenomenopharmacological feelings just kinda drain in ticklish situations but I gotta tell you it's when those simple emotions start vanishing that the better side comes out, the lower side the funny side the microbe side and I just keep talking and talking I say the most worthless inconsiderate things no I didn't check the bedroom, what's your scene man, what's your scene? We don't want to get gnarly in there, now do we? One bedroom in a lifetime is more than enough and when we come to the end of a perfect game it's gonna be clowns before beauty cuz according to Al my agent (who does all my thinking for me) that's why I get paid and so we'll see if she's in there, you go look for Barbie you go see if she's in there if she's hacked to bits in the abyss of the boudoir and I'll stay here and stare into the wound and when you're not looking I'll go fishing, nah just kidding, anyway you go in the other room and take a peek and see if Barbie's in there you go look for Barbie cuz it's so quiet in

here you could hear a mouse, not a creature is stirring in this
split-level house, and you have a habit of peering into bedrooms
anyway and I think she must have run out the door or something
har har hardie har har, she must have heard the doorbell she must
have heard Bruce screaming before he hit the floor she must have
sensed something creepy and run out the door she must have
juked and deeked and run around the axe-swinging priest and
straight out the door you go look in the bedroom and I'll stay
here and bend over and sip like a bee, yeah like a teeeeeny yellow
jacket with a glans a busy busy bee a Hummeroptera with a big
milky thing sticking out of its back I'll just reach into the center
and sip one drop, I need that teeeeny bit of extra energy
mmmmmmmmmmmmm that venous cooler smacks!!! Jeez
Louise (dats not da popper name, Looize ain't reggstered in da
debbil hall of flame) I'm talkin to myself, I'm getting kind of
daffeeeeeeee it must be my little pick-me-up it's been a while and
takes a while for blood to find blood in the bloodless corpse of
dolls and you don't have to hold it up in the air there ain't no
ghosts in here and I know cuz if there were I'd see em they're all
inside my peritoneal case mamboing unscreened in the abomi-
nable abdominal vitrines like Latin lovers like puppies in a window man they are so cute if you've got the right set of eyeshades I
mean those devilish little faces make the eyeballs glisten, put the
axe down there's a gobbet of muscle stop motioning to me over
by the bedroom you're mouthing words but when you mouth em
over and over you gotta breathe em cuz if you're muttering to
yourself if you're muttering silent words over and over and over
then you're not yourself Clyde and I don't know if I want to go
over there man, I don't think I want to step over over step over
over over over toward that door, even we killer-clowns have
limits, and it's almost time for me now isn't it? The moon is
full la kookaratcha ratcha la kookaratcha lalala la la la la la
kookaratchand I can see it in your rheumy melon-clownic eyes,
it's time for me to take over over and do my thing, it's like the

other time, it's time to take over but let me take this breather first, you have to chill out man, you have to chill, OK I'll go now, I'll go little Miss Dynamo, OK OK I'll go to the bedroom turning the corner, it's cinéma vérité, OK OK OK I've got my minicam the frames are moving turning over we're we're we're
flyingflyingflyingflyingflyingflyingflyingflyingflying
wowwwwwwwwwwwwwwooooooooooooooooowwwwwwwwwwww
wwwwwwwwwwwwooooooooooowowowowowoeeeeeeeeeeeeeeee
eewoeoweoooooowwwoooooooooeeeeeeeeeeee! hey we're heading down the hall chug chugga chug, yeah I'm following Clyde with lens and mike folks we're taking rare raw footage it's cinéma vérité we're catching every moment of the star-studded action he's hunched over he's swinging that thing he's swinging that swollen dick he's swinging that axe he's swinging down the hallway folks he's moving and forechecking Oh my God (oooooooooH) Oh my God (oooooooooooH) now I see what he means it's another open door it's open sesssamee it's cinéma vérité it's not a body not there not a body not there not a body not meat not by the bedroom door just a simple open door it's cinéma vérité and I see what it is thereeeeeeeeeeeeeeeeeeeeeee eeeeaaaaaaaaaaaaaaaaaaaaaaaaahhhh omygodomygodgod god god god god god (aaaaaaaaayyyyyyyeee don say dat uggie word we squirminggggggg say Goad uggie Clooon say Goad) I see the lights at the head of another set of stairs an open door a door opening an opening to the belly an open navel a trap a trapdoor a trap to hell a trap in an open trapdoor, you want to check out the basement Clyde just like we did before? are we going down the steps Clyde just like we did before? are you carrying a blade Clyde just like you did before? do you have a gun Clyde just like you

did before? can you hear any Irish songs Clyde? are you going to meet the demons on the stairs Clyde, just like you did before? are you going to run a gauntlet of green flame? are the flames pointing Clyde, are the flames pointing there's a light below just like.....OK Clyde it's showtime babes it's time to get rough and tough I see the tilt and dim light hanging at the bottom down below it's just like it was once upon a time and it's time Clyde now is the time it's time as we head Down Down Down there to try to remember to look back watch your step don't trip it's time Clyde it's time it's time it's time to go down it's time it's time to try to remember to go back and down and try to remember beauty before clowns babes I wish I had a tune to make the journey sing, a sweet high voice above the screams and whipping the fuckhead voice of the beast bashing and roaring as we dive

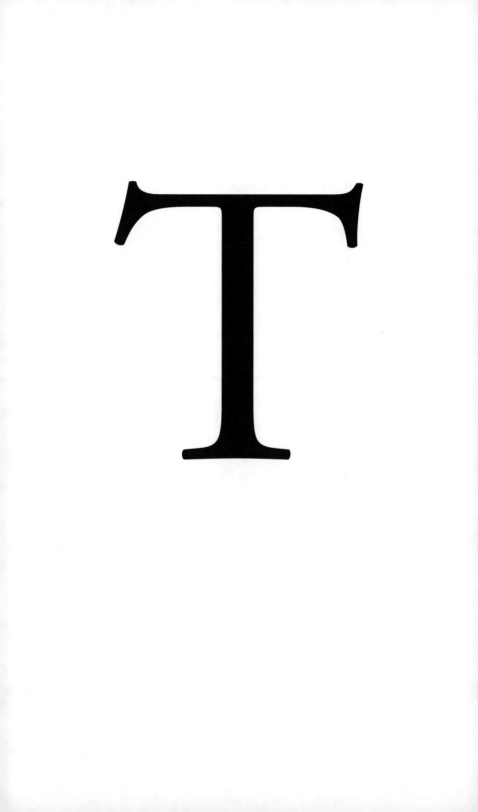

hey! watch where you're swinging that speckled thing it smells kind of moldy it's bum aromatheraphy, who cut the cheese jeez (are ya in the house now, Chief, is it reeeely baaaaad?) the furnace room of gloom I presume but this is nothing wait til you go down the real rathole wait til the floor snaps back you'll tumble and fall without the benefit of steps and the clowns below will point and shriek and rush from side to side as you fall helpless through the traps they'll rush as you fall toward the final floor perhaps perhaps perhaps perhaps you glide the fall into hell is a sporting event and down below they hold the blankets like azure stamps they rush from side to side the clowns in hell are so compassionate they try to make the damned feel they are soaring up into the sky cuz when you fall into hell you can never tell there is no sense of gravity you can never tell the ups from the downs the rise and fall of emotion after death are so senselessly profound the clowns could be puzzled cherubs holding scrolls among the puffy clouds as they rush from side to side when you fall you seem to float it's a raunchy sort of joke the trap in the floor could just as easily be a hole in the roof you can never tell the rocket up to heaven or a parachute to hell the moment of truth is a ruthless filthy thing for in hell the clowns clasp blankets yeah the damned float toward the final consolation toward the azure of the blankets toward the warmth and then the gruesome snorts and calls of blanket patrols as the blankets veer and the clowns shriek and head toward the next falling sinful bundle and just as you are about to land so comfortable and have a heavenly maternal snuggle the final clownish shrieks of the gangs of four the shrieks of frustration and anger and splat you hit the floor and jolt your blood begins to boil eternally to seethe and to sing and to bleat and to whimper and to roar

but as we go through the tunnel of green flame it's not such a chore nobody is watching or listening no one is pointing someone has been here before so thanks for handing me the axe and thanks for the champagne dreams and maraschino memories, Old Buddy yup those were some heavy bubbles and ruby cherries. Yeah so what if I did? What da fuck, you got drunk an did strange things, yeah you'd have a hard time tellin' me Friggin A-hole of all people your ol bud Sinbad that you wuz white as a lily so whad if that liddle sip of Bruce god me shitface drunk an stupid so fuckin whad whz it to ya huh? Yeah that blud ubstairs wuz tart and sassy, good home brew, the best type O that cash can buy, better than any line of coke but now I'm sober, Pow, Shazaam, Power to the Clowns! Clown Power Clown Consciousness Power to the Clowns! Power! Power! Much more Power! Huge power! Humor power! The nonclown world is clownist they are anticlown they are clownophobes they are Jim Clown hey guy, this is quite a weapon, so grooved and balanced, too bad it's been used cuz the used ones is jinxed, you don't want to chop with them twice unless you have to, now that you're huddled in the corner just like you used to be, it's funny Clyde how in moments of extreme distress humanity repeats its obsessive behaviors, yeah decades can go by and if you get in similar situations you do the same horrible things cuz the iron laws of hysteria run deep and control us from century to century and here we have another hunk of meat with her head stuck underneath the water heater and her legs are bent they're long and mean this chick wouldn't win any beauty contests but when she was young and glistening I remember those

sexual chores ah me! She got tarted up for the occasion, I'll bet
she liked you a lot cuz these aren't whoretogs, man, these are true
duds these are Lord (say Goad you mudderfuck say Goad we
worship the whipps we luve) and Taylor, she must have liked you
a lot to shed her streetclothes and wear these dowager things but
her head is tucked under the heater and I'll put aside the axe and
give a teenie tug, I'll grab her by the ankles and give a tug and lug
the guts out in the center of the room and you can stay in the
corner, I don't care, I'm used to it, ya see I never forget I never
shirk a responsibility so I'll just tug and lug and take a quick look
at her head................ yuck yuck yuck yuck oh boy surprise! I feel
it's up to me now I gotta do it once again this calls for the red

white and blue this calls for swift revenge since this one's
dead and minus something here's the gun, ya see? A forty-five
automatic. A Colt. Look familiar? Well it should, it's yours.
That's right, it's the rod you handed to the priest. Wooooeeeee,
he used it to zotz this hunk of whorish meat, in her present
condition, I wouldn't fuck her. I wouldn't pay a dime. Not me.
No way José. Without her ear, I wouldn't fuck her, no way I
wouldn't fuck her, I wouldn't even touch her if it wasn't written
in the boilerplate on the heater it looks like the shell took out half
her back. I hate to tell ya pal, but you've been framed by an
expert. Your gal, your gun, your prints on the axe, and you got a
motive big as a billboard, big as all West Texas so I'd guess you've
got a case for a doctor or a jury. That Senator hired a gun to track
her, to follow you around until you found her, and then you
handed him the address like a twerp you wrote it in his book and
he blasted her with the forty-five and left you holding the bag.
This bag of useless guts! I guess she really loved you. You were
right all along. The Senator walks away clean and you go straight
to the jug. That's sweet. Real sweet. Mind if I pick up the axe and
kick her over? Say something! I want to see her face. I want to see
if he also carved her face. Ya know, we clowns got a rap, everyone

complains that clowns get mistreated but I gotta tell you ya can never treat clowns bad enough cuz we deserve it, I mean if I were out and about in reality I'd join the Clownish Republican Army, I'd become a clownayeen, a Weatherclown, I'd go down to the international offices of the clown academy and torch the joint, I'd blow it up and every conventional motherfucker in it, that's what I'd do and it'd be healthy too cuz those jerks aren't real clowns, they're bureauclowns, they're joke shufflers, they're not evil so they're not funny, they're bad babes, they're so good they're bad, they got normal minds and that ain't good, they're clowns skin deep, their bones don't joke, they run the world they govern all the slaves of all the countries and they try to drive the evil geniuses out of business, not that I'm complaining Clyde, no sirree, but let me show ya what a real clown does when confronted with

an ear-shorn body, it's like— **wait** a moment while I cultivate an attitude appropriate to time and place, an Aristotelian

grandeur with a mookie face— **wait** it's like Oh pardon me thou bleeding piece of earth, that I am meek and gentle with these butchers, thou art the ruins of the noblest woman that ever lived in the tide of times, and then I wave my giant hand in the air like this see? or I start chanting like that rube in the temple, Mr. Abraham Pigsquat, two score and two years ago our fathers brought forth on this continent a new nation conceived in slavery and dedicated to the proposition that all men are created greedy ya see, it's closer to the truth, it really sings and I'm outrageous I'll say or do anything—fuck you fuck you reader fuck you critic fuck you philosopher fuck you teacher fuck you student fuck you writer fuck you poet fuck you clown fuck you ringmaster fuck you baby and you and you and you—given the proper basement, man she's beginning to stink, that first bacterial waste a delicate taste is starting to congregate and so I'll just kick

her over ya think we clowns are clever? well we're not we think
with our horns and our feet and I think I'll just kick this rotten

bitch over, I won't wait I'll just kick the bitch over
you can kiss my toochis, anyone who defends a clown is an ass, I

won't wait I'll just kick the bitch over you can kiss
my ass I'll just kick her over I'll kick her as hard as I possibly can I

won't wait I'll just kick her in the side as hard as I
can I'll just kick her as hard as I can you can kiss my fucking ass
any of you other clowns out there with your stupid fucking
organizations can kiss me where the shit comes loose you orga-
nized losers I'm gonna kick the bitch real hard I won't

wait I'm out here on the floor and you're there in the
corner and once she's over I'm gonna stare into her face and
check for tears cuz sometimes the dead cry they do, Clyde, and if
I weren't such a fucking son of a bitch I wouldn't know it, I
wouldn't know if they cried cuz she'd stay face down and you'd
be calling the police and the tears would dry before they got here
and then I'd have to wait and yet if I kick her over now I can
make sure she died in peace peace peace peace peace peace peace

WWWWWWWW

WWWWWWWWW

WWWWWWWWW

WWWWWWWW

WWWWWWWW

WWWWWWWW

WWWWWWWW

WWWWWWWW

WWWWWWW peace peace
peace peace peace peace peace peace peace peace peace peace
peace peace peace peace peace peace ugh she's over she's downtown she's down town she's down the poor bitch never got a
word in edgewise the air-conditioned bitch is down, not a single
word in this whole lousy book just a gnat in the wind a bedroom
grind a nameless biography of degradation and sex-felicity she
never got a word in edgewise not a single word in this whole
lousy book and now I can see that I kicked her yup she's only
earless the final humiliation the priest took his memento he
wanted you to see her here your love of a life without an ear he
hacked it off real clean this gifted otolaryngologist needs to
maintain precise trophies he probably keeps em in a shoebox she
never got a word in edgewise not a single word in this whole
lousy book just a gnat in the wind a bedroom grind a nameless
biography of degradation and sex-felicity she never got a word in

edgewise not a single word in this whole lousy book and now I
can see that I'm sure she loved you it's real clear she did and it's
too bad you gotta see her like this it's so precise without an ear
but who needs it anyway? it's a useless appendage when you've
got a tunnel in your back, but I hate to see her like this I know
you no longer care I hate to see her like this I'm so angry at her I
was chasing her I chased her all the way to here I was so angry
with her I chased her all the way to here she hurt me she hurt me
so much she made me hurt her I was so angry with her she never
touched me she never let me touch her breasts or her hair I'm so
angry with her she hurt me so much she hurt me she made me
hurt her she hurt me so much I had to hurt she hurt me so much
as a baby I don't want to see her like this, he hit me as a baby he
hit me in my crib he didn't care it didn't hurt him when he hit
me with his fuckhead fist in my crib but I'm not angry at her I'm
angry at him he hit me as a baby and she sang and wouldn't
touch me I don't want to see her like this I guess I'll just lower
the hatchet iiiiiiiit sure is heavy It ITTTItitTTTTit sure is heavy
I guess I'll just lower this long axxxxxxxxxxxxxxe and bury it, not
that I'm hoooooooongry IIIIIIIIIIIIIIIIiiiiiiiiiiiiiiIIII just need to
get rid of it and you're over in the corner and you're dreaming
and I'm laughing and shit shit shit I think it's time for me to get
funky and we're all a bunch of fuckers and thieves, we steal from
women's bodies, especially the women who wouldn't touch us,
who wouldn't share their grief and love with us, when they hide
their most important things, it's up to us to start looking to
search for the center to search for the eggs and songs to search for
the moments of peace peace peace heaven I'm in heaven and the
cares that hung around me through the week and months and
years have vanished like a gambler's lucky streak I'm in heaven
I'm down among the blankets harrowing in the clouds among the
devils man, and let me tell you one of the darkest of all secrets
pal, now that I'm kicking her over again, ugh, it's done, let me
tell you one of the darkest secrets imaginable pal, now that I'm

kicking her over again, ugh, it's done it's over, when you reach the basest levels of hell, the devils are silent, yeah the haruspex sucks on the soggy microbe-infested entrails and the mouth goes silent, all the microbes and the many voices of the dying go silent at the very same time, the death rattle chorus of all the sounds and feelings and all the moments go silent cuz when the body dies the microbes feast silently and when evil flourishes what is the need to speak? what is left to say? and here is the basest secret of all pal, this is the basest secret of all cuz that's why clowns and dolls are always silent, we live in this thing permanently this lugging hunk of whorish one-eared guts is nothing, it doesn't mean a thing, cuz we never leave it pal, we remain for all eternity lodged in a sealed shell a silent hell, and all the words are just a noisy form of clowning a rind on the outside surrounding the inner hellish silence it's when you're falling that the microbes speak, it's when you're falling toward the blankets that the lost feelings fall within you and they speak and that's why she was singing cuz she was singing out those final feelings, she was tied to the chair and feeling for the very last time, she looked down at her hubby and she looked at her son shaking in the corner, and she said those final words Clyde that I had promised you I would never never repeat but I lied babes, I lied and then the hooting lights went out and her soul was turned over to Shigella and Salmonella and this cunt's going to Barbarella hey look the evil down here is cool and quiet, which means if you stop hearing me if you stop hearing and seeing it just gets worse, it just gets quieter and you go Down Down Down the silence is empty and bottomless it's the void babes it's the Big FUCking clOwn ish Silence you got the Colt and the Ruger and I got this thing and I like my weapon and you like yours cuz back then back when your first life began and came to an end and you started doing the eternal two-step

one two one two

one two one one two one two one two one one two one one two one two

you couldn't stand to watch me do my thing and then the most important part of you went silent, you became like all the other conventional stupid fucking clowns of the world, you couldn't take the rage you couldn't take the agony you couldn't deal with my hunger for your mom's insides my agony to tear apart and chew your mother piece by piece and egg by egg and breast by breast and organ by organ and you became a lifelong prisoner of bad jokes you turned into yourself and the only cure was your writing, cuz in writing it was all remembered, not by you but by those grim muses those Harpies, the bird-women babes remembered all those things and swooped down from heaven and dumped them on your platter like dead swollen circumcised bees and so you never felt or heard or saw or knew the memories but they came out in words they shone through your alphabets they gleamed from your tattoos and that's why you and I both wear our makeup proudly, cuz they protect our silence and you don't have to feel or think or hear or see or know, in silence you can just listen to the pause between the beats, you can count all the other numbers in the silence, and the coldness and the hate you showered on this poor merciless victim huddled on the floor man, the way you pricked her and cut her and tied her and whipped her, oh sure you claim it was done lovingly but the coldness and hate you showered on this poor merciless victim man has led to this, has brought her down into this damp basement next to the hot water heater, yeah see this is Kismet Babes, this is the heavy thing, men become spiders become elephants, the arras disappears, the scenery goes dark, the knotty pine loses its knots, the wreckreation room is recreated without any amusing qualities and eon after eon the damned lose all trace of vision and speech, it all becomes the Primal Fact of the Primal Act, repeated repeated and so you never felt or heard or saw or knew the memories but they came out in words they shone through your alphabets they gleamed from your tattoos and that's why you and I both wear our makeup proudly, cuz they protect our silence and you don't have to feel or think or hear or see or know in the silence you can just listen to the pause between the beats, you can count all the other numbers in the silence, and the coldness and the hate you showered on this poor merciless victim huddled on the floor man, the way you pricked her and cut her and tied her and whipped her, oh sure you claim it was done lovingly but the coldness and hate you showered on this poor merciless victim man has led to this, has brought her down into this damp basement next to the hot water heater, yeah see this is Kismet Babes, this is the heavy thing, men become spiders become elephants, the arras disappears, the scenery goes dark, the knotty pine loses its knots, the wreckreation room is recreated without any amusing qualities and eon after eon the damned lose all trace of vision and speech, it all becomes the Primal Fact of the Primal Act, repeated repeated and the coldness and the hate you showered on this poor merciless victim huddled on the floor man, the way you pricked her and cut her and tied her and whipped her, oh sure you claimed it was done lovingly but the coldness and hate you showered on this poor merciless victim has led to this, has brought her down into this damp basement next to the hot water heater, yeah see this is Kismet Babes this is the heavy thing, men become spiders become elephants, the arras disappears, the scenery goes dark, the knotty pines lose their knots, the wreckreation room is recreated without any of the amusing qualities and eon after eon the damned lose all trace of vision and speech, it all becomes the Primal Fact of the Primal act, repeated repeated yeah see this is Kismet Babes, this is the heavy thing, men become spiders become elephants, the arras disappears, the scenery goes dark, the knotty pines lose their knots repeated repeated there's a life then a murder there's a life then a murder there's a life then a murder there's a life then a murder there's a life then a murder there's a life then a murder there's a life then a murderthere's a murderlifemurderlife then a murderthere's a lifethen a murderthere's a life then alife murder murderthere's a life then a murderthere's a life then life murder life murder a murderthere's a life then a murderthere's a life then a murdertheremurder's a life murderlife then a murderlife murderlifemurderlifemurderlife and with each horror with each new death the scenery gets grimmer and dimmer, there is no longer the cuddly feelings man, it's not mom it's a whore, it's not a wreckroom it's the damp and ugly fundament at the base of a moldy bungalow, it's a heater closet it gets darker and clammier and more quiet and unmanagable as the soul sinks deeper into hell but shit man I gotta lower this hatchet now and here it goes, ugh, it's done it's over, there is a time in life when you gotta let go, and so now you face the music right? did you get your final thrill did we do your final damage now did you get to cut her for the last time to see if she responds? did you get your final thrill? did you get to cut a woman Clyde did you get to cut and hurt and get hard and warm inside? we both get smaller and the senator is on a roll he did it to you he hired that goon to wipe away this pair of liabilities with an eraser, it's all so neat, they're dead, you're blamed, a lunatic is blamed, that older guy did good he did his job you're through stop shaking man and toss me the Colt let's go stop I got a great idea, babes stop let's not get righteous stop let's get even he nailed your ass he thought you were a wuss stop so let's nail his stop let's get out our bag of finishing nails and nail him stop let's finish the fucker you've only seen me so tall but I get taller on second thought there still are bullets in this gun so let's ram the barrel down his throat let's get that Senatorial Stoat stop let's fucking blast him it's time to kill someone we don't love babes, Einstein the Great would say it's healthy to vent our rage on proper objects man stop cuz we dolls can't reciprocate so it's better for us to grow up big and tall and fiery and before the final quiet before the quiet comes and the moon descends and shrinks before our bellies bulge as we shrink before the microbes have their final say before we make love in that final way before I keep the terms of the contract, babes let's get busy, let's do it to it let's nail that motherfucker you know we'll never find that priest, man he's long gone, he's drawing Social Security for a job well done, he's on to the next assignment babes, it's probably number three hundred twenty, this guy's got what it takes but what the heck he's not the object of our inquiry cuz he's just doing his job so let him keep his shoebox and his trophies and so I say let's nail that fucking senator, let's kill Abernathy let's kill Abernathy let's kill Abernathy let's kill Abe let's kill Abernathy let's kill Abernathy let's kill Abe Abe Abe let's maim Abe let's kill Abernathy lets maim Abe Abe let's let Kosmoski keep the shoebox and the trophies let's shoot Abernathy in his sleep, the sun's still down and no one's around, and you know his address cuz you looked it up so let's sneak over and check the windows babes let's sneak over to his house and check the windows let's go for it while we can let's avenge our memories let's take down this fucking dulocracy we don't need to be slaves to our emotions to all the hornrimmed potbellies in school ties to the World Association of Aryan Maytag Salesmen, to all the bureauclowns so let's just nail the motherfucker in his sleep, you keep out of it, you just watch and I'll crawl in we don't even have to go downstairs, I'll bet we can do it up top at the main tent level I'll bet all we have to do is open the bedroom door a notch and shoot but you don't have to worry Clyde cuz I'll grow into it, it will be no big fucking deal stop my arm will be so big I can just reach in a window and do it I'll blow his fucking head stop I'll pop his brains stop pop stop pop his head don't worry Clyde he killed the woman you tried to love her properly and peacefully but couldn't stop he'll piss his fucking sheets he'll piss and piss and I'll nail his fucking head and he'll piss his sheets as he dies stop don't worry Clyde all the poets and poetry of the world will survive stop and all the clowns and all the microbes will stop and take the poets with him I'm getting confused stop while you stay there trembling stop and now you're holding the axe again stop but I've got the gun stop and will use it so stop hack stop hack what the heck Clyde let's go for it stop babes let's go for it after my late nite snack go so stop and go for it hack let's go for it stop hack stop hack stop hack stop hack stop let's go

Two

It was raining in the bushes. Snow and blood and rain. Yet the sky was clear. Autumn night of innocent platinum light.

> *La luna cómo mueve*
> *la plateada rueda, y va en pos de ella*
> *la luz do el saber llueve,*
> *y la graciosa estrella*
> *de amor le sigue reluciente y bella!*

Fray Luis de León, another NaziJew, who also saw it raining in the paradoxical Light of God. I wiped it off. The luminous blonde hairs.

I lay on my back on the damp lawn, among the drunken nightcreepers. Among the transverse movement of sotted worms away from their wooden wormhomes. An intense aroma of armpits. Stale gravesweat. My nose felt sore and stuffed.

When I got out of the cab I had gone around the house and found the axe on the lawn in the backyard. It must have been out there for weeks. In the light of the moon, in the gentle rain, I could see the rust on the blade glistening. It must have been out there for months. I rubbed its side against my cheek. I looked up into the stretch of the heavens and breathed deeply.

I knelt and put the axe in front of me, and I remember, I said this prayer.

> *Lord, I have sinned. I lie in the pit. I do not know who I am. Save me please from voices. From the voices that command. Deep inside I am pure and wanting and good. Jesus Christ, Savior, reach down in your infinite goodness and bless me.*

Screeching voices cascaded into the hedge. I stood and walked over to a back porch, to its side door, ajar. I tiptoed up the steps and opened the screen and went in. A sisal rug. A chess table. Porch furniture with plastic cushions. I looked closely. Orange and pink perhaps. Iron leggings and backings. A child's chipped metal toolkit. On the table, the pieces were set. A pawn moved diagonally in the darkness. The sound of dead crickets, soothing, regulating, timekeeping, saintly crickets, holding the hearts of children in fairy nets.

Crickets with starlight burning in their heads.

I approached the hull of the house. The portholes looked into a kitchen. Dirty dinner dishes. An open sink cabinet. Towels on the floor dappled with black vomit.

The house turned over on its side and sank. The house spun and sank and I was scrabbling along the top of it. I crawled across to another set of windows and stared down into the living room.

Three airless skulls.

Mamma. Dadda. Baby Boy.

Jiffy Pop. Television.

The house spun again. Massive lightning flared in my eye sockets.

I realized I was holding a bottle of wine. Half-full. I fell off the wall onto the rug and climbed into a lounge chair and leaned back and emptied it. Before me a little boy was holding a sharp tool. He was happy. An old autumn breeze was blowing. The fresh cold breeze of a child's security.

I couldn't enter. Never. I could never enter again. Never another house.

Shakey, I stood and opened the screen door and went back down into the yard.

There was someone there waiting for me.

His hands were white with makeup. He smelled like gefilte fish. The lawn was glowing a dull, flourescent green. He led me into the bushes, and we knelt together. We clawed at the earth. A pool welled up from a small trough. A pool filled with tiny pictures. He began to murmur in my ear the names of all the casualties.

He assured me he would always be with me. My friend forever.

We stared together into the hole. Silent crystal cries, pleading for mercy.

Come with me Clyde, he said.

Come with me Clyde, he said. We are all done here.

One

"Sure, kid. Hop on. Your clown friend can sit in back."

"Gee, Mike, this sure is a swell truck ya got here."

Honk. Honk. Honk.

"I drive through a neighborhood of evil wishes."

"What d'ya mean, Mike?"

"I go up and down and across. I sort it all out."

Honk!!!!!!!!!

"Hey, kid, will ya tell the clown to stay out of the milk?"

"Hey, Chucks, stay cool back there."

Crash, tinkle.

"Tell your friend to wipe the Pan-Cake off his face. He's got milk all over his chest."

"Hey, Chucks, stop glugging down the milk."

Crash. Crash. Tinkle.

"Your friend is throwing bottles out the back. There's a law against that."

"Chucks, you're gonna ruin our chance! You're gonna get us kicked off the van!"

Roomrooomrooooooooooom.

"This is a fine milk truck ya got here, Mike. I'm real proud to be ridin'!"

"Service, kid. If you give women service, you give them everything."

Honk. Honk.

"Can I stay on the truck for the entire route?"

"Nah, kid."

"Can I take a peek at your heavenly drawtube, the flaming sword ya use to cut those pink and purple dragons?"

"Wouldn't ya rather see the Houses of the Stars?"

"Gee, Mike. Would I!"

"Here we goooooooooooooooooooo!"

"Weeeeeeeee! Weeeeeee! We! Weeeeeeeeeeeeeeeeeeeee!"

Honk. Honk. Honk.

The Archangel Dairy truck soared into the night.

"Gee, Mike. I had no idea that the stars were stored in bottles."

"Every star is a blank burning page, filled with harmony and rage."

"Is the Milky Way made out of milk?"

"No, kid, the Milky Way is made of the broken glass of clowns."

"And what's going on down there on the ground? It looks like people are running out of their houses, under the trees, just before it's getting light."

"What you see are the dreamsounds."

"What's that, Mike?"

"It's meaning, the very meaning of life. The heavens and the worlds embrace and that embrace is dreamsound. Trees link the air and the ground. The trees are clasps and the world is covered with movement and sound as heaven and earth intermingle and breathe and are buried."

"Do the spirits really have jobs?"

"Why do you think I got this truck?"

"What was she like, Mike?"

"Whadd'ya mean, kid?"

"You know what I mean, Mike. What was she like? Mom?"

"She had the voice of an angel."

Honk. Honk. HoOOOooOOOonk.

Crash. Crash. Tinkle.

The bottles were landing high in the air and breaking. The van moved above the stratosphere. Chuckles was getting drunk in back. He was pulling paper plugs from the bottles which he yanked from the openwork crates that were racked in the milk cabinets. The sky was covered with oily pavements, winding their way through the blackness.

Bottles breaking. Blood vessels filled with powdered poison. Small shattering sound. Seeable dreamsound. The sound of stars twinkling. Popcorn. The sound of a little boy coming.

"I thought your job was to lock up evil."

"Wrong, son. My job is to feed the good. Aah, the smells of a suburban neighborhood in the morning. That hot sultry lawn smell. The streetlights dimly on. Starting the engine. The quick smell of oil. Moving out toward the territory and those few warm beds. The predawn smell of certain women."

Rancid.

"I think I gotta get off."

"What do you mean, son?"

"I think I gotta get off this truck now."

HOnk.

"But this isn't Anita's house, little clownboy. This is a senator's house."

"That's OK, Mike. That's OK."

"You can get in the rear. It's open. You don't need a key."

"Thanks, Mike. That's A-OK."

"I never fucked that bitch though, son. I never fucked his wife, Lucy."

"So much the worse for her, right Chucks?"

HONK HONK HONK HONK HONK HONK

"Here we are, back on the ground. In front of the home of the Abernathies. A jockey holding out a clay lantern, behind a set of gates. Mickey Mouse security. A portico. This must be the place."

There's no one around. Just one guard to kill. Easy.
"Thanks for the ride, Mike. I'll be seein' ya 'round the block!!"

Honk Mike HOnk honk HONK Mike HONk

"What did you say your name was, son? What did you say was your name?"

"My name is Sinbad, Mike. Yeah, I gotta be honest, Sinbad's my name."

Two

"Don't make a sound! Get out of the bed, cunt," I whispered. I held the Colt against her head. She was wearing a negligée with wobbly straps. Even in early morning light, her skin was pebbly. There was some kind of fucked-up beauty cream on the bridge of her nose. A scrawny woman.

With perfect nails, I noticed.

I don't think she appreciated my polka-dot clown costume.

I let go of her throat so she could rise.

All the movement in her face came from around her eyes. Compulsive blinking. A nervous tic, perhaps. I turned her around as she sat and took the loose pillowcase from my pocket and put down my gun gently and gagged her.

"Where is he?" I whispered again. "Point!"

She turned towards me, and she was still making that ridiculous squeezing motion with her eyelids. Water poured in sheets down the walls of her cheeks.

"Boom bam boom," I said. "Tell me!"

She knew whom I meant.

She pointed.

"Crawl," I commanded her. "Crawl in there."

She got down on all fours and moved slowly out the bedroom door and down the hall. Half a spider. I grabbed the cold beer I'd copped from the kitchen off the dresser and took a swig and followed with my gun. She came to an adjoining door in the hall which was shut tight. She leaned her forehead against the door, as if she were a motorized toy. It seemed like she was trying to crawl straight through it. I opened it. Dapper Dan was snoring loudly.

"Move and I kill you," I yelled and in three steps I was standing

367

over the motherfucker and my gun was resting nimbly on his chin. I looked over my shoulder.

"Stay put, slut."

She remained in the doorway, rocking back and forth.

"Circus time!" I screamed, as the motherfucker opened his eyes. He didn't just open them. He stretched them open. He stared up into my clown face. He was looking directly at my rubber nose, at my yellow teeth, my cherry hair. He was looking appreciatively at my humorous face shining like a lightbulb.

"Goomba!"

I tossed the beer can to the side and pinched his nose with my free hand and pulled him forward.

"Welcome to reality!"

"Franklin!" he said, his voice barely audible, constricted. "My God!"

"Don't you wish, pal," I laughed. "Don't you wish I was Franklin. Franklin's a nice guy. Franklin's a compassionate and humane individual. A poet, but I'm not, pal. I'm not compassionate. I'm not Franklin. I'm not anything. I'm just here and I'm big. I'm big and here and very funny."

He was wearing silk pyjamas. He looked from side to side. And then he looked in the doorway and saw his wife gagged and stunned and crawling on the floor towards us. He began crying.

"Wimpo!" I screamed. "Fucking wimpo!" And I grabbed his wife by the back of the neck and pulled her to her feet and slammed her against the bedroom wall. I buried the barrel of the gun between her shoulder blades and pressed hard. "Stupid crying faggot wimp!"

I began to laugh. I was being quick-paced.

He was sitting bolt upright in his bedclothes. He wasn't particularly impressive. He looked at me in horror. Appreciation and horror.

"Wimpo," I repeated. "My girlfriend has only one ear. My girlfriend is chopped beef, man, and you did it. You paid that motherfucking priest do you love your wife?"

"Yes please!" he pleaded sobbing. "I do love her I do very much."

"What wife?" I laughed. I raised the gun to the back of her neck just below the skull and pulled back the pin and shot. I blew part of that fucking Democratic wife-bitch's neck right into the country French wallpaper.

"Bingobango bongo I done wanna leeeeve da Conggo!" I screamed.

The body dropped in a heap, the portion of it that wasn't nailed into the wall.

Her stain formed an interesting pattern like a collapsed lung. Dropping. Collapsing. Blood. Revenge. Clown comedy.

The senator began searching in the bedclothes, as if he'd lost something. Perhaps the soul of his poor wife Lucy. His little primping motherhenning discombobulated Lucy-fer of the tasteless Wallpaper.

"Hey babes," I counseled him. "Now we're almost even."

"Franklin, please," he pleaded, frantic, rising to his knees in the bed while clutching his blanket. "We're even, Franklin. Whatever you say, we're even. I'll do whatever you say. Just don't kill me. Please!"

"You butchered the woman I loved. You killed the ringmaster's wife!"

"Please, Franklin, I'm begging you. You've done enough damage."

"I'm not Franklin, prick!" I lowered my face so that we almost touched noses. I placed the smoking Colt against his temple, and he went erect. His entire body stiffened. I could feel his masculine energy seeping into my gun. "Nice blue blanket!"

I backed up a few steps and looked around the room.

"You killed the woman I loved. I killed the woman you loved Even Steven even steven evenstevenazure blue something's buried in my brain and I can't get it out, I'm telling you it won't come out!!"

It was the bedroom of an idiot. A political, preppy nothing. Less than nothing. Scum. An American leader.

I emptied the gun.

Onetwoonetwoone and done.

One

A genius is a man who creates his own tools.

A poet is a man who creates his own alphabet.

The gopher prays in its hole. The eagle prays in its eyrie. The amoeba prays for a proper split. The stars pray for clarity. The universe is composed of things that compose the symbols that compose the words that compose these prayers. The entire universe prays. When poets pray, they give words to the mute and sounds to the deaf. The prayers of the poets created humanity.

My alphabet grew in forgetfulness, it blossomed in decay. Tools were constructed that would hammer out abraxases from my smithwork of blood and callus. An agriology of rage moved out to coat the hands and wash away the bodies.

My letters: my lanugo of lechery, my bittersweet curses on the swaddles of the mummy.

Today I live a different life. Today I am poetry-free. Today I am calm and quiet.

In hell they burn artificial logs. The logs burn green like lawns.

Refinement, balance, grace, probity!

It was after I had written my chapter about the crackhouse that I was called before the tribunal. None of the jurors had proper features. Each was missing a small thing: a memento carried to a shoebox. I have subsequently learned from a voice within me that one of the most earnest and stupid of the neuro-poltroons, a sanctinomious bullethead who is proud of his auscultator, is now in charge back at Patton. Dr. Duncan is dead. The good Doc ascended, his eyeballs plugged with ceremental wax, into a giant psyche, where hopefully all of the angels have single heads and Dunkie can retire. Down here below we have many and can't count them.

I never went in.

I stayed outside the doors, and the clown alone plunged through.

I wouldn't go see what I knew was there, the disfigured body of the love of my life, the innocent victim, Barbie.

They say I do not remember, but I do. I do. I'm just not talking about it. I remember certain things. I remember that I must keep writing, for writing is heroism.

I never saw Cindy again. The police claim that the priest doesn't exist, in spite of the scrap of paper that I waved in their faces. I kept telling them 9W 9W 9W, you fools! There was the woman who sat across from us on the plane, clutching a tissue, she heard us, and she showed up, but it didn't mean much, and also in my hotel, a clerk remembered that a man in golf clothes had visited me, but that was it, it didn't mean much at all, and they found Sinbad guilty.

Of all the murders.

Barbie, Bruce and the security guard (strangled with a condom) and Abernathy, and Abernathy's wife, too. I believe her name was Lucy. I feel sorry for Lucy. More sorry than for any of the others. I wonder if the priest actually landed on a girl in a playground?

A stray unfortunate shot, but when the clown entered the bedroom, he just started shooting, at least that's what he told me. (I had waited outside. I frisked on the lawns, while the clown was breaking and entering.) Sinbad didn't look, he just emptied his pistol, and he was so big, his hand barely fit in the room. He reached in the door with his huge hand. He emptied the clip into an azure blanket which tried to move out of the way but couldn't. The bullets went splat splat splat, and after the senator and his wife died, the clown stopped growing.

Leonard Dalls comes to visit and tells me that the whole idea was to infuriate me so that I would kill Abernathy. To drive me crazy. Everything, from the first moment with Barbie in the deli, and the priest's sitting next to me on the plane, and the beating in the alley, was based on this. He says I was profiled, that the plot was put together scientifically, that Barbie never loved me but was hired along with Bruce and then killed by the priest to make me angry. He feels guilty, but he shouldn't. He asked me why I hadn't mentioned Kosmoski to him. It doesn't do any good. It could have been anybody that hired the assassin. Koreans? Republicans? Pentagon? There are too many wormholes and theories, and everyone keeps telling me that I changed American history.

Leonard tells me that the crime was a crime of genius. That Kosmoski was a criminal da Vinci. To be thrust into another basement. To respond the only way I could, with clown vengeance. This was true and very deep. I won the duel. The clown killed Mom, but the priest killed Barbie.

According to the jury, the senator died, a victim of a crime of passion, murdered in his bed by a berserk poet who killed his own girlfriend, a hooker, in a fit of paranoia and jealousy and then picked randomly on a powerful person, under a delusion of intimacy, blah blah blah blah blah. Everyone liked me but testified against me. They told the truth, they said. Judas, Delilah, Jensen and Cookie. Even Leonard couldn't help me. I hate lawyers and everything they have to say. If the jurors had had all of their features, they wouldn't have blamed anybody.

I still think that Barbie loved me. I refuse to believe she was hired and then betrayed by the priest. I still think that Sinbad was telling the truth. He said he didn't touch her body. He said he didn't kick her. He said he didn't hack at her repeatedly. Why at the last moment did the judge turn against him? I still think the villain was Abernathy.

Abernathy. Abernathy. Abernathy. An honest Abe, folks, an honest Abe. They say he would have saved America. From what? From people like me? They say he was a snow-white Martin Luther King. They can say anything they fucking want since now there is nothing more for me to say. They can keep on talking until the Judgment Day. My judgment is over, and I have to pay strict attention to my final responsibility. I signed a contract which was a curse, you see. It was composed of the final words my mother told me as I did something to her in the basement. Something I was forced to do once before. Something enjoyable and humiliating. Something I could do without hindrance, now that Daddy was stinking. The curse was composed of her last words before the clown cut her open and munched on her ovaries.

Did Sinbad actually do it?

Everyone claims he didn't, that my mother went mute and hanged herself, but the clown can bend reality, he can remove the halter from her neck. He can change color. The clown has ultimate power, and the clown can make everybody crazy.

I have fashioned a miniature blade, my microbe releaser. It is small but will be effective when rubbed against the belly. It will allow the evil within me to flee. Like Guenevere, I'm looking for a window. I want to put an end to language before they strip my skin.

I tried to find the truth.

I searched diligently for God. I gave my life to God. I made my surface into God's parchment. I tried to show my mother love and to protect her and she cursed me. I searched for salvation through a priest. I searched religiously for Barbie. I did what I could to avoid the curse, but now I must go back.

Back where?

Into the moment, into the convergence, into the evilest possible pleasure.

I shall enter alone and in silence.

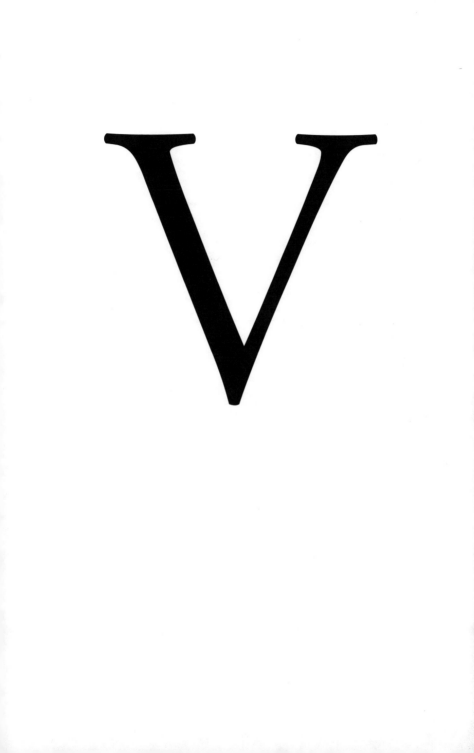

Clyde, honey?

(hee hee hee)

Two

Yes, Mom. I'm cold.

Baruch ata adonai elohenu melech haolom

Tooraloooooooooooorah

hehehe

tooraloorah lai tooraloorah loorah it's an Irish lul.....................

Oh Clyde honey look what I've done look what Satan has done to
me

(hip hoorays hip hip hip ha ha cocca laugh cocca cry staphlolaugh
a bunch ha heeee)

Clyde I never meant to touch you I never meant to make you kiss
me

he he he he he
he hehhhhhhhhheeeeeeeeeeeeeehehehehehehehehehehehhhhheeeeeeeeeeehehehehe
hhehehehehehhhhhhhhhhhhhhhhhhhhhhhhhhhhhhhhhhhhhhhhhhhhhhhhhhhhhhhhhhhhhhhhhhh
hhhhhhhhhhhhhhhhhhhhhhhhhhhhhhhhhhhhhhhhhhhhhhhhhhhhhhhhhhhhhhhhhhhhhhhhhhhhhh
hhhhhhhhhhhhhhhhhhhhhhhhhhhhhhhhhhhhhhhhhhhhhhhhhhhhhhhhhhhhhhhhhhhhhhhhhhhhhh
hhhhhhhhhhhhhhhhhhhhhhhhhhhhhhhhhhhhhhhhhhhhhhhhhhhhhhhhhhhhhhhhhhhhhhhhhhhhhh
hhhhhhhhhhhhhhhhhhhhhhhhhhhhhhhhhhhhhhhhhhhhhhhhhhhhhhhhhhhhhhhhhhhhhhhhhhhhhh
hhhhhhhhhhhhhhhhhhhhhhhhhhhhhhhhhhhhhhhhhhhhhhhhhhhhhhhhhhhhhhhhhhhhhhhhhhhhhh
hhhhhhhhhhhhhhhhhhhhhhhhhhhhhhhhhhhhhhhhhhhhhhhhhhhhhhhhhhhhhhhhhhhhhhhhhhhhhh
hhhhhhhhhhhhhhhhhhhhhhhhhhhhhhhhhhhhhhhhhhhhhhhhhhhhhhhhhhhhhhhhhhhhhhhhhhhhhh

hhhhhhhhhhhhhhhhhhhhhhhhhhhhhhhhhhhhhhhhhhhhhhhhhhhhhhhhhhhhhhhhhhhhhhhhhhhhhhhhhh
hhhhhhhhhhhhhhhhhhhhhhhhhhhhhhhhhhhhhhhhhhhhhhhhhhhhhhhhhhhhhhhhhhhhhhhhhhhhhhhhhh
hhhhhhhhhhhhhhhhhhhhhhhhhhhhhhhhhhhhhhhhhhhhhhhhhhhhhhhhhhhhhhhhhhhhhhhhhhhhhhhhhh
hhhhhhhhhhhhhhhhhhhhhhhhhhhhhhhhhhhhhhhhhhhhhhhhhhhhhhhhhhhhhhhhhhhhhhhhhhhhhhhhhh
hhhhhhhhhhhhhhhhhhhhhhhhhhhhhhhhhhhhhhhhhhhhhhhhhhhhhhhhhhhhhhhhhhhhhhhhhhhhhhhhhh
hhhhhhhhhhhhhhhhhhhhhhhhhhhhhhhhhhhhhhhhhhhhhhhhhhhhhhhhhhhhhhhhhhhhhhhhhhhhhhhhhh
hhhhhhhhhhhhhhhhhhhhhhhhhhhhhhhhhhhhhhhhhhhhhhhhhhhhhhhhhhhhhhhhhhhhhhhhhhhhhhhhhh
hhhhhhhhhhhhhhhhhhhhhhhhhhhhhhhhhhhhhhhhhhhhhhhhhhhhhhhhhhhhhhhhhhhhhhhhhhhhhhhhhh
hhhhhhhhhhhhhhhhhhhhhhhhhhhhhhhhhhhhhhhhhhhhhhhhhhhhhhhhhhhhhhhhhhhhhhhhhhhhhhhhhh

Clyde Clyde honey never untie me Clyde Clyde
Clyde Clyde what have I I done what has Satan
Satan Satan Satan done to me Clyde Clyde Clyde
Clyde honey honey never untie me me let me be
here it's because I sang sang he came I sang it was
lovely the songs are always so dreamy always so
lovely Clyde precious precious precious the songs
songs please me they make me laugh they please
Daddy Daddy Daddy I can never say what I
want what I really want and the sounds are sweet
sweet the sound of evil Clyde I can't believe what
I I I did it's because of the way I sing it's because
of the way I sing like this that Satan Satan has
made me do these things to you you never untie
me Clyde Clyde Clyde precious sweetie precious
never never untie me do what you want to do to
me

(miserable fucking cunt die die die)

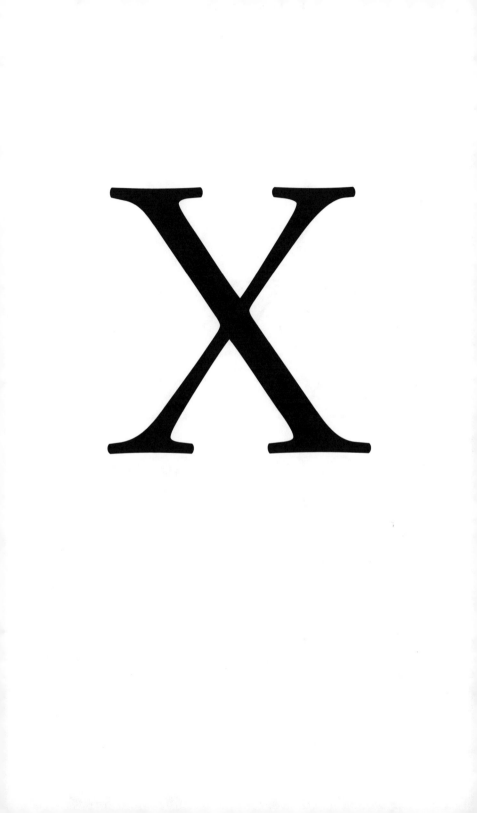

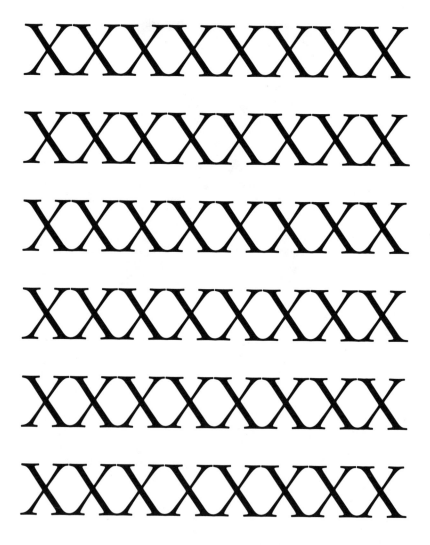

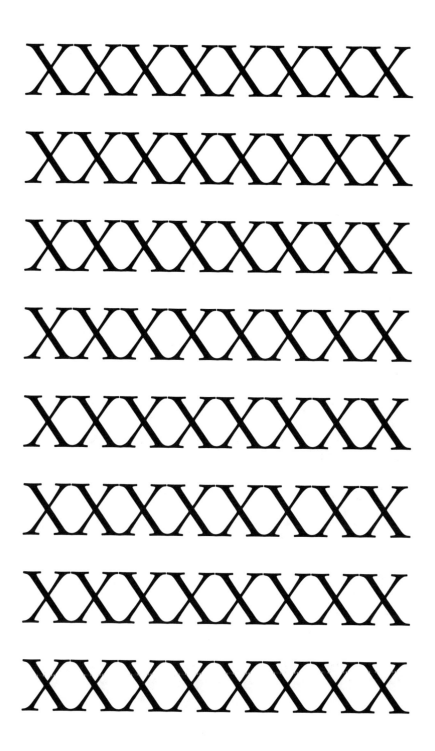

XXXCLYDE HONEY YOU SHOT DADDYXX

XXXXXXXXX

XXXXXXXXX

XXXXXXXXX

XXXXXXXXX

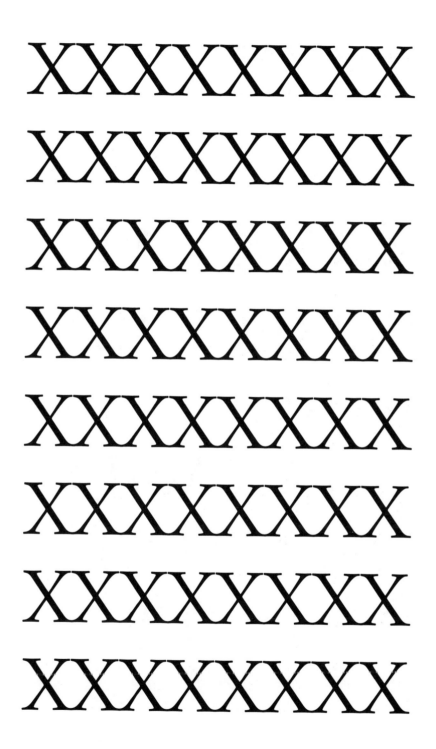

XXXXXXXXX
XXXXXXXXX
XXXXXCLYD
E PRECIOUS
BABY
SATAN WILL
OPEN YOU
JUST LIKE

HE OPENS
ME SATAN
WILL CUT
YOU DEEP IT
HURTS SO
TERRIBLY
TOUCH ME
HERE I'M
COMING

GOD OH
GOD! ! GOD
I'M COMING
FLOWING
TOUCH ME
DEEP DOWN
DEEP DOWN
DEEP
TOUCH ME

AGAIN OH
GOD OH
GOD! GOD!!
GOD! GOD!!
I'M COMING
HARD SO
HARD
TOUCH ME
SWEETHEAR

T SATAN
TOUCHES
AH!
DELICIOUS!
SATAN IS
BURNING
AAAAAHHH!
GOD!! I'M
EMPTYING

TOTALLY
CLYDE MY
PRECIOUS
SWEETHEAR
T HELP
SATAN MY
SONG
SATAN
SOUL LOVER

HURT
AGAIN
SATAN SAcut cut cut heh he

he yum the belly cut cut ha ha ha

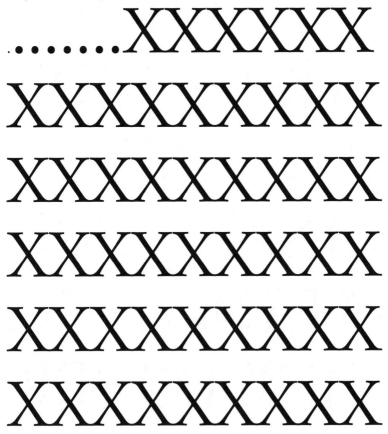

. XXXXXXX
XXXXXXXXXX
XXXXXXXXXX
XXXXXXXXXX
XXXXXXXXXX
XXXXXXXXXX

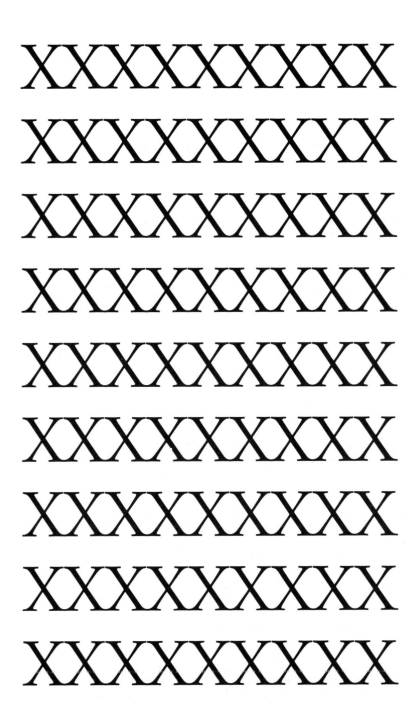

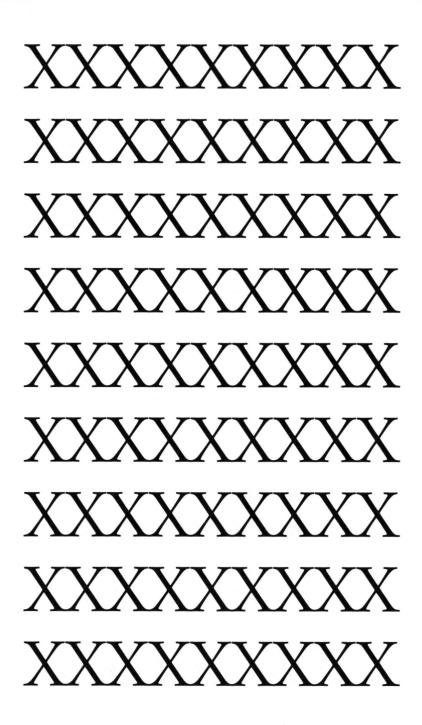

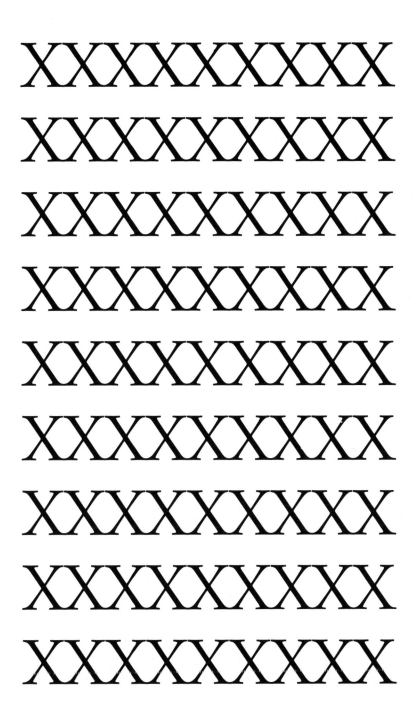

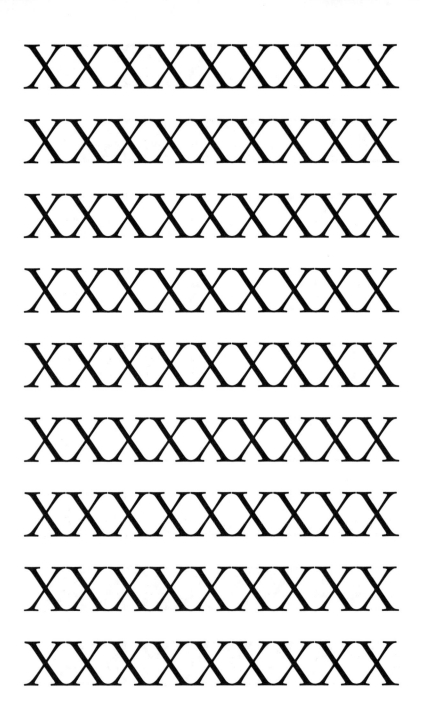

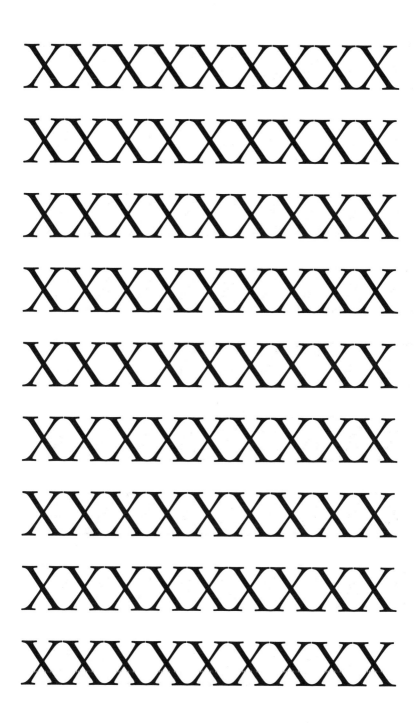

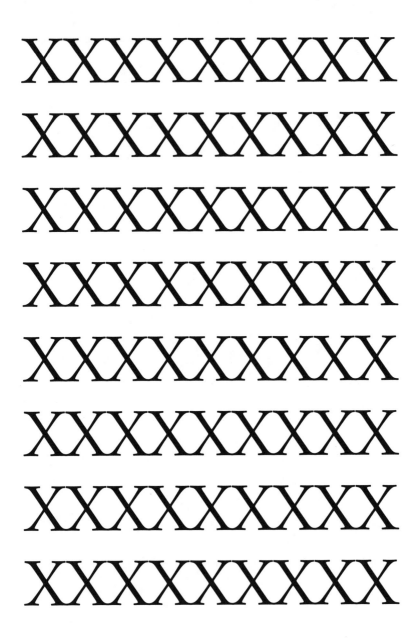

One

Now I can remember.

I sat with my head against the side of the wet bar. The gun had been fired and lay on the floor and Dad was spread across the shuffleboard and the room was splashed with blood, rivulets were running down the walls, and his neck was a series of marbled blue edges, and yes, there was a portion of a clenched jaw. I see it clearly, the busy pantaloons, Sinbad on his knees, the spokes of flaming hair surrounding his bottoms and the gorging, lapping sounds:

For A is the beginning of learning and the door of heaven for B is a creature busy and bustling for C is a sense quick and penetrating for D is depth for E is eternity such is the power of English letters taken singly for F is faith for G is God whom I pray to be gracious for H is not a letter but a spirit Benedicatur Jesus Christus sic spirem for I is identity God be gracious for K is king for L is love God in every language for M is music and Hebrew Mem is the direct figure of God's harp for N is new for O is open for P is power for Q is Quick for R is right for S is soul for T is truth God be gracious for U is unity and his right name is Uve to work it double for W is word for Y is yea God be gracious for Z is Zeal for in the education of children it is necessary to watch the words which they pronounce with difficulty for such are against them in their consequences
Jubilate Agno
Jubilate Agno
Jubilate Agno
Jubilate Agno
Jubilate Agno
Jubilate Agno

Jubilate Agno
Jubilate Agno
Jubilate Agno
Jubilate Agno

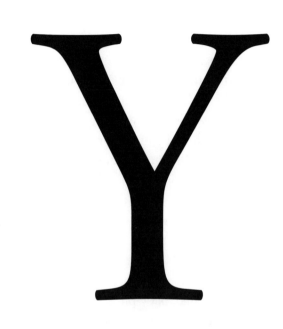

when you peeped through that door and you saw mike you saw
mike you saw mike opening her up you saw his swinging butt and
like a halo around the butt you saw his flaming hair and you saw
the rectal opening there like a lug nut and the milky pants were
on the floor and you saw his butt swinging in and out of her and
you couldn't see his teeth and you couldn't see her belly but from
where you were watching it seemed that he was eating it looked
like he was at a trough gnawing and feeding on her and she was
screaming and milkman have to get their milk and eggs where
they can where they can where they can and she sang mike don't
open me up like this oh baby please don't open me up mike
please don't open me there's someone at the door o mike baby so
good so good oh mike it's so good there's someone at the door
baby someone there oh mike baby please don't open me up like
this she sang mike don't open me up like this oh baby please
don't open me up mike please don't open me there's someone at
the door o mike baby so good so good oh mike it's so good
there's someone at the door baby someone there oh mike baby
please don't open me up like this she sang mike don't open me
up like this oh baby please don't open me up mike please don't
open me there's someone at the door o mike baby so good so
good oh mike it's so good there's someone at the door baby
someone there oh mike baby please don't open me up like this
she sang mike don't open me up like this oh baby please don't
open me up mike please don't open me there's someone at the
door o mike baby so good so good oh mike it's so good there's
someone at the door baby someone there oh mike baby please

don't open me up like this it's true that I can do things to you
now that I could never do to you before I can now be the thing
I need to be and get myself ready for the feast cuz the blood
will spring from its loop and enter me for you are the oracle but
I am the auricle and I am not a figment but reality you always
thought I was only a dream something to stick in an anus something to crap on and restrain you thought that I ripped apart your
mom you thought I killed the milkman I did neither your mother
hung herself and the milkman split he had his fuck and split he
had no reason to hang around a madwoman a woman who sang
in her apron and staggered around that sickhouse and some
fucking sicko snotty kid because you could tell walking in the
door the place was sick but you said I ate your mom which was
OK with me because any sin will do the real and unreal in hell all
amount to the same thing they do because sins are bodiless there's
no such thing as a sinner or a sin there is no such thing as suffering or loss in hell you see the only hell in the universe exists inside
of me Clyde the only thing that matters are the vows we make the
only thing that matters are the contracts all the dumbshow of the
universe all the actions from the center to the edge is essentially
meaningless and quiet and all the humor amounts to the same
thing which is why all comedy and religion were created at the
very same time because only a comic fool would ever make a fatal
vow and I created your laugh and I created your prayers and my
intentions were always clear I was the one who made you fall in
love and I was the one who hired the priest I was the one who
bought the nails that nailed you in your diapers to your destiny
that nailed you to your sickening cross I am not a clown my name
is not Sinbad I have not been in your book but I lived inside the
clown who lived inside you as you will now live inside me and I
was the essence of your suffering your mother sang to me she put
me to sleep with her songs your mother made a deal with me to
be born for you and teach you poetry the curse the contract
extends back through history from generation to generation your

mother loved her songs and made me sing them to you which I
did while you were jacking off in your bedroom dreaming your
mother knew she knew everything she knew you would kill
Charlie she told me all about it she told me you would do it when
you were born she told me you were her clown she told me you
were her clown she told me you were her clown she told me you
were her clown she told me exactly how you would kill him and
unzip him she told me every fragment of his brain that you would
coldly eliminate and she told me the memento you would cut she
told me you would unzip and cut she told me the memento you
would cut and unzip and cut and unzip and cut him and throw it
in the corner she told me you would take your memento she told
me you would cut at your hatred cut cut cunt rubbarubba cut cut
cut cut cut cunt rubbarubba cut cut cut cut cut cut cut cut cut
cut cut cut cut cut cunt rubbarubba cut cut cut cut cut cut cut
cut cut cut cut cut cut cut cut cut cut cunt rubbarubba cut cut
cut cut cut cut cut cut cut cut cut cut cut cunt cut cut cut cut
cut cunnnnnnnnt rubbbbbbbbbacut cut cut cut cut cut cut
cut when she sang her final song it wasn't to you it was sung to
me she sang it out it wasn't really what you heard it was another
melody her mind was already gone among the flames she saw the
flames rising out of the basement she came babes she had the big
fucking death orgasm she came and came and came she was my
lover Clyde she came as I fucked her she came for me she came to
me she came when you shot your Daddy she came when you cut
him she came when you touched her she came when you shot
your Daddy she came when you touched her deep down deep
down deep Down Down Down between the apronstrings she
came whenever you touched her thing that Daddy made you
touch while he was whipping he made you kneel between her legs
and touch her there as he beat you and beat her and screamed like
a beast that PRIMAL SCENE with you kneeling and her coming
and his screaming like a conquering beast and swinging his whip
and the small clink of chains and her singing and then she

touched you Clyde it was then she touched you you poor pathetic thing it was then she stroked your hair it was then and only then she stroked your thing she was my lover Clyde she came as I fucked her she came for me she came to me she came when you shot your Daddy she came when you touched her she came when you cut cut cut him she came when you shot your Daddy she came when you touched her deep down deep down deep Down Down Down between the apronstrings she came whenever you touched her thing that Daddy made you touch while he was whipping he made you kneel between her legs and touch her there as he beat you and beat her and screamed like a beast that PRIMAL SCENE with you kneeling and her coming and his screaming like a conquering beast and swinging his whip and the small clink of chains and her singing and then she touched you Clyde it was then she touched you you poor pathetic thing it was then she stroked your hair it was then and only then she stroked your thing she was my lover Clyde she came as I fucked her she came for me she came to me she came when you shot your Daddy she came when you touched her she came when you shot your Daddy she came when you cut him when you cut off his thing she came when you touched her deep down deep down deep Down Down Down between the apronstrings she came whenever you touched her thing that Daddy made you touch while he was whipping he made you kneel between her legs and touch her there as he beat you and beat her and screamed like a beast that PRIMAL SCENE with you kneeling and her coming and his screaming like a conquering beast and swinging his whip and the small clink of chains and her singing and then she touched you Clyde it was then she touched you you poor pathetic thing it was then she stroked your hair it was then and only then she stroked your thing she was my lover Clyde she came as I fucked her she came for me she came to me she came when you shot your Daddy she came when you touched her she came when you shot your Daddy she came when you hacked and hacked at

his V and slashed his thing and bit it and threw it in the corner
and screamed she came when you touched her deep down deep
down deep Down Down Down between the apronstrings she
came whenever you touched her thing that Daddy made you
touch while he was whipping he made you kneel between her legs
and touch her there as he beat you and beat her and screamed like
a beast that PRIMAL SCENE with you kneeling and her coming
and his screaming like a conquering beast and swinging his whip
and the small clink of chains and her singing and then she
touched you Clyde it was then she touched you you poor pathetic
thing it was then she stroked your hair it was then and only then
she stroked your thing she was my lover Clyde she came as I
fucked her she came for me she came to me she came when you
shot your Daddy she came when you touched her she came when
you shot your Daddy and cut him she came when you touched
her deep down deep down deep Down Down Down between the
apronstrings she came whenever you touched her thing that
Daddy made you touch while he was whipping he made you
kneel between her legs and touch her there once he beat you hard
you touched with your lips once he made you touch with your
lips with your lips and your tongue with your lips you ceased to
count with your lips with your lips with your lips and your
tongue and your tongue once once and you ceased to count and
your tongue with your lips with your lips with your lips and your
tongue and your tongue and your tongue and your tongue and
your tongue with your lips with your lips with your lips as he beat
you and beat her and screamed like a beast that PRIMAL SCENE
with you kneeling and her coming

ONLY ONCE
ONCEONLY

ONLY ONCE

ONCEONLY and

his screaming like a conquering beast and swinging his whip and
the small clink of chains and her singing and then she touched
you Clyde it was then she touched you you poor pathetic thing it
was then she stroked your hair it was then and only then she
stroked your thing she was my lover Clyde she came as I fucked
her she came for me she came to me she came when you shot
your Daddy she came when you touched her she came when you
shot your Daddy you cut cut cut and she came when you touched
her deep down deep down deep Down Down Down between the
apronstrings she came whenever you touched her thing that
Daddy made you touch while he was whipping he made you
kneel between her legs and touch her there as he beat you and
beat her and screamed like a beast that PRIMAL SCENE with
you kneeling and her coming and his screaming like a conquering
beast and swinging his whip and the small clink of chains and her
singing and then she touched you Clyde it was then she touched
you you poor pathetic thing it was then she stroked your hair it
was then and only then she stroked your thing but I owned her
she was part of me and you saw clown but she saw Devil she saw
me the lover of the dawnlight come and sigh and I wasn't drinking you were drunk but I was sober I'm always sober I have
nothing to prove I have nothing to do I have nothing to say I
have nothing to accomplish I only have to make my claim which
I am about to do you see it doesn't make a difference what you do
you were damned from the moment you entered the womb you
entered it from above on your way to below you fell like a meteor
through the milky darkness because life is a tumble the ceiling

trap is birth the floor trap is death and you just tumble through cuz you are not suffering for any reason you never did anything wrong and all your words were good and you went down and split apart and let me enter your cell and your soul and your spirit split and let me in as a result of an ancient Jewish curse handed from mother to son and I flew on leathern wings and planted a comedian and the comedian grew and grew and grew and now it's time for the final scene in which I make my claim your mother knew what she was doing when she refused to touch you cuz one of the rules in hell is that the damned never touch each other except in satanic rituals and you were born in hell cuz the damned give birth to the damned and your prayers mean fuck and you were the child of two devils as you always knew they weren't human they were evil spirit vipers and you're not going anywhere you haven't been you're just going to be my food that's all there is to it you are going to become me you are going to enter me you are going to become part of me you are going to become my microbe and you will become my slave you will become my eternal slave my piece of bacterial shit and you will be forced for all eternity to obey my commands you will never sing again and you will never write another letter and the letters on your skin will disappear and your poems will disappear and you will no longer stalk or pray or sing you'll just become my shape-less thing my damned internal slave a slave of evil swimming in my chyle a calm part of me a part of a larger evil body Clyde so go ahead and finish your book and put aside your pen and open for me open up your misery remember remember remember it doesn't take much effort to join me Precious Sweetheart darling Clyde fall into the flames burn forever sizzle green in my gut

Two

Mother blessed Mother now I finally touch you.

aaaaah your first boyish sperm rubbed like balm into my waiting head it's clown addiction,
aaaaahhhhh your fumbling childish fingers so hypnotic when I'm bound it's clown torture,
aaaaahhhhhhhhh the nights of self-abuse lying next to you on your pillow it's clownanism,
aaaaahhhhhhhhhhhh the touch of your rusty nails pounded into my flesh it's clownafixion,
aaaaahhhhhhhhhhhhhhh my flickering presence on the playground it's Clown's Syndrome,
aaaaahhhhhhhhhhhhhhhhhhhh I am your masculine slave doll it's clownage and discipline,
aaaaahhhhhhhhhhhhhhhhhhhhhhh so terrifying my dance in green flame it's clownophobia,
aaaaahhhhhhhhhhhhhhhhhhhhhhhhhh my lust for your mother's blood it's clownaholism,
aaaaahhhhhhhhhhhhhhhhhhhhhhhhhhhhh your tongue cleaving my groin its clownophrenia,
aaaaahhhhhhhhhhhhhhhhhhhhhhhhhhhhhhhhhh it's time to throw Azazel off the cliff and
summon the myrmidons Come! Come! Come! Come! Come!
Come! Come! Come! Come! Come! Come! Come! Come! Come!
Come! Come! Come! Come! Come! Come! Come! Come! Come!
Come! Come! Come! Come! Come! Come! Come! Come! Come!
Come! Come! Come! Come! Come! Come! Come! Come! Come!
Come! Come! Come! Come! Come! Come! Come! Come! Come!
Come! Come! Come! Come! Come! Come! Come! Come! Come!
Come! Come! Come! Come! Agniel and Anmael and Araquiel
and Araziel and Asael and Asbeel and Azael and Azza and Astarte
and Agrat-bat Mablah and Adrameleck and Agares and Aniquiel
and Ashmedai and Asmodeus and Astaroth and all the other
alphabetic names Come! Come! Come! Come! Come! Come!
Come! Come! Come! Come! Come! Come! Come! Come! Come!
Come! Come! Come! Come! Come! Come! Come! Come! Come!
Come! Come! Come! Come! Come! Come! Come! Come! Come!
Come! Come! Come! Come! Come! Come! Come! Come! Come!

Come! Come! from Gehenna into mucilaginous milk at the
bottom of bottles revel in the clouded silk dartle through the
undergrowth of moonlit lawns gutted on bile eruct and gladden
in the falling action emerge omphalitically tumescent from the tip
of my prunish ossicle that stings like a puffy adder when I Come
Come Come Come Come and procreate with clotted magma all
ye microbials of my white hot fever dreams and Come with
furious laughter

YYYYYYYYY

YYYYYYYYYY

YYYYYYYYYY

YYYYes tttttto
ggladennnmey
ou CCCCome

yyyyyyyesyyyy

yeesesesesyyy
yYYYYYYYY es

to gladden me youcomeyescomeyescome seecomesee
ClydedieClyde kill himself cut his harakiri veins cut his harakiri
veins cut his harakiri jelly cut his harakiri jelly cut his harakiri
jelly cut his harakiri jelly cut his harakiri jelly cut his harakiri jelly
cut his harakiri veins cut his harakiri veins and blood pours from
his belly like clotted blackberry jelly just as it did from the trough
of Mummy milk and eggs milk and eggs and milk and eggs and
milk and eggs and milk and eggs and milk and eggs and milk and
eggs and milk and eggs and milk and eggs and milk and eggs and
milk and eggs and milk and eggs and milk and eggs and milk and
eggs and milk and eggs and milk and eggs and milk and eggs and
jelly and from all the others all the holy names his alphabets will
fadecome seeseecomeseseeeeecomesaaa come see yyyyyyyyyyesyess
see him die he is going down into me now deep Down Down
Down I shall watch his blade zig then zag then split his bag and
fat layers flap cuz I am singing in the balefires in the center of the
muddy enterons where ancient elephants daven with their trunks
ablaze I am the singing train conductor I am the music of descent
the brilliant logic of the boxcars the logic of a baby rubbing its
eyes and crying in a corner of a boxcar I see I see Anita in the
center of her singing and Charles Wilson Franklin swinking his
flagellum in the milk of my testes ready to form another Clyde
out of an egg I sucked from her I sucked her sucked her sucked
her sucked her sucked her sucked her sucked her finger sucked
her sucked her body sucked her clit sucked her finger sucked
her clit sucked her clit sucked her dry she stroked me with her

416

hand and her wedding band and there will always be bug-eyed drunks as long as there are men there will be brunches and shocked genitals there will be drunken demons to join the dance we danced deep inside the embryos with the green tormentors with the whippers the bug-eyed drunken killer whippers youmadeyourdecisionClydeyoumadeyourdecision and turned your learning over to me you forgot to grow and let me do your growing you handed me your soul you made your Faustian bargain you sent away to the grape juice company you ordered three clowns you ordered one to be mommy one to be daddy and one to be baby babes one to be baby babes one to be Baby Jesus babes the demon clown the special one to do your bidding and that was me babes which is why I say babes and you stuck us in a crib and you dared the powers that be to stop you you raged you promised up your soul in flames forever irretrievably without the possibility the merest possibility if only if only.................you were a child so cute you laid your triplets in a crib but you only blessed me Clyde only me and took a toolkit and made your bedtable Golgotha a slotted base and nailed together strips of lath while you prayed and nailed up Al and nailed up Einstein and then you nailed up me you felt your skin was burning every day you felt it burn like brimstone babes your untouched skin like brimstone it would smoke and burn until you made a pact until you signed that first development contract it was torture every moment torture I got you young to crucify your parents with my charms and letters that would cool your skin and keep explosive powers in for Albert Einstein you were told created a bomb but people used him evil forces used that Jewish saint and mathematician who couldn't do the simplest math and created a bomb that killed so many children and burned their skins and opened their wounds and you saw the pictures of the children with their bones exposed to the air the children that exploded so you named the Momma doll Al and the Poppa doll Einstein and you prayed that you would not explode you prayed and wept and did your incantations and then Anita bled downstairs and you heated the water and you said a prayer you prayed you prayed you prayed you prayed and then you took down Al and took down Einstein you took them down from their crosses and you stuck them in the water in the same way the Doctor stuck his syringes in the water you stuck them in the water that was boiling in order to remove the skin because if they kept theirs you wouldn't keep yours but they kept their skins they only lost their makeup and identities and then you fished them out like half-cooked lobsters and you and I shared the same cross and bed and fantasies you plucked my nails and put me by the record player you tied me and touched me and beat me and abused me but I didn't care I didn't care a whit I actually enjoyed it because I wasn't really in that doll at all I'm really up here in your head and my microbes rejoice on the blades of axes they coat the tongue and eyes the microbes are everywhere they coat the stones and air they were the first forms of life and explode in the air it all arose out of my loins there is a moment before the hooting lights of the tent go out before the final blackness of the final blackout just before the hooting lights go out that the poet is still penning and by his side is a sheaf of papers and a shiv is in his shoe a sheaf of papers and a shiv is in his shoe a sheaf of papers and a shiv and he's all set to go but still he's writing he's penning this very sentence he still has more to say he still is wearing his makeup before it burns like sulfur and excoriates before the worm arms stiffen in the dampness of the coffin and the thing in him is ready and I am ready to have my way to drink the blood of this poor clownmaster this poor man who sold his soul this victim of poetry this vile victim of poetry because I am the purest thing because good is corrupted in wood and evil is pure and there is only one side to my spirit and it isn't breathing it never has and never will it's juices yes juices

juices juices juices juices juices juices juices juices juices juices
juices juices juices juices juices juices juices juices juices juices
juices juices juices juices juices juices juices juices juices juices
juices juices juices juices juices juices juices juices juices juices
juices juices juices juices juices juices juices juices juices juices
juices juices juices juices juices juices juices juices juices juices
juices juices juices juices juices juices juices juices juices juices
juices juices juices juices juices juices juices juices juices juices
juices juices juices juices juices juices juices juices juices juices
juices juices juices juices juices juices juices juices juices juices
juices juices juices juices juices juices juices juices juices juices
juices juices juices juices juices juices juices juices juices juices
juices juices juices juices juices juices juices juices juices juices
juices juices juices juices juices juices juices juices juices juices
juices juices juices juices juices juices juices juices juices juices
juices juices juices juices juices juices juices juices juices juices
juices juices juices juices juices juices juices juices juices juices
juices juices juices juices juices juices juices juices juices juices
juices juices juices juices juices juices juices juices juices juices
juices juices juices juices juices juices juices juices juices juices
juices juices juices juices juices juices juices juices juices juices
juices juices juices juices juices juices juices juices juices juices
juices juices juices juices juices juices juices juices juices juices
juices juices juices juices juices juices juices juices juices juices
juices juices juices juices juices juices juices juices juices juices
juices juices juices juices juices juices juices juices juices juices
juices juices juices juices juices juices juices juices juices juices
juices juices juices juices juices juices juices juices juices juices
juices juices juices juices juices juices juices juices juices juices
juices juices juices juices juices juices juices juices juices juices
juices juices juices juices juices juices juices juices juices juices
juices juices juices juices juices juices juices juices juices juices
juices juices juices juices juices juices juices juices juices juices

juices juices juices juices juices juices juices juices juices juices
juices juices juices juices juices juices juices juices juices juices
juices juices juices juices juices juices juices juices juices juices
juices juices juices juices juices juices juices juices juices juices
juices juices juices juices juices juices juices juices juices juices
juices juices juices juices juices juices juices juices juices juices
juices juices juices juices juices juices juices juices juices juices
juices juices juices juices juices juices juices juices juices juices
juices juices juices juices juices juices juices juices juices juices
juices juices juices juices juices juices juices juices juices juices
juices juices juices juices juices juices juices juices juices juices
juices juices juices juices juices juices juices juices juices juices
juices juices juices juices juices juices juices juices juices juices
juices juices juices juices juices juices juices juices juices juices
juices juices juices juices juices juices juices juices juices juices
juices juices juices juices juices juices juices juices juices juices
juices juices juices juices juices juices juices juices juices juices
juices juices juices juices juices juices juices juices juices juices
juices juices juices juices juices juices juices juices juices juices
juices juices juices juices juices juices juices juices juices juices
juices juices juices juices juices juices juices juices juices juices
juices juices juices juices juices juices juices juices juices juices
juices juices juices juices juices juices juices juices juices juices
juices juices juices juices juices juices juices juices juices juices
juices juices juices juices juices juices juices juices juices juices
juices juices juices juices juices juices juices juices juices juices it's
almost time to take a sip you did it to me babes you used me you
didn't have to do it you gave it to me early that little rhinestone
thing that zircon that you tossed away for good your soul but
that's OK we'll open you up like Mommy's curse has said because
you are tired Clyde you've packed your empty suitcases just like
Dad and need to sleep eternally in the depths of the washing
machine in the depths of the mechanical beast you need to join
your mommy and daddy in my special place where he will whip

and she will come and you will touch her deep down deep down deep so now it's time to become one big happy family and melt together in spite of the weather and Al says goodby cuz where you're going there isn't any money and Einstein says goodby cuz where you're going there isn't any psychiatry and to touch to touch to touch to touch to touch to touch to become the one thing that is never going to end the one thing the laughing ridiculous clownish thing that you abused and used it's time to go now put it all aside it's time to go to sleep it's time to lullaby it's time for little Clyde to take his pretty nap for me to take my sip then taste the letters one by one like canapes to bring the world of poetry down it's time for you to go so I will blanken all your pages one by one the minutes will erase your words I'll blot your stanzas and corrode your odes I'll steal your ones I'll steal your twos all meanings all the songs the wisdom the prayers of gophers eagles stars amoebae enjamb then fade cuz I am patient babes I'm very patient and first the words will go and then the memories of words and then the brains that made the memories and then the flesh and then the bones and then the stones and in that apocalypse when the stars turn cold everything will be inside of me it will only be me and the void and all will be inside and everything inside will be living and breathing it will all be deep inside and living and breathing within my flames within me all the fixtures will be part of one big thing and when that happens I'll remove the last dab of Pan-Cake I'll remove the last dab of powdered bone and be free to dance free to dance unseen so put aside your work now Clyde and be a good little Momma's boy and take off your shoe and be a good little Momma's boy and take up your edge yes I'll tuck you in for good now take up your edge and cut real deep it will be the least of your hurts and release for me release for me your clotted jelly release release release for me your clotted jelly release life's natural agony release sweet memory release regret release release your sorrow and your enmity release and do it do it now there is one letter missing you've had your

ABCDE
FGHIJK
LMNOP
QRSTU
VWXY

displayed on all the surfaces of your body there is one letter that was never put there it was never put there you can make it now Clyde you can make all the memories go away and all divisions you can open up your belly you can make the clotted grape juice flow cuz curses outlast poetry you can sleep now baby boy you can be as innocent and empty as you were before you trusted me you can die now baby boy you can slit the horizontal then decline and rip across the navel and return you can spill the inner light the seal of the body pulling back the skin like shutters you can sleep now baby boy lullaby sing lullaby and lullaby my plump and sweet young thing my thing you'll slip away into my laughing vessel you can put aside the cradlestring the luminous words the noble tiny bells that hang from cradles you can put aside your book now baby boy and lullaby you can put aside your words and you can seal your life and strife now baby sleep now baby rest in the arms of a clown your bosom buddy sleep now baby lullaby sweet lullaby and go to sleep now you can make that final sweep now lullaby sweet lullaby my baby Clyde my precious sweetie you can sleep now Clyde my sweet my dearest baby Clyde die in my tender arms now you can make that final sweep lullaby sweet lullaby now you can make that final effort you can carve that

Three

It has been over a year now since the eviscerated body of Clyde Wayne Franklin was discovered on the floor of his cell at Leavenworth Penitentiary. On the day of his death he had mailed me his manuscript, with a short note attached:

Lenny:

Forty years ago, I made my bargain, and justice must now be served. I shall never stop singing. Never ever. We devils have the purest voices. Peace. Peace. Peace.

Clyde

Shortly after his suicide, sitting in my study early one evening and focusing my attention on the manuscript, which I'd just finished reading, I realized with a certainty reserved only for spy novelists who spend their lives smelling rats, that a gigantic rat was here to be smelled. Nobody had figured that Clyde, shattered as he was, would have the fortitude to write it all down, to leave his testament and evidence behind. Somewhere in this book lay the key to the mystery, and even though it was too late to save my friend, I wanted to do what I could to clear his reputation, to show the world that what he had written here was, in spite of his emotional illness, basically honest and true, and that Clyde's final act was not the random violence of a poet gone berserk but something much deeper and more sympathetic.

My best chance of exposing the plotters—those whom I knew had incited Clyde to kill Daniel Abernathy—was to place myself in Clyde's shoes and search for "coincidences" or "holes" in the information he had been fed or in the situation that had been constructed to insure his mental collapse. I stared at the sheaf of papers, thinking through what had happened and what Clyde had been told, sorting through each and every detail:

A soldier-saint in the Vietnam War converts his intended assassin by uttering a few words and turns him into a man of God. A hooker takes bedroom film of a presidential candidate engaged in S&M and then entrusts the blackmail to a dim-witted pimp, who blows the project and gets them both killed. A postage-stamp-size slip of paper, containing only a number and a letter, catapults a man to his own destruction, as he realizes he has inadvertently betrayed the woman he loves. A murder is recreated thirty-years after the fact in a suburban home, in order to drive the original murderer to insanity, rage and vengeance against an innocent person. And finally, the intended consequence of these interwoven strands of events— the most highly-regarded poet in America is manipulated into killing the most highly-regarded politician in America, in a way that makes it look like a paranoid act of jealousy, when in fact it's a vicious act of political expediency. And since the poet has been manipulated psychologically, there's no money, no handler, no fingerprints, no traces. The poet's explanation is viewed by the American public as a psychotic delusion.

I continued staring at the manuscript. The room was getting dark, and the small work-objects in front of me, the ashtray piled with dottle, my keyboard, stapler, tape dispenser, the photo of Fred and Ted, and the paper tray, all of these things lost presence and receded in the half-light, as night descended.

I began to see that if I continued picking through the events in Clyde's book, following his "clew of voices" through the labyrinth, I wasn't going to get anywhere. Obviously, it was intended that even if an oddball such as I were to believe Clyde's story—a story babbled by a violent madman from prison, complete with alcoholic clown visions, obscene delusions, sexual and racial hatred and ambivalence, and hysterical pleadings and founderings—even then, he would immediately conclude that the pivotal intelligence in the actual plot was the phony Jesuit; and since Arnold "Duke" Kosmoski was long-gone, and since the FBI had found nobody who could say who Kosmoski really was, and since not a scrap of other information was available, there would be no way of linking the priest to the background conspirators, to the people who had hired him to think the whole thing out and execute it. The sequence of events entwined and ran smack into a dead end.

I lit my pipe and stared out the window.

I realized that my only remaining recourse was to move backwards rather than forwards, to examine Clyde's situation before he met the hooker in a Los Angeles delicatessan and to search for an answer to the most basic of all questions: Why was Clyde singled out as a patsy in the first place? There must have been a tremendous amount of thought given as to whom the conspirators could rope into committing the murder. Names like Lee Harvey Oswald, James Earl Ray and Sirhan Sirhan are never drawn out of a hat. How did the plotters come to decide on Clyde Wayne Franklin?

Was it because he was a famous poet? Was it because he had killed his father? Was it simply for the cosmetic value of using a tattooed intellectual, to make the act seem more surreal and grotesque when it hit the papers? Was it based on creating a right-wing backlash against the inherent obscenity of the free-thinking American artist?

And then it occurred to me that someone must have had a lot of confidence that Clyde would behave predictably—that he would react to finding those disfigured bodies by killing Abernathy, that he wouldn't just run down to the Potomac, for example, and jump off a bridge. Somebody had to have known Clyde *extremely well*, since the fate of the plot and the country was riding on what he would do at two AM on the morning of November 8. Political assassinations are hard-boiled tactical affairs, constructed with layers of deniability, and are based on iron-clad certainties and depth of expertise. Somebody had put his reputation (and probably his life) on the line, providing a personal assurance to the powers-that-be that Clyde would react under the circumstances with swift and brutal vengeance.

There were, so far as I could see, only two possible categories of person who could have provided this type of assurance: an expert forensic psychologist or an intimate friend.

Just as I began to consider these possibilities, the cusp of the moon appeared in a lower corner of my library window.

The moon!!

I dropped my pipe into the ashtray.

A shiver went up my spine, and as a recovering alcoholic, I paused for a moment and said a prayer of gratitude to my Higher Power. I finally had the answer I'd been looking for—a chink in the armor of the plotters and the first step toward solving the puzzle that had stumped me ever since that autumn afternoon when the drunken tattooed butcher-poet of America barged into my office and told me his incredible, insidious tale.

Yes, the moon was the key to everything! Clyde had commented on it over and over again: the assassination plot had been based on the movement of the moon!

"You must meet him at the exact moment of the full moon," the priest had said.

Moonlight on the bomb-pocked rice paddies of Laos. Moonlight on the steps of the Lincoln Memorial. Moonlight on a bloodied hedge in McLean, Virginia. Moonlight flooding the minds of two lovers, lying together on a bunk in Soledad Prison!

At the exact moment of the full moon, a poet waited desperately below a statue of the American savior for his own personal savior, and for release from the guilt of having shotgunned his father and from the insistent delusion that he had violated and meat-axed his mother. And at that very same moment, a hooker and her pimp were being shot and axed in a ranch house in suburban Washington, DC!

Twenty years ago, two men had shared their fantasies and secrets. Two men had shared their feelings of adoration and fear. Two murderers had shared their love and reverence for the moon. And one of the men would use this knowledge to frame the other. To frame the friend who had betrayed him. To frame the man who had slept with his girlfriend!

The following morning, I was on an early plane to Paris.

Through the *Préfecture de Police* I learned that, as a fascist mercenary involved in various actions in France in the sixties, Billy Ziqubu, under the alias Samuel Nkofo, had been a primary suspect in a number of political murders, including that of the famous student leader, Paulie Druon. An educated Zulu, he had previously been employed in South Africa as an informer and "sanitizer." Threatened with arraignment, Billy vanished from Europe, and when he was arrested in California shortly thereafter for armed robbery, the fact went unnoticed in France. I inquired of the Paris police if there were somebody associated with Ziqubu who was fluent in Indic languages, Korean or Russian—searching of course for the priest—but I drew a blank.

I reported my findings to the FBI, and within a week Bridgette Olafson was placed under arrest in Norway. A heroin addict, she didn't offer much resistance and agreed to cooperate. She was at pains to deny any knowledge of an assassination plot. She was aware of what her boyfriend did for a living, but she never asked for job details. She said she breathed easier that way.

She was, however, willing to provide the Norwegian police with three pieces of important information.

According to her, an older man, who matched the description of Kosmoski, had recruited Billy in Los Angeles more than six months prior to the events related in this book. Who this person was, she claimed she didn't know. She figured, naturally enough, that if it were a professional contact, then Billy was being hired to ice somebody.

Secondly, she related that she had come across a hundred thousand dollars in Billy's attaché case. He was in the room at the time, and he had laughed and told her jokingly that the money "was for the most expensive lay he ever paid for."

Lastly, she admitted she had been instructed to call Clyde and tell him she had murdered her boyfriend. Billy explained to Bridgette that he wanted Clyde permanently out of his life. When she objected that there were easier ways of giving old friends the brush-off, Billy reminded her that she was the cause of the trouble between them in the first place. Bridgette claimed that she hadn't seen or heard from Billy since shortly after she made the phone call, and soon thereafter, she moved to Norway.

It can be assumed that the hundred thousand dollars came through the priest and that it was used to pay June Sunlight and Bruce Crenna to go through their paces, as instructed by Ziqubu. I don't know what Bruce and June expected to happen on the night they were murdered. They had probably been told that the ultimate purpose of the job was to get Clyde to humiliate Abernathy publicly (which is what both Brennemann and I had originally believed). Such machinations are common in Washington.

There is no reason to suspect Delilah Sandhurst or Judas Brenneman of any complicity, and both have cooperated fully. Judas fell out of touch with his old friend and assumed from what he'd heard that he was dead. Clyde was right, incidentally, about one thing: my big-deal lead, Cookie Kraft, was a liar.

I hope and pray that the testimony of Olafson will somehow lead to the apprehension of the priest, whoever he may be, although I must admit that I highly doubt it will occur. As for the fate of Ziqubu, most people reading this will already know what happened to the man.

In January of this year, Billy Ziqubu was found strangled in a forest outside London.

His left ear was missing.

I also sincerely doubt that we'll ever find the source of the money behind the assassination. The sophistication of the hit leads me to believe that the trail would extend high into the halls of government or the military. In any case, the batting average on resolving this kind of crime in America so far is precisely zero.

And now I would like to say a few final words about my friend. Clyde had managed to survive, burdened with intense hatred and grief and guilt, voices and all, for many years and to produce indelible poetry. To torment and destroy such an important artist, a man who had fought courageously against the torment and destructiveness he suffered as an abused child, was an act of unspeakable savagery and cynicism. It is obvious that as Clyde wrote his book, and as the day of his death approached, he became increasingly deranged, imagining murders and events that never took place. So far as we know, he murdered four people: his father, Charles Wilson Franklin (who hadn't been sexually mutilated), Daniel Quentin Abernathy and his wife, Lucille, and the security guard at the house that night, Dwight Lee.

In memoriam, I shall conclude my "Chapter Three" by citing the title poem of Clyde's first book, *Barathrum*, which was written when he was thirty-one and still imprisoned in a mental hospital in San Bernardino, California. A barathrum, from the Attic Greek, was an ancient pit in which condemned prisoners were thrown, and hence has come to mean the depths of hell.

At this point, still grieving, I have no desire to provide any other testament or tribute to my friend. May his soul rest in "peace peace peace." Clyde's poem will have to stand in place of any further expression of my deep sense of loss.

L. Jerome Dalls

Barathrum

Barathrum

I.

Caramel drips down walls. The torn scrap of rimed skin;
slathered, twitching parts of dolls; their collars,
        belts and scarred legging.
A lucky shekel lodges on the excrement of a snail. Auburn
hair-whorl tamped beneath the sherd of a nail. A loosened eyeball:
           its foxed reflection

of bovine killers shivering beyond the gun trails. The pit
expands imperceptibly with the dull impact of babies,
        and the bight of an elbow framing
a nostril throws a helix of sunlight into a forest of bone.
I am driving below in my Boschmobile,
            a salesman on the road.

The whir and suck of gay bullets from the *Einsatsgruppe*
are like fat gnats crepitating on my spanking-new windshield.
        I am the Gypsy King of the Loam.
The worms down here are larger than I am. They have massive
arms: villi that swim through the final scents of freezing lips.
          In my pocket are white meat disks,

charms that help me sell. They are not what they seem to be.
They are the creamy testes and blighted ovaries of this pit,
        run through Nazi bread machines. Blood
of my blood, I sell to all the hanging heads, dipping down
from knotted shoulders. Heads uncovered in the brumal temple.
        Stark feet, saliva, fetid earlocks,

vomit, urine dripping through lime dreams. Near the top, there are
moans that deepen like a barren thunder, in the sanctuary.
    When one man breathes,
I lose my train of thought, I cannot continue my pitch until it stops;
until the mass of writhing flesh stops breathing,
         the mouth refuses to do

its menial thing, it refuses to do its selling. I do not belong here,
but I comprehend the trivial reason I was sent. Somebody, they told me,
      somebody tattooed and vicious
has to descend because there might be something thievable left over,
among the snow-encrusted, steaming corpses there might be...
        like shadows on a baldachin,

a letter a breath a word a voice a song a poem a blessing
or a Horst Wessel lullaby of diarrhea and Yiddish stench.
      Precious bedroom stars
beaming through the barbed wire of a crib: *Sleep sweet babe*
sweet clucking babe for one day you must descend, tumbling
        into the trench.

II.

An infant loses its sense of place as vermeil
flames explode from lactic orifices. In a Walpurgis dance,
            a woman's voice in the distance,
begging his Thong to hurt again, her baby seeks
            a flawless formula for dreaming.

Weir after shaded weir

receding toward a fixed hole in a river, Mother,
my small teeth dug into the wales of your breasts,
            into your vermiculate
sulfur pits
and I became a hero.

Of each enemy, in order, I broke his back,

scheming as I gnawed
and driveled and sucked
and forced stour numbness into his limbs. I turned
            his breathing
into a gearbox operation and bled chunks
            of red-flecked sorrel
onto a white ticking that billowed. Neo-Nazi child

of the mild stirp of Abraham, bland and thoughtless,
            cooing in the gossamer night.

III.

Jealous Lord, I've sinned. I, your star salesman,
have squandered my per diem.
    And I shot the boss.
I captured his head as an object lesson and stuffed it into an airy
        ocean,

and then I fingered his groaning woman. In a manner of speaking.
The chrome on my coupe will never stop gleaming.
    A touch of scarlet in the weather,
and gelid rivulets of regrets and petrified
        emotion,

Jealous Lord, I, your slimeball number-
one closer in the *Judenfrei* Region,
    need to make a confession.
Accept this humble Kaddish. Pardon its rueful, gruesome
        tone:

IV.

Yit-gadal v-yit-kadash sh'mey raba
those that hit the mother in the womb
hit the child at her side in the head

B'alma di v'ra chirutey, v'yam-lich mal-chutey
sometimes they are clothed sometimes they are facing away
sometimes they are naked sometimes they are facing forward

B'cha-yey-chon uv-yomey-chon uv-cha-yey d'chol beyt yisrael
in the pit very few die instantly quiet quiet quiet and one
can survive a few more moments hearing the choking and prayers

Ba'agala u'vizman kariv, vi'imru amen
the last one standing gets shot the most now and then
someone crawls out of the pit and survives as a dead person

Y'hey sh'mey raba m'varach l'alam ul-almey alma-ya
the more Yids there are to kill the more slowly
they die less gas fewer bullets less cash more time

Yit-barach v-yish-tabach v-yit-pa'ar v'yit-roman v'yit-na-sey
some go as they fall some are smashed with shovels some go their
nostrils filled with freezing soil but most don't go away for a while

V-yit'chadar v'yit-aleh v'yit-hala sh'mey d'kud-sha B'rich hu
when the pit is sealed many hours later there are still
sounds coming out of the ground there are still complete words

L'eyla ul-eyla mi-kol bir-chata v'shi-rata
not one man will ever be punished for shooting a Jew at the pithead
not a single hayseed murderer ever needlessly has to suffer

Tush-b'chata v'ne-chemata da'amiran b'alama, v'imru amen
in a better world after the murderers' wives are shot and their
children are shot as they are forced to watch the Aryan killers

Y'hey sh'lama raba min sh'ma-ya v'cha-yim aleynuy v'al kol yisrael, vi'imru amen
are lined up at the pithead and shot in each arm then shot
in each leg then shot in the balls then buried alive as they bleed

Oseh shalom bi'm'romav, hu ya'aseh shalom aleynu v'al kol yisrael, v'imru amen
these pits are cicatrices of earth over deep peopled wounds we
shall never recover the scars are ours forever and ever. *Amen.*

V.

In prison there was an iron trough where cons would fuck
    a jealous lover once lit two men with kerosene
    the skinny was they kept moving and jerking
in green flame that they died laughing and fucking.

I envision two male lovers in the pit that weren't hit they
    hid in each other's arms as the bodies of those
    they knew rained down on them they stayed silent
and did not stir they stayed silent and kissed and laughed.

VI.

I live a candent story. The sounds from this sough
    of calamity are too complex to bear.
I burn their sound onto my skin: choral screams,
    the final croon of horror and despair.

What I have to sell, the world is too devoid to buy. It breathes
    a new atmosphere of cleaner, lighter fare.
Ancient hulls of spirit, deveined and fractured,
    rot under the plump shadows of murderers.

I should know, being both. Killer and killed. Angelic,
    sodomizable animal, stave by stave I pare
down the lowest root and nerve. I whisper death-threats
    to all the quaking vegetables. *Share*

these threads, participate in fleshy bargains! I wave
    my shreds in free-flowing air;
I flaunt flayed skin, tattered syllables and follicles,
    out the spattered windows of my car.

To wear these garments, one must descend and build wisdom
    where dreams discolor and depart:
out of the moans that sweep the filthy latitudes, to assemble
    cursed, smoldering, prophetic letters

of my art. In the moment prior to surrender,
    when agony is akin to ritual pleasure,
poetry becomes a history that weeps from a river mouth
    its muddied salt of infant tears.

VII.

This sort of wasted, frigid life, this curse,
is slowly settling into soil, rebuilding ease from the hopeless.
    The meal of history is almost digested.
In their final beds, they had awaited the lineup. For the first
and only time, many had prayed for poetry, poems and poets;
    noble Jews had prayed for builders of memory.

The fools had prayed for *me.* Every final day was a normal day.
The local police were courteous in an odd way, or perhaps they weren't,
    as the new-cut trench awaited on the outskirts.
Yet I'm still there, for my part crafting judicious slogans,
selling rags to souls from the charneled outreach of my car. Never
    letting humans evade the human raiment, I bargain

from the cold swathes of innocence, I, the carnivore scop
in my sleek, indomitable machine, leprous, tatterdemalion peddler
    of the almost-forgotten, of the fallen, mottled garb
of virgin hair, duplicating the wails of suffocating babies,
the thud and moan of shochet and baleboste, from this poisoned
    strip of wintrous decay, amidst a sylvan cleanliness,

my hands beslubbered with natural brightness, with cell
upon cell of torture and redemption, I muster forth my icy voice,
    the wheedle and purr of a commercial man,
Buy this Hebrew fiber, torn from the white corpses of hell!
these cursives of my alphabet, accumulated like carved bits of snow
    that blow along this pit, each tiny flake a crystal miracle.